P9-AZV-997

the**program**

STEPHEN WHITE

the program

a Novel

DOUBLEDAY

New York London Toronto Sydney Auckland

PUBLISHED BY DOUBLEDAY
a division of Random House, Inc.
1540 Broadway, New York, New York 10036

DOUBLEDAY and the portrayal of an anchor with a dolphin are
trademarks of Doubleday, a division of Random House, Inc.

Library of Congress Cataloging-in-Publication Data
White, Stephen W.
The program/by Stephen White.—1st ed.
p. cm.
1. Gregory, Alan (Fictitious character)—Fiction.   2. Clinical
psychologists—Fiction.   3. Witnesses—Protection—Fiction.
4. Boulder (Colo.)—Fiction.   I. Title.
PS3573.H47477 P77 2001
813'.54—dc21
00-024029

ISBN 0-385-49903-5

Printed in the United States of America
March 2001
First Edition
10   9   8   7   6   5   4   3   2   1

for the Walshes of County Kerry
and the Whites of New England

Distrust any enterprise that requires new clothes.
—Henry David Thoreau

The bad end unhappily, the good unluckily.
That is what tragedy means.
—Tom Stoppard

the program

one

ALMOST FAT TUESDAY

I

"Remember this. Every precious thing I lose,
you will lose two."

The man was a good target.

Tall, six-five. Wavy blond hair that shined almost red in the filtered February sunlight. Ivory skin that refused to tan. Green eyes that danced to the beat of every melody that radiated from every tavern on every street corner in the always-tawdry Quarter. Even during a crowded lunch hour in the most congested part of New Orleans, you could spot him a block away, his head bobbing above the masses. On the eve of Fat Tuesday the Quarter was flush with tourists, and each of them was flush with anticipation of the debauched revelry that would only accelerate as the Monday before stretched into the Tuesday of, as almost-here became Mardi Gras.

The other man, the one with the gun, knew that in a crowd like this one he would have made a rotten target. He was five-eight with his sneakers on. What hair remained on his head was on the dark side of brown. His creeping baldness didn't matter much to him, though, because the Saints cap he was wearing shielded his scalp from the sun as effectively as the distinctive steel-rimmed Ray-Bans shaded his eyes. The khakis and navy-striped sweater he was wearing had been chosen because they comprised the de facto uniform-of-the-day among the male revelers wandering to join the crowds on Bourbon Street.

The late morning had turned mild, and the man's windbreaker was draped over his right hand and arm, totally disguising the barrel of his Ruger Mark II as well as the additional length of the stubby suppressor. His left hand was shoved deep in the pocket of his khakis. He had been briefed on the tall man's destination in advance and kept his distance as he followed him. At the intersection where Bienville crossed Royal the man with the silenced .22 would begin to close the gap on the man without one. That would give the assassin a little over a block to get close enough to do his job.

The tall, blond man had come from his office near City Hall. His wife had wanted to meet him downtown and accompany him to the restaurant. But he'd declined her offer. He'd made prior arrangements to stop on his way to their lunch date at an antique store on Royal to pick up a nineteenth-century cameo he knew his wife had been coveting. The cameo was a surprise for their anniversary.

The errand on Royal hadn't taken the man long, though, and he was turning the corner from Bienville onto Bourbon ten minutes before he was scheduled to rendezvous with his wife. With an athlete's grace and a large man's strides, he dodged slothful tourists with their to-go cup hurricanes and quickly covered the territory to the entrance of Galatoire's. Briefly he scanned the sidewalk and the teeming street in front of the restaurant. His wife wasn't there. He didn't even consider looking for her inside: Kirsten had a thing about sitting alone in restaurants. He hoped she wouldn't be too late; the line for lunch at one of New Orleans legendary eateries was already growing.

They had been in New Orleans for six years and this would mark the sixth time that they had celebrated their anniversary at Galatoire's. He was the one who insisted on returning year after year. She would have preferred going to a restaurant that actually took reservations.

But he prevailed. He was the keeper of the traditions in the family. He was the romantic.

The man with the windbreaker on his arm window-shopped two doors down from Galatoire's, using the storefront glass to reflect the position of his prey. He didn't worry about being spotted. There was no reason that anyone would focus on him. He was a middle-aged guy loitering on Bourbon Street just before lunch hour on the eve of Mardi Gras. One, literally, of thousands. Finally, the beeper in his pocket vibrated. With his fingertip he stilled it and began to scan the street for Kirsten's arrival. His partner up the street had paged him from a cell phone. The page was his signal that she was approaching.

She, too, would have been a good target. Like her husband, Kirsten was tall. And she flaunted it. Two-inch heels took her above six feet, and the skirt of her suit was cut narrowly to accentuate her height. The jacket was tailored to pinch her waist and highlight her hips. Her hair was every bit as blond as her husband's although the sunlight reflected no red. Kirsten was golden, from head to toe.

She carried a small gift box, elaborately wrapped. In it was a key to a suite at the nearby Windsor Court Hotel and a scroll with a wonderfully detailed list that spelled out all the erotic things she planned to do to her husband's lean body between check-in that evening and dawn the next day. She'd had the list drawn on parchment by a friend who was a calligrapher.

The man with the windbreaker spotted Kirsten down the block. As he had been told to expect, she was approaching down Bourbon from Canal. A moment later her husband spotted her, too, but he was reluctant to leave his place in line at Galatoire's. He waved. She waved back. Her smile was electric.

The man with the windbreaker on his arm moved closer to the tall blond man, simultaneously lifting his left hand from his pocket and placing it below the jacket. His right hand was now free. He stuffed it into the pocket of his trousers at the same moment he spotted his partner moving into position behind the woman.

Timing was everything. That's what he'd been told. This wasn't just about the hit; it was also about the timing. Timing was everything.

Kirsten Lord was fifty feet away when the man with the windbreaker stepped into position no more than two yards to the left of her husband, Robert. The position the man took was slightly back from Robert's left shoulder. Kirsten dodged tourists and closed the distance between herself and her husband to twenty feet. Impossibly, her smile seemed to grow brighter.

The man raised his left arm, the one shielded by the windbreaker, so that it extended across his chest. Below the jacket, the barrel of the sound suppressor was now pointing up at a forty-five-degree angle toward his right shoulder.

Kirsten's eyes left her husband's for only an instant, just barely long enough for her to notice the small man with his oddly held windbreaker. She met the man's eyes as they danced from her to Robert and back. She noticed the awkward way he was holding his arm, perceived the evil in his grin, and in a flash, she processed the peril that the man presented. The bright smile she was wearing for her husband left her face as though she'd been slapped. The gaily-decorated box flew from her hand. Instinctively, her tongue found the roof of her mouth and the beginnings of a horrified "No" left her lips just as the man in the Saints cap pivoted his hand and wrist at the elbow so that his silenced weapon emerged from below his jacket.

Out toward Robert Lord's head.

With the voices from the throngs on the street mixing with the music coming from the myriad clubs mixing with the rest of Kirsten Lord's plaintive "NOOOOO," the hushed shots from the silenced pistol were barely discernible, even to Kirsten. She thought they sounded more like arrows than bullets. Another witness later described them as two drumbeats.

Both shots found their marks. The first slug entered Robert's head just below his ear, the second higher, in his cranium. The load in the Ruger was .22 caliber. The slugs possessed neither the mass nor the velocity to find their way back out of Robert Lord's head after they pierced his skull. No grisly hunks of cranial bone cascaded against the plate glass of Galatoire's front window. No bloody gray matter fouled the clothes of the locals and tourists standing in line for lunch. Instead, the two slugs banged around inside Robert Lord's head, mixing the contents of his skull the way a ball bearing blends the contents of a can of spray paint.

The hit was supposed to be clean. And it was.

The timing was supposed to be perfect. And it was.

KIRSTEN FELL TO her knees at Robert's side just as his legs were collapsing below him. One of the two shell casings was still dancing on the concrete, finally coming to rest near the crook of Robert's neck. Kirsten seemed oblivious to any danger she might be in. No one around her seemed to be aware that her husband had just been shot. She no longer recalls what she said to the strangers who stared down at her with shock and pity on their faces.

When she looked up to identify the shooter, to confront the shooter, to accept the next bullet, he was gone. There was no way she would have known it, but by then his Saints cap was off his head, his pager was down a sewer, his sunglasses were off his eyes and he was around the corner, walking placidly down Bienville toward Dauphine. That's where the third member of the team was waiting with a car.

The band in the bar on the corner was playing some better-than-average Zydeco, and he decided that the longer he was in New Orleans the more he liked it.

His instructions had been to make sure that the lady saw the hit. He knew he'd done well.

She'd seen the hit. No doubt about it.

2

"Remember this," he'd said, pointing at me over the defense table. "Every precious thing I lose, you will lose two."

Less than a month after they slid my husband Robert's body into the only empty slot left in his family's tomb in the Garden District's Lafayette Cemetery in New Orleans, I packed up my daughter and moved what remained of our life north to a little town called Slaughter, which was bisected by Highway 19 about halfway between Baton Rouge and the Arkansas state line.

We made the move in the middle of the night. In homage to my paranoia I'd driven all the way to Picayune, Mississippi, before I backtracked into Louisiana and charged north to Slaughter. My old boss in New Orleans, the district attorney, had arranged for a Louisiana State Trooper to tail my car all the way to Picayune and then all the way back as far as Baton Rouge. I bought the trooper a cup of coffee at a truck stop outside Baton Rouge, and he finished two pieces of pie, one apple, one lemon meringue, before I allowed myself to be convinced that we had not been followed.

Somewhere between the outskirts of Baton Rouge and the town limits of Slaughter, I stopped calling myself Kirsten Lord and started calling myself Katherine Shaw. I chose the name at my husband's funeral. The inspiration? The name was written in pencil inside the prayer book that was in front of me in the pew at the church. "Katherine Shaw" it read. The name was written in a child's hand, neatly, in pencil, and I prayed that the Katherine Shaw who'd sat in that pew and sung the hymns in that church and who had spoken the prayers wouldn't mind that we now shared her name as we had shared that holy book.

Trying to make the urgent move to a new town a game to my evercool daughter, I'd allowed her to choose her own new name, too. Her class in school had been studying the Olympic Games in Sydney, so my daughter was now Matilda. I wasn't fond of the name but consoled myself with my glee that her class hadn't been studying the Nagano Games or Salt Lake City.

Together, Matilda and I danced off to Slaughter. "... *You'll come a-waltzing Matilda with me.* ..."

WHEN I AGREED to go into what I told myself was temporary hiding under the protection of the State of Louisiana, one of the reasons I'd chosen to move to Slaughter for our new home was because it was the kind of town where strangers were noticed. Where unfamiliar cars earned a second glance. Despite my still raw grief over Robert's death

I did everything I could to befriend our neighbors and I quickly became known as the mother who watched her daughter enter school each morning and who was waiting outside the door ten minutes before the end of classes each afternoon. The routine I followed didn't vary despite the fact that the upstairs window of the house that I was renting had a pretty good view of the front door of the school. For my state of mind those days, a pretty good view wasn't good enough. A half-block away was a half-block too far.

SCHOOL ENDED FOR Matilda on a much-too-sultry-for-early-June day. But the kids didn't notice the heat. They were energized and intoxicated by the prospect of their upcoming summer of freedom.

Matilda was planning to go home from school with a friend, the first social invitation she'd received since becoming the new kid in class so late in the school year. Upon learning of her plans, I invited the new friend's mother over for coffee and sprinkled the conversation with a manufactured concern that my estranged husband might try to abduct Matilda. A custody dispute, I implied. The new friend's mother said not-to-worry, she'd keep a close eye on the kids. She pressed for some dirt about my estranged husband and as I struggled to invent details to satiate her I wished I'd come up with a different story.

Eight, almost nine-year-old Matilda sensed my apprehension about her visit to her new friend's house and informed me that she could walk all the way there without a chaperone.

"Really," I said, feigning surprise, though I'd expected to hear words a lot like those from my much-too-independent daughter.

"You won't wait for me outside school?"

I raised a hand in honor and stated, "I promise."

"Mom, you *promise*?" There was a time in the not-too-distant-past that she stomped a foot every time she used that tone of voice.

I asked, "Will you call me when you two get to your friend's house?"

"Do I have to?"

"Yes, you do."

"Then I will."

"Matilda, you promise?"

"Mom."

THE PHONE RANG at eighteen minutes past three on that last day of
school. "Hi, Mom," said Matilda. "We're having lemonade and those
little cookies just like the ones that Grandma used to make. With the
jam in the middle?" "Grandma" was my mother. She'd died the previous April. My unfinished grief over her death had already been tram-
pled over by the brutal pain I felt trying to absorb the responsibility
and loss I felt over Robert's murder.

So. Matilda was enjoying an after-school snack in a house that was
three and a half blocks from our rented home, yet I couldn't bring myself to sit down and rest until I'd heard my daughter's voice on the
phone. Once I did hear the sweet melody of her call, I lowered myself
to the Adirondack chair on the front porch and resumed my daily afternoon vigil. What was it, my vigil? I sat on the porch and watched
for strange cars driven by small men wearing chinos and carrying
windbreakers.

Or I watched for anything else that might feel out of the ordinary. I
told myself that my task was like that Supreme Court justice's assessment of obscenity—I couldn't quite define what I was looking for, but
I was positive that I'd know it when I saw it.

As I sipped my tall glass of sweet tea and the ice jiggled in the glass,
the sound I actually heard was the tinkling of the spent .22 shells as
they danced on the concrete near my husband Robert's head.

That, by the way, is a killer whale.

I FELT THE distance to my daughter deep in my chest as though it
could be measured in light years and not small-town blocks and imagined what my life would be like with just one more loss and I couldn't
imagine that it could still be called living.

I caressed the cameo that hung around my neck—Robert had given
it to me for our last anniversary—and I thought about justice. The
concept was distant and imaginary, as full of promise as the Tooth
Fairy or the Easter Bunny, and just as elusive.

That's what I was doing when the portable phone rang on the table beside the chair.

I said, "Hello," my attention momentarily diverted from my emptiness and my vigil on the street.

Matilda's friend's mother said, "Is this Katherine? Katherine, this is Libby Larsen. Now tell me once again, what does your ex-husband look like, exactly? I think there's a—"

"There's a *what?*"

"It's one of those big SUVs," she said, drawing out the last letter, the V, as though its agent had succeeded in negotiating top billing. "It's a black one. Big and shiny."

"Where?"

"Under the magnolia in front of Mrs. Marter's house. It's—"

"Are the girls okay, Libby?" I was trying hard not to let my fear ignite panic in my voice.

"They're right here on the living room floor playing with—"

"I'll be right there," I said and threw down the phone. Once inside the house I wasted ten steps running to get my keys from the hook in the kitchen before deciding it would be faster to walk—no!—run, then thinking twice and backtracking for my keys after all because I might need the car to chase that SUV.

I was fumbling to get the key into the ignition when I remembered to run back inside and get my gun. Arriving at the locked case in which I kept it, I realized I'd left my keys in the car's ignition and had to retrace my steps all over again. I was losing minutes when I didn't even have seconds to spare.

"Remember this," he'd said, pointing at me over the defense table. "Every precious thing I lose, you will lose two."

The man's words had chilled me for a minute that day in court but I'd shrugged off his threat. It certainly wasn't the first threat I'd ever heard from a desperate con that I was prosecuting.

I figured that it wouldn't be the last.

But then the man in court had sent the man in the chinos to New Orleans and he'd killed Robert right in front of my eyes on the sidewalk in front of Galatoire's.

And now there was a big black SUV parked under Mrs. Marter's magnolia tree and I was sure it was driven by a small man wearing chinos but I kept thinking it's way too warm for him to be wearing a windbreaker.

The entire three-block drive I wondered what he would be draping over his arm instead.

HERE'S A BELUGA:

Before we were lovers, or even friends, even before I knew I wanted him to be my lover, Robert and I shared our first long weekend away at a mutual friend's cabin in the mountains of North Carolina. Robert and I arrived separately, and we were two of ten people sharing the spacious vacation home. The second night of our holiday, after an evening of revelry that included a sojourn in a steaming hot tub on the edge of the adjacent woods, Robert pulled me away from the group and with the softest amber eyes in the world told me that I had the most lovely back he had ever seen.

That's right. He was talking about my back. His first heartfelt complement to me was about my *back*.

If the man had been paying attention that night, and I assumed that he was, he'd had the fleeting opportunity to see my breasts, to gaze at the full length of my legs, and to study the then still-youthful contours of my ass, yet the man I would soon choose to marry wanted to reflect on the beauty of my *back*.

These are the types of things I remember now. Even at moments when I'm careening around corners and speeding three blocks to save my daughter from assassination.

I don't understand.

It's just a beluga.

THE NATURAL ROUTE to Matilda's friend's house caused me to approach the big SUV—it was one of those obscenely immense Ford things—from the front. I screeched my Audi to a stop halfway between the stubborn-looking snout of the monstrosity and the front door of the house that held my daughter, and I parked on the wrong side of the road, something that just isn't done in Slaughter.

Two men sat in the front seat of the huge vehicle. One wore a ball cap, and both shaded their eyes with sunglasses. Beyond that, I couldn't tell how tall they were or what clothes they were wearing.

Libby Larsen stood on the edge of the large, tidy lawn in front of her house, shading her eyes with the hand that wasn't supporting the toddler perched on her outstretched hip. I turned to face her and watched her mouth. "Is that him?" she was asking.

I shrugged my shoulders as I walked toward her. She tried not to move her lips as she said, "Don't look, but they're getting out of the car, now."

I barely understood her words but knew what to do next. "Why don't you go back inside with the girls, Libby? Do you have a cellar? Pretend there's a tornado drill or something, will you do that? Take them down to your cellar. You hear anything out of the ordinary, you don't hesitate to call 911."

She didn't know me well enough to know my determination about things, but she attended to my words as though I were a preacher who knew the path to eternal bliss, and she skipped away to find the girls and squirrel them into the cellar.

The two men who got out of the SUV weren't anywhere nearly as tall as it was. They both walked my way. There was no hurry in their steps. Neither of them was carrying a jacket or anything that could be used to shield a silenced handgun, though the one who was wearing the ball cap seemed to have his left hand tucked back behind his buttocks.

I watched that one, the one with the ball cap, as I fingered the trigger of my pistol, which weighed heavily inside the front pouch of my sleeveless sweatshirt. The sweatshirt had been Robert's. I'd cut the sleeves off for him. On the front it was embroidered LSU, his alma mater.

The man I was watching closely raised his free hand, the right one, and tipped the ball cap my way, saying, "Ma'am."

I nodded, trying not to be distracted from the hand that was still hidden behind his back.

He said, "We'd be looking for Missus Marter," while tilting his head back in the direction of the magnolia tree.

"Yes," I said.

The other man, the one without the cap, said, "We tried but she's not answering her bell."

I replied without allowing my attention to waver from the man with the ball cap. "Then I imagine she must not be home. Is she expecting you?"

"Indeed. Our appointment was a while ago." He tapped his watch.

"Appointment for?"

"Air-conditioning. She wants a bid to install air-conditioning."

"I'll tell her you came by. Do you have a card?"

The man with the ball cap moved, his hidden hand thrust forward with a suddenness that caused me to jerk my hand and tangle the pistol in the fabric of the pouch of my sweatshirt. I couldn't extricate the darn gun. It took too many seconds for my eyes to recognize that the hidden hand, now extended my way, held nothing more than a business card.

Leaving the pistol tangled in the pouch of my sweatshirt, I reached out and took the card from him and read it. "You're with Buster's?" I asked. Buster's Sheet Metal and Air-Conditioning. I thought I remembered seeing a sign on a ramshackle building over by the supermarket.

"Yes."

"Missus Marter will be sorry she missed you, especially on a day as wicked as this one. The summer will be a long one, don't you think?"

"Fierce," he agreed.

You betcha.

3

Matilda's new friend in Slaughter was named Jennifer. The two of them became buddies the way only little girls can. That end-of-the-school-year visit at Jennifer's house led to another at ours, which led to a sleepover at Jennifer's—"Mom, don't call her Jenny"—and to the required reciprocation. Soon, there were long nightly phone calls between the two girls and loud protests of eternal devotion that I couldn't help from overhearing.

Believe me, I tried.

By the time June was ending they'd been best friends for a fortnight and had already endured at least two spats that, in much of the animal kingdom, would have left one of their carcasses rotting in the sun.

As far as I could tell, my little girl never faltered in her quest to reinvent herself and become this child named Matilda. She fell into her ever-evolving encyclopedia of lies with an affinity that frightened me. The child could piece together the strands of her fictitious life with the facility of a master weaver. Not once did I hear her lose her place as she recounted details of her new story to her new friend. Often, I worried what bruises her fantasies were screening from my view, or of greater concern, from her own.

I was terrified that I didn't know how to measure her pain.

My own? I felt that my own bruises were invisible to others but that they were potentially crippling to me. In my mind they were like subdural hematomas. But in my heart I knew that it wasn't my brain that the swollen clots were pressuring.

It was my soul.

AT BEDTIME EACH night Matilda listened with feigned patience to my litany of concerns and my admonitions about how important it was that she understand how to react around strangers. Before long she was able to recite the rules to me the same way she had learned to recite the lines of *Goodnight Moon* as I turned each page for her when she was two years old. When she was small, no matter which book we read first, or second, or third each night, she always insisted that the last book we read was *Goodnight Moon*.

That meant that the final words before dark, the last words before "I love you," were always, "Good night noises everywhere."

After we resettled in Slaughter, we talked most nights at bedtime about Robert, her daddy, and at least once or twice a week she asked questions about the bad man who had killed him. "Did he do something to make him mad?" she'd want to know, and I told her that her daddy was the sweetest man on the planet, she knew that. "What does he look like?" she'd ask, but I wouldn't tell her about the chinos because I didn't want her to grow phobic about khakis. "Is he big?" she would wonder, but I never told her that by the time she was twelve I was sure she would be taller than the bad man who had killed her daddy.

Right from the start, though, she seemed to understand that the bad man who was responsible hadn't been caught and that we were going to hide in Slaughter until he was behind prison bars. But her grief over Robert's death was as immature as she was, and I remained worried that she hadn't shed as many tears over her dead father as I felt were required.

ALMOST A FULL month passed without another sighting of the two men in the big SUV from Buster's Sheet Metal and Air-Conditioning. I had checked them out, of course. The business was legitimate. Buster's was. And the two men worked there. I'd watched them show up for work the very next morning after I'd met them outside Mrs. Marter's house. And a simple phone call confirmed that Mrs. Marter was indeed considering air-conditioning her home, but the prices had taken her breath away as surely as had the previous July's humidity.

Slowly, as the days passed, I began to feel some renewed safety and insulation in the security provided by the routines of Slaughter, Louisiana. The call that finally shook me from that false security and stiffened my spine came from an old colleague in the district attorney's office in New Orleans.

THE MAN WHO'D threatened me that day in court, the man I was sure had arranged to assassinate my husband, the man whom I'd sent to prison for more years than even a Galápagos tortoise could hope to survive—that man—had just suffered a major personal tragedy.

The man's name was Ernesto Castro. He had been a big shot in the cocaine trade, a local boss for the Colombian drug cartels, running an operation that delivered major quantities of cocaine from Miami all the way up to D.C. and Baltimore.

When I met him, he was residing in the Mississippi River town of Welcome, halfway between Louisiana and Baton Rouge. He'd been arrested for suspicion of committing a brutal rape on a wheelchair-bound forty-six-year-old woman in the elevator of the office building where she worked as a legal secretary. The New Orleans police quickly concluded that Ernesto was responsible for at least two additional recent rapes, equally depraved, equally vicious.

Fortunately for the legal justice system, Ernesto was much more brutal than he was clever. I was assigned to prosecute him, and I had no trouble winning convictions on each and every count. I felt confident that Castro would never again see the light of the Louisiana sun as a free man.

It was the day of his sentencing that he threatened me in open court.

A day in court that began like a hundred others.

As I approached the bench at the judge's request, Castro unexpectedly stood up behind me at the defense table and raised his shackled hands. He lifted the fat index finger of his left hand, and he pointed it right at me. "You! Bitch! Hey!" he called.

I turned my head. Not even my whole body. Just my head. I wasn't even certain that I was the bitch he was talking to.

The judge pounded her gavel. I could tell that she didn't know if she was the bitch he was talking to, either. The bailiffs awoke from their revelry and moved toward the convict.

"Remember this," Ernesto Castro said before the burly bailiffs could restrain him. *Thees.* "Every precious thing I lose, you will lose two." *Doo.*

I don't even recall the look on his face as he spoke those words to me. Despite the melodrama of the moment, the threat felt relatively inconsequential, as though it were just one of too many interactions during which I'd felt soiled by the vermin I prosecuted. In my journal, on those rare days when I had the time and emotional awareness to reflect on some way I'd been treated particularly badly in court, I would note that I had been slimed that day.

That was my word for it. *Slimed*.

Do you remember *Ghostbusters*? No? It's not important. Trust me, I was slimed that day.

So what was Mr. Castro's more recent tragedy, the one my friend in the DA's office was telling me about as I hid out in Slaughter? Castro's mother had been on her way to visit him in prison when her car was hit head-on by a bread truck full of snack cakes. The driver of the bakery truck had fallen asleep at the wheel and crossed the highway median. Mrs. Castro had died in a veritable sea of Twinkies.

"Every precious thing I lose," were the words he'd spoken to me. His mother was a precious thing, right? To him? Certainly.

He could hold me responsible, right? Of course he could.

From the moment I heard the news of Castro's mother's death, I lost more sleep wondering if *Señora* Castro's death meant that I now owed Ernesto Castro one more loss of my own, or three more losses of my own?

My Robert, did he really only count for one?

Matilda, dear God, she would count for dozens.

If Castro got to Matilda, I knew I'd go all by myself to the prison where he lived and I would cut out his organs, one by one, until he died. I'd flay him open and first remove the organs that wouldn't kill him quickly, his appendix and his gall bladder and his spleen, and I'd stuff them in his mouth and I'd force them down his throat until he began to choke on his own evil.

Images like that never became part of my pod of whales. No, they never dived, they never ran deep. They became my daydreams, the thoughts that filled my head while I sipped sweet tea on the porch in the heat of the afternoon and watched the road for small men in chinos.

SHE WAS A soccer player, my Matilda. And so was her new friend, Jennifer. The Larsens had a front yard that was large enough to kick a ball around in, and we didn't. The girls spent hours that summer working on their game, which meant that they were at the Larsens' house more often than they were at ours. Mr. Larsen had constructed a makeshift goal out of PVC pipe and fishing net that he set up between some flowering bushes on the north side of the big lawn.

If Robert had been alive, he would have offered to help Mr. Larsen with the net, and he probably would have managed to totally screw up the project. Robert wasn't exactly what you would call handy. But, then, if Robert had been alive, Matilda and I wouldn't have been in Slaughter.

I'm embarrassed to admit it, but—even though I'm the one who got him killed—I occasionally cursed Robert for dying.

BY THE WEEKEND before the Fourth of July, I was complacent enough about Matilda's visits to Jennifer's house that I was able to sit and read or clean the house during her absences. But I wasn't so complacent that I would run an errand away from the house and maybe risk missing the phone call from Libby Larsen informing me that the short man with the ball cap and the chinos was back in my life.

THE PHONE CALL, when it did come, was brief, even cryptic. Libby said, "Katherine? I think you should come over. Right away."

"Is she okay?" I said. "Is Matilda okay?"

"The police are on the way," Libby said, her voice admonishing, not reassuring. "She isn't Matilda. And it *wasn't* your ex-husband."

I threw down the damn phone, grabbed my purse—which I knew already contained my keys and my gun—and drove the three blocks to the Larsens's like the mad woman I was.

A policewoman from the Slaughter force met me at the curb and was almost strong enough to restrain me from my sprint to the front porch of the Larsen home. *Almost.* Once I was past her, though, she was nowhere nearly fast enough to keep up with me. I paid no heed to her verbal protests that I stop, and I didn't knock at the front door but instead just threw open the screen and called, "Baby! Matilda! Matilda!"

Libby Larsen walked into the toy-strewn entryway of her home wiping her hands on a kitchen towel that was decorated with blue pineapples. *"Matilda?"* she scoffed. "How could you?" she demanded. She tossed the towel over her shoulder and moved her clean hands to her ample hips in the international sign of housewifely indignation. "How could you lie to me? To *us*? How could you even think about putting all the other children in danger like that?"

Her outrage deflected off of me like X rays off of lead. No penetration whatsoever. She didn't even know what danger *was*. I had a daughter to protect.

"Matilda!" I yelled.

I don't believe that I was always so callous. Perhaps I was. Maybe it was the work I did. Or having my husband murdered. I just don't know.

Libby said, "She's in the kitchen with the police." She pronounced it *poe-lease*. "I'll tell you, ma'am, but you have some explaining to do. To them. And when they're done with you, you have some explaining to do to me." She was acting as though someone usually gave pause when she used that tone of voice. Must have been her children. Couldn't imagine that it caused her husband to cower. But I didn't really know Bud Larsen. Maybe Libby was married to a wimp.

I ran past her toward the kitchen.

Matilda was sitting at the big oak breakfast table and was flanked on each side by a police officer. One was black, one was white. Neither of the two men weighed less than two hundred pounds. Their uniform hats sat before them on the table and looked large enough to act as toaster caddies. My gangly daughter was dwarfed by the scale of it all.

"Honey," I said, my voice full of tenderness now that I knew she was alive and breathing. I held out my arms.

"Mommy," she said and immediately slithered down on her chair, disappearing below the edge of the tabletop before the two big cops could figure out what to do to stop her. She was between their legs and up in my arms in seconds. "Mommy," she said again. "Mommy."

"Shhh," I whispered into her golden hair.

"They made me tell them about Daddy."

"Shhh."

"And that my name isn't Matilda."

"Shhh."

"And that your name isn't Katherine Shaw."

"Shhh."

"The bad man came just like you said he would. But it wasn't a man, Mommy. The bad man wasn't a man."

"Shhh."

"What are we gonna do, Mommy? What are we gonna do?"

"Oh my baby," I murmured.

WHAT HAD HAPPENED was that Matilda was playing defense—it was her nature—and Jennifer had kicked the soccer ball toward the net with all the might of her surprisingly strong left leg. Matilda managed to get up high and deflect the ball so that it sailed above the goal. Robert used to say proudly that his daughter had coiled springs in her legs, not femurs. Matilda chased the ball through the bushes into the next-door-neighbor's yard.

That's when she met the woman in the green halter-top and cargo shorts. "She looked just like the pictures of the girls from the Abercrombie catalog," was how my suddenly fashion-conscious preteen described the woman who was lurking on the other side of the bushes.

"Was she young or old?" I asked.

"Young. Twenty." Matilda pronounced her conclusion with a degree of confidence that I didn't share. I'd interviewed hundreds of witnesses in the past few years, and Matilda was approaching her rendition of events with an assurance that made me wary. But that, too, was her nature.

"And?"

"And she walked over to me and asked me if I'd seen her dog."

"Damn," I said.

"Mom," she scolded me. "Don't cuss. Anyway, I remembered. You told me that the bad guys might say something about losing a dog or a cat and needing my help to find them, so I was ready. When she grabbed me, I was already running, I swear."

"Don't swear. You were already running?"

"Well, not totally *running* running. But I was starting to run when she grabbed me on my arm, right here." My daughter fingered the biceps of her left arm. "See? That's where she grabbed me." The hard red outlines of the woman's fingers were clearly visible below the mahogany of Matilda's summer tan.

"Go on, Sweetie. I'm proud of you."

"Okay. It's like . . . then she reached out and grabbed me as hard as she could. But I was too sweaty and her hand was too sweaty and I was too quick for her and I got away and I ran and I ran and I screamed and I yelled just like you taught me to do and I cut back through the bushes toward the Larsens' and when I turned around to look she'd stopped coming after me and she'd started running the other way and there was a car there waiting for her and that was it."

But, of course, that wasn't it.

Not even close.

chapter

EPIDURAL

I

Alan Gregory raised the pillows from the carpeted floor and helped his pregnant wife to her feet. He asked, "So what do you think?" Lauren smiled her gratitude for his assistance and said, "What do I think? You mean about *this*?" She punched one of the pillows against his chest and said, "Here's what I think: Can you spell epidural?"

He laughed and lowered his voice to a whisper. "Is it safe for me to assume that you're not completely sold on huffing and puffing your way through the bliss of childbirth?"

She wanted to make sure he knew she wasn't kidding. When he leaned over to kiss her, one hand on her swollen belly, she was almost convinced. But not quite. With emphasis, she said, "*e—p—i—*"

"All right, I hear you. We'll get some names of anesthesiologists from Adrienne. But we'll finish the class, right?"

"Yeah, we'll finish the class. Jody wants us to finish the class." Jody was Lauren's OB. Lauren tilted her head toward the front of the conference room where they'd just attended their initial Lamaze class—First Child after Thirty—and whispered, "Do you know anybody in our group? None of your patients, I hope. That would be awkward."

"No, no patients. But I do know the woman who was sitting over by the door." He looked over in that direction but the woman had already left the room. "She's a psychiatrist from Denver. I wasn't aware she lived close to us. Her name's Teri Grady. I've worked with her a few times over the years. I like her. She's funny. I take it there was no one in here with us that you've prosecuted?" Lauren was a deputy district attorney for Boulder County.

"God forbid. No, no one I've prosecuted."

"You want to stop on the way home, get something to eat? I promised I'd take you to Dandelion if you behaved yourself during class."

"Did I behave myself?" she asked with attractive petulance.

"You did fine. You made a couple of gratuitous faces. But you did fine."

"What faces? I didn't make any faces, did I?"

He smiled. She knew she'd made some faces.

She said, "I think I'll take a rain check on Dandelion. I told Adrienne that she could start teaching me some yoga tonight. You don't mind?"

"Mind? Of course not. May I watch?"

She socked him on the arm. "Not on your life."

"Darn. She's really into it, isn't she? The yoga thing?"

"I think she looks great. Don't you think she looks great? You have to have noticed what yoga's done for her butt."

He glanced at his wife with a sideways glance. "We're talking Adrienne's butt, right? No, I hate to disappoint you, but I haven't noticed what yoga's done for Adrienne's butt."

"Well, I have, and I'm hoping it'll do the same for mine."

"Your butt, beautiful wife, doesn't need the same."

"And you're sweet."

He slid his hand perilously close to that butt as they walked from the hospital toward the car. "Don't worry about tonight—I have some calls to make. I'll make dinner while you and Adrienne do whatever it is you're going to do."

. . .

ALAN AND LAUREN lived in a recently renovated ranch house on the eastern side of the Boulder Valley, in the shadows of the scenic overlook that adorned the high point on Highway 36 as it threaded into Boulder from Denver's northwestern suburbs. Adrienne, their urologist friend, and Jonas, her son, were their only close neighbors on the dirt lane that dead-ended in the clearing between their homes.

That night was a preview of midsummer's attractions. The sun was descending toward the craggy cradle of the Rockies in a fashion that was peculiarly languid, and the evening air was more warm than cool for the first time all season. The sky was lit in the dusty pastels of Necco wafers. From one of the decks on the western side of their house, Lauren and Alan could see the lights of the parallel snakes of liquid traffic slithering slowly east and west on the Boulder Turnpike.

When Alan had first moved into an earlier incarnation of this house in the seventies, Boulder knew no rush hour. When he first met Lauren in the early nineties, the turnpike was only crowded outbound in the morning and inbound in the evening. Now? Boulder had its own suburbs. Now? Boulder had too much traffic, too much of the time. Now? The Boulder Turnpike was a pipe corroded from too many vehicles.

THEY SAID GOOD-BYE in the garage and Lauren started across the lane to Adrienne's house while Alan walked to the front door to greet Emily, their Bouvier. The dog offered him a cursory hello—a dip of her head and a little hop on all fours—before she spotted Lauren meandering across the lane and darted past Alan's legs to catch up with her. Alan called a warning to his wife who prepared herself to dart out of the way of the dog's likely overexuberant greeting.

Across the lane Jonas opened the front door of his house and squealed, "Em-i-ly! Come here! Emily!" Alan knew that their easily distracted dog wasn't going to be coming home right away. He called to Lauren, "Have Jonas bring her home when she's ready for dinner." She waved that she'd heard him.

THE HOUSE WAS lit with the light show from the western sky. A last sliver of yellow sun was crowning the peaks of the central Rockies like a thick pat of butter melting on oatmeal. Alan poured himself a glass of water that had come from nearby Eldorado Springs and grabbed a beer that had come from a brewery on nearby Canyon Boulevard. He planned to give himself a few minutes to enjoy the metamorphoses—day into night, pseudosummer into summer—before he started to make dinner.

He picked up the phone to check messages, first at home—two, both for Lauren—and then at work—two more, neither urgent. He was relieved about the work news and began to relax. One of the patients in his clinical psychology practice had been on the verge of deteriorating for almost two weeks. Today's dual stressors—her annual performance review at Celestial Seasonings, where she worked, and the final dissolution of her marriage by the Boulder County Court—threatened to take her over the edge. That she hadn't left him a choppy message in her flat monotone meant that it was likely she had survived her day.

For her, and for Alan, that was good.

The moment he finished listening to his other message, yet another in a string of cancellations from a thirty-six-year-old man whose wife thought he needed therapy much more than he did, the phone rang. Alan took a long pull of beer before he answered, "Hello."

"Alan? It's Teri Grady."

He was surprised. "Teri? Hi. It was fun seeing you tonight. I'm sorry we didn't get a chance to talk. I didn't know you were pregnant. When are you due?"

"That was my fault. Crawford needed to run right after class. He's my husband—I don't think you two have met. And I'm due in eight weeks."

"Maybe I can meet him next week at class. Or we could all get some dinner after class. You can meet Lauren, too."

"That sounds nice, but listen, I'm actually calling about something else. Seeing you tonight sparked an idea. I want to make you an offer."

"Okay."

"It's likely to sound strange."

"Then it will fit right into my life."

"There's no reason you would know it, but one of the things I do— professionally, I mean—is that I'm the regional psychiatric consultant to the U.S. Marshals Service and to the Secret Service."

"No, I didn't know it. That sounds like interesting work," Alan said, as he tried to anticipate where the conversation was going.

"You know, surprisingly enough, it's one of the few things I do that *is* as interesting as it sounds. Anyway, I'm looking for someone to cover some of my responsibilities while I'm on maternity leave. I wondered whether you have some time and whether you'd be interested."

"I'm flattered, Teri. I do have some time, a few hours, anyway. I guess it depends on exactly what you're looking for. I don't think I could squeeze in regular trips to Denver, if that's what it would take."

"All I think it's going to involve is seeing one of my ongoing therapy patients, a guy currently in WITSEC, the Witness Security Program that's run by the marshals office. You probably think of it as the Witness Protection Program. And possibly picking up a second therapy case, someone who's being processed into the same program right now and who has already requested a referral for psychotherapy. She'll be relocated to this region soon. Maybe as soon as next week. You wouldn't have to see them in Denver; both of these people could come to your Boulder office."

"That's it?"

"Probably. The local WITSEC census is as large as the Marshals Service is comfortable with right now. There's always the possibility that there will be fresh transfers in and out of the region, but most of the people in the program don't get any mental health support. So it's probably just going to be these two."

"How long is your maternity leave?"

"I'm planning on six months after the delivery. My OB is concerned about some spotting I've had, though, and he's threatened me with bed rest if it gets any worse. That's why I'm looking for coverage already."

"What about meds, Teri?"

"My guy is stable on Zoloft. John Connor—you know him from the medical school, right?—he's the psychiatrist I inherited all this federal work from. He's agreed to cover any medication issues that might come up during my leave. I don't see any real challenges on the horizon pharmaceutically, but if you need some support, he'll be available to you."

"I know John. What's the Secret Service piece?"

"John's going to handle that unless the workload gets too tough, then I imagine he would call you to do some consultation. It's sporadic work. During presidential and vice-presidential visits to the region, and during some visits by members of Congress and foreign leaders, the Secret Service has to assess risks on people in the region who they've identified as potential security threats. When the agents have a specific concern, they call and present material for consultation. Sometimes it's on the phone, sometimes they want a face-to-face."

"But it's rare?"

"Yeah. As I said, John will cover that. You probably wouldn't do any during the whole six months."

Alan watched as the last drop of the buttery sun melted into the highest valleys of the Rockies. "I have to admit that I'm intrigued, Teri. I'm always looking for ways to make my work seem more interesting, and this looks like it will do just that. But I'm curious, why me? Why not one of your psychiatric colleagues?"

"It's a fair question. First, I think you're a good match for my current patient. He's, uh, an interesting guy. But from what I recall about your style, I think it will fit him well. Second, you're flexible, and I've discovered that psychotherapy with this . . . population requires some therapeutic gymnastics. And last? I like this work a lot— a *lot*—and I don't especially want to create competition for myself within the psychiatric community. You're a safer bet for me. The Marshals Service prefers to have physicians, not psychologists, as their consultants."

Alan gave Teri points for honesty. But then, it was one of the things he always liked about her.

"I'm more than intrigued, Teri. As I said, I'm always looking for opportunities to break the routine of what I do. Let me sleep on it and I'll give you a call sometime tomorrow. Is that okay?"

"Sure, but there's one more piece to all this. You've never been in the military, have you?"

"No, why?"

"Wishful thinking. So I guess there's no reason you would happen to already have a security clearance, is there?"

"Sorry. Does that disqualify me?"

"Not at all. But no skeletons, right? No disqualifiers? Nothing that would prevent you from getting one, a security clearance? Sorry, but I have to ask."

"No problem, Teri. Actually, I did some informal consulting for some FBI types a few months back. You may have heard about it—a couple of old murders up near Steamboat Springs. The people I worked with told me that they checked into my background before they approached me, and they acted comfortable enough with what they found. I think I can pass muster."

"Good. You should be fine then. I'll look forward to hearing from you tomorrow. I hope you say yes. You have my home number?"

He said he didn't have it, and she dictated it before hanging up.

He finished the beer. By the time he swallowed the last drop, he'd already decided that he was going to say "Yes."

LAUREN WALKED IN the door around eight-thirty to a meal of shrimp lo mein. She complained of not being very limber during her initial yoga session. "I couldn't hold any of the balance poses that she tried to show me."

"Was it your MS?"

"I think so. That and being out of shape."

He said, "I'm sorry."

She gave him a "that's life" look, warning him she wasn't in the mood to feel disabled.

He told her about the call he'd received from Teri Grady.

"That's great. You're going to do it, aren't you?" was her immediate response to hearing the details of Teri's offer.

"I think so," he said.

"You don't sound too certain. Why wouldn't you do it? If I had the opportunity for that kind of variety in my work, I'd do it in a second."

"You would? Despite the fact that your new clients would be . . . I don't know . . . criminals?"

"My clients *are* criminals. I'm a prosecutor."

"You represent the people, not the criminals, and you know what I mean. You don't have to advocate for the people you prosecute."

"I don't care. It sounds like a fascinating opportunity. I think you should do it. It will help take your mind off the baby."

"I don't want to take my mind off the baby."

"Good dinner," she said, ignoring his protest. "Anyway, you know you're going to do it. You're just playing reluctant so I'll feel good that you included me in your decision."

"That's not true."

"Alan."

"Well, not totally," he said.

2

Alan's part of the security-clearance process involved participating in a rather detailed interview with an FBI agent named Flaherty, whom Alan suspected—based solely on linguistic clues—was from somewhere in the Northeast. The remainder of the screening process would apparently involve the FBI doing whatever it was the FBI typically did behind the scenes, including talking with references that Alan had provided. He'd given them the name of a friend, Sam Purdy, who was a Boulder police detective, and the names and numbers of three ex–FBI agents whom he'd worked with over the past couple of years. It turned out that Flaherty had taken a course at the FBI Academy on computer-assisted crime from one of the retired agents on Alan's reference list, a man named Kimber Lister.

Alan considered that propitious.

THE FOLLOWING FRIDAY morning he pulled his car into the garage of an imposing granite building on Cherry Creek South Drive in Denver and took the elevator to the fourth-floor office of Teri Grady, M.D. The man who greeted him in Teri's comfortable waiting room was wearing ankle-length biking Lycra and a Gore-Tex windbreaker. He said, "Dr. Gregory? I'm Inspector Ronald Kriciak—I'm a field inspector with the U.S. Marshals Service. Welcome aboard. Thanks for being willing to help."

"It's a pleasure to meet you." Alan perused the marshal's bicycle garb. "You've been riding already today?"

Kriciak fingered his lightweight jacket. "Not yet. I'm on my way right after we're done here."

"Where are you heading?"

"Not sure. Some canyon work probably. I want to do some climbing. You ride, too." It wasn't a question.

"Whenever I can."

Kriciak pointed to the open doorway. "We have a little while before we get started with Teri. I asked you to meet me a little early because I brought some material for you to read. You okay with that? I can't leave it with you. Security."

"Sure."

Kriciak handed across two files, and Alan began reading about his two new patients. Kriciak picked up a copy of *People*.

ALMOST THIRTY MINUTES later, the two men entered Teri's consultation office, which Alan could tell was at least twice the size of his own. Two huge windows faced the mountains. An old Persian rug graced a hardwood floor that definitely wasn't made of oak. Alan guessed cherry or a darkly stained maple. Teri sat, or more accurately, reclined, on a sofa that was flanked by two identical upholstered chairs. Kriciak took one. Alan shook Teri's outstretched hand and lowered himself onto the other chair.

"Teri, how's your . . . ?" He stumbled, not wanting to say "spotting" in front of Kriciak.

She forced a smile. "Let's just say this may be the last time I see this office for a couple of months."

"Oh, I'm sorry. Bed rest?"

She shrugged. "My OB would scream if he knew I was here. But screaming OBs are the least of my worries. How's your wife doing?"

"Lauren seems invigorated by the pregnancy so far. She got pretty tired during the first trimester, but since then it's been great. She started doing yoga last week, too. Seems to like it."

Kriciak cleared his throat and tapped his watch, an electronic thing that to Alan's eye appeared to have sufficient circuitry to track incoming ICBMs should NORAD develop any serious malfunctions. Teri said, "Sorry, Ron. I know you want to get going." To Alan she explained, "Ron's a bachelor and is currently pretending to be uninterested in the miracle of procreation."

"Ah."

She continued, "As I'm sure he's already explained, Ron's one of the field inspectors who's assigned to WITSEC in this region. He's been my contact for work with the patient of mine you'll be continuing with, and he'll be the contact for the new patient of yours who's being processing into the program right now. She'll arrive when? Tuesday, Ron?"

"Something like that."

I could tell from Teri's face that she'd noted that her question hadn't been answered. She didn't challenge Kriciak about it. Instead, she said, "Why don't you explain your role to Alan."

Kriciak was one of those men who sat with his legs as far apart as the chair permitted. There must have been two and a half feet of separation between his knees. He'd be hell as a companion at a theater or on an airplane. He said, "Number one, as the field inspector, I'm their monitor from the program. Number two, I'm their lifeline, at least initially. Once they arrive in their new home I help them get organized, settled, teach them what I have to teach them about establishing and maintaining their new identity, about maintaining security, about the region, the program rules, what we can do for them, what we can't do for them. The longer someone's in the program, if they're working out, the less I hear from them, and the less they see me." He smiled at Teri. "Your guy Carl's an exception to that rule. The more he's in the program, the more he figures out ways he thinks I can be of help. I swear he'd redesign the whole damn program if somebody offered him the chance."

Alan thought he detected a vein of criticism in Ron Kriciak's characterization of his what? Client? Charge?

Ron faced Alan and continued. "I'll be doing the same thing for you that I'm doing for Teri. Dr. Grady. When she needs things, she calls me. I see what's possible and whether the program can be of help. The truth is that more often than not, we can't help. You'll do the same. Here are my numbers." He handed Alan an embossed business card. "Pager or cell tends to be the best way to find me most of the time."

"Teri?" Alan said. "I'm not sure I understand. Why, during the course of psychotherapy, would I need to consult a marshal for assistance with my patient?"

Teri adjusted a pillow that supported her knees. She winced as her baby jabbed an elbow or a heel into some organ where she didn't really want it. "The work I've been doing with Carl in therapy isn't exactly psychoanalysis, Alan. Don't misunderstand—he's insightful enough, but the work's more . . . practical. Think action more than insight. I do a lot of education, guidance, even advice. Teaching, too. And when it turns out that Carl needs something specific, something concrete, that you think is prescriptive—potentially therapeutic—you need to negotiate it with Ron. Everything Carl wants to do that stretches the envelope, he needs permission from the program. And for him that starts with Ron."

"Yeah, I'm like a deputy god," Ron said with only a hint of a smile. "But Teri's got a point. Carl does like to stretch the envelope." Alan noticed him fingering his fancy watch and wondered if he'd pushed a button to time the meeting.

"What else do I need to know, Ron?"

"About Carl. Not much. You read his background. Teri knows him as well as I do, maybe better. She'll fill you in. What I need you to understand about Carl is that he's truly hot." Ron leaned forward and filled half the distance between his chair and Alan's. "He's not some low-level wiseguy grunt who's in the program because he's got delusions of grandeur or some unrestrained paranoia that a bunch of over-the-hill capos are out to get him. Carl is the real thing. If the right people found out who Carl really is and where Carl actually is, Carl would be a dead man. Do you understand?"

Alan nodded. Swallowed. "I understand. What about my other new patient?"

Ron looked briefly at Teri. "Peyton. Her program name is Peyton Francis. You watch the news, read the newspapers? If you do, then you already knew most of what you saw in Miss Francis's jacket."

Teri's face accurately reflected how perplexed she was at Ron's comment. She hadn't seen the file Alan had read in her waiting room. She said, "The name Peyton Francis doesn't sound familiar to me."

Ron said, "That pretty prosecutor down in New Orleans? The one who was threatened by that drug guy in court? Remember that story? Her husband was later gunned down in the French Quarter while the two of them were waiting to have lunch to celebrate their anniversary? Am I ringing any bells yet?"

"Yes," she said, remembering. A few months back, the story had been big news.

Alan's wife, Lauren, who was also a prosecutor, had been captivated by the whole saga. Alan recalled that Lauren had said the Louisiana prosecutor had been forced into hiding with her daughter. The feds and the local district attorney in Louisiana had argued publicly about which agency should protect her. Alan no longer had to guess how the dispute had been resolved.

Kriciak said, "Her name then was Kirsten Lord. Now it's Peyton Francis. Anyway, she's Alan's other new WITSEC patient. I've been told she's anxious and depressed. Can't imagine why." Alan wondered if he was detecting some smugness in Ron's tone.

Alan said, "Given what I remember about her story, I find it hard to believe she's in Witness Protection."

Ron actually smiled this time. "What goes around, comes around."

"Wasn't she—I don't know a better way to put it—a harsh critic of the way you guys manage the program? Didn't she testify in Congress about the number of violent crimes that have been committed by protected witnesses?"

"She's the one." Ron admitted. "The guy who threatened her in court? Same one who probably ordered the hit on her husband? He was once one of ours. No longer, of course. Now he's doing two consecutive life sentences after she convicted him for a series of rapes."

"And now you're protecting her from him? I find this incredibly ironic."

Kriciak closed his eyes for an instant longer than a blink, still fighting to hide that smile. He shrugged and said, "Small world."

Alan said, "I assume it was her idea. Entering the program."

"That's a fair assumption. We certainly had nothing to hold over her as leverage to force her to come in. My guess is that she recognized that her choices were limited because the stakes are so high. The danger she's in is severe. No one's better at protecting witnesses than we are."

"She's a witness? She knows who killed her husband?"

"Not exactly. She's a special admit to the program. She's being protected as a threatened prosecutor."

I chanced a glance toward Teri. Her expression was neutral; she wasn't sending me signals to alter my line of questioning. I asked Ron, "Isn't her being in the program difficult for the people in the Marshals Service? It puts you in the position of having to protect someone who's been publicly critical of your work."

Ron touched his chest. "Hey, am I the one in therapy here?" He leaned forward toward Alan again. "Listen, Doctor. Can I call you Alan? Good. Alan. In Witness Security I don't get to work with too many saints. Some mob informants. More and more drug informants, people who've been turned by the DEA. But mostly people who have broken more laws than most civilians know exist. People who have killed people. People who have sold enough crack or heroin to fill my garage to overflowing. I don't think about whether I like these people or not. I wouldn't get very far worrying about what's difficult for me *personally*. You know what I'm saying? Peyton Francis and I will get along because we need to. It's that simple."

"She's coming into Colorado when?"

"It's not important for you to know when she arrives. You'll meet her next week. She's asked for an early appointment to see a shrink. What can you offer me, timewise?" He yanked a Palm Pilot from an ass-pack that was on the floor by his chair and poked at the screen with the stylus.

Alan knew his open hours without having to consult a calendar. "I can do Monday at nine-thirty, Wednesday at one-fifteen, Thursday at ten."

"She'll take next Thursday at ten for the first meeting. After that you can work it out with her." He pecked away at the little computer for another ten seconds. "Your bills will come to me at the address on the card. What else? Teri, anything I'm forgetting?"

Alan thought that Teri was concentrating much more on her womb than on Ron Kriciak's questions. She shook her head.

"Well then, I think I'll be going." He stood and replaced the Palm Pilot in his pack.

Alan pointed at his riding gear, "So, what do you ride, Ron?"

Kriciak narrowed his eyes and said, "A bicycle."

AFTER THE MARSHAL left, Teri Grady said, "The amount of attitude fluctuates. I don't have my finger on it, yet. I think it's a product of his ambivalence about these people he works with. Before I was visibly pregnant, I got less of it. Now that he's not so eager to flirt with me, it leaks out a little bit more. I imagine you'll get a healthy dose."

"But he's helpful when you need something?"

"Helpful? I don't know about that. He listens, doesn't sabotage overtly, has a reasonably open mind. But he works for a secret government program that isn't eager to explain itself to me or anybody else. We get along. I don't waste energy trying to diagnose him; he's not my patient."

"But Carl is," Alan said.

"Yes, Carl is," Teri said. "Carl Luppo. I like him, by the way. Based on what I know about him, I would estimate he's killed somewhere between fifteen and twenty people. And that could be an underestimate. I've never asked for an accurate accounting." She puffed out her cheeks and opened her eyes wide in disbelief. "And despite knowing all that, . . . I like him."

Alan guessed what Teri was saying. He translated. "Transference is amazing stuff. So is countertransference."

"Tell me about it," she said.

3

THURSDAY AT TEN

Peyton Francis was early for her first appointment with Dr. Gregory. Ron Kriciak had dropped her off out front of the small house that contained his office at least twenty minutes early. She found her way into the waiting room ten minutes before the hour, and Dr. Gregory walked into the room to retrieve her exactly on time.

DR. GREGORY USUALLY spoke first during initial therapy sessions, and he usually used the same phrase to do it. "How can I be of help?" is what he'd say.

But Peyton preempted him. As soon as she sat down, she said, "I really need this. Thanks for seeing me so soon. You should know that I was hoping you would be a woman. They originally told me that I'd be seeing a woman."

Dr. Gregory gave her time to continue. She didn't. He said, "You're disappointed?"

"Yes. But I'll manage. I haven't gotten too much of what I wanted lately. Do you know what's happened to me? Have the marshals filled you in? As you can probably tell, I don't have much experience with all this. Psychotherapy, I mean. Up until now I considered myself one of the fortunate people, not one of the troubled ones."

"I know the public story and also some details that Inspector Kriciak chose to share with me. That's all I know."

"So you know about Robert? My husband? You know what they . . . um, did to him in New Orleans?"

"Yes."

She picked a thread off her dress and spun it into a ball between her index finger and thumb. "That day? At times it feels like I wasn't actually there, but I was. I was right next to him, a few feet from him. But in my head I still see it as though I was far away, like down the street from him, separated by a glass wall. No matter how much I wanted to, I couldn't get to him. Do you know what I mean?"

Dr. Gregory didn't and said so with his eyes and with a slow shake of his head.

He watched as his new patient pressed her lips together and narrowed her eyes. Her knees were locked tight in front of her, as though they'd been fused.

"It's like, when I looked up and saw the two of them, . . . I *knew* the danger he was in—even though all I saw is a man with a coat over his arm at a funny angle—but I felt in my gut that something was terribly wrong. It was the same way I can tell when my daughter has strep, or how I know when she's been hurt by something a friend has said to her. I just *know*. That day, I just knew."

Gregory watched her pause and exhale without inhaling first. The mention of her daughter, is what he thought.

"Landon is my daughter. That's not her real name. She's nine, now. Just nine." Peyton looked up and met her therapist's eyes, hoping for some sign of understanding from him. "It's like that," she said.

He digested her words, saw the fork she'd presented in the road, and picked one route. His choice was reluctant. That was nothing new for him when he did therapy. He said, "It's like a dream that feels real?"

She thought about his analogy and apparently decided that she could live with it. "Sure. Okay," she said as though the last thing she wanted to be was disagreeable. She rubbed her hands together. "Is it cold in here, or is it me?"

Minutes earlier, when she'd first come into his office, she'd had a choice between a sofa and a chair. The chair was closer to Dr. Gregory's own chair and was upholstered in leather the color of burnt butter. The sofa was farther from him and was covered in chenille. She chose being farther away, and she chose chenille over leather. Now she felt cold. Did it mean something? Dr. Gregory didn't know. He filed it away.

She apparently decided that his analogy about dreams wasn't apt after all. "No. It's not like a dream. It's more like when you're reading a book. When you know that the hero is in danger even though he doesn't know he's in danger, and *you* know how to warn him, to protect him—to save him—but you can't communicate with him, because he doesn't even know you're there. Your heart races and you read faster, and you just want to crawl onto the pages and drag him to safety. Is it ever like that for you when you read?" She looked away from him, as though her admission embarrassed her. "I like books. I really, really like books," she said, briefly closing her eyes before returning her gaze to meet his. "Does it make sense now?"

It made perfect sense, but only because he already knew the broad outlines of the story she was about to tell. He could have just said, "Yes," but his therapeutic instinct was to encourage her to sink, instead, into the crevices that most certainly meandered into caverns below her carefully chosen words. He said, "He was your hero? Robert was? Like in the books?"

She stretched her eyes open wide. The expression tightened the flesh over her cheekbones. Her tone became mildly defiant. "I don't want to cry. I've been crying for months. It feels like years. I want you to help me stop crying. Can you do that for me? I want to get on with my life."

"I don't think you can choose when to stop crying."

She dabbed at her eyes. "At some point I have to. For Landon. She needs a functioning parent, doesn't she? Am I being selfish with all this? Should she be here instead of me? God, what she's been through is way too much for a little girl."

"You're wondering if your daughter needs psychotherapy?"

Peyton nodded. "Yes."

"There's no arguing that she's been through a lot, Peyton. Are you seeing signs that she might not be coping?"

"No, no. Yes. Like what? What kind of signs?"

"Is she sleeping normally?"

"Yes."

"Eating well?"

"Yes."

"Is she moody? How's her activity?"

"No moodier than usual. And she's very active, always doing something."

"School work? Friendships?"

"She did fine in Louisiana. She's . . . fine with her friends. That's when she's at her best, I think."

"Anything else unusual with her health or . . . ?"

Peyton touched her fingertips to her chin. "Maybe I'm worried that she's doing too well. Is that possible?"

Gregory didn't answer.

Peyton asked, "So what do you think?"

He said, "I think your daughter has a mother who is very concerned about her. I also don't hear any indications that her coping skills are currently failing her. If I do hear anything, I promise I'll let you know."

"But my coping skills are failing me?"

His eyes allowed her to wonder about her own question. She glanced away from him before looking back. "Can I tell you about that day now? In New Orleans. Is that all right?"

"Of course, if that's where you want to start."

As she absorbed his simple words he watched her muscles soften and she seemed to sink two inches farther into the contour of the cushions below her and behind her. "It's where everyone wants me to start. The marshals, especially. They all want to hear either about that day or about that . . . other day during the trial. You know about that? The day of the sentencing. That's all anyone seems to want to hear."

"Hopefully this will be a little different from your meetings with the marshals. You can choose where to begin when you're in here," Dr. Gregory said. "You barely know me. I'm not about to presuppose when or how much you're going to feel like trusting me yet. Especially since you were hoping for a female therapist."

Her next move surprised him. She stood and stepped toward him and resettled herself onto the leather chair. Once her dress was tugged close to her knees, and her long legs were crossed, her feet dangled only eighteen inches from his. "I think I'll be more comfortable here," she explained. "Warmer maybe. If I don't talk about . . . that day, what will I talk about?"

He shrugged. "I can only guess what it's like to be in your shoes. I can imagine a thousand issues. If I guessed ten times what would be most important, though, I think I would be wrong exactly ten times."

Peyton said, "I'm scared almost all the time, even when I'm at home. I'm not sleeping well. I'm losing weight. I'm irritable with my daughter. I'm becoming a paranoid monster."

"See," Dr. Gregory said. "Those weren't even on my top-ten list."

Of course, he could have guessed at some of them. But he never would have placed the words in her mouth for her. She did manage to surprise him with what she said next.

"What's happened hasn't just stressed me out. What's happened has changed me. Each day now, sometimes each and every minute of every day, I find myself waiting for the end to come. A cataclysmic end. That's not me. I was raised believing in fairy princesses and knights on white horses. I'm someone who has always wanted to believe in infinity. And now I'm always looking for the end.

"I don't want to be that way. What I do want is to create something new here in Boulder. Something enduring and valuable for me and for Landon. But I'm too much of a wreck. I need you to help me, Doctor. I don't have anyone else to help me, and I'm afraid that I'm sinking."

AFTER ALAN GREGORY was finished with his session with Peyton, he was meeting his wife, Lauren, for lunch. She'd told him that morning over toast and juice that she wanted to go to Rhumba. One of the managers at Rhumba was a patient of his, however, and he wasn't comfortable doing business in establishments where his patients worked, so he planned to try to convince his wife to choose another place to eat.

Even before they were out the front door of the old Victorian, she said, "Was that your patient who just left, or was it Diane's?"

The fact that his wife was asking a question about one of his patients caught Alan's attention. She rarely mentioned his patients. There was little point in pretending that the woman who'd just walked out the door hadn't been his patient. Diane Estevez, his partner in the building, wasn't working that day. When he didn't answer right away, Lauren said, "That's right, I forgot. Diane's not here today. She and Raoul are still house-hunting."

Alan smiled.

Lauren said, "I think I recognized her. Your patient. Her hair's different, she's lost weight, she's wearing glasses, but I think I recognized her. Is it who I think it is?"

Lauren knew the rules about patient confidentiality and wouldn't press him to actually divulge a patient's identity. Alan knew he could have dropped the whole issue with a friendly reminder that he couldn't say anything about any of his patients, but his curiosity prevailed. He asked her, "Who do you think it is? Somebody you know from work or something?"

"No. It's that prosecutor who used to be in the news. The one from New Orleans. Kirsten something. Lord. Kirsten Lord. The one who was threatened in court and then her husband was murdered. You remember? We talked about her a lot, you and I, when all that was going on. People in the DA's office still mention her occasionally. Everybody wonders what happened to her. After her husband was buried it seems she just fell off the face of the earth." She paused. "Anyway, that's who your new patient is." She paused again. "At least now I know what happened to her."

Alan felt his stomach flip, but he forced a smile and pressed his open palm against his wife's taut abdomen. He asked, "How's our baby?"

She was silent for a moment, trying to make sense of the non sequitur.

Alan stepped away and checked to make sure the door from the waiting room to the back of the house was locked. When he looked back at Lauren again, her eyes were fixed on his face. Finally she said, "She's your new Witness Protection patient, isn't she?" It barely qualified as a question, and Lauren certainly didn't expect him to answer. Alan had already told her that he was scheduled to pick up two new WITSEC patients from Teri Grady.

He leaned close to Lauren and looked into her violet eyes. "The baby? How's our little one?"

She knew he was diverting, that she had gotten as much as she was going to get from him about his patient. "The baby's good, sweets. An active day." She gripped his hand tightly as they descended the old stairs on the front porch. Without changing her pace at all, she said, "If I'm right about who she is, I want you to take especially good care of her, okay? This new patient of yours. You promise me you'll do everything you know how to help her?"

"I promise," he said. "You feel like Mexican food? The baby likes Mexican, right?"

"The baby does fine with Mexican. But I thought we were going to Rhumba. I have a taste for Rhumba." She did a little quasi-Caribbean dance step to punctuate her pronouncement.

"I think I feel like Mexican. Do you mind?"

She repeated the dance step, this time more dramatically. "We want Rhumba. We really, really want Rhumba."

"Then," he said, "I guess it's Rhumba."

DR. GREGORY'S WIFE, Lauren, was a prosecutor in Boulder County. The day after Ernesto Castro threatened Kirsten Lord in the New Orleans courtroom, Lauren had heard the details at work and had told Alan the story over dinner. Not surprisingly, the very-public threat was all the buzz in the Boulder DA's office and probably in every other prosecutor's office in the United States.

A few weeks later, Lauren cried at the breakfast table as she slid the *Denver Post* across the table toward her husband. On the front page was a photograph of Kirsten stooped over her husband Robert's inert body on the sidewalk outside a restaurant in New Orleans' French Quarter.

"He did it," she said. "The asshole did it. He took his revenge on her. He did exactly what he threatened to do."

For days Lauren seemed to grieve for Kirsten Lord's loss as though she were grieving for a close colleague who worked right down the hall. Lauren mentally reviewed all the cases she'd prosecuted and recalled all the assholes who'd made oblique or direct threats over the years.

As they walked down Pearl Street toward Rhumba for lunch, Alan reminded himself that Lauren had a special attachment to what had happened to Kirsten Lord. Lauren had paid particular attention to Kirsten's tragedies. She had empathized with her losses on a very personal level. That, he told himself, was why she recognized the woman exiting his waiting room as Kirsten Lord, now Peyton Francis.

Still, Alan fought despair as they made their way toward Ninth Street. *How was Peyton going to survive all this?*

If Lauren recognized her this easily, someone else surely would. Peyton was too well known to hide.

How would she and Landon survive all this?

ALAN PULLED HIS wife to a stop in front of the Tibetan imports store on Pearl Street and waited for her to look at him. "Lauren, just for the sake of argument, let's say you were right before. About that patient you saw in my office?"

She scanned his eyes for some sign of where he was heading with his words. She didn't find it. She said, "Yes?"

"Mentioning anything to anyone about who you think she is might put her at tremendous risk."

She could hear the tension in his words. She fought a reflex to be offended. "I know that."

"Okay," he said. "That's all I wanted to say."

She laced her fingers in his and they resumed their walk.

She repeated her little dance.

4

"I go to Toledo next week to testify. You know 'bout that?"

"No. I don't. Truth is, I still don't know about much as far as you're concerned," Dr. Alan Gregory admitted to the second of his two new WITSEC patients.

The man laughed and smiled. "Welcome to the fuckin' club. The testifying? It's part of the deal. I stay in the program so long as I cooperate and testify when they want me to testify. I refuse to testify, I'm back on my own. This trial in Toledo's bogus, though, I told 'em that right from the start. I'm basically going to say I saw so-and-so going into such-and-such a meeting. That's it. I wasn't in the meeting. I don't know who said what. Somebody came out later, somebody let's say I do know, and they told me I might be doing a piece of work in Indianapolis. That's all I know. Who wanted this guy taken care of? I don't know that for sure. That's what I'll say when they ask me. For that little bedtime story I'll spend a day being babysat by a couple of marshals barely older than my oldest grandson."

From Dr. Gregory's briefing by Ron Kriciak, he knew that the man sitting across from him in the leather chair was discussing his previous career. "Doing a piece of work" was a euphemism for planning someone's murder. Dr. Gregory tried to act nonplussed and immediately questioned whether or not that was the right therapeutic move.

He asked a meaningless question. It was one of the things he did in therapy when he was nervous. He asked, "When you testify at these trials, you fly in and fly out in the same day?"

"Nah. Fly in the day before. Spend the day in a jail cell somewhere in solitary. Fly back here when the U.S. attorney's done with me. Marshals hold my hand every step of the way."

"You okay with this?"

The new patient raised his chin a smidgeon as though his tie were too tight. He wasn't wearing a tie. "You mean the traveling or the squealing? Know why I'm here? In the program? They turned on me after I stayed quiet for twelve years. The people I stayed loyal to turned on me. After I honor my word in the federal pen for twelve years, they turn on me. What do I owe 'em after that? Tell ya, I don't owe 'em."

Dr. Gregory tried to recall the man's history. Fifty-two years old. Referred originally for depression. Responded well to Zoloft. Secondary diagnosis, PTSD. Post Traumatic Stress Disorder. Symptoms: sleep disturbance, anxiety. Precipitating events: his previous employment, his years in prison, and loss of contact with his family. Dr. Gregory decided that PTSD could certainly be considered an occupational hazard of being an enforcer in organized crime.

With another patient, Dr. Gregory would have allowed the silence in the room to spread, like a heavy gas, until it filled the room. Not with this patient. He wasn't comfortable with this man being anxious. Not yet, anyway. He asked, "Are you okay with the change?"

"You mean you for Dr. Grady? Too early to tell, you know what I mean. She was a good problem solver. She seemed honestly interested in helping me adjust, if you know what I mean. I liked that. If you're a good problem solver, you and me we'll do fine, too."

"What kinds of problems did you work on with Dr. Grady?" He knew he wouldn't have asked another patient the same question. He knew it.

The man smiled, and to Dr. Gregory his eyes looked older than they had before. "I'm going to treat you like a rookie," the man said. "But that's okay. I'll be teaching you about the program and about the life— you'll be teaching me about living. Because I'm coming to learn I don't know shit about that."

"What piece of living should we start with?"

"Right now, I got too much time on my hands. I don't do these trips to testify very often. Don't know if Dr. Grady told you, but I did a semester of college already, in Denver at Auraria, but I'm not sure that's the best thing for me. I think instead I gotta get a job, or start a business, or something. That's where we should start. Talking 'bout how to do that."

"Do you have ideas?"

"I have lots of ideas on how to make money. I'm a practical man. I see voids, if you know what I mean. You could call it vision—it's always been one of my things. But I don't know much about business. Running a business, that is. Dr. Grady kept trying to convince me that the skills I have from my other life don't translate too well to . . . this world."

"You would need to do this on your own? Find work? Set up a business? The marshals don't help?"

Carl Luppo puffed out his cheeks in exasperation. "You know much about fishing? You don't, do you? I can tell. You don't seem like the type. Anyway, the point I was going to make is that Witness Protection is basically a catch-and-release program. After they snare you and you agree to cooperate they drop you into a new pond and they give you enough money to get settled and then they basically tell you good luck. Well, me? I haven't been in a pond that wasn't behind bars for twelve years. And the pond I was in before that one didn't have the clearest water around, you know what I mean. So I don't know much about being effective in this life with the skills I have. The money they gave me at the beginning— that's your stipend—if that's all I had, I'd be one dead flounder."

Dr. Gregory was reluctant to ask. But he asked. "What are those skills you have?"

The man raised his chin a centimeter or so before he said, "I was a gorilla." Then he paused. "And I'm good at it. At least I was."

"A gorilla?"

"I intimidated people. Some a little. Some a little more than that. Usually just needed my eyes. Sometimes my tone of voice. On rare occasions I had to beat on my chest, you know?"

Dr. Alan Gregory could only imagine.

5

THE FOLLOWING THURSDAY AT TEN
Peyton took the initiative as her second session began with Dr. Gregory. "My memories? They're like whales. I think of them sometimes as though they're a pod of whales. Is that weird?"

Alan Gregory didn't understand the analogy Peyton Francis was making but assumed she would explain it further. From the look on her face he couldn't even be certain whether or not she was embarrassed by her admission about how she conceptualized her memories. He waited. He did a lot of waiting while he was doing psychotherapy. Sometimes he considered it the most important and the most difficult thing he did.

She'd arrived for this session, her second, with a lollipop in her mouth, the white stick tucked all the way against the corner on the right side. She touched the stick infrequently and had only removed the lollipop from her mouth once in the few minutes she'd been sitting with him. Her new therapist thought it might be a Tootsie Roll Pop, but he wasn't really up on lollipops.

When she spoke again, he was amusing himself by trying to decide whether to say something interpretive about an oral fixation.

"Most of the time, they're submerged. Invisible. I'm talking about the whales. But they always surface eventually—it's as though they need to come up for air. Sometimes they surface when I expect them to, you know, someplace close to where they were the last time they went down. I'll see a picture of Robert and I'll remember something especially happy or especially sad about him, about us. Other times the whales seem to migrate and pop up where I don't expect them. Lately they've been coming up in the middle of the night. They do seem to like to surface then."

"They don't ever really go away?" Dr. Gregory asked. With his question, he was dancing a little. What he really wanted to know was whether her metaphor about whales was her way of talking about repressed memories, those that are inaccessible from consciousness, usually due to trauma, or whether she was referring to memories that had simply faded from her awareness.

He was still distracted by the lollipop.

"The big ones? The whale memories? No. I wish sometimes that they would go away. I marvel sometimes that, uh, Landon is already forgetting things that happened to her when she was only three and four. Even special times that have to do with her father. I would think she'd cling to those as though they were a life preserver. That worries me mostly, but sometimes I feel envy, too. Because I don't believe my whales will ever, ever totally fade away. I don't think I'll ever be able to forget some of the whale memories. The best I hope for," she smiled sadly, "is that when the bad whales dive, they go down so deep that I can't find them for a while, can't even feel the disturbance they make as they swim through the deep water."

He didn't know where she was going next and said nothing.

She arched one eyebrow, then the other. A trace of a smile was visible in her eyes. "Some of them I actually adore," she admitted. "The memories aren't all evil, not at all. The ones I adore are the ones that appear in my mind like daydreams and float me away to some-place special that I once cherished and that I fear I will never . . . ever . . . have again. They're my friendly whales. I call them my be-lugas."

"But some of the memories aren't so friendly?" Dr. Gregory assumed that Peyton's intent was to talk about the whales that weren't so friendly, but he silently questioned the redirection he'd encouraged the moment the words were out of his mouth. It wasn't part of his job to assume what patients intended.

"Absolutely not. God, no. Those are my killer whales. Robert being murdered." She looked away and stared at a blank spot on the wall. "Getting the phone call about my mother dying. And . . ." She closed her lips tight around the tiny lollipop stick and shut her eyes for a mo-ment. "The day they tried to kidnap Landon—Landon was Matilda then. You probably don't know about that, do you? What happened . . . was never in the news. That's the whale that keeps visiting during the night these days. I wake up, and I get out of my bed and move from my room into her room, and I lie—is that right? Is it lie or is it lay? I don't know, I can never remember. Anyway, I lie beside her in her bed before I can fall back to sleep. I smell her here, in the crook of her neck," she said as she touched herself right above her collarbone. "I just stick my nose right into her hair and inhale her sweetness, and I swear it's like a narcotic for me. It calms me. And hours later I wake up and I'm still in her bed. And when I do, that whale is no longer on the surface."

Dr. Gregory had trouble concentrating. His mind had already traveled from his patient's daughter's bed to his own wife's womb, to the sweetness growing there. He was momentarily lost wondering about his baby's sweet aroma, the perfume in the crook of his son or daughter's neck. Then the word *kidnap* resonated in his consciousness and he asked, "They tried to kidnap your daughter?" trying to keep the *Oh my God!* out of his voice.

Peyton nodded. "After my husband was killed, we went into hiding. Landon and me. But he found us, his people found us, found her. Matilda, I mean Landon. She did all the right things, though."

"You weren't there?"

She lowered her chin and shook her head, as though shamed. Without Dr. Gregory noticing, she'd managed to move the lollipop stick from one side of her mouth to the other. "She was at a new friend's house. They were playing outside."

The truth was that despite all the times Dr. Gregory had seen Kirsten Lord's face on the news, he wasn't sure he would have recognized her. Her long blond hair was now carelessly short and had been cosmetically darkened to the color of weathered mahogany. She wore rimless glasses instead of contacts and simple clothes suitable for both Boulder and her new profession.

Since she'd arrived in Boulder, she'd been working as an unpaid intern in the kitchen at Q's, arguably one of Boulder's finer restaurants, doing something she'd always thought she might love. She'd joked to herself that she was auditioning for the role of being just another burned-out lawyer looking for something new to do with her life.

Teri Grady had warned Alan Gregory that money is an important issue for most people in the program. WITSEC provides some transitional financial support, though program participants are expected to move quickly toward self-sufficiency. But Peyton didn't have those concerns yet. Her husband's life insurance and their joint savings were more than adequate for the short term for her and for her daughter. She could afford to apprentice in a restaurant kitchen and pursue her dream to learn how to cook.

.   .   .

"I DON'T REALLY want to talk about that today. I trust that's just fine with you, Dr. Gregory." Her voice, he thought, was mildly teasing.

"It is," he said while he palpated the tease for signs of flirtation.

"What I want to talk about is my daughter." She waited.

He said, "Yes."

She pulled the lollipop from her mouth. The candy that remained on the end of the stick was no larger than a pea.

Dr. Gregory knew that he would have chewed the little nub of candy off the stick long ago. He was beginning to appreciate that the woman sitting across from him had an abundance of patience.

"Do you know much about kids?" she asked.

As a psychologist he'd heard the question before, of course. He hated it a little bit more each time he heard it anew.

"Yes," he said. Technically—academically—his answer was truthful. But he felt like a liar. The kid he knew the most about was the one who hadn't yet been born, the one still in his wife's body.

She fished into her purse and retrieved a camel leather wallet. The picture on top was of her daughter. She handed it to him.

He struggled for the right words. "She's lovely. She looks a lot like, oh, you know . . ."

She finished his sentence by saying, "The way I used to look?" She smiled with her mouth, but not with her eyes. "Thank you for saying that. It's a compliment for me. Though she looks a lot like her daddy, too."

"But you have some concerns?" he said, attempting to reel them both back to her prologue.

She nodded. "Of course. What she's been through. Robert's murder. Two major moves. Two new schools. The kidnap attempt. All my paranoia. She's been through . . . hell. And it's all because of me."

"You feel responsible," he said, injecting some empathy, yet hoping not to interfere with whatever direction she'd chosen to go.

Her eyes moistened. "Landon is all I have left. My parents are dead, so are Robert's."

"How is your relationship with your daughter?"

Peyton smiled with her eyes *and* with her mouth and said, "She's my buddy. She's a dream. She's just nine years old. Oh, sometimes she's more like four, and sometimes she's more like nineteen. Sometimes she wants me to be her best friend, and sometimes she wants me to be her mommy. Every hour, every minute, I have to figure out what she needs, and I have to be there for her. Truth is, she's the only reason I decided to volunteer to go into the Witness Protection Program. And she's the only reason I'm still sane."

She paused, waiting for something. Dr. Gregory wasn't clear what.

She said, "Yoohoo, Dr. Gregory? I am still sane, aren't I?"

"As far as I can tell."

"Now there's damning with faint praise." Her eyes fell to her lap. "I'm having a problem about Landon with Inspector Kriciak. I'd like some advice."

He allowed her request to linger in the space between them for a moment before he said, "I'll do what I can to help."

"Landon lives for two activities. She loves soccer—she plays goalie. And she's a phenomenal little speller. You know, like spelling bees? Ron doesn't want her to compete in any events where there's likely to be media coverage. No regional soccer tournaments or soccer camps, no spelling bees outside her school. I think he's exaggerating the risk to her. What do you think?"

He recalled Lauren's reaction to seeing Peyton in the waiting room. He said, "I can see how there could be some risk of your daughter being recognized."

Peyton was prepared to argue. "Her hair's different. She's growing like a weed. What's even more relevant is that she needs soccer and spelling for her . . . self-esteem, you know? It's part of how she sees herself. They were two things that she did with Robert. Her father. For her, doing them is a way of keeping his memory alive."

He weighed his words before speaking. "Even if by doing them she increases the risk of not keeping the two of you alive?"

His question was too direct. She took a moment to compose herself. She touched the lollipop stick and then the collar of her shirt. She tried to smile, but failed. "I'm not even comfortable leaving her alone with a babysitter. When I'm at the restaurant, I call home twice an hour to check on her. She wears a beeper so that I can reach her. I wear one so she can reach me. For me, this whole move to Boulder has fresh nightmare written all over it. I'm beginning to recognize the signs. I'm afraid that this is going to be the birth of a new whale."

"Is it a killer whale or a beluga?"

"That's the question I'm struggling with," she said. "That's the question. There's another category of whales in my pod. The humpbacks. They sing to me when they're close to the surface. Long, brooding songs. When they dive they disappear, and when they resurface, they come back up as belugas or killers. But I don't ever know which. This one—this whole question about Landon's freedom, her soccer, her spelling—it's singing to me now; it's starting off feeling like a humpback." She sighed. "You see, the whole thing is especially complicated because Landon has already tested into some summer competitions that will prepare her for the regional spelling bees."

Dr. Gregory waited. Peyton waited. Finally, he spoke. "That must make you proud, Peyton."

"Proud? Absolutely. But terrified is more like it. I have only one daughter. I couldn't bear to lose her."

He nodded as though he understood her words at the deepest of levels. But he acknowledged to himself that he probably didn't. Once again his thoughts went to his wife's womb.

"Don't you see what's happening?" she said. "Landon and I are all that's left standing after fate has bowled its first ball down the lane. That's it—two pins left standing. And we're just waiting . . . paralyzed . . . waiting for the next bowling ball to come down the lane, waiting to see if fate's a good enough bowler to pick up the spare. Coming to Boulder, all that accomplished was moving Landon and me from Lane One to Lane Thirty-three to try to protect us. But fate will find us down here, too. You watch. Fate found Robert, didn't it?"

"You're not completely sure you want her in that spelling bee either, are you, Peyton?"

"No," she admitted. "I'm not. But I can only protect her so far. We changed where she lives. We gave her a new name, altered the way she looks, even gave her a new birth date. But we can't change what's in her soul, Dr. Gregory. We can't tell her to love something new and different. Some things about children aren't malleable. Some things parents can't change."

"You want me to talk to Ron Kriciak?"

"Please."

"And what would you like his blessing to do?"

"She wants to go to the summer spelling competitions. She'll stay away from the cameras. Even if she qualifies for the regionals, she won't go. That's what we'd like his blessing to do. That's all."

6

Dr. Gregory didn't laugh when I told him about my whales, didn't even seem to be hiding too much of a smirk. I wonder if he knew it was a test.

I wonder if I did.

I'd been in Boulder with Landon—gosh, it was so hard to remember to call her by her new name—for only, what? Ten days?

Yes. Ten days.

I KNEW THAT Kriciak, the inspector who was supervising me for the Marshals Service, was going to go nuts when I told him that I wanted to allow Landon to participate in soccer and spelling. Kriciak's style was to act cool, but underneath it all he had a temper, a cop's fuse. In my years as a prosecutor I'd worked with a dozen cops just like him.

I could have already predicted his arguments about why I shouldn't allow Landon to participate.

He'd say there was a chance she'd be recognized. People might be looking for her to surface.

He'd say it will be too hard for us to protect you. Your tormentors are quite determined.

And anyway, he'd say, think about Landon.

None of the marshals who had assisted me during my orientation and evaluation at the safe site had mentioned any possible relocation sites. No one pretended with me that I might have a choice about where I ended up. In fact, they made it clear to me many times that I didn't. I prayed for a city that might have good restaurants. After what happened in New Orleans and what almost happened in Slaughter, I knew that working as an attorney again, especially as a prosecutor, was out of the question. I'd already decided that I wanted to follow another passion of mine: I wanted to learn to cook in a fine restaurant.

When I heard I was going to Boulder, I was elated. I thought Boulder would offer more opportunity for fine restaurants than a place like Fresno, California, or Amarillo, Texas. I imagine that sounds insulting to the people of Fresno and Amarillo, whom I don't even know. I'm sorry, but that's what I was thinking at the time. Though I admit I wasn't at my best then, thinkingwise.

The marshal who eventually told me I was going to Boulder was a young woman. She was black and had eyes as comfortable as the softest pillow on which I'd ever rested my head.

She questioned me relentlessly to determine that Boulder wasn't a hot spot for me, that it wasn't in what she called my "danger zone," which included, as far as I could tell, only Louisiana, Florida, and the Baltimore–D.C. corridor. There were no known associates of the man they suspected of murdering Robert living in Boulder. They had asked me to be sure, and I wracked my brain for two days and nights and couldn't think of anyone I knew in Boulder. No old friends. No colleagues who had relocated there. No one from law school. No one who would recognize me and blow my cover.

I LIKED IT in Boulder. The sun in Colorado is sharp and brash, and I found myself attracted to the brazenness and to the clarity of the light. The Rocky Mountains rise provocatively—almost majestically—from the western edge of town, and I felt their vaulting presence as a protective wall for me and for Landon, as though they functioned like a moat at a medieval castle. During the first few days in town, I found myself turning my back to the Rockies the way I'd started sitting against walls in restaurants, always facing the open door, always scanning for short men in chinos.

Rationally, I didn't suspect that the next assault would come from the same man who'd killed Robert or even another man dressed the same way. But I had a face for the old monster, and I cherished it in much the same way that I cherished the cameo that hung around my neck.

It connected me to something essential, to my survival.

THE FIRST BRICK pavers of the Pearl Street Mall begin only a couple of blocks from Dr. Gregory's office. I walked to the Mall after the session when I'd confessed about the whales and looked for a place to sit outside in the sun. I had time to kill before I needed to be at Q's to begin the evening prep, and I was fighting a strong, strong urge to park myself outside Landon's door and listen to the childish sounds she made as she played. The sounds would soothe me like nothing else could.

The urge was a daily one. I swear my blood pressure went up twenty points the moment the little girl was out of my sight.

I'd just selected a pleasant spot on the Pearl Street Mall, at an open table under the outdoor awning at the café beside the Boulder Bookstore. I'd been to the café a couple of times before, and on one of the previous visits a waitress had told me that it was right next door to the old New York Deli, the one where Mork used to work—remember Mork? No? It's not important. The New York Deli's gone now, replaced by a sushi bar called Hapa. Mork's gone, too.

Anyway, that's where I was about to sit down when I felt someone looking at me.

My antennae resonated with some alarm, and I hesitated while I decided which seat at the table to choose. Intentionally, I looked down before I glanced back up, and I knew I'd succeeded in catching the man turning his head away from me as though he didn't want to be nabbed—what did Landon call it?—gaping. He didn't want to be caught gaping.

He was ten yards away, sitting on the edge of one of the brick planters in the middle of the Mall, the one at the end of the block beside the flat bronze sculpture of the old man who spits. Next to the man—not the one who spits, the one who was gaping—sat a large shopping bag from Abercrombie & Fitch.

The man who'd been eyeing me wasn't tall, maybe five-eight. He wasn't young, wasn't old. He had most of his hair, but it was short. I guessed that he was in his late forties, maybe early fifties. He wore sunglasses but no ball cap. He wore chinos and good leather shoes.

Yes, chinos.

Without glancing back my way, he stood and hooked the handles of the shopping bag with his fingers and lifted it from the bricks. The bag didn't distort as though it contained an extra heavy load. If the man had a gun, it wasn't stashed in the Abercrombie bag.

He took steps my way.

I didn't panic. I didn't run. But I moved away from the spot I'd chosen at the café and walked purposefully down the Mall. I fought an impulse to begin to pray, and I avoided looking over my shoulder. I was calmer than I might have been. Why? For some reason I didn't think that it was going to end like this.

I didn't feel a whale being calved.

After I crossed Broadway, I paused in front of a little store called the Printed Page. I spotted him on the other side of the Mall. He appeared to be window-shopping. I increased my pace and made my way down Thirteenth toward Canyon. I stopped at the light but didn't see him any longer.

My main hangout in my brief time in Boulder was the Dushanbe Teahouse. It is a stunning structure that was a lavish gift to Boulder from its Tajikistan sister city of Dushanbe. The bright, airy building was handcrafted in Asia and then disassembled and shipped in pieces to Boulder. It sat crated for years until the City of Boulder found the will, and the funds, to permit Asian artisans to reconstruct the exquisitely carved cedar columns, mosaic panels, and painted ceilings into a remarkable room.

I walked inside, got a table, and ordered tea. I was waiting for it to arrive when I saw the man with the Abercrombie bag walk in the door.

He stepped away from the entry, stared open-mouthed at the lavish decorations in the room, and then he spotted me. Without any further hesitation he stepped toward the empty seat at my table.

His approach paralyzed me the same way that I felt stopped in place by the man on Bourbon Street, the man who killed Robert. I considered screaming, running. But I couldn't afford to create a scene and bring attention to myself.

I didn't know what to do.

By then he was standing right in front of me. He was smiling. "May I?" he said, pointing at the empty chair. Even hearing only those two little words gave me some information. His accent was flavored with the eastern seaboard of the U.S.

Where exactly? *The Baltimore–D.C. corridor?* I couldn't tell.

Know thine enemies, I thought. Then I thought, *if this man wanted me dead, I'd already be dead.* Almost involuntarily my mouth said, "Um, I guess. Have a seat." I wasn't expecting him to reach into the Abercrombie bag and blow me away with a silenced weapon. All along, I thought I'd know when that was about to happen. This didn't feel like the time.

He lowered himself heavily, as though his ample weight was a bit much for one of his joints, a hip or a knee. "They got espresso here?" he asked me, his tone light, friendly. His cheeks rose when he smiled, chipmunklike.

"I don't know. I always have tea," I said, sliding a menu his way. His eyes intrigued me. They were the same blue as Landon's, even had the same amber pebbling in the irises.

"You're new in town?" he asked, but it wasn't really a question.

I didn't respond.

"You are," he said, leaving things momentarily at that.

I felt a shiver and wondered how he knew. Was it the way I was dressed? I was wearing a simple sundress; I no longer wore chinos. Ever.

He raised his hand from his lap, and my heart skipped a beat before I recognized that it was empty. He was offering to shake my hand.

"Carl Luppo," he said. "Pleasure."

For a moment I couldn't remember my new name. *Katherine?* No!

That was the old one. *Kirsten?* Can't use that one. *Peyton?* Yes! "Peyton Francis," I said, almost proudly.

He smiled. "Takes a while to get used to it, doesn't it. All the lying and pretending. It's unnatural. Took me months. I still f—— Excuse me, I still screw up sometimes, give stuff away that I'm not supposed to. You know?" His eyes remained friendly.

What? How does he know about the lying? What does he know about me? I swallowed, but I was more curious than frightened. I reached an instantaneous conclusion that this man was a marshal. He represented some kind of test that Ron Kriciak had arranged for me.

The waitress came and delivered my tea. Darjeeling. Carl Luppo ordered an espresso and after the waitress went on her way, he said, "I know I'm gonna be disappointed. I watch 'em make it sometimes and sure enough it comes outta the right machine, but it doesn't taste like it's suppos' to taste. The espresso? That's what I'm talkin' about." He offered me a pleasant little shrug that was more neck than shoulders. He had a robust neck, too large for either his shoulders or his head. His accent was definitely East Coast, but I couldn't begin to guess whether it was Miami or Boston or Newark or somewhere in between.

Like maybe the Baltimore–D.C. corridor.

My stomach flipped, and impulsively I almost asked him if he had kidnapped Landon. Figured maybe that's why his hand hadn't held a silenced gun. If he had my girl, he didn't need a gun. But my gut said that he didn't have Landon. My gut said something else was happening.

This was a WITSEC test, had to be.

He spoke. "I wasn't gonna talk to you today. Was gonna wait till another time. Hope I didn't spook you. That wasn't my intention." He scratched his head with his left hand before he smoothed his hair with his palm, a habitual gesture of someone who was accustomed to having more hair than Carl Luppo had right then. "But you made me over there when I was eyeing you. Over when I was sittin' on that planter on the Mall? That was good, that you made me. Generally, I'm not that easy to make. I'm pretty good at being invisible." He winked at me.

Involuntarily, I smiled back at him. But I was thinking that that's what people had said about the man in the chinos who'd killed Robert. The witnesses all said he was almost invisible. They'd hardly noticed him.

Carl Luppo waited until he'd captured my eyes in his own and said, "Me and you, Peyton Francis, we have a lot in common."

A cloud intercepted the sun, and the light around the Dushanbe Teahouse fell into shadows. The colors in the carvings seemed to come even more alive. "We do?" I managed to say.

"Sure we do."

The waitress brought his drink. He waited for her to move on to another table before he raised his demitasse cup from its saucer and touched the rim to his lips with his eyes closed, the way Robert used to when he was pretending he knew something about wine. "The espresso's all right—I'm surprised," he said. "Pleased, even. Not the same as back home in . . . but . . ." The neck shrug again. "What are you gonna do?"

"You said we have something in common," I said.

"Yeah, I did say that. We have the same doctor, for instance. That's something, right?"

God. That was it. Damn. He'd followed me to the Mall and then here from Dr. Gregory's office. I wondered why and fought a shiver that wanted to snake up my spine. What did he want with me?

"And . . . we have the same babysitter."

I lost my calm. I yelped, "What did you say?" Now I had to question my instincts. Maybe this was about Landon. Or was it? I only had one babysitter for Landon. She was a Hmong woman named Viv. She'd told me her name meant sister in Hmong. She watched Landon while I was working at the restaurant. Viv had told me she didn't work for any other families. Landon was actually learning some Hmong.

Weird.

Carl Luppo recognized the panic that lit in my eyes. "No, no, no," he said, making a dismissive gesture with his left hand. "It's not like that. Not about *kids* and babysitters. The babysitter I'm talking 'bout is Inspector Kriciak. He's *your* babysitter, right? Well, he's *my* babysitter, too. He's something, I gotta tell ya."

Suddenly, I knew exactly who this man was. "You're in . . ." the next word, whatever it was going to be, stuck in my throat.

"The program? Yeah. Ten months." He sounded like an alcoholic dating his sobriety.

It was the last thing I expected to hear from a stranger on the street. It was something I never expected to hear from a stranger on the street. The reality of what was occurring struck me. I'd been in the program for less than a month and I'd already been discovered? *Made.* Great. Just great.

I felt a hollow in my stomach that could have housed a herd of spelunkers. I wanted to run from the table and find my car and go find Landon and take a flight to the moon.

Carl Luppo said, "You're a newbie. It's hard, I know. But I think maybe I can help. The marshals aren't always going to be so helpful themselves. Pretty soon, Kriciak will stop dropping by so often. How often do you see him now, once a week?"

I nodded. "Twice maybe."

"Soon it will be every two weeks or even less than that. He calls you now, doesn't he?"

I nodded again. "Every other day or so."

"That'll stop. He won't call you so much on the phone, maybe not at all, or he'll only stop by when he has your stipend check or he wants something from you. He'll begin to see you as an occasional appointment he has to keep, not as a curiosity. Not a priority, you know what I mean?

"The problems you're having in a while won't be the same ones you have now, but there'll still be problems. You still won't know who to trust. And every day something will be hard. Awkward." Carl Luppo shook his head. "This is something I know about, believe me. Why? Because it's still hard for me after almost a year in the program. Want to know what's the hardest part about being in? Do you?"

I opened my mouth to reply. Closed it. Finally I stammered, "Sure. What's the hardest part?" I told myself I hadn't really acknowledged anything by asking the question.

"I miss my family. That's the hardest part. Knowing I can't see them, no matter what.

"The second hardest part? I feel useless now. I once had a role in life. I felt like I did important things. Now?" He did that shoulder shrug again. "I don't have a role. My role is waiting. Eliminate those two things—the family and the being-useless thing—and I swear I could do it. The time I'm doing in the program. Prison was easier than this in some ways. I spent some time there—a lot of time there, who am I kidding?—before I came into the program. I missed my family there but at least I wasn't useless. I had a role, a reason, a place inside, you know what I mean?" He drained his tiny cup and placed it haphazardly on the saucer. When he looked up he was smiling. "Here, though, at least there's better coffee than there was inside. And I can have wine with my dinner. Listen," he looked at me, "I've upset you with all this. I'm sorry, that wasn't my intent. My apologies." He feigned a little bow.

I'm a lawyer. I'd signed a Memorandum of Understanding that outlined my rights and responsibilities when I'd agreed to be placed in WITSEC. My mind started searching my memory of that document for a clause in the agreement that might have restricted my contact with other WITSEC participants. I couldn't recall one, but then I wouldn't have paid much attention to it anyway. I never expected to have a meeting take place like the one I was having.

I asked, "Are we allowed to do this?"

Carl Luppo was enjoying himself more than I was. "What?" he asked. "Sit in a pretty place like this and drink coffee? I think so. The program has some crazy rules but I don't think there's a rule against that." He paused and his eyes twinkled. "Truth is that this is probably considered a breach of security. Marshals knew we were here, we'd both probably be given the paper. But it's not my intention to jeopardize you unnecessarily. So you want me to get up and leave, I'm gone. History."

"What's 'given the paper'? What does that mean?"

"The paper is your ticket out of WITSEC. You want out, you ask them for the paper. They want you out because they think you violated security, then they give you the paper."

My indignation came out of hibernation. "Then you jeopardized me by following me here?"

"What I have to offer is worth it, I think. The risk is small. But you decide that, not me. Like I said, say the word, and I vanish like Tinkerbell."

I was off balance, way off balance. I made a perplexed face as I asked, "So you're really not going to tell Inspector Kriciak that we met?"

He smiled at me as though I were a lunatic. "What?" he asked. "You gotta be kidding?"

"Yes, I'm just kidding," I said, recovering.

I'm a good girl, always have been. I follow rules. I play by the rules. Sitting here breaching WITSEC security with this man frightened me. But along with the terror I was experiencing, I was feeling something else. I was captivated at the prospect of learning the ropes from somebody who had done what I was doing. I asked, "How did you find me, Mr. Luppo?"

"Call me Carl, please. But that was a good question you just asked me, Peyton Francis. Shows me that now you're thinkin'. If you want to stay in the program and you want to stay alive, it's important that you keep thinking. Disappearing—it's not as easy as you might imagine. It's important not to get complacent."

The word *complacent* surprised me coming from Carl Luppo's mouth. I said, "Well? How did you find me?"

He took a moment before he responded. "I don't expect much from people anymore. I used to. Respect, honor, loyalty. They were big deals for me. And honesty. I couldn't stand the f——, the people who wouldn't be straight with me. So . . . this is all a roundabout way of explainin' that I found you by accident while I was checkin' on Ron Kriciak's honesty. I was tailing him for a few days when he told me he didn't have time to do something for me. Turns out he was sittin' on *you* almost the whole time I was on *him*. One of the times I followed him was the time he dropped you off at Dr. Gregory's office. I put two and two together. Same place I go once in a while. I've always been pretty good at math so . . ."

I wondered if Carl Luppo was trying to give me an indirect message about Kriciak. "I'm not sure I understand. Why would you need to check on Inspector Kriciak? He's here to help you, isn't he?"

Carl said, "You'll learn. Some of the marshals, they're here to help. Others are here for another reason. What? You ask me, they're here to do what they can to get you tossed from the program."

"What?"

He leaned forward over the table. "Yeah, I'm serious about this. Some of the marshals, they can't do enough for you. They're like your mother's sister's kid, you know. Like family. Others? They get a hard— Excuse me, they get excited waiting for you to screw up. They sit on you, park outside your place, follow you to work, all the time waiting for you to commit a little breach of security—then they report you to Washington and you're gone. That's when they give you the paper."

I asked, "So what exactly did you discover when you were following him? Was Ron Kriciak being straight with you?"

My words earned me another smile. "Another good question, Peyton Francis. Maybe with my help you'll do okay in the program." He closed his eyes briefly. "The answer to your question is, I'm not sure yet. That time he was. But the jury's still out on Kriciak."

AND THAT'S HOW I met Carl Luppo. Everything about him told me he was going to be a beluga.

Everything about him also screamed "MOB!"

Hello.

7

What I knew about organized crime I'd learned from Al Pacino, Robert De Niro, and Robert Duvall. I had no context for understanding Carl Luppo. None. He seemed like a nice guy. After having tea with him, I felt that he could have been somebody's uncle. Somebody's father.

I also felt certain that he would have spent the whole afternoon chatting with me while sipping espresso in the Dushanbe Teahouse, but I had to get to work. I excused myself when it was time for me to walk the few blocks to begin my voluntary servitude at the prep table at Q's in the Hotel Boulderado. Carl stood quickly to help me slide back my chair.

"We should do this again," he said.

I wasn't ready to commit to that. Inadvertently breaching security once was one thing, plotting to do it again, something else entirely. I tried to deflect him by saying, "I'm curious about something. How could you be sure that Inspector Kriciak wasn't meeting me here today?"

"Ron doesn't do meetings in restaurants. He's too restless. I'd hate to see Kriciak after two or three coffees. Haven't you noticed? You seem perceptive. I'd have thought you'd notice."

He was right about Ron, of course. He was a walk-and-talk here's-the-plan kind of guy. Reminded me of a man I dated in college. No, not fondly. "Can I think about it, Carl? Doing this again. Maybe give you a call."

He looked crushed at my words but managed to conceal his disappointment behind the shrug that he seemed to have patented. "Sure, sure," he said. "Lemme give you my number." He scrawled it on the bottom of the receipt from the teahouse—he'd paid cash—and handed it to me. "I'm there a lot of the time," he said in a manner that amply communicated that he was lonely and bored and wished he had other things to do with his time. I'm sure he was hoping that I'd offer him my telephone number. But I didn't.

I felt repulsed by the sentiment my radar was detecting. I didn't need anyone to need me right now. For anything. No one but Landon.

And sometimes not her.

"I'll think about it. I promise," I said, pocketing the receipt with his phone number, and then I slid past him toward the bricks of the Mall. I was tempted to turn my head and offer a parting smile, but I told myself I shouldn't, and I didn't.

8

Ron Kriciak phoned Dr. Gregory a few minutes after eight on Saturday morning. Alan was already up and his wife, Lauren, was already out the door. She was someplace in town doing yoga with their neighbor Adrienne.

Ron didn't even bother with the banality of feigning concern that he might have woken Alan by calling so early on a weekend morning. They covered the how-are-you niceties in record time. Then Ron asked, "You planning to ride today?"

Alan was, but he wasn't looking for company. Most of the time he preferred riding alone. "I hadn't thought about it, Ron. But probably. On days as pretty as this one looks like it's going to be, I usually do."

"They say that the winds are going to come up this afternoon. They were over seventy miles an hour at Wondervu yesterday. I was thinking this morning would be better."

"Were you? Are you inviting me to go for a ride, Ron?"

"I guess. I've been thinking we should talk a little bit more about your new clients. Thought a bike ride might be a good idea, a nice way for us to get to know each other. Is there a route you like to do from your house? I'm thinking a hard ninety minutes or two hours."

"You want to climb?"

"No. Not today. Something flat."

Alan was already beginning to wonder what Ron wanted to discuss about his new WITSEC clients. "The releases they signed only permit me to share basic information with you Ron, not the details of what they might be talking about."

He was dismissive. "I know that. You have an idea where we could go?"

"Sure, there're some places we could go from my house. Do you know where I live?"

"I'm guessing Boulder."

"County, not the city. It's actually a little east, near the scenic overlook on 36."

"Morgul Bismarck neighborhood. I'll throw my bike in the back of my truck. Give me directions."

Alan did.

Ron said, "I can be there by nine."

"Then I guess that I'll see you then."

Alan couldn't recall the last time that he'd had a telephone conversation that conveyed less warmth with someone who wasn't in the process of goading him to change his long-distance carrier.

KRICIAK ARRIVED TEN minutes early. As Alan scurried around trying to get ready to ride, Ron kept saying, "Don't worry, no hurry," while he stole glances at his fancy watch. Alan was tempted to tell him to screw the ride but recalled Teri's caution about how essential the inspector's role was in the work that she did for WITSEC.

Ron's bike was an almost new Serotta Legend titanium road bike. Ron had customized his with components that probably brought its cost to slightly less than that of a good used car. A very good used car. Alan complimented him on it, and Ron replied by looking at Alan's three-year-old Specialized and saying, "Yeah. Yours is okay, too. I used to have one of those."

Alan led Ron away from the house on a northern and western route over country roads that climbed the undulating prairie and pasture of eastern Boulder County. Five years earlier, they might have had to slow for a farm tractor or even wait as a dairyman moved his herd of holsteins across a road from one grazing pasture to another. Not anymore. Now, Chevrolet Suburbans and Ford Expeditions filled the narrow lanes from shoulder to shoulder, shuttling young soccer or lacrosse players from Boulder's suburbs to their Saturday morning games against the kids from the city.

Ron stayed right on Alan's tail until they were well past Niwot and had started to skirt the farmland-gobbling developments around Longmont. At a point where it seemed they might have the road to themselves, Ron materialized next to Alan and said, "You been thinking any more about the material I let you review about our friend?"

"Which friend?" He'd given Alan plenty to think about regarding both Peyton Francis and Carl Luppo.

"What's-her-name, Peyton."

"Yes, I have."

"So how far are we going?"

"Thought we'd turn around near Hygiene. Is that okay?"

"I've never heard of it. Are we close?"

"A few more miles. It's before you get to Lyons."

Ron reached down and grabbed his water bottle and started sucking at the nipple. When he was finished taking a drink, he said, "We'll take a break and talk then." His bike trailed back behind Alan's so he could catch the slipstream.

Alan wasn't convinced Ron was a team player. He muttered, "Aye aye, Captain." So far, he wasn't having a good time.

THE MATERIAL RON was referring to had been in the two files that he'd permitted Alan to read before the meeting they'd had with Teri Grady to introduce him to his role with WITSEC.

The material about Peyton had been interesting to Alan, not so much because of the novelty—he knew the broad outlines of her story already—but because of the point of view that a retrospective look affords. It turned out that the initial threat made against Peyton Francis, then Kirsten Lord, had been small news. The news media had paid only passing attention to the little open-court soliloquy by Ernesto Castro that had so clearly threatened Kirsten Lord and her family. The entire coverage consisted of a brief article in the New Orleans paper and a short piece that had been run by AP. The only people who'd paid close attention had been other prosecutors.

Most of the media attention on Kirsten Lord came earlier and came later.

The earlier coverage focused on her eloquent diatribes against the U.S. Marshals Service and its management of the WITSEC program. Long before the arrest of Ernesto Castro for the elevator rape of the wheelchair-bound legal secretary, Kirsten Lord had been a vocal critic of WITSEC policies in regard to the handling of felons with records of violent crimes. Ms. Lord's pointed criticisms of WITSEC propelled her from the local news section of the *New Orleans Times-Picayune* to a guest column on the editorial page of the *New York Times,* a panelist's chair on *Larry King Live,* and to a remote hookup with Matt Lauer on the *Today* show.

The *Time* magazine profile followed soon after, as did a capsule biography in *People* that was accompanied by a photo of Kirsten holding a little white dog.

The bulk of the coverage that came after the infamous day in court when Kirsten was threatened by Ernesto Castro focused on the murder of Robert Lord, Kirsten's husband. Subsequent articles, mostly in the *Times-Picayune,* examined the public spat that developed between the district attorney in New Orleans, on one hand, and the local U.S. attorney and the regional WITSEC administrators, on the other hand. The local and national authorities were arguing who was best equipped to protect Kirsten and her daughter from further reprisals from whomever Castro had enlisted to carry out his threats.

ALAN PULLED OFF the road at a Diamond Shamrock station near Hygiene. He had to pee and asked Ron if he'd watch his bike while he went into the restroom.

"Let me go first," Ron said. "I'm about to explode."

He was off his bike before Alan had a chance to complain.

AFTER ALAN'S TURN in the bathroom, he walked back outside, the cleats on his bicycle shoes clacking on the concrete pad. Ron was at the compressed air machine, checking his tire pressure. Alan waited for him to finish.

"You see the news yesterday?" Ron asked as he walked back.

"Yes," Alan said, but he had no idea what in the news Ron was referring to. Maybe he wanted to talk about the Rockies current road trip or the Broncos annual sojourn to Greeley.

"The story from New York? LCN? La Cosa Nostra? The guilty plea in the RICO trial? You pay any particular attention to that?"

"Can't say that I did."

"The reason that they got the guilty plea was because of our boy, Carl. That was his doing."

"I thought Carl was in . . . I thought he was someplace else." Alan almost slipped and revealed confidential information from his session with Carl Luppo. Keeping the privilege intact with Ron Kriciak felt odd to him since he couldn't imagine that Ron didn't know where Carl had gone to testify the previous week, but he told himself that the cautionary reflex was healthy.

"Where did Carl tell you he was? These guys lie." Ron laughed and waited to see if Alan was planning to answer. After a moment of silence, he said, "But what are you going to do?"

Alan shrugged. He didn't know what he was going to do.

"His testimony just aced this guy in New York. That's why they got the guilty plea out of him. Before, I told you that Carl is hot? Well, if Carl was hot before, Carl is sizzling right now."

Alan's impression was that Ron was proud of Carl Luppo.

A Dodge Ram pickup pulled up next to them. Ron looked up at the driver and held his gaze a long time, as though he was considering asking the young woman who was driving for either her license and registration or for a date on Friday night. When Ron was done staring, he pushed his bike to some shade that was spread below a billboard on the side of the lot. Alan followed him.

"Carl's a handful. Smarter than most of the protected witnesses we see, oh, I'd say by about a light-year. Conservatively. Some of these wiseguys we get, let me tell you, they're not the brightest bulb in the scoreboard. But Carl? He's something else. Even though he spent most of his time as a high-ranking soldier, the man's got a mind of his own."

Alan thought that Ron wanted a comment, so he said, "Is that so?"

"Not a lot of formal education. I actually doubt he finished high school, but wise, nonetheless. Street-smart, yes. That's a given. But smart-smart, too. You'd be better off with him if you remember that."

Alan wanted to encourage Ron to keep talking, so he said, "I imagine having that level of intelligence would help Carl adjust to the challenges of being in the witness program."

"You imagine wrong." Ron cleared his throat and spit something disgusting up at the billboard. It stuck, making it twice or three times as disgusting. "The protected witnesses who do best are the ones who let their inspectors do most of the thinking, especially at first. That's not Carl's style. He does things his way. His fear never overrides his will. That's the exact opposite of most of our witnesses. For most of them, their will never overrides their fear. Carl's fearlessness and his willfulness makes him a tough handle."

Once again, Alan thought Ron wanted a comment from him. He was thinking of saying that the same trait probably helped Carl succeed in his earlier career. Instead he said, "I'll keep that in mind."

"Her, too. Peyton. She's way too smart. She knows she's smart, and what looks like it's even more of a problem for us is that she doesn't trust us. It makes it double hard for us to do our job."

Alan considered the possibility that Ron was grouping himself with Alan. Were they the "us"? he wondered. Alan asked, "She doesn't trust whom?"

"WITSEC. The marshals. Me, specifically."

Alan recalled the history. "There's a tough history between her and WITSEC, isn't there? A lot of suspicion to overcome. One of your other witnesses is responsible for killing her husband. Then attempting to kidnap her daughter. Now forcing them both into hiding."

"We're not a perfect organization. We supervise our protectees real well, but we're not perfect. And our witnesses are far, far, far from perfect people. Still, do you realize that fewer than ten percent of our witnesses are ever picked up for a serious crime while they're under our protection?"

It sounded like a lot of potential lawbreakers to Alan, but Ron's tone told him that he considered it a good number. Alan made a neutral face and kept the editorial opinions to himself.

"You know," Ron said, "be nice if you could help her overcome it, her distrust." Ron looked up at the mountains as he spoke these words. Alan felt that the diversion he was witnessing almost under-scored the importance of the message Ron was sending his way.

The message? Ron was trying to interfere with Peyton's therapy. A yellow caution flag descended into Alan's awareness. He wanted Ron to continue talking. "Really?" Alan said. "Me?"

"No joke."

"How would I do that?"

Ron laughed and tapped Alan on the shoulder, like they were good buddies. "How do you guys do whatever you do? I don't know and that's not my problem. What is my problem is that she's not de-pending on me the way she should, not looking to me for guidance. Usually, at the beginning, the protected witnesses treat me as though I'm only slightly less fallible than the Pope. Not Peyton. I think she's holding back. I'm afraid that if there are signs of danger around her, she won't let me see them. That leaves me in a difficult place. It's a trust thing, I think. Some residue from her earlier con-cerns."

Alan was struggling to read Ron's subtext. He asked, "Are you sug-gesting Peyton's afraid that there are people inside WITSEC—I guess I mean the marshals—who are more interested in harming her than protecting her?"

Ron straddled his bike and buckled his helmet strap. "She's pissed off a lot of people. She was our most vocal critic outside of Congress. People lost jobs. Careers were destroyed. A lot of people in the orga-nization feel that she unnecessarily jeopardized their work."

"I'm not sure I follow. Does that mean that there are people in WIT-SEC who want to harm her?"

"Can't say. I'm sure there are people who wouldn't shed a tear if something bad happened to her. Or if she screwed up somehow and got herself canned from the program."

Alan tried to read Ron's eyes but couldn't discern any nuance through the smoky lenses of his sunglasses. "Given what you're telling me, Ron, it seems possible that Peyton has good reason not to trust the program."

"No. The folks who were vocal in their opposition to bringing her in for protection don't know where she is. She's on special status in the program. Only a handful of WITSEC staff in the country even know her location. All information on her is tightly restricted. She knows all that, but still she's cautious. She needs to trust me. You need to trust me. We going to ride or what?"

He took off to the southeast.

Alan followed him, thinking *we could have done this on the phone*.

chapter

three
KHALID

I

During the first few days after I'd met him I concluded that my reaction to Carl Luppo had more to do with my feelings about Witness Protection than it had to do with my feelings about his participation in organized crime. My history with organized crime goes back only as far as Mario Puzo and has no more basis in reality than does my history with the Millennium Falcon. But I do have a history with WITSEC that goes back to my early days as a prosecutor in New Orleans.

IT TOOK ONLY one encounter with federally protected witnesses for me to cement my bias about WITSEC.

That first run-in had been with a man named Billy Foster.

Billy Foster's ticket to WITSEC was typical. In his earlier, pre-WITSEC life, Billy was a clumsy drug dealer named Wayne Simkin who was doing time in Nevada's state prison system after being busted for offering a commercial quantity of crystal meth to an undercover officer in a sting set up by the Reno Police Department. Once inside the walls, Wayne flipped and offered to inform on some of his fellow inmates in return for protection inside, and later, outside of prison.

The information that Wayne provided turned out to be valuable enough to the DEA that he earned, as part of the protection-on-the-outside-of-prison part of the deal, a WITSEC ticket to Louisiana and a court-ordered name change to Billy Foster. He found a job as a truck driver with a frozen-food delivery service. Within six months of his arrival in the South, Billy was arrested by the New Orleans police on a sultry August night on the edge of the French Quarter. Billy had just knifed a local drug dealer named Armando Jones.

Billy Foster claimed self-defense in the knife attack on Armando Jones. Running Billy Foster's fingerprints through AFID led the local police straight to Wayne Simkin. Self-defense, it turned out, was the precise claim that Wayne Simkin had used the two previous times he had been arrested for similar knife attacks, once in California, once in Nevada. One conviction, as a juvenile, came from the two arrests. Simkin's name, of course, led straight to WITSEC.

I caught the Simkin/Foster file. Although I was a baby DA at the time and didn't really have the standing to protest the way I did, I made a stink about the whole thing with my boss, the New Orleans district attorney. In a general staff meeting, I questioned the policies of a federal program that inserted lowlifes such as Billy Foster into communities like ours with little regard to the well-being of the law-abiding residents who lived there. One of my colleagues argued that Armando Jones was not exactly a law-abiding member of our community. I persisted anyway. After my diatribe I expected to be called naive and shuttled back to my desk. Instead, the DA took advantage of my youthful enthusiasm and moral outrage and quickly collected the files of five other cases of protected witnesses who had been arrested in his jurisdiction over the previous few years. He instructed me to become an expert on the cases, and on WITSEC procedure and strategy, and soon he appointed me to act as the liaison between our office and the local WITSEC representatives from the regional office of the U.S. Marshals Service.

I took Wayne Simkin/Billy Foster straight to trial, though he believed right until the end that WITSEC would ultimately save him from prosecution for his latest crimes. To their credit, they didn't. While I was readying my case against Foster, I did a little public prosecuting of WITSEC. I became a pain-in-the-ass to the local WITSEC team. One of the local marshals, a field inspector like Ron Kriciak, actually accused me of making a living chewing on his hemorrhoids.

Before long, our local congresswoman invited me to testify before a congressional committee investigating WITSEC abuses. After that splash, I did interviews with a dozen newspapers and magazines. I did CNN and CNBC and some late-night program on Fox that I wished I hadn't done. A producer from the *Today* show bugged me to talk live with Matt Lauer. I did. I was hoping for a trip to New York, but all I got was a remote hookup from the local affiliate.

The public arguments always had the same general tone. Usually a media representative from WITSEC was invited to participate. He— it was always a man—argued conviction rates based on protected witness testimony and the Marshals Service's exemplary record of protecting the safety of witnesses and the great inroads that had been made in prosecuting organized crime and drug cartels. I responded by arguing public safety, and I underlined the cost to the general public of having convicted violent felons released into our communities.

The truth was that, after a few weeks, the public grew tired of the argument. A few weeks after that, so did the media.

It seemed my fifteen minutes were up.

Then along came Ernesto Castro.

That one day in court he pointed his fat finger at me and he said, *"Remember this. For every precious thing I lose, you will lose two."*

With those words, I was granted fifteen fresh minutes and a half pod of fresh whales.

DURING MY THIRD visit with my new doctor he asked me the obvious question: Given the bad blood, given all I knew about the worst aspects of the program, how did I make the decision to agree to enroll in the Witness Security Program?

"They're good at what they do," I said. "Protecting witnesses.

There's nobody better. After what happened in Slaughter with Landon—Matilda—whatever, I knew I needed the best protection available for her. Ernesto Castro's people had found me in Louisiana. I don't know how. I don't know why. But I knew that they'd found me. I also knew that I needed better security than what I was getting in Louisiana. I felt WITSEC was my only real option, so I asked some friends to approach the U.S. attorney for me. See if he would sponsor me."

"But you don't truly trust them?" Dr. Gregory asked.

I hesitated before I said, "I trust them more than I trust Ernesto Castro."

"Which means what, Peyton?"

I liked the way this therapist pressed me sometimes, forcing me to take the next step. Robert never pushed me when I expressed discomfort. I'd dangle a painful feeling out there and act as though it scared me half to death, and Robert would amble forward and give me a hug and kiss me on top of my head. I could always hear him inhaling as he got close, sniffing for my perfume.

That memory—Robert smelling my scent—that's a baby beluga. It still warms me and brings tears.

I do believe that Robert often knew what I'd meant by my evasions. I also recognized that the problem was that I hadn't always had to acknowledge what I'd meant by my evasions. Robert saved me from that. Robert actually liked saving me from that. He so much liked being the husband. The only real problem in our marriage was that being the wife wasn't always that good a situation for me.

Dr. Gregory was still waiting for me to respond to his question.

I said, "Which means what it means." I knew that I was testing his resolve. I was aware that I wouldn't be disappointed if he rose from his chair and came over and hugged me and kissed me gently on top of my head. I wouldn't have minded had he inhaled my perfume along the way.

He didn't blink. He didn't get up. He said, "Yes. Go on."

I reached into my purse and unwrapped a lollipop. A DumDum. This one was cherry though I didn't care much about the flavor. Mostly I just liked having them in my mouth. My lollipop consumption had doubled or tripled since that day outside Galatoire's. I'd gone from a couple of bags a year to a couple of lollipops a day. Dr. Gregory would probably have a field day with that information. For the present, I kept it to myself.

"Some things I don't like to say out loud," I said as I crumbled the small waxy square of DumDum wrapper into a tiny ball. The trash can was across the room beside his desk. I couldn't decide what to do with the wrapper. I held it in my hand and rolled it between my fingertips.

"The benefit of not saying those things out loud is . . . ?"

"I don't know," I said. I was worried that I was beginning to sound petulant. Landon would be on me in a second; she had radar for petulance. She had a lot of her father in her. It was one of the things that made me love her so much that I ached at the danger she was in.

Dr. Gregory said, "Perhaps it's so you don't have to confront the fact that you don't trust me, either."

That surprised me. "What?"

"You said you trusted the Marshals Service more than you trusted Ernesto Castro. Perhaps you're unwilling to explore that further—out loud, at least—because you don't really trust me with what you might have to say."

He said it matter-of-factly, as though he was giving me directions to a new restaurant, or informing me of an approaching cold front.

"You don't think I trust you?" Deftly, I slid the lollipop across my tongue so it rested on the other side of my mouth.

He leaned forward a few inches, shifted his weight on the chair. "I'm actually pretty certain that you don't trust me, Peyton. I'm wondering why it's so difficult for you to acknowledge it."

I felt trumped by his words. "The odds that Ernesto Castro would keep his promise, that he would hurt Landon or that he would hurt me, are very, very high. The odds that someone in WITSEC will hurt me, or her, are, I think, lower. The risk exists, but it's muted. By agreeing to become a federally protected witness, I was playing the odds."

He said, "Have you suddenly decided to trust me?"

"Isn't that what you wanted?"

I expected him to say "yes" or to say "no." Instead he asked, "Is it important for you to do what I want?"

. . .

LATER, WHEN THE session ended, I left his office without having told him about Carl Luppo or all my trips to the bank, or about Khalid Granger.

I had to admit Dr. Gregory was right. I guess I didn't trust him.

I knew that I didn't trust Ron Kriciak. No reason to. The stakes were way too high, and Ron wasn't the kind of guy I was likely to trust easily. When I was a prosecutor, he was the kind of cop I was always reluctant to put on the stand. From the first day I was spirited away to WITSEC orientation, I had decided to take what the marshals had to offer and cover every one of my bets.

Just in case.

CARL LUPPO WAS waiting on the sidewalk outside Dr. Gregory's office. He was in plain sight. He wasn't trying to be invisible. His plump hands hung by his sides. No jacket over his arm. No Abercrombie bag hiding a Tec-DC9.

I'm not sure why, but I wasn't unhappy to see him. "Your turn next?" I asked him, hooking my thumb back toward Dr. Gregory's building. I didn't slow, though, and Carl had to hustle to keep up with me as I marched in the direction of the Pearl Street Mall. I didn't have a particular destination in mind. Landon was at a spelling prep session. I had hours to kill.

"Therapy? No, not today. I came to see you. See how you been doing. I've been feeling sorry I haven't heard from you."

I felt much more brazen with Carl Luppo than I did with Dr. Gregory, though I wasn't sure why. Certainly he was the more dangerous of the two men. I said, "Since that day we met and had coffee, I've been curious about something. Why are you in the program, Carl?"

From the corner of my eye I watched him shrug his thick neck. He didn't prevaricate.

"I spent much of my life in La Cosa Nostra. You probably guessed that already, though, right? I've been told that I wear the Italian flag on my sleeve. That was actually a line from my last therapist. The one Dr. Gregory's replacing. After I was arrested and put inside, things developed so that some of the people I used to work with broke some promises they'd made to me. I moved to protect my own. That's why I'm in the program." His tone was matter-of-fact. No pride. No regret. It's as though he was six feet eight inches tall and was acknowledging that he'd played a little basketball. He concluded with the simple words, "What did I do? Mostly, I was an enforcer. A gorilla. Along the way I killed some people. That's what I did."

Those last words he'd spoken felt unreal, and they settled unevenly in my thoughts, like a mouthful of unpalatable food. I didn't want to swallow them, couldn't fathom spitting them out.

Carl Luppo had said, "I killed some people."

Huh? It was as though I was listening to someone mimicking the dialogue from a movie.

Some part of me was able to respond to him. I suppose it was the part of me that was always good at conversations with strangers. Robert said I was a star at cocktail parties. I don't know if that's true. I do know that I loved looking across a crowded room and seeing his eyes locked on mine.

That's a baby beluga.

What I said to Carl Luppo was, "No, I hadn't guessed that about you. You seem Italian, though. If I thought about it, I guess I might have suspected the organized crime part."

He noticed the omission I was making. "The other part? The killing part? I sometimes feel I should acknowledge that up front. People tend to have trouble understanding it."

I said, "I guess." My friend Andrea felt the same way about letting dates know she had herpes. She always told them up front, over drinks. Not the kind of thing she wanted to blurt out once she was already naked with her legs spread.

"What about you? Why are you in the program?" His tone was conversational. He had no intuition that he'd struck a match to a fuse that was ticking down to a keg of emotional dynamite. We were waiting for the light to change at Pearl and Ninth. I found it ironic that the hit man standing next to me was waiting patiently for the light to change.

I wondered if the man who killed my Robert is someone who would have waited for the light to change.

At some level I knew that with his question Carl was trying to distract me from what he'd just told me about the Mafia. I allowed the distraction. The light changed and once again we began to walk. I tried to adopt his matter-of-fact manner as I told him about the arrest of Ernesto Castro and the threat he'd made against me in court and about Robert's murder outside of Galatoire's.

I didn't tell Carl Luppo about the woman who had tried to kidnap my baby while she was playing soccer. The woman my daughter thought was dressed in clothes from Abercrombie.

"What they did to your husband? We called hits like that 'suicide moves.' It's real risky to clip a guy on the street like that with so many witnesses. Drug people," Carl said, spitting to the side. The spitting was an obvious demonstration of disgust. "They have no respect. I wouldn't ever have killed someone in front of his wife. Never. If I saw family close by, I'd bag the work and plan it again another day. But these new drug criminals, they're like animals. Animals. No rules, no respect. Everything changed when the drugs started flowing. I remember the days before the poison was on the streets. I'm old enough."

I said, "But you killed people who had wives?" Somehow, the voice coming from my mouth resembled my natural tone even though the reality of what this man had done was becoming crystal clear to me.

Carl Luppo was one of those men in chinos. He carried silenced handguns and ended other peoples' lives.

"I did," he said. "It was my job."

My impulse was, of course, to run. I didn't. I saw an opportunity to learn about men in chinos. And I needed to learn about men in chinos. I prepared myself to be slimed.

"Your *job?* Like driving a bus? Or being a foreman at a factory? Killing people was *your job?*"

He shrugged again. Was he embarrassed by my outburst? I don't know, but I doubted it.

"Let's say it was a piece of my job. It was all part of the life I was living back then. The people who ended up getting whacked—by and large they knew the rules, they knew what they could do, they knew what they couldn't do. There were customs that were followed. Protocols. Sometimes, for whatever reason, these people chose to cross the line. When they did, part of them knew deep down that eventually I'd be there. Me, or someone like me."

"Someone *like* you killed my husband," I said, aware at some level that I was poking at a grizzly bear with a sharp stick.

"No," he replied without altering his stride or raising his voice at all. His defiance was apparent, nonetheless. Something about the way he said the word *No* carried all the defiance that was necessary. People like Carl Luppo didn't have to protest loudly to have their protests register. "If they felt you had crossed the line, my people might have had *you* killed. But not your husband. That's not the way we worked. And it would not have been done in front of him. Never. We respected families. It separated us from those that pushed the drugs."

"You . . . *respected* families? Would the widows of the men you killed and their fatherless children agree that you respected families?" I couldn't believe what I'd just asked him. The voice in my head screamed, "*Shut up, Kirsten!*"

We walked a few more steps before he responded. "Okay, okay. I deserve this," Carl Luppo said. "Listen, I'm very sorry about your husband. And I'm sorry that you've been forced into the program, and I'm sorry for why you're in the program. Me? I've spent a lot of years thinking about my fate, and I decided a long time ago that I have no one to blame but myself for where I am in my life. But you? No. What happened to you isn't fair. I listen to your story and it sounds like you're a victim, pure and simple. I can understand that."

"What?" I didn't want his compassion. It cheapened my pain. It cheapened Robert's sacrifice. "You understand that I'm a victim? What on earth are you saying to me?"

He seemed to react physically to my outburst. "I deserve this," he repeated. "The acid that's coming from your mouth." We were in front of the *Daily Camera* building. He checked the sidewalk in both directions before he resumed speaking to me. "I'm not saying I like it, but I won't argue that I don't deserve it. Listen," he said, his voice suddenly an octave lower, "you should know something. Ron Kriciak is following you. Occasionally? Frequently? I don't know. And I don't know why he's doing that. But I thought you should know that he's been tailing you. It could be important."

I stared at him as though he had spoken to me in Italian and I didn't understand the words. "You have my phone number," he said, and he turned and jaywalked across Pearl Street.

I stood still and watched him hop up on the curb and disappear around the corner past Tom's Tavern.

A couple walking by jostled me from behind; otherwise I might have remained frozen in place where I was.

I kept thinking, *Carl Luppo is a hit man*.

A hit man.

Jesus.

2

The truth was that I'd literally been running for my life since Robert was killed but somehow had managed to end up in terrible shape anyway. After a night standing at the prep table at Q's earning my nonexistent wage, my thighs felt like a couple of Virginia hams.

I'd decided that I wanted to start walking my way back into shape, but I didn't feel safe being out in the open by myself, and it was too pretty in Boulder to think about working out indoors.

So that was another problem: Getting in shape. Virtually everything in my life felt like a problem.

EACH MORNING AROUND ten o'clock I hovered near the mailbox and scoured the horizon for the approach of the postman's Jeep. I was anxiously awaiting the arrival of my new Peyton Francis credit card and my new Peyton Francis First National Bank of Boulder scenic

Flatirons checks to arrive in the mail. My new life was difficult without them. Merchants weren't eager to take temporary checks from a person who sometimes stumbled over her own name.

Who was going to blame them?

During moments when I felt grateful about anything, I was grateful that I came into the program with enough cash assets that I could afford to guarantee my new MasterCard myself. The accountants at the program somehow managed to get all my assets moved from my old name to my new one. How did they do it? A judge helped, I'm sure. Ron Kriciak told me that few WITSEC participants come into the program with any legally obtained liquid assets. Most are forced to go through the laborious process of establishing credit from scratch, unable to guarantee their own credit.

The marshals who oriented me to the program warned me what it was going to be like. Ron warned me what it was going to be like. They all said there would be plenty of little humiliations as the fact that I was living without a history caught up with me. The marshals would do nothing to help me create a false history. No fake credit reports. No forged letters of recommendation. Whatever lies I employed would have to be of my own invention.

The marshals also told me there would be plenty of loneliness.

And isolation.

They were right about everything.

ALMOST EVERY DAY while Landon was away I'd think about calling someone I knew from our past. Sometimes I would play out conversations in my head with one of my old friends from Florida, but usually it was with someone in Louisiana who knew Robert, too. My agony over the changes in my life was somehow less when I could imagine sharing it with someone who knew him and could appreciate the depth of my loss.

Sometimes I held the phone to my ear and listened to the dial tone and it soothed me like a squeeze of a teddy bear.

Ron Kriciak had given me lots to worry about when he gave me the lecture about contacting people from my past. I was surprised to learn that it wasn't expressly forbidden. But he advised me not to do it. Period. The rule I'd learned in my WITSEC orientation was that I could never give out my number, my new name, or my location to anyone from my previous life, but I could call them from telephones that had been blocked to caller ID. During my orientation the marshals warned me that phone company blocks on caller ID were notoriously unreliable. Quite simply, the blocks didn't always work. Sometimes blocked numbers showed up on caller-ID screens. So, caution. Always caution. The marshals also taught me to be extra cautious about using 800 numbers, because they automatically identify the phone number of the caller, even if the caller ID on the line was blocked, as mine was. That's right, every time you use an 800 number the person on the other end knows who called.

The phone company doesn't tell you that about 800 numbers.

Ron instructed me not to tell old friends where I was, of course. So I didn't, even in my fantasies. In my imaginary calls I would tell my old friends that I wasn't in the South anymore and that it was pretty where I was living. In the calls that I fantasized some of my friends would play twenty questions trying to tease the location out of me, and others would act as though it was the last information they might ever want to learn.

A few wouldn't even ask my new name.

I DECIDED TO make an exception to Ron's caution about calling old friends. I made the exception, I told myself, because of Khalid.

Yes, Khalid. You'll see soon.

The first call I made from my present to my past was from a pay phone in the lobby of the Boulderado Hotel, using a phone card I'd purchased at the Total station on Twenty-eighth Street where I got gas. I blocked caller ID and called my old friend Andrea Archer in Sarasota. To say she was surprised to hear my voice was an understatement. She asked me where I was almost immediately, and then she apologized profusely when I told her I wasn't allowed to reveal my location. She wanted me to divulge my new name two minutes further into the conversation. I told her my name was Peyton. And she made me laugh as she wanted to know, "How the hell did you come up with that name?"

"Peyton Place," I admitted.

She howled. "You despised Peyton Place."

I hadn't told her my last name. If I had, she would have gotten a kick out of the fact that I'd chosen it because of how much I detested Connie Francis. Andrea had always mixed her up with Anita Bryant.

I said, "The witness protection people said to pick a name that no one could tie to me. So I picked two names that I hated."

"If I did that," she said without hesitating as long as it takes a hummingbird to flap its wings, "my name would be Menstruate Pantyhose. I hear something else in your voice, though, don't I?"

"I wanted to use Roberts as a last name. They wouldn't let me. Too obvious, they said."

"You're too sentimental. You know that?"

From Andrea I knew it wasn't a criticism. I said, "He was the sentimental one, not me. That's what's ironic."

"You know what Robert's doing right now, don't you? He's probably sitting around in heaven, enjoying the view, pointing out all this irony to his new cronies. You know he's holding court up there."

Andrea could always make me laugh, and she could usually make me cry. I knew she was right; Robert was certainly holding court up there. But I spent more time wondering if he'd found someone new in heaven than I did wondering about his relationships with his new angel cronies. As much as he loved me, I always felt that I was replaceable.

Me, yes. Landon, never.

He could never replace Landon. I liked to think I was part of her package. It gave me solace.

When we hung up, I told myself that it had been okay to call Andrea. The next time I spoke with her I'd deal with Khalid.

THE SECOND TIME I called Andrea from Boulder I did it from my home. The phone number was blocked to caller ID, and I used a convenience-store phone card to place the call so it wouldn't show up on my bill. Andrea was thrilled to hear from me again, and the sound of her voice soothed me like a scalp massage from Robert, but the conversation quickly developed into something that left me feeling as though I were trying to swallow chicken bones.

Khalid. Here he comes.

The conversation started off in a manner that would've surprised me from almost anyone else I knew, but not from Andrea. She wanted to know if I'd taken her advice from the previous conversation and consulted a nutritionist yet. "A real one," she elaborated. "One who knows something about herbs."

"Herbs?"

"You know, an herbalist? Because I've been reading this stuff that I got from a guy who lives up in Winston-Salem—you're not there, are you? That would be a stitch. And he's not only a nutritionist but he's also an herbalist, and by the way, he's willing to do a consultation over the phone. I mean it, he'd do both of us at the same time, a conference call for the same fee; the man is not into the money at *all*. He'd actually like to set up a foundation, if you can believe it. So that this information is available to everybody. And from what I've read already, I've got to tell you that the orange juice you drink every morning? Bad. Got to go. Wrong way to start your day. And I think we're eating the wrong fish and we need to trade in some of the cooked vegetables for more raw vegetables and soybeans. Raw cauliflower especially. I don't pretend to get it. But that's easy enough, right? Cauliflower? Who'd have guessed?

"The main thing is, we have to start with a cleansing fast. That comes first. And massages with essential oils. But only the right ones. Apparently the body can't accept some of the essential oils until your diet is balanced, the same way we can't digest some of the things we need until our diet is balanced. Makes sense, right? But the main thing, first, is that orange juice. Has to go, okay? Do you have a fax machine? This material I have is only about nine pages; I'm sure you'll be as excited as I am when you read it."

Andrea didn't exhale at the end of her speech. But I did it for her. "No fax on my end, Andrea. Sorry. I'd have to give you a number, and

I'm not allowed to do that." With some pride, I announced, "Hey, I got a credit card in my new name today, Andrea. I'm official."

What she said in response took a lot of words but basically amounted to, "That's nice." Andrea wasn't usually lacking in the empathy department, but I assumed she was still recovering either from my tepid response to her Klaxon call for me to examine my nutritional well-being or from my refusal to trust her with a phone number. Regardless, I was beginning to accept the reality that the daily vexations that are inherent in not having an identity are hard to understand until you haven't had one.

It was her next sentence that started my problem with the chicken bones. "Remember Khalid Granger?" she said.

"Of course," I responded, feeling the first sharp edge of something catch on my epiglottis. Asking me if I remember Khalid Granger was like asking me if I remembered my father. She knew that.

But she'd brought him up, I hadn't.

"Scuttlebutt around the courthouse is that the decision on his final appeal is due this week."

"And?" It was all I could manage to say. Andrea's forced nonchalance on the subject of Khalid Granger was not contagious. She'd always been totally comfortable with what happened to him. What we did to him.

She said, "If he loses the appeal—or *when* he loses the appeal—the judge will probably set a date for his execution."

I cleared my throat and asked, "Commutation?"

"Not likely. Not in this state. Not with this governor. Not in this environment. Not given who the victims were."

She said, "Are you ready to have it behind you?" The words didn't surprise me as much as the inflection did. I didn't think that her tone was begging me to answer affirmatively.

The moment she mentioned Khalid, I'd carried the phone to the kitchen, rushed to the sink, and poured a glass of water from the tap. One of my new neighbors had informed me that the local water came from a glacier near the Continental Divide. I remembered that information as I sipped, momentarily wondering how it got from there to here. Then I replied, "I guess."

"What's wrong? You sound funny."

Andrea could always tell. "I think I'm coming down with something," I lied. "The climate's so different here."

I used to be a truthful person. Now the lies sprouted from my tongue like tulips in the spring.

Andrea said, "The herbalist will help. You're not eating right. We both know it, babe. You're under stress, and we know that stress is not your best thing. What kind of different is the climate?"

A KILLER WHALE

This one's been submerged for a long time. When I talk to Andrea, I always feel the motion of the water as this huge creature slithers deep below the surface, but I rarely catch sight of its dark flesh or its white underbelly. But she usually doesn't mention him to me. I'm grateful for that.

Khalid Granger is the whale.

Back then? He was a twenty-seven-year-old black man living north of Sarasota, Florida.

Me?

Back then? I was a twenty-seven-year-old white prosecutor living in the same county as Khalid Granger.

For some amount of time he and I walked the same streets, breathed the same air, shared the same birth year and even the same month. But socially, racially, and economically Khalid and I never really even lived on the same planet.

So what brought us together?

Khalid and I collided over the bodies of an elderly vacationing Mennonite couple from Lancaster County, Pennsylvania, who were shot to death during the aftermath of a gas station robbery that couldn't have gone worse even had the perpetrator meticulously planned it to be an unmitigated disaster.

The details of the crime start out mundane, become almost comical, and end in abject tragedy.

It goes like this:

A solitary black man wearing a ski mask approached the counter of a convenience store on Highway 41 just north of Sarasota, raised a handgun, pointed it at the store's clerk, and demanded money. The clerk, a nineteen-year-old woman named JoBeth Reynolds who had a psychiatric history longer than Khalid Granger's criminal record, took one short look at the robber's handgun and fainted flat to the floor. Jo-Beth busted her head on the terrazzo as she completed her fall, and she stayed unconscious for the duration.

Her participation in the robbery was officially over.

The robber then took a single shot at the security camera that was suspended from the ceiling about six feet behind the counter and actually *hit it*. Square in the lens. A *single* shot.

Lordy.

The videotape record of the event was officially over.

My account of what happened after the onset of JoBeth's unconsciousness and after the camera's demise is a necessary mixture of police supposition and forensic science, some parts of the story heavier on the supposition, some parts more reliant on the science.

The police surmise that the robber was unable to operate the cash register without the assistance of JoBeth, the unconscious clerk. And they decided that the robber wasn't a particularly patient man. They reached this conclusion because the method that the suspect chose to open the cash drawer was to lift the whole big Casio machine off the counter and drop it on the floor in front of the candy display. A whole mess of gum and Life Savers came down with it.

The method was inelegant, but it was reasonably effective, though dents on the machine indicate that it took at least two tosses before the cash drawer popped. Loose coins spread as far as twenty-six feet from the cash register. Two quarters were found actually touching each other beneath the toe-kick on the soft-drink dispenser at the back of the store. What are the odds of that, do you think?

The bills from the cash drawer subsequently all disappeared from the scene.

While the robber was on his hands and knees scooping up the bills, he made a serious error in judgment: He turned his back to the front door.

Enter the elderly Mennonite couple from Lititz, a small town in Lancaster County, Pennsylvania. The husband held the door for his wife, who stepped into the store first and was likely immediately distracted by the site of the cash register upside down on the floor and the young black man in the ski mask scurrying around it on all fours hustling up money.

The lead detective on the case, a man named Mickey Redondo, theorized that the elderly Mennonite lady's next move was to step on a roll of dimes—though his partner Jack Tarpin was a proponent of the stepped–on–a–roll–of–Life Savers theory—whereupon she immediately did a header. Postmortem examination showed that her right wrist had been broken badly in the fall, as had her right hip.

As she fell, and perhaps screamed, the robber heard the commotion behind him and, probably in panic, he came up firing.

The first shot caught the elderly Mennonite gentleman in the thick of the throat, slightly off center, barely missing his Adam's apple but definitely decimating his carotid artery.

The blood spray was profuse.

The second shot flew out the still-open door of the store and was ultimately recovered from behind the display on the gallons meter of the premium gas pump outside the convenience store.

The third and fourth shots that the robber—now the murderer—fired entered the supine body of the Mennonite lady. She died quickly from her chest wounds.

THE LOCAL POLICE department was on the case in a flash. The only witness to the aftermath of the robbery and the two homicides was a man who had been pulling into the parking lot of the convenience store to buy gas and who reported seeing a solitary black man walking quickly from the scene, heading north. The man who witnessed the black man leaving the store was also the person who discovered the two dead bodies and the unconscious clerk behind the counter. Given the scene he stumbled on inside the store, the man was a frantic wreck and not the most reliable of witnesses by the time the police arrived.

Enter Khalid Granger, who fit the general description given by the witness at the scene. The witness had reported that the man he had spotted leaving the parking area of the convenience store wasn't wearing a mask. He was a solitary black youth, not a teenager, but not too old, either. As I said earlier, Khalid was twenty-seven years old at the time of his arrest. The witness remembered that the suspect sported a pencil-thin mustache, and so did Khalid. And the witness estimated the size of the suspect at five-ten, one eighty or so. Khalid stood five-eleven and weighed in at an intimidating one ninety-five. Both men were wearing baggy pants slung low on their hips.

Khalid was walking on the sidewalk about three and a half blocks from the crime scene when patrol officers who were scouring the nearby streets for any signs of the suspect stopped him and questioned him about the crime that had just occurred at the convenience store. Khalid denied any knowledge but was subsequently detained for further questioning. The probable cause for his detention was that his appearance matched the physical description given by the witness. In addition, the officer's report noted that Khalid was discovered in the vicinity of the crime scene.

In law enforcement, "vicinity" is a notoriously elastic concept. Almost as elastic as "probable cause."

On Khalid's person the officers discovered one hundred and forty-three dollars in small bills rolled tightly and bound by two rubber bands. The roll was comprised of two twenties, six tens, seven fives, and eight singles. The amount closely matched the estimated proceeds from the convenience-store robbery, which was later determined to be one hundred and thirty-six dollars. Khalid's wad had been crammed into the top of his left boot.

After further questioning, Khalid was arrested and ultimately charged with armed robbery and with the murder of the Pennsylvania tourists.

To make a long story shorter than it deserves to be, I helped convict Khalid Granger of the two murders, and I assisted in getting him sentenced to die in the infamous Florida electric chair for his crimes.

But even before that day—the day he was sentenced—Khalid Granger had become one of my killer whales.

Now he was one of the oldest whales in that pod.

ANDREA ASKED, "DO you want to know when the decision on the appeal comes down? I'll let you know."

"On Khalid?" For some reason I'd never called him "Granger." To my memory, not once. Maybe in court I'd referred to him as Mr. Granger. To me, he'd always been Khalid.

"Yes, on Khalid."

"No, I don't think so. Maybe I'll call you and see . . . you know, what . . . I don't know."

"I can leave you a message somewhere. Let you know if a date's been set for the execution."

"That's not necessary, Andrea. I'll keep an eye on the news from Florida. *USA Today* likes to cover those things. I like talking to you. You know I'll be back in touch, soon."

"What about the conference call with the herbalist? Can we do that? I *really* want to do that."

"I have to talk with somebody to make sure that's okay. See how to set it up from my end. Security, you know?"

"Hey, honey, I've been yakking so much about myself, I haven't even asked. How's your little baby?"

"Not little. But she's fine, Andrea. She misses her daddy. But all in all she's taken all that's happened and all the moving more in stride than I have. Her defenses are better."

"She still doing the same stuff? Soccer and spelling? No interest in boys, yet, I hope."

"Not that I've noticed, which is fine. I'm not ready for that. That was going to be Robert's department. But yes, she's still in love with soccer and spelling. She still studies her spelling lists all the time. All the time. And her room looks like a shrine to Mia Hamm and Briana Scurry."

"Who?"

"Never mind."

Andrea was quiet for a moment on the other end of the line. Then she brought tears to my eyes by asking, simply, "You really miss him, don't you?"

I had to swallow and squeeze my eyes shut before I could speak. "I wish the pain would start to ease. Everybody told me that if I cried enough and talked enough and enough time passed that the pain would start to ease. I don't know why it hasn't been true, yet. I still reach for him in the middle of the night, and I shock myself wide-awake when I realize that the sheets are cold on his side of the bed. I pick up the phone to call him sometimes when I'm feeling lonely at work. I dream about him sometimes at night, and I fantasize during the daytime that he'll be waiting for me at home to rub my neck and give me advice."

"You're working? As a lawyer?"

I laughed at the very thought of it. "No, Andrea, believe it or not I'm cooking in a restaurant. I'm like an apprentice. I want to learn. For now, I don't really need the money."

"In a restaurant?"

"Yes. I like it. Nobody's threatened me yet."

"You must not have burnt the borscht."

"It's not that kind of restaurant."

"Well tell me, what kind is it? Is it healthy?"

"You wouldn't like it. We serve meat."

3

Andrea pushed the button that would silence her office speaker-phone and turned to the man who sat on the other side of her desk.

Andrea said, "You got all that, I hope. As I've been telling you, she's just not there, yet. I told you she wouldn't be."

He was resting his chin on his hands. "I could understand most of the conversation. You're sure she's not coming around? That thing she said about clemency?"

Andrea shrugged. The gesture was lost on Dave Curtiss. He'd lowered his head back down, exposing the bald spot near the crown. In color and size it reminded her of a glazed jelly donut. Glazed jelly donuts reminded her of her ex-husband, Patrick, and Saturday-morning sex. The combination of the two images caused a swell of nausea to rise in her gut. She said, "She has so much on her mind."

"But she's not with us on this?"

"Not yet, no. Why should she be?"

His voice had an edge to it that was whiny, desperate. "But she may be moving that way? You think that's possible? If you read between the lines?"

"I'd be guessing, Dave. Khalid Granger isn't her highest priority right now. You heard her—she sounded surprised to hear me mention him."

"Well, since I got that letter, it sure as hell is my highest priority."

"I know that, Dave. It's mine, too."

"We need to know where she stands, Andrea. Actually, we need to know she stands right next to us." He slapped the arm of the chair. "The decision on the damn appeal is due any day. If the three of us are united on this, we have a small chance of success. If it's only two out of three of us . . ."

"What are we gonna do? It's not as though I can go plead with her. One, I don't know where she is. Two, things are too sensitive for that. She's been through too much, Dave. Given all that's happened, maybe she doesn't care what we do about Khalid."

The man across the desk was only two years older than Andrea but looked twenty years her senior. He wore his anxiety like a plumed hat. You couldn't miss it. His upper lip was dotted with sweat. His face was the color of watermelon flesh. He was cracking the knuckles on his hands sequentially from pinkie to thumb, then back again, ending with the thumb once more. After the sequence was complete, he switched hands and started over. When he took a break from the knuckle cracking, his free right hand rubbed absently at his chest just above his sternum.

"We can't risk that. We accuse the cops and then she goes public and contradicts us? We'd be fried. You really don't even know where she is?"

Andrea said, "No. I don't. Someplace with a climate that's unlike Florida or Louisiana. That's all I know."

"Drier? Like a desert, maybe?"

"Maybe. Or mountains. Or maybe she's in North Dakota or Minnesota. I just can't tell."

"She doesn't even trust you to know where she is? You're one of her best friends."

Andrea used a sarcastic tone as she said, "I'm trying not to take it too personally, Dave. Who knows, she may have her reasons. You know she probably shouldn't even have called me."

The man stood and misbuttoned his suit jacket so that it hung on his large frame like a crooked painting on the wall. "We have to do something. That's all there is to it. I can't live like this. I'm losing weight and I can't sleep. My partners are beginning to look at me funny." He turned and started toward the door but stopped short of it. "One more thing. No more cell phones when you and I talk about this. My firm keeps records. I'm sure your office does to. So no office phones either, or home phones. You know those records can be subpoenaed. This has to be pay-phone city."

"*Pay-phone city?* Dave, don't get any weirder on me, okay? I don't mind using pay phones when I talk to you, but I don't have any choice about what kind of phone to use when I talk to Kirsten. I can't call her now, remember? It was pure luck that she called while you were here. If she wants to talk, she calls me. She might call me here at the office. She might call me at my home. I have no control over that. She won't give out her number."

"Caller ID! Get caller ID."

"You don't think the Witness Protection program is bright enough to block her number, Dave? We're not dealing with fools."

He placed his hand on the doorknob and turned his head. "We need to know where she stands, Andrea. We can't go public with our concerns until we know where she stands."

"That might be too late for Khalid, Dave."

He grimaced. "I don't want to hear about it."

4

Peyton had asked Dr. Gregory for an additional session. They met on Friday morning.

"What you said about me trusting you, that it's a process that will take time—that's not true anymore. There's something I've decided that I can't deal with on my own, so I need to trust you. And today, I've decided to go ahead and trust you."

Alan Gregory inhaled slowly, filling his lungs gradually so that his patient wouldn't notice. His first thought was to hope that he was prepared to hear whatever he was about to hear. His only word to her was, "Yes?"

"There's a man on death row in Florida."

As Dr. Gregory took in her words she shifted her gaze toward the windows. Something was distracting her momentarily.

When she looked back at her doctor, she added, "The man's name is Khalid Granger. He was convicted of killing two people in a convenience-store robbery."

Dr. Gregory waited. He wondered what the connection was between Peyton Francis and Khalid Granger.

"I helped convict him," she said. "It was a long time ago. I was twenty-seven and it was my first capital case prosecution. I was living in Florida then."

So, the psychologist thought, *whatever the issues, whatever the connection, the stakes are high. Life and death.* He was aware of trying especially hard to appear as nonjudgmental and neutral as possible while at the same time appearing to have more compassion than a tree.

Peyton said, "The problem is that I'm no longer convinced that he did it. I'm not sure Khalid killed those people that day. I'm not even certain he was even in that convenience store."

She expected him to say something here. Needed him to say something here. He said, "That . . . presents quite a dilemma for you, Peyton."

"Yes," she said. "It does." She was relieved that he seemed to grasp what was on the line for her.

IT TOOK MOST of the session for Peyton to explain the details of Khalid's alleged crime to her doctor and to identify the holes that the police and prosecution had plugged in order to gain a conviction.

As soon as her presentation was done, she began arguing to reinforce her case for doubt.

"When the police picked up Khalid for questioning, he was actually walking *toward* the convenience store, not away from it. Now tell me, why would somebody who was trying to get away from a crime scene be walking right back toward it? That's always bothered me. Always. The money Khalid was carrying in his boot? Although it was close to the right amount, it could never be tied to the robbery. Not one piece of it had JoBeth Reynolds's fingerprints on it. Not one solitary bill. Jo-Beth was the clerk who was there that shift. She handled every one of the bills that were in the cash register that day. Her fingerprints should've been on some of the money."

Dr. Gregory could tell from the accelerating pace of Peyton's words that she wasn't done with her argument.

"Khalid Granger was, and probably still is, an evil man. The kind of man you don't want to meet on the street, the kind of man you absolutely want in jail. Priors? You bet. He'd been arrested eleven times by the time he was twenty-seven years old. That record includes two arrests for domestic violence against girlfriends, and two arrests for violent street crimes. I think the street crimes were both stickups. He'd stolen cars as a kid. Been picked up for possession and possession-for-sale. If my memory is right, at the time of the convenience-store murders he'd been out of the state prison system for all of eight months and two weeks.

"Something else that is still troubling to me after all these years is that all four of Khalid's prior violent crimes were committed with a knife. Khalid Granger was a cutter. And believe me, he was a *proud* cutter. He was known on the street for his knife skills. His knife was on his person when he was picked up. But he didn't have a gun with him. And nobody we talked to had ever seen him with a gun. In fact, the gun used in the crime has never been recovered."

Dr. Gregory said, "I assume this man, Khalid Granger, was tested for gunshot residue after he was arrested." He knew all about GSRs from his wife, who was a prosecutor.

Peyton raised an eyebrow. "Good for you. How did you know to ask that?" She didn't expect him to answer but paused just in case he planned on revealing something about himself. Finally she said, "Yes, he was given a GSR. He tested positive."

"So he'd recently fired a gun?"

"The test results that we received from the police show that he tested positive for trace metals on his GSR." She glanced back outside. "But, today? Right now? I actually don't think he'd fired a gun at all."

"I'm not sure I understand. Are you suggesting an error in the analysis? Or are you suggesting that the results were faked?"

"I've never said this out loud before. But over the years I've begun to think that it's possible that Khalid was set up."

Dr. Gregory tried to gauge how convinced Peyton was by her own accusation. He said, "The man who was in the convenience store, whoever he was, was quite a marksman, wasn't he? The kind of shooting skill you described earlier? Hitting a surveillance camera with a single shot? That takes some significant practice."

"Or—maybe—he was one lucky amateur. That was the police argument. Mickey Redondo, the lead detective, figured that the killer had a one in a hundred chance of hitting the surveillance camera with a single shot from that handgun. And he concluded that the day of the robbery was the shooter's lucky day. The police theory was that Khalid decided to use the gun, and not his knife, for the robbery and had a hell of a first day on the job."

"And the shots at the elderly couple?"

"The police made the same argument for the second shot, the one that hit the gentleman in the neck. It was either a lucky shot from a tough angle or a bad miss on an attempted body shot. Who knows? The killer missed with the next shot. The man was falling already, and I think that's why he missed. Regardless, the slug hit the gas pump outside. Shots four and five? He stood above the woman to shoot her when she was on the floor. No skill involved there."

Dr. Gregory asked, "Have you decided what to do with your doubts?"

"I can't put Landon at any more risk. I know that. And I can't let Khalid be executed for a crime he didn't commit. I know that."

"It seems to me that by going public to save Khalid you will put yourself at risk. Putting yourself at risk puts your daughter at risk."

Her eyes flashed. "Don't you think I know that? That's my dilemma."

Alan Gregory waited before he spoke. He wanted his patient to digest some of the intensity she was feeling. "When you first came in today, you said that you needed to trust me. Trust me with what, Peyton?"

She reached down and grabbed a lollipop, unwrapped it, but didn't put it in her mouth. It was a DumDum. "I've always had backup in my life. Always. My parents were wonderful people who stood behind me through my successes and my mistakes. And Robert was a dream, a better man than I ever expected to find. Maybe a better man than I deserved. He completed me in so, so many ways. Even during Khalid's trial I wasn't lead prosecutor. I was second chair." She allowed her words to hang. "I'm not denying responsibility for whatever role I played in Khalid's conviction. There was a time that I was proud of it. I'm just trying to teach you something essential about me. About who I am. I'm someone who hasn't performed without a net very often in my life." She placed the DumDum on the left side of her mouth and asked, "Would you like one? A lollipop?"

Dr. Gregory shook his head, said, "No, thank you," and considered following Peyton down the lollipop road. He quickly decided that he would have ample opportunity to explore that lane in the future.

He said, "What about your campaign against Witness Protection? You were pretty far out there on that one."

She shook her head. "The DA in New Orleans was behind me every step of the way. I think he had his own ax to grind with the marshals. I wouldn't have done any of it without his support. The moment he told me to drop it; I would have dropped it."

"And now, what? You would like me to be your backup? Your net?" He wasn't quite sure what the words meant to her.

"I need you to believe in me."

He knew he didn't comprehend her meaning. He said, "I'm sorry, but I don't think I understand."

"If I begin raising questions about Khalid's conviction, there may be serious casualties. Serious casualties. One of the casualties may be my best friend from Florida, a woman named Andrea Archer. And her boss, the trial deputy, a guy named Dave Curtiss. Andrea was the lead prosecutor, the one who handled the case. I don't recall her ever having any trouble with the evidence. She and Dave may have been complicit for all I know. Assuming that I'm right, that my doubts have merit, the other casualties would be whatever police officers were involved in concocting the case and fabricating the evidence."

Dr. Gregory paused, waiting for her attention to settle. When she was looking at him once again, he said, "And one of the casualties may be you."

Peyton nodded. "I don't know what to do. I can't put Landon in any more risk. I just can't."

"Why now, Peyton? Why not five years ago? Why have you decided to talk about this today?"

"Because the whales are surfacing. Because the courts are about to rule on his final appeal. Because . . . taking someone's life is more complicated for me now than it was back then. That's why." She grimaced and raised her fingertips to her eyes. "I'm worried that I may be guilty of something here, something serious. I'm afraid that I may be guilty of believing that because we arrested and convicted a bad man—a man who probably deserved to be in prison for *some* crime— that what we did was right. And whatever I might have believed deep down about the holes in the case, I never really allowed myself to believe that Khalid shouldn't be in prison. I was sure he belonged there. I was *sure*. I probably still *am* sure.

"But if he didn't rob that convenience store and he didn't kill those two old people from Pennsylvania, then he doesn't deserve to die." Peyton thought of Robert and then of Landon, and she wondered if Khalid Granger had a family. She tried to recall the facts, but she couldn't remember any details about Khalid's background. She found it hard to imagine him with 2.2 children and a golden retriever. The white picket fence wouldn't even come into focus.

"You know," she said, "after the trial was over, Mickey Redondo—

the detective I told you about?—he came up to me in the courthouse and he said, 'That's one more evil man off the streets. Good day of work, Counselor.' Looking back now, I know that Mickey didn't really care whether or not it was the right evil man who was off the streets. And I suppose I didn't care enough, either."

"And your friend, Andrea? Did she care enough?"

Peyton looked down at her hands. "I don't know what she knew back then. As we prosecuted the case we weren't questioning what we had; we were always busy trying to prop the case up. We weren't looking for holes. Would she have conspired with the police to frame Khalid? I really doubt it. Would she have looked the other way if she thought justice was being done anyway? Maybe. Andrea was always more ambitious than me. Her work was bare knuckles. She never considered criminal justice to be a game for the weak of heart."

Dr. Gregory watched Peyton remove the lollipop stick from her mouth, swallow, and then return it to the middle of her tongue. Her cheeks collapsed into craters as she sucked hard on the candy.

He said, "It's not enough, is it? If I'm hearing you correctly, all you have right now are your suspicions that the police may have acted in-appropriately. My understanding of the process is that it's quite diffi-cult to get death sentences overturned this late in the game. Don't you need proof?"

She rolled the lollipop from her tongue to the snug confines of her left cheek. She seemed lost in thought but managed to say, "Yes. To overturn a sentence you need proof."

"Is there proof?"

She acted as though she hadn't heard him. He repeated his ques-tion.

"What? Proof? I don't know about any proof. I don't think I can prove any of it. To anyone."

He cocked his head and narrowed his eyes. "Where did you go just then, Peyton?"

She didn't hesitate. "Robert. I was thinking about Robert."

Dr. Gregory didn't know what to ask next, so he asked nothing.

"When I used to get discouraged—okay, bitchy—about work . . . or people . . . or life, Robert would listen to me ever-so-patiently, and at some point in the conversation he'd say something like, 'Life is what it is, babe. Hey, mostly the three of us are blessed. Come tomorrow or the next day, this passes and the good life goes on.' "

"Which meant what to you, Peyton?"

"It meant, be grateful. Appreciate what we have."

He waited.

"But after Robert was killed, I wasn't sure I wanted life to go on. I didn't feel blessed anymore. My complete life had been Robert *and* my baby *and* my work. Now all I have is my baby and as much as I love her I haven't been able to feel like what I'm living is a complete life anymore. He used to say that all the time. He'd say, 'Life is what life is.' Well, I want what life *was*.

"And I feel that's wrong of me."

Dr. Gregory composed his next words carefully. He asked, "And this has what to do with Khalid?"

She said, "Something, but I don't know what. But I think I need some legal advice. Consultation. About my position."

"From another prosecutor?"

"Yes."

"Can you do that confidentially?"

She nodded. "Sure."

"Do you know someone whose advice you would respect?"

"There are people I could call. People I know from New Orleans. I can't really call the people I worked with in Florida."

"But?"

"I'd rather find someone I don't know. Someone who doesn't know my history. You understand?"

He didn't. "But you would also like me to be your net?"

"Yes."

"What does that mean?"

"Robert would warn me sometimes. He'd see me struggling with something about work, or life, or our daughter—something—and I'd ask him how he dealt with it inside, how he never seemed to be conflicted or troubled by the things that would torment me so much. And he'd say, 'You have to learn to cover your heart, K.' That was one of the ways he was my net. When I was most vulnerable, he'd warn me when it was time to cover my heart."

"Was he doing you a favor?"

"What?"

"I'm just wondering whether he was doing you a favor by encouraging you to insulate yourself from your fears."

"What are you saying?"

The therapist paused and considered his words. "Maybe Robert wasn't always right with his advice."

"And you are?"

"I'm not aware that I'm giving any."

She seemed taken aback. Her next defense of her dead husband was clumsy. They both sensed it. She said, "He was a good man."

"Yes."

Peyton pulled the lollipop from her mouth and pointed the little nub of candy at her therapist. "I don't understand. What are you saying?"

He moved slightly in his chair, shifting his posture slightly in her direction. "From your descriptions, it sounds like Robert protected you from your feelings. He encouraged you to hide from them, especially when whatever you were feeling made you uncomfortable. I wonder if he was really protecting you or whether he was protecting himself from things he didn't want to face with you."

"He didn't need protecting. Robert was strong."

"Perhaps so are you."

"He protected me."

"Did he?"

5

Prowler's work space was tucked into the gable end of a hypercooled attic in a renovated antebellum house not too far from Atlanta, Georgia. The attic space was devoid of decoration or affectation. It contained two state-of-the-art computers—one PC, one Mac—both with twenty-one-inch monitors. A T1 line for the modems. Two fax machines, one of them color, on separate phone lines. Two televisions, one tuned to CNN, the other to MSNBC. Prowler was considering adding a third set for FOX News.

The floor in front of the machines was a polished gray terrazzo. The man scooted from keyboard to keyboard to phone to fax on the wheels of a Herman Miller Aeron desk chair.

One of his telephones chirped shortly after noon. He adjusted the microphone on his headset and poked a button to answer. He said, "Yes?" The second the phone chirped he'd made a silent guess about who was calling, and his caller ID had already confirmed that he was correct with his assumption. Prowler was always pleased when the caller ID worked even though the call was originating from another state.

The voice on the other end asked, "Prowler?"

"Yeah."

"I'm returning your call. I hope you have something for me."

Prowler had already decided how he was going to handle the problem with this client. He said, "The task may not be as easy as I had hoped. We still don't know where she has been relocated. My contact at WITSEC doesn't have access to any of her placement records. He says she's buried deep, but we suspected that she would be. If he looks around any more closely, he's sure he'll draw undesired attention to himself. We can't risk having anyone know we're looking, right?"

"And?"

"And . . . I'm exploring other avenues."

"My friend and I? We don't have unlimited time."

Prowler hated the way this guy referenced his "friend."

"I'm aware of the time constraints. What I need from you is more information on the child. Whatever you can put together. Her friends, interests, hobbies, clubs, sports. School performance, strengths, weaknesses. Medical history. Confirm her birth date while you're at it. Quickly."

"You think that you can find her through—"

Prowler lightly touched the phone button that disconnected him from the call.

As a favor to another client, he had agreed—reluctantly—to work for this man's friend. He felt no responsibility to be cordial to the flunky who was acting as intermediary.

6

After my extra session at Dr. Gregory's office I called in sick at Q's.

I didn't really need to lie about my symptoms. The tendons at the back of my head had solidified into pipes, my temples were pounding, and it took a conscious effort for me not to kneel down and vomit the contents of my stomach into one of the brick planters full of flowers on the Pearl Street Mall.

The sous-chef at the restaurant was more understanding than I would have been were I in his shoes.

I used a pay phone to call my Hmong babysitter, Viv, and told her that I would meet Landon at the school myself. I felt so good that she asked me if I was enjoying the weather. I told her that I was. The code I'd worked out with her dictated that if I called to change any plans about babysitting, any plans at all, even by only a few minutes, she should ask me if I was enjoying the weather. If I said that I was enjoying the weather, that was my message to her that everything was cool. If I said anything else, it meant that Viv should immediately take Landon to another location, one I'd already chosen and shown to her.

Before I drove home I went into the bank. Inside, I stopped twice and looked around casually, checking the foot traffic on the Mall, looking for Ron Kriciak. I didn't see him lurking anywhere. At the teller window, I cashed yet another check. This one was for eight hundred dollars. I took the money in fifties and twenties.

Even if Ron were following me, he'd think I'd gone into the bank to cash a check for pocket money or make a deposit or something. That's all. He wouldn't know I was collecting so much cash. He certainly wouldn't know why.

Why was Ron Kriciak following me?

Landon wanted to study some new lists of spelling words that a tutor I'd found for her had given her to prepare for the next big bee, one of the school district's qualifiers for the big state contest. She disappeared into her room and moments later I heard her switch on a CD in her little boom box. I couldn't have identified the group she was listening to if my life—or hers—depended on it. Girl singers, though.

I thought they were girl singers. It could have been prepubescent boy singers. There were a lot of those around.

I had to get more involved with that part of her life. Robert, where the hell are you? Her music was your job, damn it.

The eight hundred dollars from the bank were still in my purse. I removed the money and placed it with the rest of my stash inside a book I'd hollowed out. The book was *The Cider House Rules* by John Irving. I bought the big hardback at a used bookstore that was going out of business on the Mall. I'd read the book once before in Louisiana and I loved it and it broke my heart to cut it up inside. But it was the only book that I had with me in Boulder that was fat enough for all the money I needed to hide.

LANDON AND I lived in a rented townhouse on the east side of the Foothills Parkway, near Arapahoe Road. If you've never been, that's on the side of Boulder that's farthest from the mountains. The layout was townhouse typical. Downstairs was a living room, dining room, and kitchen–family room combination. Upstairs were two bedrooms, each with a bathroom. A laundry closet with one of those stacked washer/dryers opened onto the landing at the top of the stairs.

I didn't feel safe in the townhouse.

I hadn't felt safe anywhere since Slaughter.

That's not completely true. Right after we'd left Slaughter, the marshals had taken us in a van with darkened windows to a location that was more than a day's drive from Louisiana. From there they'd driven us to a city that I guessed was Washington, D.C., but I was never really sure. They put us up in a little apartment that was in some big government building. The tidy apartment had no windows. It was inside that building that the marshals began to examine me and evaluate me and orient me to what I might expect life to be like in WITSEC.

For those few days in that boring government building I'd felt safe.

THE FURNITURE IN our Boulder home was rented. All that Landon and I actually owned in the townhouse was a small television and some kitchen things and a few personal items and our new clothing. The marshals had arranged storage for everything else before we'd moved to Boulder from Louisiana.

I wanted to feel safe again before I sent for our things. Safe and settled. I knew that meant being out of the program. Why? Because the marshals had made it clear that they would never let me possess anything that tied me back to my life with Robert. And those were the only things I really wanted to have with me.

I wondered sometimes when I was despairing if I'd ever send for our things, ever see them again.

The truth was that I felt as though my life was in storage along with our belongings. The assassin had killed me just as cleanly as he'd felled Robert.

The only difference was that I hadn't yet died.

FROM THE KITCHEN I couldn't see the landing at the bottom of the stairs, so I sat instead on the dining room floor, precisely where the dining room table would rest if I had bothered to rent one, which I hadn't. I wanted to make sure I could hear Landon's approach if she was coming down the stairs. But I didn't want to be so close that she might overhear my conversation.

I held the portable phone in my hand. I'd already memorized Carl Luppo's number. I hadn't tried to remember it, but like an annoying commercial jingle, I couldn't get the darn thing out of my head after

I'd read it once from the piece of paper that he'd handed me while we were leaving the teahouse that first time.

I tapped the number into the phone and waited while I listened to three sequential rings. I was about to hang up when I heard, "Hello."

"Carl?"

"Hello, Peyton." The greeting wasn't enthusiastic. No inflection at all. I wouldn't even characterize it as pleasant.

"How did you know it was me?"

"I don't get too many calls. Anyway, I recognized your voice. A little accent, you know. Me too, I'm told."

Although it was tempting, I skipped the small talk and prepared to use my DA voice. It felt odd. "Earlier, when we were walking on Pearl Street, you remember?"

"Yeah."

"You said that you think Ron Kriciak is following me. Is that right?"

"You got it mostly right. But I didn't say 'I think.' I know he's following you. I thought you'd want to be aware of it, too."

"How do you know? Were you following me, Carl? Or were you following Ron?" I tried not to sound accusatory but I'm sure I failed. I couldn't pull it off with Landon, either. Robert used to tug me aside and tell me when I was backing her into a corner with my questions about her friends or her schoolwork or about her un-done chores.

He'd tell me it was the tone of my voice that was the problem.

That's a baby beluga, by the way.

Carl paused in response to my verbal challenges and I considered the possibility—no, the likelihood—that he was using the time to construct a lie. I was constructing a prodding follow-up question when he surprised me by saying, "I'm not sure you're prepared to believe my answer. So why should I give it to you?"

I exhaled my exasperation in a little burst. Carl had to have heard the noise I made. Had to.

He said, "Face it. You're not who you used to be, Peyton. What you've gone through has changed you. Am I right? Well, the same for me. I'm not the man I used to be."

"But . . . you were a *killer,* Carl." I whispered that part so that Landon couldn't possibly overhear. "*That* changes?"

I could almost hear him shrug over the phone. "You know what? Maybe you're right. I haven't been to mass in twenty years and I still consider myself a Catholic. I haven't killed anybody in more than a dozen years, but maybe in my heart I'm still a gorilla and I'm just kidding myself that I'm not. It's something I'll ponder some more. These days I have plenty of time to ponder."

A gorilla?

Carl continued. "In case you care, and I think you do, Kriciak followed you to that big old place on Baseline Road up near the mountains. You know the place? It's like a park or something. But with a lot of buildings. Chautauqua? Is that what it's called? I think so. There's a place with that name in New York, I think. You went into the restaurant there."

"Yesterday?"

"Yeah. Is it good there? I've never been."

"Oh God. Landon was with me. A little girl was with me? That's my daughter, Landon."

"A little girl, yeah. She's pretty. I have a granddaughter 'bout that age. But I haven't seen her in a while. Actually she was a baby when I was last with her. I didn't know till I saw you two that you were in the program with a kid. I would think that would be better in some ways and worse in some ways. You'd have family with you, you know. That would be a blessing. A true blessing. But I'm sure you worry about her, too."

I think he wanted to talk about his family. The one he'd left behind in Philadelphia or Boston or Miami or wherever he was from. I was too consumed with terror about my own situation to digress and talk about Carl's family. I felt guilty as I asked, "Why would he follow me, Carl?"

He paused for half a breath. Then he asked, "You been threatened at all since you moved here?"

"No."

"Any reason to think you've been made by anyone?"

"No. No one's acted like they've recognized me. Ron's never said anything. But I suppose that it's possible. What'd Ron do once he followed Landon and me up to Chautauqua?"

"I like her name. Landon. Pretty. I suppose it's not real. It's like Carl and Peyton, right? Ron drove away after he saw what you were doing."

"You mean while we were in the restaurant?"

"Yeah."

"He didn't wait around until after we were done eating?"

"No. Maybe five minutes after you went into the Dining Hall, he left."

"Do you know where he went?"

"No."

"Why, Carl? Why would he follow us? Is that part of what the marshals do at first for people who are new to the program?"

"I'm no expert on the marshals. But I don't think it's usual. I'm 99 percent sure that nobody followed me around at the beginning. I'm pretty good at covering my rear and I never noticed a tail. Certainly not one as sloppy as the one that Ron was painting on you."

"Then why?"

"I don't know why Kriciak's all over you. Maybe the marshals have a reason to be concerned. Maybe they've heard something, got a tip, something that they think makes you . . . you know, hot. Maybe it's something else. Like I told you once, far as I'm concerned, the book's still out on Kriciak."

"They wouldn't tell me if they thought I was hot?"

"They give you that 800 number in Washington? The one to call in an emergency?"

I said, "Yes."

"Then you're hot enough. I had an inspector tell me once that not everybody gets that. But I don't know exactly how the marshals think. Been trying to figure them out since I joined up. If they think the risk is acute enough—and I can promise you this is true—they'll whisk you and your little girl away to someplace new with a couple of babysitters before you can open your mouth to complain."

"You mean we'd have to move again?"

"That's the way it works."

"No warning?"

"No warning."

"Have you had to move?"

"This is my second stop."

"You don't trust Ron do you, Carl?"

I could almost hear him shrug.

"Why don't you trust him?"

"You develop a sense for these things," he said. "It's how you survive in the jungle."

And that, I thought, *is where the gorillas live.*

"I'm gonna go now," he said.

"Wait. Please. There's another part of my story I should tell you. Something I didn't tell you before."

"Yeah?"

"When I was a prosecutor in New Orleans? I was a . . . critic . . . a very public critic . . . of the Witness Security Program. I'm sure I made some enemies with my criticism."

He made a grunting noise before he asked, "How public were you?"

"I testified before Congress. Did a lot of interviews. Even went on the *Today* show once."

"You've been on *TV*?" I thought his voice carried alarm below the surface, the way the surf drags seaweed to the shore.

"Yes. Quite a few times. And I was in *People* magazine. I got my fifteen minutes. Maybe half an hour."

"You're talking about a lot of exposure. Makes it harder to hide. In fact, that's how Sammy the Bull got made. Somebody recognized him after they saw him on the tube. I bet there's plenty of people who could recognize you after they saw you on TV, too. They change your looks much when they brought you in?"

"My hair, my eyes. I used to wear tinted contacts. Now I wear glasses. My hair's dark; it used to be blond. You know. No surgery, if that's what you mean. I've lost some weight."

"Give me some details about your criticism of the program. One thing you'll learn about WITSEC is that it doesn't like attention. Doesn't seem to much appreciate advice, either."

I did. I told Carl Luppo about Billy Foster who was really Wayne Simkin and all the problems I caused for the Witness Security Program while I was in New Orleans. For some reason I even told him about Ernesto's mother and the bread truck full of Twinkies and Ding Dongs. I told him about the attempt to kidnap Landon in Slaughter, Louisiana.

As I told my story, Carl called Billy Foster "a drug loser," and then he called Ernesto Castro "another drug loser."

He also said, "Really? Twinkies?" They were his only three interruptions.

When I was done, I asked, "Well, what do you think, Carl?"

"I can see some potential problems."

My stomach sunk to the floor. "Such as?"

"Like it's possible that there's someone working inside the witness program—I'm talking a marshal or somebody—who doesn't like what you said when you were a prosecutor. Be easy for them to leak your location back to that guy—what's his name?—Castro. And that Castro guy you put in prison seems to have the means to reach out. You already know that, right? And you already know that he's the type of guy who seems to hold grudges. You know what I mean? I'm making sense here?"

I knew what he meant. I could hear the spent shells tinkling on the sidewalk beside Robert's ear.

"Or . . . it's possible someone inside the program might be willing to compromise your security on his own. You know? To make a point."

"Ron?"

"That wouldn't make much sense. You get hit on Ron's watch, it won't look good for Ron. Maybe he's heard something, some rumblings from his buddies, and that's why he's all over you."

As Carl finished speaking I pulled the phone away from my ear and listened for any sound that might be a sign of Landon descending the stairs. I heard nothing. I moved the mouthpiece close to my lips and tried to summon enough courage to ask a question I'd been dying to ask.

Finally I said, "Carl?"

"Yeah?"

"I don't know a polite way to ask this. But what was it like to . . . kill someone you didn't even know?"

He didn't answer immediately. I thought he sounded a little sadder when he finally spoke. "You wondering what it was like for that guy who did your husband?" His question surprised me for its simple insight.

"I guess I am. I'm not sure."

"I think maybe you are. I can see why you'd wonder. You wondering about guilt?"

"I don't know, maybe."

"Don't. I imagine for him it was just another piece of work. Nothing personal. The shooter wasn't alone that day, I promise you that. He was part of a team. They were told to do it—probably given the circumstances they were even told how to do it—and they went and did it. From your description of what happened, I'd say they had plenty of experience, you know. A hit like that was a risky job and the guys were pros. I don't think the shooter knew either of you—you or your husband. I'd guess it's possible the guy was hyped, you know like adrenaline-hyped, for a few minutes after he clipped your husband. Maybe he had a couple drinks to help him come back down. Talked it over with his crew after. Maybe he went and saw his girlfriend or else found a hooker. A friend of mine used to do that. He'd go to a hooker. Usually the same hooker each time. Once she told me he cried one day after he was done with her. I don't know about that, but I had no reason not to believe her.

"Some guys I know took naps after. But mostly it wasn't that big a deal to whack somebody. People lived. People died. The violence was part of being a made guy. Life went on."

"Not Robert's."

"No, you're right, of course. Bad choice of words. I'm sorry."

"What did you do? After?"

The silence became prolonged. I wasn't at all sure he was planning on answering me.

Finally, he said, "I'd do what the other guys did. We all—everybody—drank too much. We'd go to clubs, joints, places our friends owned. But then, usually, I went home. If I had a girlfriend, I'd go see her first, maybe."

I could hear him breathe as he paused for what felt like an eternity. Maybe it was ten seconds.

"Once we got an okay to hit a guy who was made. It was a big deal, didn't happen often. Made guys were usually untouchable. We did him in his car, then buried the whole fuckin' thing—him and his car—

at an excavation site. Took half the night. I remember that after that one I went home and played ball with my kid. He'd pitch. I'd catch. We'd do it for hours. Pitch and catch. I liked to pretend I was Yogi Berra catching Don Larsen's perfect game.

"I liked to listen to music, too. Crooners. Sinatra. Sometimes I'd surprise everybody and cook a meal. Pasta was my thing. My wife used to yell to the kids, 'Clear the decks, the penne king is on board.' "

"But when you were done with your, your—"

"Piece of work."

"With . . . your piece of work, you wanted to be with your family? That's what you did?"

"Never thought about it that way, but yes, I guess I did. First I was with my boys, that family, and then I'd go home and I'd be with my other family. Yeah, I usually went home after. Eventually anyway."

I thought that talking about his family might have left Carl momentarily off balance. I asked, "Were you following me yesterday, Carl? Or were you following Ron Kriciak?"

Before he could say anything, the sticky sweet melody of Landon's CD suddenly blared louder from the open door of her room. She called from the top of the stairs, "Mo—ther!"

"Just a sec, Carl," I said into the phone. "I'm down here, babe. What's up? What do you need?"

"Have you seen my scissors?"

"Check the shoe box on top of your dresser."

"I did. They're not there."

"Did you look in your desk drawer?"

"They're not there, either."

"What about—?"

"Mom? Can you come help me look?"

Her voice was instantly whiny, too desperate for the circumstances. I knew the feeling. I felt that way a lot lately myself. I had to go and comfort her. "One minute, and I'll be up," I yelled up the stairs.

"Your daughter needs you," Carl confirmed. "That's a good thing. You gotta treasure that."

"Yes."

"To answer your question, I started off following Ron. When I saw who he was following, I started following both of you. Now that I hear your story, I think you might have something to be worried about."

"Thanks for not lying to me," I said. "Now I have to go to my daughter."

7

Prowler waited until he heard a gruff greeting rasp from the speaker in his ear, then he said, "I told you my plan would work. We have three possibles. I'm sending someone to check them out in person. I should have something for you in thirty-six hours max."

"Tell me how you got where you are."

"According to the records you provided, the subject's kid is a spelling wiz. Since she was six years old, she's done all the big spelling bees, and she's done them well. Kind of a little spelling *wunderkind*. I searched the state and regional spelling tournament listings for kids about her age who are appearing on the roster in their state or region for the first time. Most of these tournaments are sponsored by newspapers. That helps; they keep good records. I succeeded in accessing records for forty-three states accounting for 93 percent of the U.S. population."

"That must be a lot of kids."

"It was."

"Good work."

"Thank you." Prowler's sarcasm was intentional.

"Go on."

"I began to rule out kids based on how long they'd lived at the address on their registration form and how long they'd attended their schools."

"You can get that data? I'm impressed. Good again, I'm still with you."

"Next I ruled out kids whose birthdays differed from our target by more than six months. I can't see WITSEC altering the kid's birth date by more than six months. I think three is more likely. Or even one. But my goal was to be conservative. And that whittled the list down to eleven."

"Eleven's a long way from three."

"I ruled out four kids in Louisiana and Florida. I don't think WITSEC would risk placing her in either state. The kid's mother is too well known in both locations. The marshals would consider them 'hot' territories."

"Agreed. We're down to seven."

"I ruled out the other five children one at a time. Turns out that two kids live in segregated neighborhoods and attend segregated schools, one in the south side of Chicago, the other in East St. Louis. WITSEC can't hide a kid who's as white as the one we're looking for in neighborhoods like either of those. Be like trying to hide a grain of rice in a box of red beans."

"That's five."

"One kid had a feature written about her in her local paper. I have the photo. It's not our girl."

"One to go."

"I couldn't eliminate the next one right away. Then I realized that our kid wouldn't have a sibling in the tournament and one of the remaining girls had an older brother registered."

"I'm impressed. Where are the final three girls?"

"A suburb of Indianapolis, Indiana, called Carmel. A town in California called Oceanside—it's north of San Diego. And Boulder, Colorado."

"I like Indiana."

"I do, too. It's our first stop."

"Your plan is?"

"We have the addresses. My people will do surveillance and achieve visual confirmation of the identities of both mother and daughter. I should have digital photos to you within an hour of confirmation."

"Excellent."

Prowler asked, "Your own surveillance? Any fruit from that tree?"

"We have that bug in his home. Still not in hers. She's in a security building. It's felt too risky. And neither of their offices. So far I mostly get to listen to his daughter talk to her friends about boys."

Prowler said, "Let me know if you get something."

"Will do. My friend will be pleased with the progress."

"I'm so happy to hear that."

chapter

four
TWELVE STEPS

I

About halfway between Peyton's townhouse and the sharp rise of the Rocky Mountain foothills, Lauren and Alan were meeting after work to begin shopping for a crib. The plan was for him to meet his wife at Kids and Co. on Arapahoe near Twenty-eighth, next door to Grand Rabbits toy store. When he arrived at the furniture store he spotted Lauren in the back admiring an ornate mahogany crib with lathe-turned spindles. The look was vaguely Victorian.

Lauren's black hair was still cut short. Her neck was bare, and from the rear he could hardly tell she was pregnant. He paused for a moment and admired her profile, concluding that he didn't see how doing yoga with Adrienne was going to improve upon that butt. "Hey, pretty lady," he said when he was still a few steps away. "I was wondering—you doing anything later?"

Without turning to face him she replied, "I don't know. My evening is pretty full. I was planning on doing some work to update my baby book. And maybe see if I can figure out how my new breast pump works." She put a seductive lilt in her voice and added, "Are you interested?"

"The breast pump part sounds interesting enough."

She turned and kissed him. "This was probably why you were available when I met you. You wasted all your best pickup lines on women in maternity stores and baby furniture shops."

He gazed into her eyes and thought she looked tired. He constantly fought concerns about her health. Pregnancy and multiple sclerosis. Multiple sclerosis and pregnancy. He quipped, "But all my friends told me that that's where the women were."

She smiled. "Fortunately for me, all your friends were complete fools. You like this crib?"

He was still trying to gauge her mood. "Should I feign interest or tell you what I really think?"

"It's early in the process. Feign interest."

"Well, in that case, I will say that it seems to be about the right size for a baby. That's a definite plus. And, given the design, it has some definite potential should we decide to name the kid Beatrice or Arthur."

She kicked him lightly on his shin. "Humor me, Alan. I'm pregnant. I'm tired. And I'm hungry."

He looked at his watch. "I think the store's open until nine. You want to get something to eat before we do this?"

"Full Moon Grill?"

"You read my mind. We have reservations."

"I know I read your mind," she said. "Especially about the breast pump."

THEY WALKED WEST a few hundred feet while enjoying a view of the parking lot of the Safeway Supermarket across Arapahoe and of the soaring flat rock faces of the distant Flatirons. At the restaurant they were escorted to a pleasant deuce by the windows.

"You know what? I really want a beer," she said.

"Sorry, sweets. You want to order a nonalcoholic something? A Sharps or a Cutters?"

"No, I don't think so. I've decided that abstaining is easier. Near beer is like having sex without orgasm."

He thought about it for a moment. "There are worse things."

"I'll remember that the next time we're—"

"That's not . . . what I meant."

The waitress walked over and smiled a smile that was too kind for strangers. Alan ordered a beer. Lauren asked for a large glass of lemonade. The waitress spun on her heels and departed.

Alan asked, "How are you two feeling?"

"We two are doing fine. Like I said before, we're tired and we're hungry. Maybe a little cranky."

"Let's order something to start, then." He pointed to the list of appetizers on the menu. "But you're just usual-tired and usual-cranky? Nothing special I should be concerned about?"

"Just the usual," she said. "How was your day?"

"Okay. I think my new government patients are going to provide me with a constant source of amusement and challenge."

Lauren was instantly intrigued. She asked, "In what way?"

He'd opened the door to her question and had to figure out a way to tell Lauren what he wanted without breaching his patients' confidentiality. "Maybe it's not too surprising, but my impression is that nobody involved seems to trust anybody else very much."

"You mean your patients and the government?"

He reached across the table and tore a crust off a hunk of bread. Didn't say yes, didn't say no.

Lauren said, "I would think that the witnesses would be quite beholden to the marshals who are protecting them."

"That's what I thought at first, too. But apparently once your life has been threatened, trust doesn't come too easily."

Lauren waited until she was certain that Alan wasn't planning to continue, then she said, "If that patient of yours is who I told you I thought she was, she has plenty of reasons to mistrust the Witness Protection people." Lauren didn't take her eyes off the table as she spoke.

Alan felt a need to distract Lauren from drawing him further into a conversation about Peyton. "Have you ever dealt with them? Professionally, I mean. Has the Boulder DA ever prosecuted a protected witness?"

"No, not that I'm aware of." She lifted the napkin that was covering the bread in the basket and perused her choices. "Sweetie?" she said.

"Yes."

Lauren leaned forward and lowered her voice to a whisper. "I know that you can't tell me about her. About your work with her. But I know what I saw in your waiting room. Okay? What she did in calling attention to problems in the Witness Protection Program—"

"Technically it's called the Witness Security Program."

"Whatever, you idiot. Don't try to distract me—it's not going to work. In my eyes, what she did in focusing attention on the problems with protected witnesses was flat-out heroic. What happened to her after she took that risk—God, I can't imagine it. It's my biggest fear about my work, that somehow I'll do something that will draw some crazy guy back into our lives—yours and mine and the baby's—and he'll seek his revenge on us.

"I feel so deeply for her. I can't begin to express how glad I am that you're helping her, and I wouldn't dream of doing anything to jeopardize the work that you're doing with her. Please understand that. But if there's anything I can do, any questions I can answer, anything I can teach you about being a prosecutor that you don't already know, please ask. I won't pry into your therapy with her. But it would feel great to me to be able to help her, even in the smallest possible way. Do you understand what I'm saying?"

"I think so."

The waitress returned with their drinks and asked if they were ready to order. Lauren said, "Sorry, we haven't even looked at the menus." The waitress forced another smile and moved on to another table. Then Lauren said to Alan, "I mean it. I want to help any way that I can."

"I don't know what to say. But if I think of anything that you can do to help me with my work, I'll let you know. How's that?"

"That's fair," she said. "You know, last night I dreamt that our baby is going to be blond."

He looked at her with puzzled eyes. Lauren's hair was as close to true black as hair could be. His own was sandy brown. "Blond? Where did that come from?"

"You're the psychologist, you tell me."

He sat back on his chair and smiled at her. "You're inviting me to interpret your dreams?"

"You're right. Bad idea." She reached across the table and took his beer and wet her upper lip with foam. "Forbidden fruit," she said. "So, I've been wondering, do you think we should get a regular audio monitor for the baby's nursery or one of those new video ones?"

Alan exhaled, "Something tells me that you've given this more thought than I have."

THE REMAINDER OF the evening proved that they were no closer to agreeing on a crib than they were to agreeing on a name for their baby. Lauren's view of the nursery was much more romantic than Alan's. He saw the room as a kid's bedroom and thought her image of the space more closely resembled a postnatal spa.

They agreed to disagree, temporarily, and after leaving Kids and Co. they drove east to their Spanish Hills home. Once the garage door had closed on their cars and Emily had been greeted and had peed, Alan and Lauren sat together on the sofa that faced the western windows. The city sparkled below them, and the glacial faces of the Divide radiated below a three-quarters moon. Alan said, "I have a question for you. It's a hypothetical situation that a prosecutor, someone like yourself, might find herself involved in."

"Yeah." Lauren's voice was soft and had a husky burr on its edges. Sleep was close.

"You're tired. I can ask you tomorrow," he said.

"No, now. I'm fine." She swallowed a yawn.

"Hypothetically, okay?"

She murmured something that he took to be an assent.

"Let's say you were involved in a prosecution years ago. Maybe eight, ten years back. A second-chair situation for you on a big case, a capital murder. The facts you were working with looked good at the time, not great, but the only suspect you had was excellent for the crime. He was in the neighborhood and could be tied circumstantially to the murders. He's scum, with multiple priors."

"Mm hmm."

"You get the conviction after a straightforward trial. Defendant's defense was adequate, but nothing as imaginative as David Kelley could do. The guy is sentenced to die for his crimes. You feel justice was served and your life goes on—you have new scumbags to prosecute, right? Without much effort, you put the whole case out of your mind. Later, as time passes and you get more prosecutorial experience under your belt, you start to develop some lingering doubts about some of the evidence that the police produced during the original trial."

"Yes." Lauren was growing more alert.

"The guy's on death row this whole time, of course, and he's running through his appeals like a ten-year-old kid goes through his allowance. Soon there's only one appeal left. But with every failed appeal, your doubts are growing stronger. Truth is, you're no longer convinced he did it."

"Yes?"

"What do you do?"

"A couple of questions first. My colleagues? The ones I tried the case with. What do they think?"

"You don't know what they think. You don't work with them any longer, but you're not convinced that they share your doubts. Regardless, you suspect that they would prefer to let sleeping dogs lie."

"Do I have any evidence that might support my doubts?"

"You think someone tampered with a GSR, though you're not sure whether it was the detectives or the lab. Most of the rest of the case was equally circumstantial."

"But I have other doubts as well? Not just the GSR?"

"Correct."

"Do I suspect the police?"

Alan thought for a moment before he responded. "Although you're reluctant to admit it, you probably do."

"Do I suspect my colleagues?"

"You're trying not to. You would like to believe that they weren't involved in tainting evidence."

Lauren stood up and said, "Hold that thought. I need to pee." She walked toward the bathroom.

Alan stretched himself at an angle to the corner of the sofa, kicked off his shoes, and stared at the Open Space south of the Flatirons, toward Eldorado Springs. Traffic was stopped outbound on the Turnpike. He guessed there was a traffic accident. His eyes tried to find the pulsating beacons of approaching police or rescue vehicles, but he couldn't spot any.

Emily's stomach growled noisily.

Lauren returned and settled herself beside him, against his chest. She'd shed her work clothes and was wearing a chenille robe. She reached down and grabbed both of his hands, placing them on the contours of her rounded belly. Then she launched right back into character. "I'm thinking that I may have another problem. In the years since this trial, I may have changed my life, let's say changed my life dramatically, and I may be reluctant to return to my former life to follow my conscience and do the right thing in this old death-penalty case. Who knows? I may be severely reluctant, even. Does that fit your scenario?"

"Sure," he said. His fingertips had found a sharp edge poking at the flesh of Lauren's abdomen. He was guessing that the protrusion was an infantile elbow or knee. He pressed on it. His child pressed back. He found the interaction amazing and looked for another place to prod.

"I don't know what the hell I'd do," Lauren said. She rolled slightly toward him and made eye contact. "That's not true. Sure I know what I would do. I just don't know how I would do it."

"What would you do?"

"I'd do whatever I needed to do to erase my doubts. I'd have to convince myself all over again that this guy was guilty."

"How would you go about that?"

"Reinvestigate. Especially the weakest parts of the case. Talk to the people who were involved with the gunshot residue test. The detective who administered the kit, the lab guys who analyzed it. See who acts squirrelly."

"How would you solve your other problem? The not-wanting-to-surface problem?"

"I don't know," she said. "I don't know the answer to that. That's not a prosecutor question. That's a heart-and-soul question."

"What do you mean?"

"I have one more concern. See, hypothetically, it turns out that I have a child." She smiled and gazed down at her baby. "A child who might be placed at risk if I make a stink and decide to try to save the life of some lowlife who may or may not belong on Death Row. So I have to make a choice."

Alan shifted his weight so that he could more easily caress his wife's belly. "How hard a choice is that? Try this on: If the situation were different, if you walked into an armed robbery, a bank robbery say, and you found yourself in a position to push this very same criminal into the line of fire to save your child, or alternately to push your child into the line of fire to save him, your choice would be clear, wouldn't it?"

"Sure. Of course. I'd sacrifice him to save her. In a second."

"There you go, then."

"But it's not that simple. The problem is that in this scenario that you've created, the prosecutor—me?—I'm not just the mom, I'm also the bank robber. I'm not only the one pushing somebody to his death, I'm also the one who's holding the gun that will kill him. That's what makes my choice so difficult." She paused and caressed his hands. "The only solution I can see is to put down the gun."

"How do you do that?"

"First? I have to find out how my colleagues feel, see if I have any allies in my doubts. If it turns out that my old colleagues aren't too fond of my questions, I can use the fact that they don't know where to find me as a shield."

"Okay."

"If it turns out that I have an ally, I use that ally to begin to investigate. Cops. Witnesses. Lab. Whatever."

"If you don't have an ally?"

"Things get sticky."

"Sticky?"

"Yes, sticky. Heart and soul, remember? I have that child I'm worried about."

"Yes, you do."

2

Late Friday morning, Andrea Archer dropped two coins in the slot of the pay phone outside a Burger King in Sarasota and punched in Dave Curtiss's office number. The aroma of grilling meat wafting from the restaurant caused her vegetarian stomach to flip in protest. The morning had been gray along the coast, but when she turned her back to the phone to try and catch a sea breeze, she spotted a sliver of sunshine sparkling off the waters in the distant Gulf of Mexico.

Maybe the day would improve.

As the connection went through and the phone began to ring, she pirouetted on one foot and gazed at the unfamiliar surroundings near the restaurant and thought to herself that this must be Dave's Pay-Phone City.

A receptionist said, "Good Morning. Larkspur, Granita, and Warren."

"Dave Curtiss, please."

A moment passed before another anonymous female voice said, "Mr. Curtiss's office."

"May I speak to Mr. Curtiss please? This is his sister."

A moment later Dave Curtiss said, "This is Dave," uncertain whether the person on the other end of the phone was his actual sister, Judy, calling from Ohio, or whether it was Andrea Archer using the code he'd asked her to use when calling his office.

"Did you hear?" asked Andrea, her voice urgent.

"No. What? You found her? You know where she is?"

"No, I still don't know where she is. I'm calling because the decision came down earlier than we expected. Khalid's final appeal was denied. The date's been set for his execution."

"Shit! We need time, Andrea. Shit, shit, shit." He paused. "When is the execution?"

"Beginning of next month."

"We can't wait another day. We can't. We have to know where Kirsten stands on this."

Andrea said, "I've been thinking, Dave. Maybe she doesn't care one way or the other what happens here. You know, her own problems are pretty severe. She can't exactly take a public position on this."

"She's too damn moral, Andrea. She's the original Miss Law and Order. These death penalty issues are big deals for her. You know I'm right—you know her better than I do. Before this goes any further, we have to be certain where she stands or we could go down, too. If she decides to publicly disagree with us, we're sunk."

"What do you suggest we do, Dave? Call the Witness Protection people and ask for her address?"

"She hasn't called you again since that day I was in your office?"

"No. But she might call now. Remember, she told me she's been reading USA Today, trying to keep up with the Florida news. Hopefully a story about the Khalid Granger appeal will be in tomorrow's paper." Andrea felt something rough against her ear and examined the earpiece of the pay phone. Someone had filled most of the holes with yellow mustard. Andrea thought shower. No, even better, sauna.

While she was examining the phone she'd missed something Dave was saying. She picked it up in time to hear, ". . . that's the way I see it. When she calls, you need to find some way to press her for information on how she feels about the decision on the appeal. We need to know what she thinks. Then we'll make a decision about what to do next."

"Have you thought this through, Dave? Have you actually considered what you're going to do if you discover she's not on the same page that we are?"

"What *we're* going to do. Last I looked, we're in this together, right? I'm a hopeful man, Andrea."

"Yeah, and I'm a supermodel. You, a hopeful man? I've known you since law school at Penn, Dave. Who are you kidding?"

3

Carl showed up a few minutes late for his Monday morning appointment with Dr. Gregory. As always, he sat on the far end of the sofa, closest to the wall.

"I want to go back to what we were talking about before. Me and my ideas for a business. Remember? But my inspector, Ron? I ran them by him, and he's not too hot on any of my ideas. He wants me to come up with something portable, something he says I can just walk away from, need be, or take with me. He says he's wary of bricks and mortar with someone in my situation."

Dr. Gregory asked, "What do you think? Can you see where he's coming from?"

"Sure, I guess. Being a protected witness doesn't always mean security, you know? If I open a coffee bar over on the Mall over there—and I mean a real Italian place, no mochas and shit, that's one of my ideas—and someone from my old life shows up and makes me and I gotta run, then what happens to my investment? The damn espresso machine alone costs as much as a late-model Lincoln. What happens to all that shit? I think that's Ron's worry."

"So his position seems reasonable to you?"

Carl shrugged. "I don't know. I know I gotta do something, Doc. I mean what can I do that doesn't take some investment? Write songs, maybe? Twenty, thirty years ago I used to write songs that I wanted Sinatra to sing. I wrote dozens of them for him and for that other guy, Engelbert something. Just lyrics, though, not the music. Yeah, and Robert Goulet. I liked Goulet. You liked Goulet? Is he dead? I think he's dead. I could write songs again I suppose. But who listens to ballads anymore? You know, I think all three of those singers are dead. But that's what I like to write—ballads. But they're all dead. All the guys who sang them and half the guys who listened to them. Dead."

Dr. Gregory wasn't sure the crooners were all dead. But he didn't argue. He waited to see if Carl wanted to talk more about music and songwriting and ballads. It seemed he didn't.

"What about getting a job, Carl? Just a simple nine-to-five?"

"Two problems, there. One, what could I do? I got no references. And like I already told you, I got no real skills, so I do what? I could be a bouncer in a nightclub, maybe. Second problem is that I'm used to getting my own way. That's a serious problem. I don't think I'd make a good employee. If a boss gave me a hard time, I'd probably intimidate back a little. I don't think that would work to my advantage. I think it's best that I find a situation where I'm the boss. I'm thinking maybe something on the Internet. That's what I'm thinking."

Dr. Gregory waited. When Carl spoke again, he was glad that he had waited.

Carl raised his chin and briefly averted his eyes. He said, "I met somebody. You know, a girl. She's nice."

To Alan Gregory it appeared that Carl was on the verge of saying something more, but he didn't. He just shrugged. Dr. Gregory composed a welcoming look on his face, thinking that Carl Luppo might actually be at a loss for words. The psychologist was eager to witness the process of Carl trying to find his place.

Carl said, "The girl? She's younger than me. By a lot, maybe twenty years or so. I don't know, I'm not that good at ages. But younger than me. Not that that matters much cause my interest isn't romantic or anything."

Carl was sitting on the edge of the sofa. His elbows rested heavily on his knees. "It isn't. I'm married, you know? Still married. Being in the program doesn't change that. Vows are vows." Carl's voice trailed away with the thoughts of his wife. Dr. Gregory was left to wonder whether he was witnessing his patient's longing for his marriage or his patient's lament over the fact that he was still burdened with a wife. In the few therapy sessions thus far, Carl hadn't spoken much about his family.

Carl looked up, shrugged again. "So you gonna say something, or what? You just going to sit there? In case you're wondering, I don't find that particularly helpful."

"When I have something useful to say, I'll say it." He tried to sound matter-of-fact. Certainly not petulant. Not with this guy. "I'm not sure where you're going yet. I don't want to get out in front of you. I'd just be in the way."

"You think I'm going somewhere? I don't know about that. I'm just telling you I met somebody I've been spending some time with. I don't have too many friends since I came here, you know what I mean?" Carl smiled, swallowed a little laugh, as though he found the thought of having friends amusing.

"But you like this girl?"

"Yeah. Met her at that tea place across Broadway. What's it called? Dushan something. It's from Tibet, I think. No, no, not Tibet, one of the 'stans. Uzbekistan. Afghanistan. Whatever, some gift to the city from someplace in Asia. I read about it in the tourist guide."

"Dushanbe." Alan knew it was from Tajikistan.

"Yeah. Dushanbe. You seen the place? The carving and the painting? Almost as pretty as something done by Michelangelo or Bernini. You close your eyes a little bit and soften the focus, it almost looks Italian. Like a little Sistine Chapel or something. Not that I've been there in a long time. Hear they cleaned it up since I was there." He paused for ten seconds, maybe fifteen. "Anyway, it's nice. I'm guessing that she's lonely, too. The girl? Like me in some ways. She has . . . what do you say? Issues. She has issues."

"Issues?"

"Yeah. Issues."

"What do you like about her, Carl?"

"One thing is, I like that she's not scared of me. Not so much, anyway. We talk."

"Why would she be scared of you?"

Carl shrugged again. "I'm told I'm a scary kind of guy. When people on the outside smell wiseguy, even if they don't recognize the odor, they tend to cross the street."

"You think she smells wiseguy?"

"Look at me. Listen to me. What else you gonna think? I have to wear a sign around my neck or something?"

Alan eyed Carl from his head to his toes. He said, "I see a guy with a friendly face. A man wearing boat shoes, Dockers, and a nice polo shirt. I don't see or smell anything that says wiseguy."

"You stupid or are you pulling my leg?"

"Hopefully, neither."

"She does. She smells wiseguy."

"You're sure?"

"I'm sure."

"But she spends time with you anyway?"

"Not much time. A little. Couple of times I've seen her. We talk about her troubles. Her issues. I listen. Like I told you, it's not romantic or anything."

"You like being helpful to her?"

"Is that a problem?"

"Hardly."

"Good. I was hoping you'd say that."

4

I went back to work on Monday even though I didn't feel all that much better.

My last break at work was at four, long before the restaurant was busy for dinner. I wasn't hungry, so I used the time to call Viv to check on Landon and then tried Andrea at her condo on Longboat Key in Sarasota. She seemed so happy to hear from me that it brought tears to my eyes.

I missed Robert most of all. After him, I missed my friends.

"I wondered if you'd call. Hoped you would. You must have heard the news today," she said.

I thought, *oh boy,* and softly sang, "Four thousand holes in Blackburn, Lancashire."

"What?" she said. She didn't recognize the old Beatles lyrics from "A Day in the Life." It was on *Sergeant Pepper,* one of Robert's favorites.

"Never mind. It's not important. Yes, I saw the little blurb about Khalid in *USA Today.*"

"I didn't see that one, but I bet a couple of paragraphs didn't fill your cup with too many details. Anyhow, with his appeals exhausted, the Khalid story is almost over for us. The case sure brings back memories, doesn't it? You and Dave and I made quite a team till Robert kidnapped you and took you to New Orleans."

I heard something unexpected in her tone but couldn't be certain what it was. I asked, "You still see Dave since he defected to the private side?"

"We run into each other professionally. Not socially, though. His wife thinks I'm out to steal her man."

"Dave Curtiss? You?" Peyton laughed.

Andrea said, "His wife is not a well woman."

"I like to think that you and Dave and I did some good things on the prosecution side back then, Andrea."

I thought I sensed a hesitation, maybe even a quick intake of air before she asked, "Are you including Khalid on that list?"

I stuck a toe in the water. "Should I? Since I saw the newspaper this morning I've been wondering how I'm supposed to feel about being instrumental in someone else's death. Doesn't it give you pause?"

Again I sensed the hesitation before she responded. Even thought I heard the same inhale as before. "Honey," she asked, "when you talk about being instrumental in someone's death, are you talking about Khalid Granger or are you talking about your Robert?"

Just hearing someone suggest out loud that I was culpable for my husband's murder could cause tiny fangs to tear at my heart. I fought the pain and tried to respond. "That's just it, I don't know. Sometimes these days I think I'm talking about Robert no matter what else I'm talking about. With my mom dying last year and then with Robert, I don't know. Tell me honestly, does this sound crazy? Do you know what? I was actually considering going to see that woman whose husband died at Columbine High School. The teacher who died in the shooting there? I've been thinking maybe his wife could teach me something that would help me move on."

"You'd just call her out of the blue?"

"Or go talk to her. It's not that far from here." My breath caught in my throat. "*Oh my God!* I shouldn't have said that. Please pretend I didn't say that."

"I guess you just told me that you and your li'l darlin' are living in Colorado, didn't you?"

"Please forget I said that. I didn't just say that, okay?"

My plea settled like the dust of the day on the silence between us.

Finally she said, "So what exactly is your plan? You'd just knock on this woman's door and say you want to have some tea and talk about your murdered husbands?"

"You think it does sound crazy?"

She paused again, then she said, "Whatever gets you through the night is what I think."

I felt a shiver crawl up my cervical spine. "Andrea, I wonder if that was my first slip. Sometimes I have so much trouble keeping all my secrets straight. I'm so hesitant about things. I even have to stop and think before I tell someone what my name is."

"I can only imagine how difficult it must be."

We fell silent for too long, the deadness on the line poignant and awkward between old friends.

She broke the silence. "Is it pretty where you are? I've never been, just seen pictures."

"Gorgeous. The weather is better here than I ever thought it was. It's a good place for me and Landon, I think."

"Landon?"

"I didn't tell you? That's Matilda's newest name. Landon. I'm starting to like it. It's the kind of name Robert would have chosen for her when she was born if I would have let him. He wanted something special for her. Something she didn't have to share with a hundred other girls. Listen, I have to get back to the hotel where I work. I'm on break."

Her voice took on urgency as she said, "Wait, please. I need to know something, Kirsten. What you said before about being instrumental in someone's death? Do you have any doubts about Khalid?"

Hearing my real name shocked me. "Call me Peyton, okay? What kind of doubts?"

"Any kind."

A million. A billion million. But I didn't know why she was asking, so I couldn't tell her. I wanted to believe she shared my doubts. I said, "Andrea, I'm late getting back. I'll have to call you another time."

I hung up the phone and walked slowly back toward the kitchen at Q's. I hoped—I prayed—that I wasn't about to slip and fall on the beans I'd just spilled.

AN HOUR OR so later I finished cleaning my station. I wasted a few minutes changing out of my checked chef's pants and shedding my double-breasted chef's blouse before I walked down Thirteenth toward my car, which I'd left a couple of blocks away between Spruce and Pine. My car was a late-model four-door something that Ron Kriciak and I had picked out from Hertz's used car selection the day after I'd arrived in Boulder. The car looked like five thousand other late-model four-door somethings that lined the streets of downtown Boulder at any given point in time. I knew that was the point. Once already, in the parking lot at Target on Twenty-eighth, I'd tried to get into someone else's late-model four-door something instead of my own.

I missed my Audi.

I was quietly singing the few lyrics that I could remember from "A Day in the Life"—*A crowd of people stood and stared/They'd seen his face before/Nobody was really sure/If he was from the House of Lords*—when I spotted Carl Luppo waiting for me on the steps of the church at the corner of Thirteenth and Spruce.

Chinos, yes. A light jacket, yes, but over his shoulders, not over his arm. He almost looked preppy. No Abercrombie bag. Instead, his hands were in the pockets of his chinos. I guessed they were Dockers.

I wasn't in the mood for Carl. I now knew that after he had killed strangers on the street he had gone home to his family and played catch with his son. I didn't slow to greet him, didn't even shift my eyes his way as I passed. I said, "Not now, Carl. I'm not in the mood." The words didn't come out the way I'd intended. I was afraid I sounded like I had a headache and wasn't interested in sex.

"Fine," he said gruffly. "But you should probably know that Ron's waiting for you over there. He's parked on Pine in sight of your car. He's not driving that big pickup truck of his this time; he's driving an even bigger Ford Expedition. A white one. Bet it's a DEA confiscation. Go check it out yourself."

I stopped walking and spun on the concrete sidewalk. I was furious at both of them. Ron and Carl. But Ron wasn't available, so I turned on Carl, who *was* available. Robert always used to tell me that I never picked my enemies with the care with which I chose my friends.

Robert, it seemed, was a damn genius.

"Who appointed you?" I hissed. Landon hated it when I hissed. She could shrug off my yelling and my screaming, but she would cower when I hissed. I tried to save it for special moments.

Carl didn't cower. He looked at the fingernails of his left hand, pushed a cuticle back with his thumbnail. This, of course, wasn't a man who was accustomed to being hissed at. He stood up. Since he had been sitting on the third or fourth step of the church, he towered above me when he stood, despite his diminutive height. "Nobody appointed me," he said. "Tell you what, I think maybe meeting you here was a big mistake. I'll just be going. See ya."

I put my hands on my hips and immediately felt silly. Taking them back off my hips would have felt even sillier. I said, "Maybe I arranged to meet Ron after work. Did that possibility ever occur to you? Did it?"

"But you didn't," he said. "You know you didn't. Listen, I've been trying to be helpful to you. Friendly. Thought maybe you could get used to being around someone who gives a shit. Someone who knows maybe what it's like to be living the life you're living."

"You know nothing—*nothing*—about my life."

"Whatever. Maybe it's more selfish then. Maybe what I'm doing is I'm making amends. You ever consider that possibility?"

I didn't want to be having this conversation at all and certainly not on a busy sidewalk in downtown Boulder. I climbed two steps so I could get closer to him and I lowered my voice but I tried to keep the hiss in it anyway. "I don't want to be part of your 'amends,' Carl. What do you think this is I'm doing with my life? Running some twelve-step program for hit men? I've got an idea for you. Why don't you go down into the church basement and give your, 'Hi, my name is Carl and I'm-a-hit-man speech' down there? It'll go over better with the other twelve-steppers than it will with me, I promise." Considering the venom in my words, even I realized that the continuation of the hiss was pure redundancy.

A whale surfaced right then. Right in front of my eyes, like an apparition. It was a Robert whale. Surprisingly, it was a beluga.

ROBERT AND I having one of our rare fights. About what? I didn't recall—anyway that wasn't the point. Robert striding forward slowly and taking my face in both his hands. Robert saying, "Your mind is as sharp as a diamond, K." Sometimes Robert called me K. In my mind I spelled it C-a-y. Why? I never knew, always figured it was a Florida thing. He said, "You can wield it like a surgeon with a scalpel, or you can slice up people like a street thug with a bowie knife. So how exactly do you want this argument to end? Do you want to heal me or make me bleed to death?"

The honest-to-God truth? Right then and there I wanted to wield the bowie knife and I wanted Carl Luppo to bleed to death on the granite stoop of the First Congregational Church of Whatever.

HOW DID CARL respond to my tirade? He shrugged the way he does and said, "If that's the way you feel."

But I couldn't just let him go. I couldn't just let him walk away. Why? Because I couldn't get the Robert whale out of my mind. I dropped my hands to my side and said, the hiss now absent, "So what if he's following me? Why is it any of your business whether Ron Kriciak is following me?"

I could tell that he wasn't sure how to react to my suddenly softer persona. I wasn't quite crazy enough to think that Carl had been able to see the Robert whale surface and frolic around in my private sea. He said, "It's not my business. It's your business. But you can't really make it your business unless someone tells you it's happening. So I'm telling you it's happening. That's all. You want to ignore the information, then that's your right."

I'd been on my feet nonstop since I'd crawled out of bed at six-thirty that morning. My legs were still attorney's legs, not cook's legs, and they were killing me. Muscles in my calves hurt that I didn't even know I had. I glanced at my watch to see how much time I had before Viv had to leave Landon and go home, then I sat on the flagstone stoop and patted the cold stone next to me. Carl sat, too.

Pretty women can get men to do all sorts of things. I was a pretty woman and I knew that.

But Carl sat farther away than the spot I had been patting. This retired Mafioso's survival skills were still very much intact.

"You think this is important, don't you, Carl? All this cloak-and-dagger stuff with Ron. Why can't I just assume that Ron's going to some extra effort to keep an eye on me?"

He sighed. "You can assume that if you want. But the whole point of them putting you into the program and moving you here was that once they've ripped your life out from beneath your feet and shredded it into a million little pieces and taped it back together so you can't even recognize it, then nobody should have to keep an eye on you. I mean that's the whole point of all the disruption, right? So the fact that Ron is following you means that—"

"It means that somebody in the program thinks I may still be in some danger. That's what you're saying?"

"Yeah," he said, swallowing a little burp. He placed an open hand over his mouth. "Excuse me. While I was waiting, I had one of those empanadas from that place over there." He gestured back toward the Mall. "They're new for me, but I think maybe I'm developing a taste."

I knew the little empanada place. It was only a couple of blocks down from the hotel. I liked it, too. "Okay, Carl, what you're saying makes sense. Show me where Ron is right now."

We stood and I followed him down Thirteenth to Pine. At his direction we crossed over one at a time to the north side of the street and reconnoitered behind a FedEx truck. Carl said, "Peek your head out and you'll see his white Expedition. Three cars from the corner, the other side of the street."

I peeked. I saw a man sitting in the driver's seat of a big white SUV, his elbow resting on the window ledge. I couldn't see the man's face but had no reason to believe it wasn't Ron Kriciak. I still didn't know what to make of it.

I stepped back behind the FedEx truck and moved to within a foot of Carl Luppo. He was wearing a subtle cologne that I hadn't noticed the last time we'd spoken. Something with lemon in it. His nose was slightly crooked and his skin was soft and unwrinkled. Did this man never worry? Even women my age would envy the texture of his complexion. "Same question as last time, Carl. When you spotted Ron today, were you following him or were you following me?"

Carl's tone was mildly admonishing, as though he was reprimanding a favorite daughter. "You're too smart to ask that question again. Don't you see? Following you, following him. It's become one and the same thing."

I held his eyes. "So what should I do?"

"I'm not sure. You want me to, I'll think on it."

"I'd like you to, Carl," I said, then I stepped back, suddenly uncomfortable with our physical proximity.

"I've been thinking something else, too," he said, and my breath caught in my throat. I feared he was about to ask me for a date. "I've been thinking that with your permission I'd look into this guy in prison, this druggie, the one who had your husband whacked."

"Ernesto Castro." Just saying the name turned my stomach.

"Yes. Ernesto Castro. I was thinking I might make a call or two to some people I trust and see if I can learn his current intentions. See whether he's been active, what he's been thinking." Carl touched his hand to his chest, right above his heart, as though he was about to recite the *Pledge of Allegiance*. "Of course, I would make these calls only if that's what you wanted."

My own chest felt suddenly as if my lungs had been filled with fluid. I didn't seem to be able to inhale at all. I finally managed to say, "What do you mean 'his intentions'? What are you saying?" I was afraid that Carl was using some Mafia vernacular that I was unable to translate.

"I'm wondering, I think, exactly what you've been wondering. Is this Castro guy still looking for you? Does he have people who might have tracked you here? Is that maybe why Ron has punched up the security? Maybe the program has heard about some new threats or maybe they have some intelligence that causes them to worry. It's possible I could find the answers."

"I assume that Castro is still looking for me. I live every day believing that Castro is still looking for me."

"You might be right. But you might be wrong about that, too. Occasionally people lose interest. Grudges are sometimes carved from granite. Sometimes they're carved from ice. Those are the ones that melt. I've been there—I know. Your Ernesto Castro is in prison now. Prison causes people to have new priorities. I've been there—I know that, too."

I wanted to believe him. I said, "You think?"

"I do. I also think maybe I could check on Mr. Castro's intentions without too much difficulty. I could make some calls. Maybe I have some friends who are locked up where he's locked up. I could reach out to them, ask a favor. What prison is he in?"

I told him. "You can do this without giving away my location?"

"Your location is my location. I'm a little vulnerable here, too. I try to be extra careful."

I have to admit that I'd forgotten that Carl, like me, was on somebody's hit list. I said, "Let me sleep on it."

"You let me know then."

"I will. And I'm sorry about before. About the way I acted on the steps at the church."

"God forgives." He shrugged. "Who am I to hold grudges?"

CARL WALKED AWAY in the direction of Broadway. I retraced my steps to Spruce Street and made my way toward my car by the same route I would have used were I coming from the restaurant.

Carl was worried about Ernesto Castro's intentions. That day my instincts told me to worry more about Ron Kriciak's.

I drove home slowly. Only once did I lose sight of Ron Kriciak's big white Ford Expedition as he trailed behind me. He was wearing sunglasses and a baseball cap of some kind.

Robert would have known the team for sure.

5

The phone still in her hand, Andrea walked to the sliding glass doors and stared at the waters of the Gulf. She drained her wineglass and placed it on the cute little rattan bistro table by the window before she punched in Dave Curtiss's number and waited for him to answer.

While the phone was ringing she paced in front of the glass doors and ignored her cat. As soon as she recognized Dave's voice, she said, "Meet me in twenty minutes. You know where."

"No. I'm alone with the kids. I can't leave. Anyway, I can't stand this any longer. I'm an absolute wreck. Vicki says I'm getting hives. Do you know I had a chance—I mean a real opportunity—to go into investment banking instead of law? I ever tell you that? Well, I did. And I should have done it. I wouldn't be in this pickle, I'll tell you. There's no capital punishment in investment banking. If you have something, for God's sake tell me now."

"I'm at home, Dave. This isn't Pay-Phone City."

"Don't push me, Andrea. I'm not up for it. I hope this means you finally talked to her?"

"I did."

"Then tell me what she said."

"She accidentally told me she's in Colorado. Someplace close to the mountains. She's working in a restaurant in a hotel. That's all I know."

"Restaurants need lawyers?"

"Bad ones do, I imagine. No, she's learning to cook. Oh, and wherever she is, isn't too far from Littleton."

"Littleton?"

"You know, where Columbine High School is."

"Jesus. My daughter's in junior high. I don't even like to think about Columbine High School. What did Kirsten say about Khalid?"

"Not much. She's Peyton now, by the way. We ran out of time. She said she'll call back. But I think she may have some doubts."

"What kind of doubts? Death-penalty doubts?" His voice actually bordered on being hopeful.

"She had to hang up and go back to work at the restaurant. I don't know what kind of doubts."

"She'll call you back when?"

"I don't know, Dave. Soon, I hope."

AN HOUR AND fifteen minutes later, Prowler's phone rang in the Atlanta suburbs. He answered on the first ring.

"Forget Indiana," the caller said. "My tap finally produced. She's in Colorado. Get your people moving now."

"Of the three possibles, that would have been my last guess. You have confirmation?"

"Yes. She just now told her friend she's in Colorado, somewhere near the mountains. She's working in a hotel restaurant. So, of your three possibles, it has to be Boulder."

"How certain are you?"

"One hundred percent. I have it on tape. Do you want to hear it?"

Prowler considered listening to the recording, but said, "That won't be necessary. Did you get additional details? The name of the restaurant? The name of the hotel? Anything useful?"

"No, I can't walk you right to her door. But I found the haystack she's in. And I located the section of the haystack she's in. All your people have to do is find the damn needle."

Prowler processed the criticism and chose not to respond. He said, "As long as all of your information is reliable, you can consider that your original request will be accomplished in a timely fashion."

"Don't worry, my information is golden. But my friend doesn't want any deviation from the original plan. No deviation. This has to be coordinated. You'll send me photos before you take any action?"

"That's the plan."

"Good."

Prowler added, "If the second payment is delayed like the first one was, you won't like the consequences."

"Don't worry. It was just an account number mix-up on my friend's part. I told you that already."

Prowler said, "Tell your friend I don't worry. I act."

chapter five

BARBARA BARBARA

I

The United flight from Indianapolis to Denver was approaching DIA from the north, which afforded Barb Turner an inspiring view of the mountains from her window seat on the starboard side of the plane. This was Barb's first visit to Denver, and she was mesmerized by the sight of the light fracturing above the mountains as the sharp teeth of the distant Rockies gnawed on the liquid underbelly of the setting sun.

While the plane taxied, Barb reached down and checked her carry-on bag to be certain nothing had been tampered with during an earlier trip to the lavatory. She felt for both of her cameras. She touched her wallet. Everything was in its place.

She found the Denver airport disconcerting. Bright, brash, new. And big. Too big for the city she expected to find. In advance of viewing Denver for the first time, she'd already concluded that what they had built was a size-fourteen airport for a size-eight city. Barb especially didn't like the new airports that had their own train systems. But she had done her homework, had memorized the layout at DIA, and she quickly found her way around. Her rule-of-thumb was to follow a herd of business people off the plane. One lone traveler might be as lost as she was. A whole herd usually meant familiarity. Turn right if they turned right. Follow them straight to baggage claim or to ground transportation.

As always, the strategy worked. Within minutes—using pedestrian walkways, escalators, and the dreaded train—she covered what felt to her like miles and found herself standing in front of the fountain in the center of the main terminal. She craned her neck and examined the soaring translucent roof above her head. She was intentionally acting like a tourist. She faced the fountain and saw an Avis counter to her right.

BY THE TIME Barb Turner had retrieved her solitary suitcase from baggage claim, signed for her rental car, and picked her route from the airport to Boulder, night was almost done replacing day. The mountains were silhouetted against a pale charcoal sky, and the peaks appeared much farther away than they had when she was gazing at them from the window seat of the plane. The woman at the car rental checkout booth had told her to expect about a forty-five-minute journey to Boulder.

She played with the radio controls, trying to find a station from the town she was about to visit, and began to prepare herself for the reality that was Boulder. She felt as though she already knew the town but was cautious about her knowledge because she knew that she knew Boulder the same way she knew Brentwood.

Brentwood was O.J.

Boulder was JonBenet.

Towns like Brentwood and Boulder had become infamous because of the work of amateurs. Barb Turner wasn't an amateur. She was a professional. And she planned to leave no mark during her visit. No one on MSNBC would be talking about the mess she left behind.

. . .

SHE HAD NO hotel or motel reservation in Boulder. Although she was a planner at heart, she insisted on doing some things by feel. Picking where to spend the night was one of those things.

She stayed on Highway 36, the Boulder Turnpike, until it turned into Twenty-eighth Street and curved north into Boulder. As she made the transition into town, she noticed a motel on her right called the Broker Inn. Next came the Boulder Inn, followed by a Ramada Inn and then a slightly funkier place called the Lazy L. She felt a moment's magnetism for the Lazy L but wasn't fond of the locale. Twenty-eighth Street was too much of a main drag. Down the road a bit, on her left, she spied a multistory place called the Regal Harvest House.

No. None of them felt right to her. The cross street at the next big intersection, Arapahoe Road, was lined with commercial and retail activity, so she turned left there. But the retail district turned out to be small. Within a couple of blocks she found herself driving on a two-lane, tree-lined road that was a mix of commercial and residential properties. It could have bisected a thousand small towns anywhere in the Midwest. She passed a big school that a stone sign identified as Boulder High School. The school was followed by a few more shops.

Barb drove on, hesitating at the intersection at Broadway, another big street, searching left and right from the corner, trying to spot another motel. On the other side of Broadway, Arapahoe Road became mostly residential. Brick bungalows mixed with some stately Victorian homes and some anachronistic apartment buildings and condos. She guessed that the brick homes were as old as the house in which she'd grown up in Iowa.

She passed a new library and then a turn-of-the-century school as Arapahoe Road climbed gently toward the west. The mountains loomed large in front of her. After a few more blocks, she had to lean forward over the wheel and crane her neck upward to even begin to glimpse the dark sky above the vaulting peaks. The mountains were close and they beckoned. She drove on, slowing to circumvent a series of traffic circles that were placed in locations that made no sense to her at all. She was about to acknowledge that her instinct had failed her when she came upon another small commercial district. Some small office buildings. A couple of little stores. A park along a stream.

Arapahoe Road narrowed and became one-way. And then, on the left side of the road, a red "Vacancy" sign emerged from the darkness. The adjacent "NO" was unlit. The rest of the sign was dark. She drove closer until her headlights illuminated the marquee. It read, Foot of the Mountain Motel. AAA approved. HBO. Above the sign, on a little rise, she spotted the motel. She guessed there were a dozen rooms in three or four old log-faced buildings. Barb counted six cars in the meandering lot.

She pulled in front of the cabin marked OFFICE and killed the ignition on her car. She was confident that she'd found her temporary home away from home.

THE LITTLE OFFICE was dimly lit by an old desk lamp. Some tourist brochures and flyers were stacked on a rack that was placed on the counter along one wall. The high counter separated the room roughly in half. A young woman sat at the small desk behind the counter. She was pecking away on a laptop that was surrounded by open books and reprints of articles from journals.

Barb knew that Boulder was the home of the University of Colorado. She asked, "Writing a paper?"

"Due tomorrow. I'm a procrastinator. May I help you? Are you looking for a room?"

"Yes, I would like a room. Please. And please tell me you're not full. I don't have a reservation."

"We are full but I just had a cancellation, a family that had booked two rooms. Let me see . . ." The young woman grabbed a loose-leaf notebook full of sheets covered with a calendarlike grid. "We have . . . a tiny double . . . and a double with a killer view but old plumbing. I can give you either of those. The one with the view is my personal favorite. But you can only have it until . . ." She checked the same sheet of paper. "You can have it for four nights."

Barb asked. "That's not a problem. How old is the plumbing? Are we talking flush toilets?"

The girl laughed and stood from the desk. She towered over Barb, who guessed that the young woman was at least six-one. "Don't be

silly. Some of the others have new fixtures. The owners haven't re-
modeled that one yet, that's all. The bathtub's a little funky but everything works fine. Sometime before football season they promise they'll
get to it."

"If it's your personal favorite, I'll take it."

"Good. Want to fill this out, please?" She slid a registration card toward her new guest. "How long will you be staying?"

"I'll take all four days," Barb said. "That should work out to be just
about right for me." Barb expected to be gone in two.

"Where are you from?"

Barb momentarily lifted her eyes from the registration form and
made fresh eye contact with the young clerk. "I'm from Indianapolis,"
she said.

"You here on business?"

"Yes," Barb Turner said. "I have some meetings at the university.
What's the paper on?"

"Abnormal psych."

Barb said, "I'm in education. I'm afraid I don't know anything about
that."

HOW CLOSE TO the Rocky Mountains was the Foot of the Mountain
Motel? The next morning at first light Barb could see that if the motel
were a house, the Rocky Mountains would start in the middle of the
motel's backyard. The Foot of the Mountain Motel was actually in the
mouth of a wide canyon. Another steep ridge of rock rose a few hundred feet from the front door.

Before getting ready for bed the night before, Barb had used the
local Yellow Pages to prepare a list of the establishments in Boulder
that called themselves hotels, and that offered their own restaurants.
There weren't many. One was the Regal Harvest House, one of the
places she had passed the night before on her way into town. But the
closest hotel on her list was a place called the Boulderado. She
planned on going there for breakfast.

She was confident that she would find the woman she was searching for before the day was done.

. . .

IT TURNED OUT that Barb was right.

Earlier that day, Barb had used a pay phone to call both the Harvest House Hotel restaurant and Q's, the restaurant at the Boulderado Hotel. Each time she asked to be connected to the kitchens and each time she asked to speak to Peyton in the kitchen. She was told that no one by that name worked at the Harvest House. But whoever answered the phone at Q's said that Peyton wasn't working right then, but that she was working a short shift later, from one to five.

That's how hard it was for Barb Turner to locate Kirsten Lord in Boulder, Colorado.

AT THREE-THIRTY, BARB used a public phone on Spruce Street to call a familiar phone number in Georgia. Prowler answered after a solitary ring.

"Prowler," he said.

"Hey, it's me. I found her. She's working at a restaurant called Q's. Just capital Q, then apostrophe s. She's like an intern or something. I haven't actually seen her yet. As soon as she shows up for a shift, I'll get a picture to you. Afterward, I'll follow her home and begin to put together a plan for the next phase."

"The name I provided is correct?"

"Yes. Peyton something. No address yet, though. I should have it and a last name by tonight, tomorrow at the latest."

"After you transmit the file, our client should be able to confirm her identity within hours."

"Excellent."

"Good work, Barbara."

Barb said, "It's why I get paid the big bucks."

Prowler laughed. Barb enjoyed the moment. She knew Prowler's laughter was an infrequent sound.

2

Ron Kriciak thought that he might have met Fenster Kastle on one of his training junkets for the U.S. Marshals Service. That seminar in Dallas, maybe. Didn't Kastle do a talk on something? Security issues in traffic? Was that it? Ron really felt he should remember. *Fenster Kastle?* The guy's name sounded like some monument in Great Britain, for God's sake. Ron prided himself on his ability to remember people, and when he ventured into his mental archives for an image of Fenster Kastle, he retrieved a picture of a round black man with small teeth and dark button eyes. A man who was round the way ex-athletes are round. But Ron didn't remember Kastle as a soft man. Quite the contrary.

He remembered Fenster Kastle as the kind of guy Ron would be reluctant to arm wrestle in a bar.

Ron hadn't enjoyed an opportunity to test his memory for accuracy, though. Every one of Ron's recent contacts with Fenster Kastle had taken place by phone or e-mail. And every one of those recent contacts had concerned their mutual WITSEC charge, Peyton Francis.

Kastle was the headquarters honcho who was coordinating Peyton's participation in WITSEC.

This latest contact that Kriciak received from Kastle was as impersonal as the ones that had preceded it. The e-mail read, "We need to talk. Call me on a secure line. ASAP."

"Fenster? Ron Kriciak in Denver."

Ron could hear muffled voices on the other end of the phone along with the scratchy sound that people make when they're trying to cover the microphone with their palm. Finally, after one long last screech, Fenster Kastle said, "Listen, I just have a minute. Things are crazy here, and I need to alert you to some fresh red flags in regards to our friend."

Ron grabbed a pencil. "Yeah." He didn't want to sound like a supplicant but immediately questioned his reply. Too casual? Not sufficiently deferential to Kastle's authority?

"We've detected a couple of attempted internal searches in our computer system. Basically it appears that someone's been trying to identify her placement location. The firewall caught both of the attempts, but the user was sophisticated enough that we haven't been able to detect the source of the inquiries. Just that they were internal. The geeks are checking to see if they can do better on the tracing and to see if they can reassure me that nothing actually pierced the veil, but for now you and I need to be aware that we have some people trying to find her. At this moment we think they've been thwarted, but we're concerned that they're looking."

"You're certain that it's our people?"

"That's affirmative. It's internal."

Ron decided to grab the lead in the conversation. "Any rumors I should be aware of?"

"We still have a lot of colleagues who don't think we should be protecting this woman. That hasn't changed. The popularity of that point-of-view may actually be increasing. Beyond that, I don't have anything new."

"The number of people who know her new identity and know where she is? Has it changed?"

"It's stable."

Ron pondered the news from headquarters. Decided he wasn't too surprised or too alarmed by it. His own assessment was that one of his colleagues in the U.S. Marshals Service was trying to be the first to be able to say he tracked down Kirsten Lord within WITSEC. Ron had seen it happen before with some of the bigger Mafia fish after they were buried in the program. Ron called the practice deep-sea fishing and knew it was all about bragging rights.

It didn't mean that anyone was actually thinking about hurting anybody. But it might mean that one of the other marshals might be trying to compromise Peyton's security. That happened sometimes.

Ron said, "Fenster, I'm thinking that the problem may be more of an internal, macho-type thing. Somebody wants to find her, prove they can beat the system. We've seen it with some of the LCN celebrities we've buried. Do you really think she's at risk from inside?"

A long pause later, Fenster Kastle said, "Yes, as a matter of fact, I do. And Ron? If you know what's best for yourself and for our friend, then you do, too. Do you understand?"

To Ron, the words didn't sound like the words of a *soft*, round man.

Ron didn't like getting warned by some guy in some office back east. Without even being aware that he'd decided to create a diversion, he asked, "Hey Fenster, let me ask you something. You ever play any ball when you were younger?"

"Yeah."

"Where?"

"Savannah State. I played with Shannon Sharpe. You're in Denver, you've probably heard of him."

"Shannon Sharpe? The tight end? No shit?"

Fenster Kastle wasn't easily distracted. "Don't get lazy on me, Ron. We lose her, it won't look good for either of us. I've already been reminded by my superiors that as bad as she made us look when she was a DA in New Orleans, it's nowhere near as bad as she's gonna make us look if we can't protect her properly now. Especially from some of our own people."

Ron was silent.

Kastle said, "I'm waiting for you to salute."

"Yes, sir. I agree."

"Along those lines, I want to hear from you if our friend has insect problems in her new home, if she gets a funny rash on her hands. I want to be the first to know if her daughter's grades drop, if the darn wind begins blowing funny anywhere close to her. Do you get my drift?"

"We're on the same page, Fenster. She's getting a lot of special attention already. I'll be certain that she gets some more. What position did you play at Savannah State?"

"Defense, Ron. Defense. For me, it's always been about defense."

3

Landon wanted spaghetti for dinner on Monday night, and I didn't care any more about the specifics of dinner than I had about the specifics of breakfast or lunch. I started to make spaghetti. She hovered for a while to be certain that I was making the sauce the way that she liked it, smooth, with no discernible chunks of tomato. My daughter appreciated tomatoes in most of their permutations, but she didn't like chunks of cooked tomato. I didn't understand the distinction. She and I had actually argued about it once while she was picking the tomato chunks from a glorious meal in a funky restaurant called the Gumbo Shop in the French Quarter. Robert ate the culled tomatoes and refereed the argument, and we'd all ended up laughing.

That's a baby beluga.

Landon ate twice as much dinner as I did. I cleaned up the kitchen while she bathed. Afterward, she begged, so I quizzed her on a hundred spelling words before bedtime and read her two, not just one, chapters of the new Harry Potter book before she dozed off to sleep. My daughter was a Harry junkie.

It was eight-thirty when I descended the stairs and retrieved the cordless phone from its charger. I carried it in my hand as I walked from the living room to the dining room to the family room hoping to find the right place to sit.

I tried the kitchen but soon moved back to the floor of the dining room. I was already fearing a night without sleep, and the prospect of the empty hours before dawn drained me of any hope I might have husbanded from my day.

The barren dining room offered no real comfort so I carried the phone to the kitchen and drank a glass of water while I decided what to do next. I didn't know what to do about Ron Kriciak or Ernesto Castro or even about Carl Luppo. But I did know what I needed to do about Khalid Granger. I had to erase my doubts. So I phoned Andrea in Florida for the second time that day.

She answered after two rings.

"It's me again. Am I calling too late?" I said.

"Kirsten, hi," she replied. "I'm sorry—Peyton, I meant Peyton. Hi. No, I'm still awake."

It was an oddly moving experience to have someone recognize my voice when everything else about me had changed. I said, "I need to know something, Andrea. Are you feeling good about what's happening with Khalid? About his appeal?"

"No," Andrea said, her voice a loud whisper. "I'm not feeling good about Khalid at all. And neither is Dave. Are you?"

I felt a lightness buoy me, a swell lifting me higher in the water. For a moment I could see lights flickering on the distant shore. I knew the feeling wouldn't last, that every swell—every last one—was followed by a trough. I said, "I've been thinking he may be innocent, Andrea. I think it's possible Mickey and Jack may have done something to set him up."

I heard her exhale—loudly. "Dave and I have come to the same conclusion. We were afraid that you were going to fight us if we went public. I didn't know how to reach you to ask for your support. And I didn't want to burden you—you've been through so much."

"Thank God I said something. I was afraid I was the only one with doubts. I was thinking that I couldn't really do anything if I was the only one who thought there was a problem. What are our options? What can we do at this point?"

"Unless you know something that Dave and I don't know, we don't have much to work with from an evidence point of view. But we think we know where to look. Even if we find something though, you know as well as I do that it's not going to be easy getting the sentence overturned at this stage," Andrea said. "Do you know something specific? Please have something that might help."

I hesitated, wanting to give her a basket full of promises. I finally said, "No, nothing. Just my gut feeling that Mickey was dirty."

"That's where Dave and I started, too, after Dave got the letter. You don't know about that. He got an anonymous letter in the mail a couple months ago that said that Khalid didn't kill those two Mennonites."

"Really? What kind of letter?"

"Do you remember Mickey Redondo's old partner?"

"Jack Tarpin. Sure."

"Good. Then I'll tell you where we are."

FIVE WEEKS EARLIER Dave Curtiss had received a handwritten note at his law offices in Sarasota. The letter-size envelope had been delivered by the U.S. Postal Service but did not have a return address. The cancellation mark indicated that it had been mailed in the Florida Keys.

The note misspelled Dave's last name, not an uncommon occurrence. The letter was two lines long. It read:

> Mr. Curtis:
>   Khalid Granger did not kill those two Mennonites. Check the timing on the GSR.
> Sincerely,
> A friend of justice

Inside the envelope, along with the short letter, was a clipping from a week-old *Miami Herald* article about Khalid's upcoming final appeal.

Dave hadn't recognized the handwriting on the note, and after he called Andrea and showed her the letter over drinks a couple of nights later after work, she hadn't either. But she'd quickly reached the same conclusion that Dave had.

"It's got to be a cop," she said. " 'Check the timing on the GSR'? Who would talk that way? It has to be either a cop or a criminalist. Somebody on the job."

Andrea was still in the system, working at the DA's office—and Dave, in private practice, wasn't—so Andrea pulled Khalid's voluminous old trial records and began scouring the handwritten police reports for a handwriting match. She never found one. She'd hoped the handwriting would match Jack Tarpin's, but it wasn't even close.

She dug deeper into the case files and pulled the copies of the reports on the GSR, the gunshot residue test, that had been performed on Khalid Granger shortly after his detention. The administration of a GSR involves swabbing the suspect's hands, arms, and face with specially prepared sponges that are designed to capture specific chemicals and microscopic trace metals that are emitted with the explosive gases that escape during the discharge of a firearm. The microscopic particles come to rest on the skin and clothing of anyone in close proximity to a gun being discharged. The swabs are then analyzed in an electron microscope.

Khalid's GSR had been damning. It showed unequivocal evidence of trace metals on his hands and forearms. The presence of those metals constituted circumstantial evidence that Khalid Granger had been in the vicinity of the discharge of a firearm.

Andrea continued to wonder what the anonymous note writer had meant by "check the timing on the GSR."

She went back to the reports and checked the timing. The official report stated that the GSR samples had been collected from Khalid at two-fifteen on the afternoon of the murders, only four to five hours after the shootings in the convenience store, and well within accepted time limits for appropriate use of the test. The samples had been collected by Jack Tarpin.

The receipt accompanying the samples was signed by Jack Tarpin.

The caution in the anonymous note that had been sent to Dave Curtiss made no sense.

Andrea phoned a friend at the police department and asked him if he knew where Jack Tarpin had gone after he retired.

"Jack? He's trying to supplement his pension running fishing charters out of Plantation Key. Not doing too well as a captain is what I hear but otherwise enjoying the good life. Why?"

Andrea replied, "I need to talk with him about an old collar of his. You got a number for him?"

"Is he going to be sorry I gave it to you?"

"No. This is dot-your-*I*s-and-cross-your-*T*s-time for me. Just covering all my bases before a trial."

"He won't want to testify."

"He won't have to."

Andrea's friend gave her Jack Tarpin's number on Plantation Key.

ANDREA HAD NEVER gotten along with Jack Tarpin. Not from the first time they had met.

At the time Khalid was arrested for the convenience-store murders, Jack was an old-timer in the force. Tarpin had gone through two marriages and outlasted three alcohol rehabs before he could get either a wife or his sobriety to stick around. For the last dozen years he was on the job he was perceived as a burnout just putting in his time. If you asked his fellow officers about Jack's main goal in life, nine out of ten would have said that he was trying to stay both alive and invisible long enough to get his pension.

The third wife, the one who had stuck with him, had family down in the Keys and she and Jack were planning to retire down there and do some fishing after he was done upholding the peace in Sarasota.

But Jack had his sympathizers, too. The people on the force who didn't consider Jack Tarpin an aging loser often discovered after spending some time with him that they actually liked the guy.

Andrea was one of the people who thought Jack was an aging loser.

Dave Curtiss had always liked the guy.

Andrea quickly decided that whether Dave liked it or not, he would be the one to make the call about the letter. She volunteered to run the GSR results by some people she knew at the state crime lab to see if they could spot any anomalies.

DAVE CURTISS HAD known Jack Tarpin well enough to know that Jack wouldn't tell him a thing about Khalid Granger over the telephone. Dave knew he'd have to drive all the way down to Plantation Key and look the man hard in the eyes if he had any hope of finding out what Jack knew about the GSR he'd performed so many years before on Khalid Granger.

Dave Curtiss also knew that getting to Plantation Key meant driving through Miami. Dave hated Miami and he hated the tourist-infested drive south to the Florida Keys.

Dave would rather have another sigmoidoscope than make that drive.

He called Jack the following Wednesday and spoke with Jack's wife, Pamela. Dave gave a fake name and said he wanted to talk to Jack about a charter. Pamela had said that her husband was out on his boat right then but that he'd be home the next day if Dave wanted to call back. Dave didn't call back but instead got up early the next morning, called in sick to work, and did the dreaded drive, arriving at Pamela and Jack's home shortly after lunch.

. . .

JACK TARPIN DIDN'T tan.

That was Dave's initial impression of the man who came to the door of the little frame house that he shared with his wife. Jack's face, hands, arms, and legs displayed more shades of red and pink than a greeting card shop on Valentine's Day.

But Jack didn't bluster, either. After narrowing his eyes at his visitor—giving Dave a clear indication that his presence at the front door wasn't particularly welcome—Jack pushed open the screen door and said, "Hi, Dave. Come on in. We were just sitting down to sandwiches and iced tea. You'll join us."

It wasn't an offer as much as it was an expectation.

IT TURNED OUT that Dave enjoyed Pamela as much as he'd always liked Jack. Her laughter and self-deprecating humor put Dave at ease, despite Jack's obvious consternation at the visit. Pamela had stringy brown hair, was skinny as bamboo, and had a smile so wide it seemed to link her ears together. She wore a man's sleeveless T-shirt and a pair of cotton drawstring trousers that had faded to the color of key lime pie. The outfit made it simple for Dave to come to the conclusion that Jack's boobs were easily twice the size of his wife's.

THE SANDWICHES THAT Pamela served for lunch consisted of fat chunks of grilled fish swimming in a sea of Tabasco-laced mayonnaise and chopped onions. The fish mixture was stuffed into big sections that had been sliced out of a long roll of supermarket Italian bread and then topped with thick slices of pungent pickles. After weeks of processed turkey and nonfat mayo sandwiches—his wife's idea of a heart-healthy lunch—Dave took one bite of Pamela's grilled-fish hoagie and thought he'd died and gone to heaven.

"Caught that yesterday," Jack said with pride as he watched Dave chew and swallow.

"I cleaned that yesterday," Pamela said. "Wasn't anywhere near as much fun as the catching, I'm telling you."

When the plates were empty and what was left of the tea was just a clump of cloudy ice cubes melting together in the bottom of an old Kool-Aid pitcher, Jack said, "You didn't drive all this way just for lunch."

"If I knew how good lunch was going to be, I might have. But you're right, Jack, it's about an old case you worked on."

"I'm waiting," Jack said.

Dave watched Pamela avert her eyes and stand to clear the dishes from the table.

"Khalid Granger," Dave said. "I'm sure you remember him. His appeals are up, and there're some lingering questions about the GSR that was done after he was picked up." Dave had already decided not to mention the letter unless he had to.

Jack scratched his scalp vigorously enough that it looked to Dave as though it had to hurt. He sighed and said, "Course there are questions. I'm surprised it took so long for someone to ask. You found the problem?"

"Not exactly," Dave said. "We've been looking but we haven't been finding. That's why I drove all the way down here."

"You said 'we've' been looking? Who else?"

"Remember Andrea Archer? She's still with the DA's office. I'm not—I went into private practice before you retired. Andrea pulled the old trial records for me so we could try to figure out what was going on with that damn test."

Jack said, "She and I never got along. She thought I was a hopeless drunk."

Dave tried not to look embarrassed. Finally, he nodded and glanced over at Pamela who had started rinsing the dishes at the nearby kitchen sink. Jack followed Dave's eyes. He said, "Don't worry about Pammy; she knows about my reputation and she knows about Khalid. The day I handed in my badge was the day I stopped keeping secrets from her."

Dave said, "This isn't about helping Andrea, Jack."

"Yeah, I know. But it's you two who are doing the wondering? Nobody else? What about that other DA who prosecuted this with you?"

"Kirsten? Kirsten Lord?"

"Yeah, her."

"We'll talk to her if I come up with anything here today."

Jack nodded.

"Okay. Thing is, I don't get it, Jack. It doesn't make sense. You gave Khalid the GSR a few hours after the shooting. It lit up positive. Andrea and I don't see a problem with the timing or the test. It's all kosher."

"If that's the case, then who's asking all the questions? I figured that if this conversation ever took place I'd be having it with some public defender trying to save Khalid's ass."

Dave pushed his chair back from the table. "Lot of people have questions. Andrea and I feel particularly vulnerable since we prosecuted Khalid. But people are raising caution flags."

"What people?"

"Anonymous people. We're getting letters."

"Letters." Jack winced. "You worried about yourselves or you worried about the little prick?"

"If Khalid did it, Jack, I don't have any problems with him frying to death in that chair. That's the honest-to-God truth. He won't be the first man I convicted to end his life there. My reason for coming all the way down here to see you is simple. I want to know if there was a problem with the GSR or with anything else you and Mickey came across during your investigation. That's all."

Jack pushed himself back from the table and laced his fingers together behind his head. He stared at Dave until he saw him shift his weight on his chair and avert his eyes. "Problem? There was no problem unless you count the fact that it wasn't Khalid's test that lit up."

"What?"

"They're about to fry him, right?"

"Khalid? Yes."

Jack rubbed his stubbled face with the back of his hand. He said, "He's pond scum—you know that, don't you? He cuts up women, he deals drugs, he strong-arms his own neighbors. Nobody's crying that the man's in prison. I mean nobody. I bet his momma's glad he's there."

"I know that, Jack. That's not the question. The question is whether or not he actually killed those two old folks in that convenience store. I'm not trying to get him out of prison."

Jack tilted his tea glass up to almost vertical, trying to dislodge an ice cube from the bottom. The tactic didn't work. He said, "Mickey Redondo was the worst fucking partner I ever had, and I had some assholes over the years. That doesn't mean I want to cause him any trouble over scum like Khalid."

Dave said, "I understand that, Jack," hoping that Jack wasn't about to become uncooperative.

"Well, I meant what I just said. I'm pretty sure that Mickey switched out the GSR before it got to the lab."

"I don't get it."

"You drove all the way down here. Now your belly's full. So I suppose you have time for me to tell you a story. Well, here's what happened that day."

4

The story Jack Tarpin told Dave Curtiss the day that Dave visited Jack and his wife Pamela down in Plantation Key went something like this. Keep in mind that I heard it from Andrea, of course, and not from Dave.

JACK SAID, "AFTER the uniforms stopped him and detained him, Mickey and I interviewed Khalid together. We did the interview at the station, and right away we already liked him for the murders of those two old people at that store. Khalid fit the description of our only witness, he had the right amount of money on him, he was in the wrong place at the wrong time, and he had a list of priors longer than my long line. Plus, he was full of attitude. Pissing on us every chance he got. But he's been busted like a thousand times before and he knew how to play us, and the truth is, we didn't get much from him that helped us develop the investigation. My take was he figured he was gonna walk."

As he began to tell the story, Jack had pulled a crinkled bag of sunflower seeds from his pocket and immediately started throwing them into his mouth in fives and sixes. He was able to shell the seeds with his teeth and tongue, not using his fingers at all, but the pile of soggy hulled shells he was collecting on a napkin on the table in front of him was quickly growing large and relatively disgusting.

Dave was quiet while he waited for Jack to spit out some seeds and find what felt like a good place to pick up the story.

"Then Mickey got a telephone call. A uniform stuck her head into the room where we were working on Khalid and told Mickey that someone wanted him on the phone. He told her we were busy, to take a message. Instead, she comes on in and whispers something directly into his ear. He laughs out loud and says, 'No shit,' and he tells me he better take this call. I told him no problem, I'd do the GSR while he was gone. And I did. I already had a kit with me and I swabbed Khalid up real good, right according to the book. The whole time I'm swabbing, Khalid was doing his song-and-dance about how I'm wasting my time, that everybody knows he's a knife-man, not a gun-man. Give him back his knife and he'll be happy to show us his skill. He was kind of a funny guy, a regular Chris Rock. Whatever, I got the test done. Then I marked the samples, sealed the envelope, filled out the stupid form, and I signed the thing."

The pile of spent sunflower seeds grew bigger as Jack talked.

"Anyway, Mickey comes back a few minutes later and his whole attitude has changed. He doesn't want to bust Khalid's chops anymore. Suddenly Mickey's just all polite and businesslike, and he doesn't have any more questions for Khalid about the double murders. Before I know it, Khalid's on his way down the hall to get his ass booked for two counts of first-degree murder and assorted lesser charges. Khalid's like going ape-shit; he can't believe it. Totally lost his sense of humor. But Mickey's happy. He takes the GSR that I did on Khalid and some other forms and shit from me and says he'll make sure everything gets checked in.

"Me? I'm wondering why this guy—who in the two years we've been together won't even pour me a cup of coffee when he's already up getting one for himself—is suddenly being so generous and helpful to me. I say something like, 'That must have been some call you took.'

"Mickey's eyes flashed at me for a second, then he said, 'Just someone letting me know that I've got my man.'

"I asked him what that meant, and he told me to forget about it."

Jack paused as though he thought Dave should be able to piece it together from there. Dave told Jack he still didn't see the problem with the GSR.

"Well here comes your problem. Next day I get the results of the GSR from the lab. And it's obvious that despite all his 'I'm-a-knife-man not a gun-man' denials that our man Khalid had been busy firing a firearm. Results show that he has residue everywhere I swabbed him. Everywhere. As evidence goes, it's circumstantial, sure, but if you recall, Dave, it was a damn good piece of our case against Khalid. Still, I have other work to do and don't think much about the GSR after that. It's not going to convict him, right? You with me?"

Dave was.

"Okay. Next time I'm thinking at all about that GSR is when I'm sitting in court up on the witness stand at Khalid's trial and your friend Andrea Archer is putting me half to sleep showing me reports and forms and evidence and asking me over and over again am-I-familiar-with-this and am-I-familiar-with-that and am-I-familiar-with-this-other-damn thing, and I'm saying yes, I wrote that, or yes, that there's my signature. Then she hands me the receipt that I filled out that went along to the lab with the GSR I did on Khalid, and she asked me if I recognized it. I said yes before I even looked at it, but then out of the corner of my eye I could see that it wasn't the same form I'd filled out on Khalid. So as nonchalant as could be, I quickly added, 'Yeah, I signed that.' "

Dave sat forward, avoiding the teetering pile of sunflower seed shells on the table between him and Jack. "What do you mean it wasn't the same form?"

"It wasn't my handwriting. It was my signature on the bottom all right, but it wasn't my handwriting on the form. It was Mickey's."

Dave leaned forward and rested his elbows on the table, careful to avoid the Vesuvius of sunflower seed carcasses. "I assume you asked Mickey about the discrepancy?"

"Course I did. During the next recess."

"And?"

"He told me he spilled coffee all over the other envelope, and that he gave me a fresh form to sign and he sealed it back up himself in a new envelope."

Dave pressed. "Jack, did he really give you a fresh form to sign? Do you remember?"

Jack shook his head. "I'd be lying if I said I did. And I'd be lying if I said I didn't. But if my partner had asked me to sign a form like that, I probably would've signed it. Even if it was Mickey Redondo doing the asking."

"But now? You're saying you think Mickey actually switched out the samples? Why do you think that?"

Pamela had finished rinsing dishes at the sink and she rejoined the men at the table. Jack immediately stopped eating sunflower seeds. Some unwritten code between them, Dave thought.

"I told you already, I was suspicious about Mickey, about that call. I went back to the lab to see what time the evidence had been checked in for Khalid. Turns out that the GSR didn't make it to the lab until almost eight o'clock that evening."

"That's unusual?"

"He took it from me at what, three-thirty? Lab's in the same building we were in. So what was Mickey doing with it for over four hours? Damn right it was unusual. It's even more unusual when you consider that sometime between six and seven that evening Mickey Redondo had spent thirty minutes of those four hours taking practice at the police firing range."

"He was at the range? I take it that's unusual, too?"

"Mickey hated the range. Had to be dragged there most of the time. Didn't even want to go out there when he was due to qualify. And for him to take time out of a day when he has two fresh homicides to investigate to go to the range?" Jack laughed. "Yes, that's unusual."

Dave asked, "How do you know he was there?"

"Like I said, I got suspicious. I checked the logs." Jack smiled for his wife's benefit. "Hey, I used to be a detective."

Dave wanted to hear Jack voice his suspicions. Dave said, "So you're thinking that after he went to the firing range he did a GSR on himself and that's what he turned into the lab?"

Jack said, "Yeah, that's what I think. He switched out the GSR he did on himself after he was at the firing range with the one I did on Khalid at the station. Which has left me with one inescapable conclusion. Why go to all this trouble unless Mickey somehow already knew that Khalid's GSR was going to be negative? And unless he absolutely didn't want that to be true."

"The phone call he got," Dave Curtiss said. "That must have been one important phone call."

"That's what I thought, too," Jack said. "What I figured later, after the trial, is that whatever Mickey heard on that phone call included the actual identity of the person who killed those two old folks in that convenience store. Only way Mickey could be so sure that Khalid didn't do it is if he knew who really did, right?"

"So I went back and found the uniform who originally brought him the phone message during the interrogation and asked her if she remembered who it was who had called that day."

"And she did?"

"Oh yes. She did. It was Pat Lieber."

Dave's heart skipped a beat or two, then started racing. "Really? You kidding me? The football coach?"

"Think I'd bullshit about this? She said the guy called right up and said he wanted to talk to Mickey Redondo."

"And even though he was interrogating a homicide suspect she immediately went and she found Mickey?"

"She did. You would have, too, if he had called you. You know how big Pat Lieber is in Florida. Even back then. Bear Bryant and Vince Lombardi all rolled into one."

Dave Curtiss sat back and balanced his weight on the back two legs of his chair. His chest burned. He chewed on a Pepcid and asked Pamela for a glass of cold water.

She smiled politely, stood, and moved to the sink.

"Pat Lieber, huh?"

Jack nodded. "Pat Lieber."

"He asked for Mickey? Not for whoever was working the case? I got that right?"

"Yeah, she said he asked for Mickey by name."

"Did Mickey know Lieber?"

"Over the years, I came to believe they knew each other before that day. Nothing I could prove. Occasionally Mickey'd get football tickets I would have died for. A couple of times I fished a little bit about where they came from. The impression I got is that they came from Lieber."

Dave wondered what interest the most revered football coach in the State of Florida could have with Khalid Granger. He said, "You can't prove any of this, can you, Jack? Any of what you think happened?"

Pamela delivered the water.

Dave thanked her.

"Prove it? Prove what? I testified honestly at the trial—that was my signature on the receipt for the GSR. And Mickey going to the range that evening? I imagine you can still get those logs and prove that yourself 'cause he was there. And that he got that phone call from Pat Lieber during Khalid's interrogation? The officer who came to get him is still on the force. I'd bet she still remembers getting a call like that. But even then, you have all that, so what you going to do? Mickey will never admit to what was said during that phone conversation. And Lieber? He's going to deny any call ever happened. Mickey's no fool. If he took money from Lieber, you're never going to find it. What I got? It's not nearly enough to get a judge to give Khalid another look. We both know that."

Dave knew that Jack was right.

"You never looked into Lieber's connection to all this?"

"You kidding me? Investigate Pat Lieber in Florida?" He laughed. "That's like investigating the Pope in the Vatican. I don't need that kind of trouble," Jack said. "That's the beauty of it. I can stay down here in the Keys and keep my hands clean—"

Pamela interjected, "Jack Tarpin, your hands haven't been clean since the day I met you."

Jack smiled at his wife. ". . . and allow people like you to do what you can to save Khalid's sorry ass from Old Sparky. And you know what's even better? Now that I've told you all that happened, maybe I can sleep all the way through the night again. That'd be something positive."

"He doesn't sleep well," said Pamela. "Tosses and turns so much that sometimes I get seasick in the bed next to him."

5

It took Andrea almost an hour to finish telling me about the letter and Dave's visit to Plantation Key.

No surprise, but by the time I hung up the phone I had already begun jousting with my whales.

Usually, the whales that visit me on the surface come to my attention as picture memories, visual images evoking something I either yearn to relive or dread to remember. Sometimes the whales turn my head and arrive in the form of familiar scents—vanilla or magnolias or the smell of Robert's hair. And sometimes they swim in the dark and I only recognize them by their sounds. Most rarely they swim in tight waters beneath my skin and flicker into my consciousness as feelings. This time, it was the feeling whales that ruled the pod.

THERE ARE FEW moments in my life when time has actually slowed. I can count them and recall them all. Vividly.

Once, when I was seventeen, I crushed my daddy's new car into the back of a city bus. My head had been turned toward the radio, and I never saw the bus stopping in front of me. When I called home to tell my parents what I'd done to the car, the phone seemed to float in my hand and the moment that was actually only a fraction of a second seemed to last as long as my freshman year at Miami. My daddy broke the silence by saying, "Are you all right? Nothing else matters, baby. Are you all right?"

The next instance that time stopped was my second experience making love to Robert. Not the first, but the second. Our first had been impulsive and awkward and almost adolescent in its intensity. We went from sharing a beer on my sofa to acrobatics on my coffee table in record time. I admit though, even now, that the memory holds a certain charm. But the very next time—oh Lord—there was a moment between *almost there* and *there* when my heart stopped beating and every clock on the planet ceased ticking for what felt to me like forever. The moment stretched before me like the light of a late-summer dawn. Wide and bright and infinite. Robert never quite took me to that place again, though bless him it wasn't for lack of effort, but reaching that plateau at least one more time in my life became a goal for me, like reaching heaven.

The third event that caused time to stop was after the birth of my baby. Right after I followed the dictates of my doctor and pushed for what she promised would be the last time—ha!—expending what I was certain were the final calories of energy that remained in my body, I heard Robert's voice sing above the rest of the sounds in the birthing room. He said, "K, it's a girl, a beautiful, beautiful girl," and I swear it was an hour later, maybe even longer, before I was handed that little bundle and was able to lay my eyes on the tiny thing that had already started ruling my heart forever. Why it took them an eternity to hand me my beautiful baby I'll never understand.

Robert says it was actually two minutes, maybe three.

Robert wasn't always right.

And the fourth instance that time stopped?

It was, of course, the day that Robert was murdered.

We were meeting for lunch at Galatoire's in the Quarter, as we'd done every year we'd been in New Orleans. It was our anniversary.

He'd arrived first and was holding a place in line. Robert was almost always taller than everyone else in his vicinity and I spotted his blond head as I was walking toward him from half a block away. I'd closed the distance between us to less than ten feet when I first noticed the man in chinos with the jacket held awkwardly over his bent arm. I don't know why I found him curious enough to capture my attention. Maybe because his eyes jumped to Robert and then back to me and then once more to Robert, and I felt the traces of a smile begin to creep across his face. His smile burned me somewhere deep.

I remember even now that I could feel the man's smile as though it was a vial of acid being splashed into my eyes.

Time stopped right then, there.

For how long? It stopped long enough for me to transport myself back to court, to the very day I heard Ernesto Castro promise, "Remember this. Every precious thing I lose, you will lose two."

Time stopped long enough for me to know that this man on the sidewalk outside Galatoire's was the embodiment of Ernesto Castro's promise being kept. Time stopped long enough for me to know with great certainty that the man in the chinos and the jacket draped over his arm was about to try to kill my Robert. How did I know? I don't know how I knew.

I just knew.

Time slowed and captured my shouted warning and my screaming protest and locked them somewhere in a prison in my chest, and time has never released them.

Time stopped long enough for me to feel my certainty as a sense of inevitability that almost drained me of my will. Time stopped long enough for me to feel a total sense of inadequacy that I would be able to intervene before my husband was killed in front of my eyes.

Time had slowed so much *that* day that to *this* day I swear I believe that I actually saw the leaded slugs as they exited the shadows below the draped jacket and crossed the few feet of lazy, humid Louisiana air that separated my husband's unsuspecting head from the dull metal barrel of the silencer on the handgun.

What I felt during the lifetime that I endured between the second I spotted the man in chinos and the instant I recognized that my husband was dying in my arms was an entire lifetime's worth of the most debilitating mixture of responsibility and inadequacy I could imagine. I knew in the fibers of my heart that it was I who had lured the gunman to my husband's side, and I knew that it was I who'd been unable to fly ten miserable feet to stop the assassin from killing him.

THE WHALES THAT joined me on the surface after my conversation with Andrea were two of the feeling whales that I knew intimately. These beasts were the responsibility whale and the inadequacy whale. When they visited me, they tended to swim together.

Why were they visiting then?

To remind me, I think, that I had been part of the effort that had led an executioner to Khalid's cellblock door. Yes, inadvertently. Yes, without malice. But the hooded man was lurking outside Khalid's bars, nonetheless. And now I feared that I was going to prove unable to stop that executioner from carrying out his awful duties.

His *lawful* duties.

How did that knowledge feel? Well, if I looked into a mirror at that moment, I thought I would see my reflection twice.

I would be the man in chinos with the silenced .22.

I would also, once again, be the woman on Bourbon Street in the pretty suit. You know, the woman with the scream caught in her throat.

I CHECKED AND double-checked the locks on the doors and flicked off the downstairs lights one by one. Upstairs, I found that Landon was sleeping sideways on her bed, more on top of her covers than under them. I rearranged her and pulled the blanket up to her chest. Her favorite stuffed bear never left the crook of her arm. I kissed her hair and then her shoulder and then once more her hair. I whispered, "I love you, baby. Good night."

Out loud, I said, "Goodnight noises, everywhere."

My bedroom at the front of the house was dark. I left the lights off as I walked to the window and peered through a slit in the drapes. I wasn't gazing at the view of the mountains or scanning for constellations in the night sky. I was searching the parking lot and the adjacent streets for a big white Ford Expedition with a sleepy federal marshal in the front seat.

I didn't see Ron Kriciak but didn't think for a moment that not seeing him meant that he wasn't there.

After keeping the vigil for a few moments I retraced my steps to Landon's room. She had already kicked off her covers. I replaced them, this time only up to her waist. I was her mommy; it was my role to keep her warm.

And safe.

I really, really wanted to believe that the marshals could protect me from Ernesto Castro. Deep in my heart, though, I knew the only one who could protect me from a renegade marshal was me.

I wondered who Khalid was counting on to protect him from Florida's infamous electric chair. I bet it wasn't me or Andrea or Dave. I bet it wasn't Jack Tarpin or Mickey Redondo.

I wondered if Khalid had given up hope or if he even knew what hope was.

I was, I thought, beginning to empathize, to begin to know what it felt like to have your appeals dwindle toward zero.

chapter

six

D O G S E C

I

Barb Turner didn't like collecting data. She was an action person. A doer. It's why teaching fifth grade in Galveston had turned out not to be her thing. Oh, the part with the kids in the classroom had been okay. Mostly she could keep them moving, doing. But the dealing with the parents part? And the jousting with the administrators part?

She'd always ended up feeling like killing somebody.

So she decided to honor all the unsolicited advice she was receiving from her friends. To a woman, her best friends told her to find a passion and just follow her heart.

BARB ALMOST MISSED Peyton's arrival at work that day.

Barb had begun staking out the restaurant entrance at eight o'clock in the morning, just in case. A half dozen different women had temporarily piqued Barb's interest in the next three hours, but none of them had been a disguised Kirsten Lord. Barb had actually focused her camera on Peyton as she was walking down Thirteenth toward the Boulderado but rejected her as a Kirsten Lord wannabe before something, some intuitive something, caused Barb to swing the camera back in the woman's direction. Barb refocused her lens, recapturing the image of a lanky woman in a floral sundress who was taking long purposeful strides in the direction of the entrance to the Boulderado Hotel.

Barb tightened the zoom. *Maybe,* she thought. She snapped off one picture. *Dark hair. Short hair. Maybe,* she thought again as she narrowed the zoom further and snapped off another shot. *Glasses—those are new.* She whispered, "Come on honey, please take off your sunglasses. Give me a look I can send off to Prowler. Come on, come on."

As if on cue, Peyton did remove her sunglasses. She folded them and stuffed them into a case and put the case in her purse. She removed another pair of glasses, frameless with clear lenses, and adjusted them onto her face just as she began to climb the flagstone steps that led up to the hotel entrance.

Barb managed two more quick images. *Click, click.* In the age of digital imaging, there was no distracting whirr as film advanced. "Gotcha, Miss Kirsten," Barb Turner said, as she lowered the camera. "I think I gotcha, babe." She inhaled deeply and exhaled through tightly pursed lips. "Next time no shutter, I'm afraid. Next time, love, I think I'll be pulling a trigger."

FROM ACROSS THIRTEENTH, Carl Luppo watched the woman's lips moving as she lowered the camera and placed it beside her on the seat. The woman was sitting on the passenger side of a dark blue Dodge that was parked across Thirteenth Street from the entrance to the hotel. Carl had already reached the obvious conclusion that the woman had been photographing Peyton.

Now, he wanted to know why.

BARB NEEDED HER computer to send the digital images from her camera over the Internet to Prowler. She figured she had at least a few hours to get the download accomplished and get back to the hotel in time to follow Peyton home.

Barb started her car and took Pine back to Broadway and then Broadway toward Arapahoe. Within five minutes her car was back in the parking lot of the Foot of the Mountain Motel.

Carl Luppo arrived in the same vicinity about fifteen seconds later.

He was troubled.

BARB PULLED HER car right in front of her cabin and carried her camera inside. She removed the diskette from her camera, loaded it into her PC, and checked the quality of the images on her screen—good, not great—before transmitting the files to Prowler. She added an e-mail message promising to send the target's home address and some photos of the spelling-bee kid by the end of the day.

When she changed careers, Barb Turner actually had a much easier time dealing with the new computer technology than she did with her weapons.

From the very beginning she found that ironic.

CARL LUPPO HAD pulled his car to a stop in the parking lot at nearby Eben Fine Park and was hanging out on a big rock on the banks of Boulder Creek waiting for the woman in the motel to make her next move. He read the paper while he waited.

Carl Luppo killed a lot of time before he watched Barb Turner get back in her car midafternoon.

By then, Carl Luppo had left his perch on the rock by the creek and was sitting on the front seat of his own car, listening to a Rockies broadcast from Florida on the radio. The local team was losing six to one in the second inning. He wondered how it was possible that one baseball team could give up so many runs.

And he was still troubled by the woman in the cabin at the Foot of the Mountain Motel.

. . .

BARB HEADED BRIEFLY west on Arapahoe before curving over to Canyon and backtracking east. Carl followed her car. His visor was down. He was wearing shades and a weird round Orvis hat that almost covered his wide forehead. He guessed that the woman would be going back to the Boulderado to wait for Peyton, so he wasn't surprised when she turned from Canyon to Thirteenth and continued down the road toward the hotel.

Barb took the only open parking place opposite the hotel. Carl was getting accustomed to downtown Boulder's parking dilemmas and had already decided on an alternative plan. He drove past the woman's car, crossed Spruce, and then turned right on Pine and began driving back and forth between Spruce and Pine on the numbered streets east of the hotel. It took him almost five minutes before he spotted Peyton's car. She'd parked it half a block west of where she'd parked the day before.

AT THE END of the day, Barb Turner followed Kirsten Lord/Peyton Francis from her job at the hotel restaurant to her town house in east Boulder. Barb took a calculated risk, pausing long enough outside her prey's town house to snap a couple of digital shots of the exterior and, luckily, a couple of the kid. The girl actually came out of the house as though she was hitting her mark. Right on cue, just like her mother had removed her sunglasses earlier in the day as though she could hear Barb's plea.

The final photographs taken, Barb spent the time driving back across town to the Foot of the Mountain Motel, making initial plans for the hit. Prowler had already told her that there would be a limited window of time to accomplish the work. What he'd said was, "She needs to be done at the same time as the others." Barb didn't know who the others were and she didn't really care. Didn't know who was doing the other work. She preferred not to know, as a matter of fact.

What she did care about was whether or not she was going to be instructed to do the kid. She'd never done a kid and didn't really want to start now. The girl was just about the right age so that she could have been one of Barb's students in her classroom in Texas.

Once safely back in her cabin at the motel, Barb checked her e-mail and got the message she had expected from Prowler. "The bird you spotted there is the same one we've been looking for here. Await instructions."

She moved the diskette with the four new images from her camera to her laptop, checked the pictures for quality, and sent them on to Prowler in Atlanta along with an encrypted e-mail containing Peyton's Boulder street address and a simple question, "What do you want done with the other inhabitant of the nest?"

Barb had a new DVD with her. *Wild Wild West*. She ordered pizza from a company called Blackjack because she liked the name, got two cans of Sprite from the garish machine by the motel office, and settled onto her bed with her laptop and its DVD player resting on her thighs.

She just loved Will Smith.

2

The next day was Tuesday. Once again I stopped at the bank on the Mall on the way to work. While I was driving across town I kept checking my mirrors and didn't think anyone had followed me. At the bank I withdrew four thousand dollars in fifties and hundreds, the largest amount I had pulled out yet. I stuffed the thick wad of money into the pocket of my chef's pants and kept it there through my entire shift at the restaurant. When I added it to my stash at home at the end of the day, I would have almost eleven thousand dollars in cash stuffed inside *The Cider House Rules*. The mutilation of his book aside, I thought John Irving would be pleased.

During my hours at the restaurant I beat egg whites until my forearms ached. I julienned squash until the little sticks I was cutting were as uniform as little Nazi soldiers. I peeled and seeded two flats of tomatoes, and parboiled and hulled ten pounds of fava beans. I enjoyed a much-needed lesson in stock reduction and learned how to render duck fat.

When the day was done I thought my legs hurt less than they had the day before. I called it progress.

I half expected Carl Luppo to be waiting for me as I strolled back to my car to go home midafternoon after work. I was leaving early to take Landon to a qualifying bee at her school. Carl wasn't there waiting for me. I was aware of being both relieved and just the slightest bit disappointed. I was beginning to appreciate having him at my back and in his absence I felt a little twinge of vulnerability, as though my guardian angel had taken the afternoon off.

I tried to be vigilant while I was driving back to my town house, and my mirrors told me that Ron Kriciak hadn't followed me home. I was acutely aware that I was no longer viewing Ron as my advocate. Despite Carl's warnings, though, Ron hadn't yet crossed the line and become my adversary. But whatever responsibility I'd allowed Ron to assume for guaranteeing my safety and my daughter's safety in Boulder had once again become my own.

As Carl had said the very first time I'd met him, the jury was out on Ron Kriciak.

VIV HAD SOMEPLACE to be and rushed away as soon as I got home. Landon pounced on me the moment her babysitter was out the door. She wanted to go to the park and play soccer after the spelling bee.

"You promised," she told me.

I didn't remember promising. But I didn't remember not promising, either. I cursed Robert under my breath. Kicking soccer balls with our daughter was definitely supposed to be one of his things. I said, "Sure, babe, if we're done on time we'll come back here after the bee and change our clothes—then we can go to the park. Maybe we'll go out and get some dinner after."

"Can we get sushi?"

Robert's idea. Introducing our daughter to sushi. Raw fish is not my thing. I said, "I'll think about it. I was thinking maybe Mc-Donald's."

She said, "Oh," and I felt guilty. I didn't even know where to get sushi in Boulder. I guessed I could find someplace decent downtown near the Mall. Maybe that place that used to be the New York Deli. But then, I didn't eat raw fish. How would I know decent?

Ten minutes later we were driving to the school for the spelling bee.

The district qualifying bee was being held at a school not too far from our house. Assuming I'd get lost, I allowed ten minutes to make the five-minute drive. I used the time with Landon to retrace some ground we'd covered when I'd agreed to sign her up for the spelling competition.

I said, "Babe? You know this is the last bee for now, don't you? No matter how well you do, we can't risk having you appear at the district finals."

"I know," she said. "Because of the TV cameras, right?" The tone she attached to those two words conveyed the fact that not only did she know, but that she didn't particularly want to be reminded, and that she still thought the whole darn thing was unfair. It was hard to disagree with her. In her *so there* voice, she added, "But I'm going to qualify anyway. Just so you know."

"And I'll be proud of you. Even though you can't go any farther. Just so *you* know."

"Tell me again—how many qualify, Mom?"

"Only three kids from this bee, babe."

"Piece of cake," she said. "The kid who comes in fourth is really going to owe me when I back out."

I smiled. When we arrived at the school, I drove around the perimeter twice, checking for men sitting in cars looking as though they didn't belong in the neighborhood. Finally, I pulled into the parking lot.

"You looking for the bad man?" Landon asked.

The perspicacity of her question deflated me like a punch in the gut. I briefly considered lying to her, but I didn't. I nodded. "Yes, babe. I've always got an eye out for him," I said.

"Then I'll keep an eye out for him, too," she said, and she peered intently out the windshield.

I started to cry when she said that and quickly pulled into a parking space and climbed out of the car, hoping she wouldn't notice my tears.

We followed two other mothers and daughters into the school and down some sterile hallways into a small, equally sterile theater. Landon said, "See you later," and scurried away to join the other children on the raised stage. I moved a folding chair to the side of the room so I could watch the audience when I wasn't watching the kids on stage. I checked the room carefully for news cameras.

As was often the case at spelling bees, the first three rounds served to winnow the contestants. After only thirty minutes the twenty-six kids on stage had been reduced to eight. Landon was one of the eight. I smiled as she aced *synergy*.

My smile vanished as a solitary man entered the back of the theater. He was about my age, a stocky guy with short, wispy blond hair and small frameless glasses that seemed to magnify his blue eyes. He was wearing a navy blazer. When he paused near the door and crossed his arms, I thought I spotted a bulge below his left arm, toward his back.

My heart jumped as I factored in the bulge, and I temporarily lost track of the competition on stage. The man took a seat near the rear of the small theater and spent at least a minute scanning the audience, his eyes, it seemed, resting momentarily on every parent in attendance but me.

I refocused my attention on the stage. Six kids remained. Landon was the smallest of the four remaining girls. She was on deck. My eyes jumped from her to the man in the blazer and back as though I were watching a tennis match, not a spelling bee. The boy in front of Landon flubbed *diminutive*. A mother groaned.

Landon's name was called and she approached the microphone.

Her word was *lissome*. Or maybe *lithesome*. Tough draw. I wasn't sure how to spell it.

As my daughter leaned too close to the microphone and repeated the word and said the letter "l," the blond man stood and stepped into the aisle.

I stood, too, and began to edge closer to the stage so I could be in place to insert myself between the man and my daughter.

Just then an ear-shattering ringing filled the theater, a sound so fierce and sharp that it hurt to be in its vicinity. The two adults on stage jumped immediately toward the children participating in the bee. A woman standing near me took me by the elbow and pointed me toward the doorway at the back of the theater. I yanked my arm free and tried to find the blond man in the blazer.

He was almost to the steps that led up to the stage.

I tried to get to Landon but when I turned I ran smack into the woman who had been urging me out the door. We both went flying. She fell with a grunt so loud that I could hear it above the cacophonous ringing. I feared she was hurt, but my compassion for her would have to wait. I scrambled to my feet. I couldn't spot Landon, but the blond man was all the way up on stage.

Someone was yelling, "Please, parents. Parents, please. It's the fire alarm. Single file out the back door. Please."

Yeah, right. I sniffed the air for smoke, sensed nothing suspicious. I'd already decided that the alarm was a ruse. Something the blond man had manufactured to create confusion.

I hurdled the woman that I'd knocked to the floor and I vaulted up to the stage. The children had already disappeared stage right, and the blond man's back was just visible as he was entering the same wing. My mind forced my eyes from his blazer to his trousers.

He was out of my sight before I could determine whether or not he was wearing chinos.

I was aware that someone was screaming at me to get off the stage.

Every precious thing I lose, you will lose two.

Give me two more seconds, I thought, and you can be sure I'll be off the damn stage.

A DOORWAY LED from the stage to a dimly lit school corridor. On one side of the corridor the walls were tiled to shoulder height. The other side of the hall was lined with lockers. I listened for the sounds of retreating footsteps, or children's voices, or—God help me—Landon's screams. But the bitter clanging of the fire alarm blocked out every sound but the ever-present echo of Ernesto Castro's threat.

I sprinted off in the direction of a solitary green EXIT sign. With each step I felt jostled by the reverberations of the relentless bell. The linoleum began to sparkle in the spot that the corridor intersected with another hallway. I turned to my right down that hall and headed toward the distant brilliance of some glass doors.

Partially silhouetted against those doors at the end of the corridor I saw the man in the blue blazer. He had a child under his arm, the child's sneakered feet kicking wildly in the air.

I screamed, "STOP!" I screamed, "BABY!"

The man didn't slow. I ran faster than I'd ever run in my life, faster even than I'd run that day in Slaughter, yelling reassurance I didn't feel to my sweet daughter, screaming at the man to stop.

I was maybe twenty feet from him when he reached the door. As I opened my mouth to once again yell "STOP!" the fire-alarm bell abruptly ceased, causing my shrill exclamation to fill the end of the corridor. The man's feet stopped moving, the child's didn't. I heard her squeal. He looked back at me over his shoulder.

He'd heard me.

"Put her down," I said.

"Are you a teacher?" he asked.

"Put her down," I repeated, closing the distance between us.

"She has to get to the orthodontist," he said. "We're already late."

The orthodontist? Hell!

I spoke crisply. "Put—her—down. NOW!"

He put her down between himself and the door. I waited for him to go for the gun that was stashed below his blazer. I wondered what I'd do, how I'd distract him long enough for Landon to get away.

And then an orca breached and I heard the timbre of spent shells dancing on a New Orleans sidewalk.

With a distracting tilt to his head, he asked, "Are you a teacher? She's all done at the spelling bee. She's out. I'm just taking her to the orthodontist."

With a big metal smile on her face, the child peeked around the man's thick waist and looked at me. She said, "She's not one of my teachers, Daddy."

I stared at her mouth full of braces and her unfamiliar face, and I stammered, "I thought you were . . . someone else. I'm . . . so sorry."

The man narrowed his eyes and shook his head at me the way I do sometimes at drivers who have cut me off in traffic. He took his daughter by the hand and disappeared into the brash southern sunlight.

He was wearing tight white jeans. Not chinos.

I backed against the tile wall and slid to the floor. I started to shake before I started to cry.

FIVE MINUTES LATER I found the kids from the spelling bee lined up on a basketball court on the north side of the school. Landon was there. She saw something in my appearance as I approached her, maybe the tremor in my hands, or the redness in my eyes. Maybe the desperation in my voice as I said, "Hi, baby." I'm not sure what she saw exactly, but she stepped out of line and walked over to me.

"Are you okay?" she asked.

I nodded. Smiled weakly. "Sure. I'm fine."

"Did you see the bad man?" she asked.

Damn. I shook my head. "No," I managed. "The fire alarm before? It surprised me, that's all."

She exhaled and took one of my hands in both of hers. With gravity in her voice totally inappropriate for her nine years, she said, "The first rule of fire drills, Mother, is 'Stay calm.' Remember that the next time, okay?"

I fought more tears as I said, "Okay. That's good advice. I'll try to remember that."

TRUE TO HER promise, Landon placed in the top three in the spelling bee, securing second place. The word that finally tripped her up was *funicular*. She was in a good mood as we drove home.

I remained unsteady from my experience with the fire drill. I answered warily when the phone rang in my bedroom as I was changing into shorts and sneakers to fulfill my promise to go to the park to play soccer.

Carl Luppo said, "It's me."

"Hi," I said. I surprised myself by how happy I was to hear from him. Given what I'd just been through, my tone was friendlier than I would have imagined possible.

"Hey, listen, remember that thing we were talking about yesterday? That thing with the big white . . . Hey, I don't have to spell it out for you, do I? You know what I'm talking about here, right?"

"Yes." His evasiveness warned me that something was up. My knuckles were turning to chalk on the hand that gripped the phone.

"Well, it appears there's another one, now. A different one, but the same kind of thing. This one is more confusing to me. I'm not so, I don't know, cavalier about it as I was yesterday. You and me, we should talk somewhere I think. Soon."

Cavalier? Did Carl Luppo say "cavalier"? I bet Landon could spell it.

"How soon?"

"Like now. Now soon."

I fought panic. "Okay."

"I was thinking that place I mentioned that serves those things that give me a little touch of indigestion. You remember that place?"

He was talking about the empanada place that was on Thirteenth, just off the Pearl Street Mall. "Yes, I think I do. You said you thought you were developing a taste for them."

His voice took on the timbre of a smile. "Exactly. Say, twenty minutes? We'll meet right there."

I remembered my commitment about soccer and sushi. I said, "I have someplace to go first. With my daughter. Let's say seven o'clock. Will that work?"

He exhaled before he said, "Not a good idea. Being out of your house somewhere with your daughter right now."

My heart stopped. I felt a whale being calved.

I lowered my voice, but my next words came out in a swirl. "What do you mean? What—?"

Carl's voice stayed level. "Not here. Not now. Not on your home phone. Outside phone lines or face-to-face. Trust me on this."

"Twenty minutes you said?"

"That'll work."

I hung up the phone and counted to ten. I said a silent prayer before I called out to Landon. "The bus leaves for dinner in two minutes. Little change in plans, we're having empanadas. Are you ready?"

She said, "Have you seen my shin guards? *Mom?* What are *empanadas?*"

"Your shin guards are down here by your shoes. But we're not going to play soccer right away. Bring some clean socks instead. Empanadas are South American food. They're like little baked sandwiches."

"*Mom.*"

"I think you'll like them."

"What's in them?"

"Different things. You can choose. Let's go, honey. Please. It's really, really important."

"Do they have any with sushi in them?"

I didn't respond because I didn't know how to respond. How many nine-year-olds would ask that question?

My mind was spinning. Carl had discovered something that had convinced him that Landon and I were in danger. He must be thinking that someone else was following me. Someone besides Ron Kriciak.

Before Landon came downstairs, I went to the bookshelf and transferred all ten thousand eight hundred dollars from John Irving's mutilated book to a spot in the bottom of my purse.

I checked for my keys.

Good.

I heard my daughter's footfalls on the stairs. But my heart was the loudest thing in the room.

What was I forgetting?

Ernesto Castro? Have you really found me so fast?

3

The wide lawn that stretched between the courthouse and the fourteen hundred block of the Mall was almost deserted when Landon and I arrived to meet Carl. The street people I was accustomed to seeing there had retreated from their grassy domain earlier than usual that evening, and the adolescent kids who were usually hanging out waiting for their friends to show up had apparently found something better to do with the rest of their day.

After we finished our empanadas and lemonade, Carl offered to kick the soccer ball with Landon for a few minutes on the courthouse lawn. He wasn't what I would call agile but was quite enthusiastic and showed a flair for the dramatic that I hadn't seen in him before. When he finally joined me in the long shadows near a big tree across from Antica Roma, Landon elected to stay on the open part of the lawn and continued to work on her dribbling. I kept my attention divided between her and Carl.

It took Carl a few minutes to catch his breath after running around with Landon. He said, "I like your kid. She's sweet. Kind of spunky, too. I like girls who like sports, you know what I mean?"

I was hoping he wasn't thinking I might be one of those girls. I said a silent prayer that he wasn't going to ask me something about football or baseball. "Thanks," I said. "She is both those things. The spunkiness hides the sweetness sometimes—if you know what I mean."

He chuckled. "My granddaughter, Amanda, I hear she's like that, too." He pointed to Antica Roma. "That place over there," he said. "The trattorias don't really look like that in Italy. Not in the south, anyway. I've been a few times to visit family. This one here's a bit too Disney World. Like a tourist version of the real thing, you know what I'm saying?" He smiled. "But from here the food smells all right. You think? You ever eaten over there?"

I said, "No," and to focus his attention I grazed the top of his hand with my fingers. He seemed startled by my touch, immediately caressing the same spot I had just touched. I asked, "Carl, how do you know it's safe for Landon and me to be here? I mean out in the open like this. You seemed pressured earlier on the phone—now you're nonchalant."

"Like I told you when you got here, the woman followed you home from work, and she waited for a while outside your place with her camera. Your daughter came out the front door to say good-bye to that woman, the one you said was watching her."

"That's Viv."

"Whatever. Your daughter was out for just a minute or so. The woman snapped a couple, three pictures, then she took off again. I stayed with her and tailed her back to the motel where she's staying. It's up Arapahoe, near the mouth of the canyon, by the mountains."

"And you don't know who she is?"

Carl shook his head. "Sorry."

"Is she a marshal?"

Carl made a soft fist and covered it with his open hand. "Doesn't make sense for the program to put a marshal up in a motel like that. WITSEC could use somebody local if they wanted to tail you. Hell, they'd just tell Kriciak to do it—he's been doing it enough anyway. Or they could put a transmitter in your car and make it easy on themselves, right?" I nodded. He went on. "The office here has plenty of people in it. I've been babysat by at least half a dozen different marshals on my witness trips. And the camera? I can't make any sense of the camera at all. WITSEC has plenty of pictures of you and your daughter. Both before and after your entry into the program. I don't see any way it adds up that the lady is a marshal."

I thought about his words and the underlying argument. On the drive downtown with Landon, I'd covered some of the same ground myself. "Then there's no escaping the fact that Landon and I are in some danger, Carl."

He looked down before he spoke, picked at some long blades of grass and twirled them between his fingers, braiding them into a single thick strand. When he looked back up at me, his eyes said, "No shit," but the words he spoke were, "I'm afraid I have to agree with that appraisal, Peyton."

"Do I tell Ron about the woman?"

He shrugged. "I think you have to. The important information, I think, is how he reacts."

"What if the woman is a marshal? Someone still angry about my criticism of WITSEC. Someone trying to set me up, get some retribution. You know, catch me in a security breach. Get me . . . the paper."

"If Ron's not part of a setup like that, then it's a problem for him. Puts him between the proverbial rock and the proverbial hard place."

I considered Ron's conundrum, thought it paled in comparison to my own. "Do I lose anything by telling Ron about the woman with the camera?"

Carl laughed ironically. He said, "If your point is right—that that lady's a marshal with her own agenda and that Ron's in on this—then he already knows where to find you."

"Will he believe me?"

"You mean if he's not in on it? That somebody from WITSEC might be tailing you without his knowledge? Probably not. That there might be forces within WITSEC that want you out? If he's not in on it, I don't think that will go down too easily for Ron, but it won't surprise him."

"What about the woman with the camera? How do I tell him about her? How do I tell him I know about her? I can't tell him about you and me."

"No, you can't tell him you know me. I suspect that Ron won't deal with that in a mature manner. Just tell Ron you saw the woman with the camera out your window. You were keeping an eye on Landon when she went outside, and you saw the woman sitting in her car taking pictures of your daughter."

I thought about his suggestion for a moment, didn't see any obvious flaws. "Yeah, that should work. But I want Ron to know where she's staying, don't I? I mean which motel."

"I'll call that in anonymously, somehow. I can think of a way to do it. I'll give them the license plate number of her car while I'm at it, too." He shifted his weight and his leg ended up only inches from my thigh. I felt some heat radiate my way. "There's something else you need to be thinking about, too."

"What's that?"

He rested his weight on his elbow and craned his neck to look at Landon before returning his gaze to me. His eyes narrowed. "What if the woman with the camera is not a marshal?"

My lungs seemed to stall. I forced an exhale and said, "Then it must be somebody sent by Ernesto Castro."

"*Every precious thing I lose, you will lose two.*"

Instinctively, my eyes scanned the courthouse lawn until they found Landon. She had begun playing one-on-one with a boy a little younger than her. She was smoking him. It made me smile.

Carl said, "Castro's the guy who ordered the hit on your husband?"

I shivered at the ease with which the words exited his mouth. Ordering a hit was like ordering a pizza margherita for Carl Luppo. I said, "Yes."

Carl nodded, scratched his ear. "See, I don't think so. *Señor* Castro doesn't seem like the type to send a woman for this job."

I tried not to be offended by Carl's contention but wasn't about to mount a spirited argument that murder was one of the jobs women could do just as well as men. I said, "Maybe Castro is trying to be clever. By using someone I don't expect him to use. Like her."

"Your Ernesto Castro doesn't sound clever to me. Look at his life, you want to call it that. He's not sharp. He's not a scalpel, not even a knife—he's a hammer, a blunt instrument. He sells people drugs. And what use does he have of women? He beats up prostitutes, is that right? And then, what, he goes and rapes a lawyer in a wheelchair? And he goes and rapes some other women, too. I got that correct, don't I? No, this Castro's not going to hire some woman to do his dirty work. He's not the type. Women clean up his blood; they don't spill it."

"It was a woman who tried to grab Landon when we were living in Slaughter."

"Grabbing ain't shooting. He wouldn't send a woman to clip you."

The irony didn't escape me. I was sitting in the light of dusk on a tranquil lawn just steps from the Rocky Mountains chatting with a retired mob enforcer—a self-described gorilla—and he was pontificating about the character flaws of the lowlife scum who'd ordered my husband killed. I blinked rapidly a few times and had to make a conscious decision to close my mouth so that my jaw didn't hang open.

Carl Luppo seemed confident of his assessment about Ernesto Castro. And a sharp twang below my ribcage told me he was probably right about it. I didn't like the conclusions I was left to draw.

"So who then?"

He held up one thick finger, said, "You got your Ernesto Castro." He flicked up a second, making a peace sign. "You got your pissed-off federal marshals." He grabbed the ring finger with his free hand. "Who's number three? Anybody else who isn't particularly fond of you, Peyton?"

I shrugged. "Isn't two enough?"

"In my experience, enemies always seemed to come in packs. You're strong—there're no buzzards in the sky. You bleed a little, and the black birds come out of the clouds waiting to peck on you."

The dusk was still shimmering, but I felt the darkness like a pillow over my face. It was threatening to suffocate me. I tried to lighten things up. I joked, "Just how many mortal enemies can one girl have, Carl?"

"Usually, in my experience, the answer is one too many."

"What about the press? Maybe it's a reporter who's following me," I said.

"Like who?"

"I don't know. A tabloid like the *Star* or the *Enquirer*. Maybe they've decided to track me down."

He looked puzzled. "Why?"

"Why do they do any of the things they do?"

"Yeah, you're right. I can't argue with that. But exposing the whereabouts of federal witnesses? I don't know, Peyton. That'd be asking for a whole new level of trouble."

I didn't respond and he didn't press me further.

After a minute or so he spoke. "You want coffee?" he asked. "We could walk over to Dushanbe. I always like an espresso after I eat."

I caught his eyes with mine and recognized the awkwardness of the longing that hid in the recesses. This wasn't an offer of a beverage. This wasn't an offer of assistance. Carl Luppo was asking me out on a date. I wasn't sure he was even aware that he was asking me out.

But I knew it.

I had to answer him. Before I could, though, a whale breached. I tried to shake it off, force it to dive, but I couldn't. It was something about Robert and Robert's eyes and me knowing that he wanted me. The feeling was one of warm pleasure, of power mixed with lust.

I shushed it away.

I said, "Not tonight, Carl. I'm too worried about Landon. I need to go home, call Ron Kriciak, decide what to do next."

"Can I offer Landon an ice cream? There's a place right down the Mall. It'd be a treat for me to buy her an ice cream. It would make me happy." He pointed west, toward the mountains.

I knew he didn't want to say good-bye. It made me think of all the losses he was responsible for, all the good-byes that he'd forced in his life. I said, "I don't think so. I should get home. Call Ron."

Carl looked down. "When you tell him all of this, he's gonna relocate you, you know that? You'll be out of your place tonight and into a safe house. Be in another safe place tomorrow, and you'll be in Topeka or someplace by the weekend."

For some reason I thought of the money stashed in the bottom of my purse. The marshals would search me. The money would raise questions. How would I account for it?

I looked west, toward the mountains. The sunset was monochromatic, as golden as fresh butter. The yellow light softened and disappeared as it dripped down into the canyons. I said, "Where we go next, it probably won't be this pretty."

"Who knows?" he said. His eyes were heavy, and it seemed to take some extra effort for him to find the energy to continue speaking. "Maybe there's program room in Bermuda, or Honolulu."

I laughed.

"Listen, whoever's looking found you real easy. They're sharp. They have contacts. Good contacts. Odds are they'll find you again. You'll have to stay on your toes. Promise me you'll do that." He was using his father-talking-to-his-favorite-daughter voice again. The sexual tension between us had risen from the air; its heat had carried it higher. Carl and I were left close to the ground with the density, the sadness. I felt it from him.

I felt it in myself.

I tried to make my voice playful. "Who'll look after me next time? I won't have a Carl Luppo when the next plane lands, will I?"

"Carl Luppos are one of a kind," he said.

"Yes, they are," I replied and kissed the hit man on the cheek.

God, how my life had changed.

4

After a quick dinner, Prowler took the private elevator from his basement apartment to his attic office. His tenants in the four apartments in the building didn't even know that there were offices tucked under the roofline of the building. Nor did they know that the free DSL Internet access that their landlord provided to his tenants also provided their landlord access to an additional phone line that he'd rewired from each apartment to the attic office. He insisted that each tenant receive the DSL service from the phone company in their own name and submit the monthly bills along with their rent checks. Prowler then deducted that amount from their next month's rent. The system gave Prowler four untraceable lines for making or receiving local calls.

To unlock the attic space required a key, a six-digit alphanumeric code, and an iris scan. The correct combination in the correct order not only unlocked the door, it also deactivated the computer security system, which was programmed to instantaneously format all the drives in the room in the event of unauthorized entry, unexpected movement, or the sound of broken glass. The windows on the third floor did not open; they were all opaque and all made of fixed glass. Radiant tubing provided heat to the space, and the diameter of the ductwork used for the air-conditioning system was too narrow to permit human access.

As far as the security system was concerned, the only authorized entrant was Prowler.

Upon entry, Prowler reactivated the system on "Stay" mode, which deactivated the motion sensor.

He accepted the arrival of the new digital images from Barb Turner with hardly a glance. A few key strokes and he saved them to three different hard drives. Prowler didn't believe in portable media. It was entirely too hard to destroy and way too easy to steal.

Kirsten Lord's kid didn't interest him and he'd assumed that Lord's address would be on its way because Barb Turner had said it would and she had become his most reliable man. That's how he thought about her. For Prowler, Barb Turner was like a guy in disguise. And her disguise helped her blend into the most unlikely of locations. Like Boulder, Colorado.

He e-mailed back to her that he didn't see any reason to disturb the rest of the nest. He figured that would ease Barb's mind. Prowler wouldn't hire anybody who could kill a kid without at least a little compunction. Nor would he hire anybody who wouldn't kill a kid if instructed to do so.

Prowler was busy planning the coordination of the next phase when his phone rang. He straightened the microphone on his headset with one hand and guessed the identity of the sender before he glanced down at his caller-ID screen. The number on the screen told him that the call emanated from Washington, D.C. That meant Marvin. Prowler hadn't guessed that Marvin would be calling. First time he'd missed all day. He punched a button.

"Prowler," he said.

"There's some noise here at headquarters."

"I'm listening." And saving to disk.

"My man has picked up on some e-mails that are circulating in rarefied air. Okay? Is that clear? It seems that some security flack detected some active attempts to penetrate files at headquarters, including the files of a person of particular interest to us. Whether they picked up my contact's earlier attempts to get through the firewall or whether there are some independent efforts under way, that's unclear."

Prowler processed the problem instantly. He said, "Then clarify it. If it's your contact that they're picking up evidence about, be prepared to clean up after yourself without delay."

"We're trying to determine what they know right now. My man has to be especially careful not to leave any electronic fingerprints. That would only make matters worse. We don't want that."

Prowler sensed indecisiveness. He didn't like indecisiveness. "Are you prepared to sever ties, Marvin?"

"It won't be necessary, Prowler."

"You should know that *I* am prepared to sever ties. I'm told that a little role-modeling can be a wonderful motivator for a subordinate."

Prowler could hear the man on the other end of the phone gulp before he said, "You know me. I'll take care of whatever needs to be taken care of. You can rest assured of that."

"I rest fine. I assume plans are in place."

"They are."

"Good."

Prowler clicked off and punched eleven numbers on the phone keypad.

The phone was answered after three rings. A man said, "Krist." He pronounced it Christ.

Prowler appreciated the irony. He said, "We're ready at this end. What do you have?"

"You still want an accident? Or do you want I should send a message?"

"This is a whisper job all the way."

"If I have some latitude timewise, I can do them together. Car in the water. Lots of water down here."

"What kind of latitude?"

"Three days, maybe four. They get together with some regularity to discuss our client."

"You don't have that kind of latitude. It needs to be over within twenty-four. Noon tomorrow would be better."

"Then she goes in the water. He has a heart attack. She's careless and the man is a coronary waiting to happen."

"So be it," said Prowler.

"Then it's a go?"

"It is a go."

5

I refused to believe that Landon and I would be leaving Boulder within hours, and I told myself that was why I refused to say good-bye to Carl

Luppo as we left him behind at the Pearl Street Mall. Although I couldn't imagine an innocent explanation for why a woman with a camera would be following my daughter and me around Boulder, I was trying to convince myself that such an innocent explanation did exist.

Carl had walked us to our car, which was parked on Thirteenth, near the hotel where I worked. When I was inside the car with the window rolled down, Carl Luppo leaned in toward me and said, "I want you to know that helping you out has made me very happy. Very happy." I could feel his breath on my face and could smell his scent, some blend of lemon and sunshine.

"Thanks, Carl. For everything. I mean it."

From her spot in the middle of the backseat, Landon piped up. "Yeah, thanks a lot for the empanadas and lemonade, Uncle Carl. And for playing soccer with me. And I mean it, too."

As she said, "Uncle Carl," he smiled the broadest smile I'd yet seen on his face. His eyes sparkled like Santa Claus's.

LANDON DISAPPEARED INTO her room the moment we got home. Somehow the night seemed normal to her. She wanted to listen to music and study her spelling lists before she went to bed.

I was wondering whether or not Ron Kriciak and the Marshals Service would even permit her to wake up in the same bed the next morning.

What had I done to my little girl?

I TOOK THE phone downstairs and sat on the dining room floor where the table would be if we had one. I sat smack in the middle of the room, right below the tacky smoked-glass-and-fake-crystal chandelier that was hanging from a faux antique bronze chain. I started to punch in the number of Ron Kriciak's pager but stopped one digit short of completing the sequence. I disconnected the call, then checked my purse for another number instead, found the business card I was looking for, and dialed. I listened to a long message and was prompted to leave a message of my own and then dial another number to activate a pager.

For my message, I said, "Hi, this is Peyton. I'm really sorry to bother you, but something's come up and I need to talk with you right away. It's real important, obviously."

I dictated my number before I hung up.

I dialed the second number, punched in my number, and I waited.

Two minutes, three. My watch told me that it was eight fifty-seven. The watch was too elegant for everyday use, but I wore it anyway. It had been a gift from Robert. But it wasn't engraved. After a protracted argument during my initiation, the marshals had relented and allowed me to keep it.

Finally, the phone rang. I pressed the talk button after less than half a ring. My greeting sounded hoarse. I wondered if I was getting sick. Couldn't possibly be related to stress.

"Peyton?" my therapist said.

"Dr. Gregory, thanks for calling."

Ten minutes later, not really expecting an answer, I asked my psychologist, "So, do you think I should call Ron?"

I felt him hesitate before he responded. When he spoke, he said, "I wish I was in a position to offer advice on that, Peyton. I could argue it either way—calling Ron or not calling Ron."

I put some despair in my voice, the way I used to do with Robert when I felt that he was resisting me unreasonably. "I'm not sure what to do. I could really use some advice."

Dr. Gregory's reply surprised me. "Advice is tricky for me. You know what advice is? Advice is me standing on the sidelines telling you how to maneuver yourself and your daughter through a minefield. Let's say I suggest that you step somewhere and it happens to be the wrong place—boom!—you're both screwed, but I'm still just fine, standing on the sidelines. Giving advice."

"You have part of it right. This sure feels like a minefield," I said. I was still disappointed, but I was feeling a little lighter on the despair.

I'D STARTED OUT the conversation telling him everything I knew about the woman with the camera and about my suspicion that Ron Kriciak had been following me around Boulder for a few days. But I hadn't told Dr. Gregory everything. I hadn't told him about Carl Luppo's help.

I'd also admitted, "I just don't know who else to trust."

Other than myself, my daughter, and a retired mafioso.

And you, dear doctor, I thought.

Sort of.

HE RESPONDED TO my minefield comment by saying, "What are you going to do, Peyton?"

What?

What did he mean asking me that?

My daddy wouldn't have asked me that. My daddy, bless his heart, would have decision-treed me to bored tears, frowning at every feint I made down the wrong branch, turning up the corners of his eyes in a smile as I found the stem he wanted me to choose. Problem solving was like a treasure hunt with my daddy, and I always loved to play because he let me cheat.

He loved for me to cheat.

Robert wouldn't have asked me what I was going to do, either. Robert, at this exact moment in my passivity, would have spelled out precisely what my choices were and then whittled away at the perimeters of the ones that he thought were asinine until it was clear that any reasonable person—*and I am a reasonable person, aren't I?*—would choose the one that Robert in his wisdom had rightfully, and righteously, decreed should be left standing.

"I don't know what I'm going to do," I said to Dr. Gregory. "I'm thinking I should call Ron."

I silently cursed the impersonal quality of the phone and in my mind pretended that I was staring hard at him in his office, eyeing him the way I did when I was trying to pin a witness I was certain was about to lie to me. Even in my mind, though, Dr. Gregory's eyes didn't waver. They stayed locked on mine. His face was impassive. His crossed legs unflinching.

I wanted a cue.

I got nothing.

Frustrated, I reached over and fumbled inside my purse and dug around until I found a solitary lollipop. It was a pale red one. Did DumDum make watermelon? Yeah, they did.

But this one was strawberry. I unwrapped it and placed it on the center of my tongue, trying to keep the hard candy from clanking against my teeth.

Finally he said, "Yes?"

I replied, "I told you once that I trusted the marshals more than I trusted Ernesto Castro, didn't I?"

"I think you did."

"Well, that argument tells me I should call Ron and let him know what I'm thinking."

Apparently it wasn't the right answer. He asked, "Right now, what are you concerned about, Peyton?"

You mean besides some stranger wearing chinos or maybe the latest from Abercrombie trying to kidnap my daughter? You mean besides that and maybe besides that same someone trying to blow a hole or two in my head with a silenced .22? You mean other concerns? The direction of the Supreme Court? The price of gasoline? The instability in the Balkans?

"The moment I call Ron," I said, "my control evaporates. He takes over. He decides what happens next. For all I know, he'll have me out of my house by midnight and out of Colorado by tomorrow morning. Landon leaves more new friends. I lose a job I like and Landon and I once again become pieces that are moved around on some big WIT-SEC board game."

Two beats of my heart passed before my therapist said, "You haven't had much control, have you?"

His words made me cry. I wasn't sure why. I tried not to sob into the phone. I didn't want him to hear me sob. I moved the lollipop from my tongue to a hollow in my cheek.

After I garnered some composure I followed him, meekly. I said, "Not since that day at Galatoire's, no."

He said, "I'm talking about even before that. Katherine Shaw certainly didn't have any control. Peyton Francis doesn't have much, either. The surprising thing—maybe to both of us—is that I think you're telling me that Kirsten Lord didn't have much either."

He remembered all my names. I was touched. Some days I couldn't even remember all my names. "What do you mean?" I said, protesting his contention about Kirsten Lord being out of control.

"I think you know."

I did.

"Is there some message in what you're saying? Something that might help me know what decision I should make tonight?"

He read between my lines. "I wish I knew what was best for you, Peyton. If I did, I'd tell you."

Daddy always knew what was best for me. Robert always knew. My bosses always knew. I said, "I wish you did, too." And I almost meant it.

"I think other men in your life have been willing to act like they knew what was best, weren't they? If you were willing to act helpless enough."

I swallowed, forcing down a rebellious rise of anger. I wanted to disagree, even if only for form.

"Robert," he said.

I was sure he could hear me breathing. I made a conscious effort not to suck on my DumDum.

"Your father."

For some reason I wanted to catch the train before it left the station. I felt stupid standing alone on the platform. "Are you suggesting I conspired with them? That I encouraged them to make decisions for me?"

He started to speak, then hesitated before he said, "In order to rescue a damsel in distress, first, I think, requires a damsel."

Me, a damsel?

Robert would laugh at the thought, and upon hearing it he would rush up to me and he would kiss me hard, at least one hand on a cheek of my ass, and he would be perfectly content with the description.

"You're *my* damsel," is what he would say.

The reflection on Robert didn't warm me. It didn't even qualify as a visit from a whale. I said, "Maybe . . . maybe tonight I shouldn't play the damsel. Maybe that's the message."

"Maybe," my therapist said.

"Trouble is," I said, "I'm not quite sure what role she was supposed to be playing tonight."

He laughed. It sounded like music to me.

LANDON WAS ASLEEP in her clothes sideways on top of her bed. Her CD player was spinning a tune by some group whose fame would certainly have evaporated by the time I learned who they were.

Unless she was ill my daughter slept like she was in suspended animation. I undressed her and pulled a nightgown over her head without hearing even a whimper from her. The possibility of waking her so that she could pee and brush her teeth crossed my mind, but I decided against it. It would take a bushel more energy than I possessed to rouse her from her slumber, and the truth was that I envied both her innocence and her sleep.

Before I flicked off the light I quieted her CD player and knelt by the side of her bed. I quickly read the Spartan language of *Goodnight Moon*. The bedtime ritual went much more quickly when I didn't have to share the pictures or laugh as she pointed out the mouse on each page.

My last words before "I love you" were the almost as familiar "Goodnight noises everywhere." I closed the book and leaned over to touch my lips to her cheek. I tasted salt when I kissed her.

My daughter, the little Mia.

I WAS FEELING so languid that the walk from her room to my own felt interminable, like crossing a continent. My fatigue was a midafternoon on a hot New Orleans day kind of tired. Siesta tired. Ceiling-fan tired. But I knew I was too anxious to sleep. I still had a riddle to solve—whether or not to end the evening—and most likely my stay in Boulder—by calling Ron Kriciak and telling him about the woman with the camera who was staying at the motel near the mouth of Boulder Canyon.

My bedroom was dark and I left it that way.

I tugged open the drapes and scanned the sky for shooting stars. None. I scanned the parking lot for unfamiliar cars. None. I tried not to look in the bright space between the parking lot and the night sky, because in-between was what I would be losing when I left. Boulder and all its promises, Colorado and all its loveliness.

I heard a muffled cough, a swallowed little growl, and stood silently, controlling my breathing until I was certain that Landon wasn't waking with a cough.

I counted to ten. Nothing.

With one quick motion I crossed my arms and pulled my top over my head and then stripped off my bra. I unbuttoned my shorts and allowed them to drop on the floor exactly where I was standing. I stepped backward one step and stood there in my panties while I welcomed a whale.

Robert usually sensed when I was naked—I don't know how he knew, exactly—and he could always be counted on to *care* that I was naked. He'd slip up behind me silently and reach around and cup my breasts in his big hands or he'd run his fingernails down the long muscles of my back or he'd shed his own clothes before he approached me and he'd turn and fit his long back right up against my own and he'd thread his fingers into mine and ass-to-ass, we'd dance naked.

He'd sing a song, something romantic.

Or something silly.

NOW, AT THIS time in my life, no one cared that I was naked.

No one even knew.

The Robert whale was swimming away when I heard another muffled cough.

This time I turned.

6

Alan Gregory hung up the phone after talking with Peyton and rejoined his wife on the narrow deck off their bedroom. He wrapped a lightweight chenille throw that was the color of Dijon mustard over her shoulders before he sat back down.

In front of them the sky was gray, streaked with silver. The air had begun the transition from hot to warm.

She murmured thanks for the blanket and they sat silently for a few minutes. Emily was at the end of the deck intently watching the narrow trail that wound through the prairie grasses just west of the house. It was the trail that the red foxes used during their nightly prowls. Emily wouldn't bark when the first fox stepped onto the tableau, but every muscle in her strong body would tense and she'd lower herself to be ready, her snout just over the edge of the decking.

For what was she getting prepared? A leap into the dusk? Alan and Lauren had never guessed.

Alan was about to say something about the apparent increase in the critter population around their house when Lauren asked, "Was it a real emergency?" She was referring to the page Alan had received. He had just returned from returning a call to the number that had flashed on his pager.

He thought for a moment. "In my patient's mind it was."

"*Was?*"

He laughed at himself. "I guess I'm not that much of a magician. *Is.* In her mind it is."

She fished. "Her? And you're feeling okay with things the way you left them with her?"

He guessed, incorrectly, that Lauren was concerned that this emergency page might be the first in a series, that it would interfere with their evening. He said, "No, I'm still worried about her actually. I wouldn't be surprised if she calls again."

Lauren's eyes narrowed but she didn't look his way. "Should I be worried about her, too?" she asked.

His breathing changed. He knew it. He knew that she knew it. He tried to erase the alteration in his breathing from the universe by reaching over and touching her and saying, "All you need to worry about is our baby."

Lauren nodded and wondered what was going on with Kirsten Lord that felt like an emergency her husband could solve. She lowered her hands to the underside of her swollen belly and grew silent.

Alan said, "I actually considered asking Sam to send a patrol car by this patient's house tonight. She has some . . . fears."

"Yes?"

"I ended up deciding that the issues . . . the fears . . . were more psychological than . . . actual."

Lauren felt her pulse rise. The baby gave her a couple of swift kicks in the kidneys. "You don't sound totally confident in your decision. What could it hurt to send someone by?"

"Let me think about it," he said.

She got up. She had to pee.

She always had to pee.

7

Carl watched Peyton and her daughter drive away from the picnic they'd had together on the Mall before he walked back to his own car. He changed his clothes from a duffel bag he kept in the trunk. First he swapped out his sunglasses, then he pulled on a purple Colorado Rockies windbreaker, and then he topped the outfit with a brimmed hat celebrating the Bronco's second Super Bowl victory. Quite early in his brief sojourn in Colorado, Carl had discovered that this particular outfit was suitable for virtually every public occasion in the Greater Denver Metropolitan area, with the possible exceptions of weddings and funerals.

So far he hadn't attended any of those.

He climbed into his car, backtracked to the south, and headed west on Arapahoe until he pulled into the parking lot at Eben Fine Park. After a short walk he spotted the woman-with-the-camera's car right in front of her cabin where he'd hoped to find it. That was good.

He watched a pizza being delivered to her room by a young man whose Toyota Tercel had a Blackjack Pizza sign attached to the roof. The pizza delivery was good news. Carl figured that the woman in the cabin would be home for a while.

As far as Carl knew, Peyton had never seen his car, so he used it to drive back east on Arapahoe past Thirtieth and then past the Foothills

Parkway to the cluster of town houses where Peyton lived with her daughter. He cruised the neighborhood once, trying to spot Ron Kriciak or another follower from the Marshals Service, but he didn't see anyone suspicious. Carl found a spot to park under a tree on an adjacent street and climbed out of the car.

Out loud, he said, "She's not gone yet, right? So our job's not done? Am I right, or what?"

A little yip emerged from the backseat.

"Let's go for a walk. Whattya say? I think both of us could use a little walk. Come on. Come."

CARL LUPPO'S DOG was a miniature poodle, maybe sixteen pounds. When he got the dog from a breeder a few weeks after he'd arrived in Colorado, it was already six years old. The dog was in the process of being retired—Carl assumed forcibly—from life as a stud and was saddled with the unfortunate moniker of Christopher. The dog had a peculiar habit of standing with his front legs bowed out, as though he was posing for a doggie bodybuilding magazine. Carl thought it made Christopher look tough, so he'd immediately renamed the black dog Anvil.

Years before, when he was still in *the* Family and still lived with *his* family, his wife had always had standards, the big poodles, and she'd insisted on spending a damn fortune grooming the two dogs so that they looked fey. "Fey" was a word Carl had heard on the streets growing up, and he wasn't sure exactly what it meant. But he was pretty sure it applied to the way his two dogs looked after they were clipped and shaved and combed out to appear as though they'd each swallowed about a dozen inflated hairballs.

Despite his perception of his wife's sartorial mistreatment of the family dogs, Carl had learned to adore the character and poise of his two poodles, Lois and Clark, and started looking for one for himself as soon as he was settled in Colorado. The day Carl found Christopher, he'd had to endure listening to the owner go on and on about how one of the dog's first sires had actually made it to Westminster. But Carl was smitten by the dog, so he put up with the owner, and after being granted the great honor of purchasing her dog, he'd immediately had

Anvil regroomed to disguise any underlying feyness that might be lurking in the dog's genes.

Carl was aware that with Anvil's new haircut, his new home, and his fresh name change the dog could have been safely ensconced as a participant in the Federal Dog Security Program.

Carl decided to call the new program DOGSEC. And Carl not only ran the program, he ran it well.

The only dog enrolled in DOGSEC was so well disguised he didn't have to worry about a thing. Carl figured that the newly reincarnated Anvil could take a dump in his old owner's front yard and the woman wouldn't be able to recognize him anymore.

ONCE ANVIL HAD jumped from the backseat of the car to the front, Carl clipped a retractable leash to his collar and grabbed a couple of plastic bags from the glove box to corral the dog's inevitable poop. The two of them started to stroll Peyton's neighborhood. Carl didn't underestimate the benefit of having a dog on a leash when he wanted to blend into a residential area. Shortly after acquiring the dog, he had learned that Anvil was also a reliable chick magnet, as his older daughter used to call it. When he was lonely, which was often, Carl considered the chick-magnet thing a good deal. When he was trying to be inconspicuous, Carl wasn't so sure. But he'd also learned that the dog was so cute that the strangers who approached him rarely even bothered to look his way.

Sometimes that was fine with Carl.

8

Please don't have a cough; bad time to catch a cold, baby, is what I was thinking as I stepped toward Landon's room. My path to the bedroom door took me right past the foot of my double bed.

Along with virtually everything else in the house, I'd rented the bed shortly after I arrived in Boulder. It was utilitarian. A mattress and box spring sat on a metal frame that was attached to an oak headboard that was dressed up with some inlay. I'd tried to soften the hard lines of the ensemble with nice linens and a bed skirt and had even added a couple of upholstered pillows I got at Pier One.

It was okay, what I'd done. Sure, the walls above the bed were bare. And, of course, the night table was oak veneer, not antique bird's-eye maple. The room certainly didn't evoke memories of the romantic hideaway I'd put together for Robert and me in our home in New Orleans with its linens and accessories from Frette in Manhattan, but . . . Robert was dead and I doubted if I would ever see New Orleans again. What had once felt like an absolute necessity of mine— to feel Frette sheets against my bare skin each night—now felt like a laughable indulgence.

I had walked almost completely past the bed when I heard the stifled cough for the third time.

It wasn't Landon.

The sound came from my right, not from the open door in front of me.

I began to turn my head and barely caught sight of the motion that was rising at the edge of my peripheral vision. It appeared as though the pillows resting against the headboard were levitating and hanging in the air above the bed. When I turned my head to look they actually began flying at me from across the room and the mattress began rising rapidly from the frame, head over foot.

I froze in my steps as I struggled, unsuccessfully, to make sense of what I was seeing.

I heard a deep bass groan from below the erupting mass of bedding and I thought, *Landon!*

A loud cough followed, this one unmuffled.

Landon!

The mattress kept coming up toward me, all the way to vertical, then beyond. The chenille bedspread that covered the sheets slid to the carpet near my feet and the mattress started to soar at me. It was about to pin me to the wall when I crouched, leapt forward, and pounded hard on my hands and knees toward the door. My only thought was that I had to get to my baby.

"Every precious thing I lose, you will lose two."

The second I broke free of the falling mattress I felt the grip of a strong hand around my right ankle. The pressure that closed suddenly on my leg felt like the grasp of the devil. Hot and strong and unrelenting in its pressure. I was dragged backward by the force, away from the door, away from my daughter.

I thought about chinos and silenced weapons.

I screamed, "Baby, run! Run! The bad man is here!"

Before the words were out of my mouth I felt the weight of him cover me as one of his gloved hands masked my face. I bit at the fabric of the glove that covered my mouth—it was a rubbery material covered with tiny round nubs—but I couldn't get my teeth spread far enough apart to get his fingers between them.

My next scream died in his hand.

The bad man is here!

But why is it a man? Didn't Carl say that the person following me in the car was a woman?

The thought disintegrated as I tried to squirm out from beneath him. I couldn't. The mass on top of me seemed to be equivalent to the weight of a car. I was flattened face first into the carpet, a killer's hand smashed furiously into my mouth.

"Run, baby, run!" I tried to yell again. But all of the volume was in my head.

My mind jumped. I thought about damsels and needing help and calling Ron Kriciak and telling him I was being followed. But I thought mostly about my little baby, and I prayed that she hadn't managed to sleep through the ruckus.

"Every precious thing I lose, you will lose two."

I imagined her running down the stairs like Mia Hamm streaking toward the goal, flying like the wind.

"Score, baby, score!"

The man had moved a knee to the middle of my back, and he was sticking something over my mouth. I could barely breathe.

I didn't want to be tied up. I so much didn't want to be tied up.

He started securing my wrists behind my back. He was using tape. I could smell the adhesive. I struggled, temporarily freeing one arm from his grip. He increased the pressure on my spine with his knee. When I was afraid my back was going to snap, I relented.

He finished my wrists, then he did my ankles.

I felt trussed.

After he was done cinching me he never said a word. But he gave me a hard whack on the side of my head with his hand. It felt like a warning about what was to come.

He stood and stepped over me. For a second, in the darkness of the room, I could see the outlines of his shoes. Black, rubber-soled lace-ups. I hung onto the image as though it were as important a piece of evidence as a strand of DNA. I repeated it to myself. "Blackrubber-soledlaceups. Blackrubbersoledlaceups."

The man cleared his throat and swallowed. He said, "You can't hide." Then he walked out the door of my bedroom and closed the door behind him.

I struggled onto my side and lifted myself to my knees before I lost my balance and fell over again, closer to the wall with the window, farther from the door.

Farther from my baby.

Oh Landon!

Using the window ledge for balance, I somehow managed to get to my feet. I was just about to turn my back to try to manipulate the crank with my cinched hands in order to call for help when I saw a man standing on the sidewalk in front of my town house. He had a small dog on a leash.

He was staring right up at me in the window.

His mouth was open.

The dog on the leash was a little black poodle, its front legs bowed out like Popeye's arms.

The man was Carl Luppo.

I didn't know who the dog was.

9

Carl and Anvil had walked past Peyton's town house once and were looping back to return to his car when Carl sensed some movement in one of the upstairs windows and figured he'd been made. He shrugged and glanced up where he thought he'd seen the movement.

Carl Luppo later chided himself for noticing that Peyton was mostly naked before he noticed that she had a band of tape over her mouth. The two perceptions happened so close together in time, however, that it didn't slow Carl's decisiveness.

Anvil acted as though Carl's sudden sprint to the front door of the town house was an expected part of their evening stroll. The dog flanked his owner step for step, prancing on the end of the lead with his head held high, his prior-life showring memories providing all the behavioral guidance he needed.

Although Carl Luppo wasn't a huge man, his mass wasn't insubstantial, either. Once he'd arrived on Peyton's porch and determined that the door was locked, he lowered his left shoulder and threw his dense weight against Peyton's front door with a ferocity for which he'd found no particular use since his release from prison.

The door didn't budge.

Carl examined the lock. There was a latch *and* a deadbolt. He cursed and tried to ram through the door once more. Twice. The door was made out of metal textured to look like wood. The result of his pounding was the same each time: no movement of the door, definite movement of the structure of Carl's shoulder.

At the sound of the concussions that were made by his master ramming the door, Anvil dropped his tail from an almost perfectly vertical position to a location solidly between his legs.

Convinced the door wasn't going to give, Carl ran to the side of the town house looking for another way in. Other than the big garage door, there wasn't one. He ran back to the front door, took the Longmont Dairy milk box off the porch and threw it through the window that was closest to the front door. He then yanked off his purple Colorado Rockies windbreaker and wrapped it around his right forearm and fist and used the bundle to clear the rest of the glass from the window frame. Then he reached through, turned the dead bolt until it clicked free, and twisted the doorknob.

Carl was inside. The staircase rose straight ahead, the first step maybe ten feet inside the door.

With the commotion of breaking in coming to an end, Anvil regained his composure. He was back in familiar territory at his master's side. His tail popped up and he stayed at Carl's left side as they moved toward the stairs.

Carl hesitated a moment at the foot of the stairs to get his bearings. As he leaned over to touch Anvil on the head, he thought he heard a little cough from the back of the town house. Was that the little girl, he wondered?

Was she down here?

He immediately adjusted his plans, which had been limited to getting upstairs to assist Peyton.

Before he moved in the direction of the cough Carl picked up the dog and placed him on top of a sideboard near the front door. Carl knew that no matter what happened Anvil wouldn't jump from the perch; the dog seemed to be paralyzed by heights—a "height" for Anvil being anything above thirty inches or so.

Carl searched the living room adjacent to the entryway for something he could use as a weapon and came up with a heavy glass vase. He dumped the flowers and water onto the floor and tested the heft of the crystal, holding it by the open end. He smacked the base against his open palm. The base was as solid as a hammer. It would have to do. He grasped the vase in his right hand and moved in the direction that he thought he'd heard the cough.

A narrow hallway led to an empty dining room and then to a galley kitchen and family room. Carl proceeded carefully, examining each space as his eyes adjusted to the darkness. All three rooms appeared empty. Three pine doors led off the kitchen and a sliding glass door separated the family room from a small yard. A broomstick lock braced the sliding glass door. In the distance, Carl could see the silhouette of a wooden fence marking the perimeter of a tiny backyard.

All the doors were closed. He'd have to check them one by one.

10

Landon? Did you run, baby?

As I pressed myself against the window I could hear and could even feel Carl's efforts as he tried to pummel his way through the front door. But he was below me, hidden by the covered porch, and I couldn't see him pounding away.

Cheering him on in my head. *Do it Carl. Do it Carl.*

Finally, after a series of deep thuds, I heard the sound of glass breaking and seconds later could even hear the front door finally swoosh open. I waited to feel the concussion of Carl's heavy footsteps on the stairs.

But the reverberation didn't come.

I wanted to yell to him, "Go check on Landon, first. She's down the hall." But the gag stifled me.

Straining, I thought I could hear him moving around downstairs. But he said nothing to me. He didn't call and tell me he was going to check on my baby. I tried to hop to the door, to get down the hall to her. Instead I fell hard on my face.

IF I COULD have had my dreams come true I would've wanted to say, "Don't worry about Landon, she's gone. She flew away like Mia Hamm. She's safe."

But my dreams were under the control of devils, and instead of all my dreams coming true—instead of that—all the clocks in the house had stopped ticking and my lungs had ceased processing oxygen and my synapses had stopped firing and all the time in my universe stood still. Totally still.

Again.

I was waiting for his next words, it seemed, forever.

Tell me how my baby is, Carl. Tell me how my baby is.

. . .

I HEARD A door open downstairs somewhere and I began to count. At six, the door closed again.

A second door opened. I counted to eight before it closed.

A third door opened. I didn't even get to the number one before I heard a deep hollow thud, the kind of thud that sends shudders through a mother's heart, the kind of thud that says that a child's head has met a dense object and that the object has proved less resilient than the child's head.

I almost threw up into my gag.

A groan, a masculine groan, resonated through the house. It felt as though the baritone wail was going to go on forever, and then the sound stopped as abruptly as a radio being turned off.

For a few seconds no new sounds emerged from downstairs. Then I began to hear scraping noises, as though something was being dragged across the kitchen floor below me.

Another door opened. I remembered to count and got all the way to thirteen before it closed. For almost five minutes I heard nothing else.

Then, finally, I heard footsteps on the stairs and Carl calling out to me, telling me he was going to check on Landon.

I DON'T REMEMBER exactly how I did it, but somehow I hooked the gag on a sharp edge of the bed frame and yanked it from my mouth.

I yelled, "Carl? Landon?" and waited another eon for an answer.

II

Carl came back inside from the garage and paused for a moment before he turned toward what he remembered was the front of the house, in the direction of the stairs that would take him up to the room where he'd seen Peyton standing in the window. He took the pause to allow himself time to begin to catalog all the surfaces he may have touched during the scuffle.

At the front of the house Anvil was sitting precisely where Carl had left him, his perfectly vertical tail wagging maniacally. Carl lifted the dog from the sideboard and lowered him to the floor and side by side the two of them mounted the stairs and moved in the direction Carl had first spotted Peyton.

At the top of the stairs he called out. "Sit tight in there. It's me, Carl. I'm going to check on your kid first." Earlier, Carl had seen the gag in Peyton's mouth; he didn't expect a reply.

He dropped Anvil's leash and took measured strides down the short hall, poking his head into the doors that opened off the second-floor landing. The tiny bathroom was empty. Laundry closet? No, she wasn't there. Another door led to a linen closet that was almost devoid of bedding. Finally Carl entered the door that led to Landon's bedroom and he stopped in the doorway, aware that he was feeling something he hadn't felt in years.

His heart seemed to hollow itself of blood, and he thought for a moment he was going to faint.

Anvil stared up at Carl, his tail still wagging, the retractable leash trailing behind him like a ten-ton anchor on a skiff.

12

When Carl finally walked into my room, I didn't say hello or beg him to untie me. I leaned left and then right to look past him, over his shoulder into the hall, to see the spot where I was sure he'd left my sleeping daughter as he came to untie me.

But she wasn't there.

He helped me to my knees and spun me around and reached for my wrists. He started talking to me, but I couldn't process anything but the sight of the empty hallway. Over my shoulder, I looked again, searching up at the ceiling, down, everywhere. The volume of tears that were flooding into my eyes almost kept me from seeing anything at all.

Finally I heard him. He was saying, "Just one man? That's all?"

The bad man? "Yes. One man. My baby?"

"I told you, she's sleeping. She's all right. It's like nothing happened down there at all."

"My baby, she's all right?"

"Yeah. She's all right. I tell you she's sleeping."

He dropped down to my ankles and tugged at the tape that bound me there. I tried to pull out of the restraint too soon, almost falling on top of him.

"She's breathing?"

A mother's question.

"Sleeping, breathing. The whole thing. I tell you she's fine. The guy who did this to you, I found him downstairs. He came after me. Let's say I prevailed. He's in the trunk of your car right now. Hey, where's Anvil? You see my dog?"

But I was already past him. Down the hall, into her room.

Carl was wrong. My little girl wasn't sleeping. She was sitting up in bed. A little black dog was curled back onto her chest like it was his favorite place to be in the whole world.

Landon looked up at me, puzzled. I realized I was standing almost naked in the doorway to her room. She certainly saw Carl behind me, added two plus two, and got lord-knows-what.

Trying to keep my evaporating terror from dripping into my voice. I said simply, "Hi, baby."

Landon hugged the little animal closer to her, if that was possible. She said, "Mommy, look. Uncle Carl brought his dog."

CARL WATCHED ME pull on my bra. I didn't glance his way to see if he was looking, but I could feel his eyes. I didn't care. I had a thousand questions to ask, a million things to remember.

I said, "I'm not sure what to tell her. When she gets up, she'll see the busted door and the broken glass."

"There's some blood in the kitchen, too. The guy was like hiding in the pantry. I heard him cough."

"Jesus. Me, too. He told me I couldn't hide."

Carl said, "He said that? I wonder what the hell that meant. Tell your kid you scared a bad guy away. Maybe that'll be enough. With kids, sometimes less is more."

I was surprised at his perspicacity. "With her, I've always called him the 'bad man.' The man who killed her father and chased us from Louisiana."

"Fine. Tell her you scared the bad man away. And that Anvil and I came over to help."

I tugged a T-shirt over my head. I couldn't see Carl's face as I said, "I can't figure out who it was, Carl."

"I can't either," he said. "He looked like a damn marine. I think maybe a cop."

"A marshal?" I asked.

"I don't know. Didn't say that. You want to go see him?"

"Did he say he was a marshal?"

"By the time I was done making introductions he wasn't doing much talking. No ID on him. You want to go take a look, see if you recognize him?"

I took a deep breath and asked, "Is he . . . dead, Carl?"

"Nah. Unconscious though. I hit him on the side of the head with the vase you had in the living room."

I shivered. The vase was crystal. Cheap crystal. But crystal. *Ouch.* "What was he going to . . . ?" Finishing the sentence meant imagining a sequence of things that was too horrible to imagine. Instead, I asked, "He was hiding when you came in?"

"Maybe he heard me out front trying to get in. Temporarily hid in the pantry and was planning to run when I went upstairs. But I didn't go upstairs."

"It's possible," I said. But I was puzzling out the bigger question, wondering why whoever it was *was* hiding under my bed. If he was already in my house long enough to hide in my bedroom, then he would already have had plenty of time to hurt Landon, or grab her. Or to go through the house and steal something.

"Carl, do you think the police are on the way?"

He shrugged his shrug. "Maybe. You can never tell about neighbors. Sometimes they hear things. Sometimes their TVs are on and they don't hear jack. Sometimes they call the cops. Sometimes they don't want to get involved. In my experience, there's no telling what the general public's gonna do. One of the great mysteries of my business. My former business."

I turned my back to him before I pulled on some jeans. I don't know why I did that. It felt less like modesty, more like something else.

"Carl?" I said.

"Yeah."

"Can you give us a ride somewhere tonight?"

He digested my request and answered with a question of his own. "You going on the run?"

"Do you really want to know? It could be complicated for you."

His eyes twinkled. "I've been thinking that my life's way too simple. Yeah, I want to know."

His sarcasm made me smile. "Then yes, we're going on the run." It felt odd saying it out loud.

He asked, "You never called Ron Kriciak?"

"Nope."

His eyes narrowed. I could almost watch him think. "It's not easy, you know. Disappearing. Especially on your own."

The phone rang. I listened as the machine picked up and as whoever was calling hung up without leaving a message.

I said to Carl, "Too many people are after me. I don't trust the marshals. I don't feel we have much choice left." He didn't respond. I added, "I bought some books, you know, on how to disappear. I've been preparing since the minute we got to Boulder." I wanted to appear thoughtful, not impulsive.

"You'll need money."

"I have money."

"Cash. I mean cash."

"I have cash. Quite a bit."

"I'll help you."

I felt that he meant the gesture in a grand way. I was unwilling to commit to that since it required trust I knew I couldn't muster and reliance I didn't think I could risk. I said, "You've done so much already, thanks. But maybe a few more little things. The closet downstairs, the one by the front door? There're two duffel bags in it. Grab them for me, okay? Put them by the door. Oh, and get the cooler out of the pantry in the kitchen. Put it by the sink. Throw some ice cubes into the bottom."

He said, "Sure. I'll be a few extra minutes. There's some things I have to wipe first, in case anybody shows up to dust for prints." He headed out the door toward the stairs, stopped. "You should take a look at this guy, see if you can make him."

"Yeah. I'll be down."

Some damsel I am.

Think, Peyton, think! Duffel bags—check. Money—check. Food—check. Purse—check.

Landon—check.

I called to her down the hall. "We're out of here in two minutes, baby. You're dressed?"

Despite the hour, Landon was wide-awake, cooperative, and energetic. She loved commotion and intensity when it was right in her face. It focused her. It was her goal-keeper mentality. "I'm all set, Mommy. Can we bring Anvil?"

"Anvil will need to stay with Uncle Carl. We really can't take a dog with us tonight."

"Where are we going?"

"On another adventure, baby. On another adventure."

"Back to Louisiana?"

"I don't think so."

When she asked, "Do I have to keep my old name, Mommy. Or do I get to pick a new one?" I heard excitement in her voice but also something else, something unexpected, some wariness.

Give her a little control. "We'll decide together, you and I. How's that?"

"Cool."

"What about Uncle Carl?"

Yes, I thought, *what about Uncle Carl?*

"I have to check something in the garage for a minute with Uncle Carl. Will you take care of Anvil?"

"Sure!"

chapter seven

RUNNING IN PLACE

I

I didn't have to think about what to do next. I'd already carefully choreographed the next few steps, although Carl's willingness to help with the plan gave me some unexpected flexibility.

Of course, if the police showed up before we were out the door of the town house, everything would go to hell. I hadn't counted on broken front windows and men trying to bust down my door.

WHAT WAS NEXT? I called Yellow Cab and ordered a car.

When the dispatcher asked me for a destination, I said DIA, Denver's airport. The driver arrived about five minutes later. I loaded the duffels and the cooler into the trunk and hustled Landon into the backseat. I kept my face down as I told the driver to take me to the Boulder bus station, the one downtown between Canyon and Walnut near the Pearl Street Mall.

"I thought we were going to the airport?" He sounded indignant and disappointed. The fare he would earn had just dropped by about fifty dollars.

"No, I told your dispatcher I was taking a bus to the airport. We just need to get to the bus station." The ruse was a small misdirection that I hoped might cause the marshals a few moments of confusion as they tried to determine whether Landon and I actually took a bus or a plane to get out of town.

The driver muttered "Shit" under his breath, and I watched Landon roll her eyes. She was still at a stage in her life where she was amused at the inappropriate behavior of grown-ups.

The drive across town took a little more than ten minutes. I think we missed every light, and I think I imagined that every car next to us had at least one passenger who peered into the backseat of the cab.

I lugged our stuff into the deserted waiting room on the Fourteenth Street side of the bus station and five minutes later, exactly as I'd requested, Carl and Anvil drove up to the curb. Carl stayed in the car as I transferred my daughter and our belongings into the backseat.

Anvil was happy to see us.

At my direction, Carl drove into a residential area behind the University of Colorado—an area the locals call The Hill—and backtracked down some small streets west of Sixth. It's an old neighborhood with mature trees and houses that look like their eyes are always half-closed. I asked Carl to pull over to the curb right on the curve where Sixth runs into Euclid. We watched the road in both directions for over a minute. While he spied the macadam for tails, I joined him in the front seat, pulled a floppy hat over my hair, and tugged a black cotton cardigan sweater over my T-shirt. I threw a baseball cap and a polyester soccer jersey at Landon. The baseball cap read "AF" and the jersey read "Scurry" on the back. Ever since the '99 World Cup, she had been Landon's favorite goalkeeper.

Landon pulled the jersey on without protest. I was shocked at her generous cooperation. And I was grateful. I assumed that Anvil was responsible for her benevolent mood.

"I don't see a tail. Certainly don't see that big white thing that Ron's been driving lately," Carl said. "So what's our destination? Canada or Mexico? I'll probably need to get gas."

His humor was so dry that I almost missed it. I pointed straight out the windshield, up the steep slope that Sixth Street makes as it climbs south toward the Flatirons. "We're going right up there, Carl. I rented a cottage at Chautauqua. There's a whole bunch of little cabins that the festival built back at the beginning of the century. I paid my new landlady with cash and gave a fake name. She's a sweet little thing in her eighties who thinks I'm hiding from an abusive husband. So that's where we're going. At least for a while."

I watched him raise his eyebrows a little, whether in response to the thoroughness of my preparations or in response to the trust I'd just placed in him, I wasn't certain. He changed his position on his seat, stretched his thick neck, and fiddled with the vent on the driver's side of the dashboard even though neither the heat nor the air-conditioning was turned on.

He said, "You're running in place then?"

"That's the plan for now. Until I know who I'm up against. I've been preparing for this from the moment I arrived in Boulder. I assume that the marshals are going to think I'm going someplace else."

"That's why you were so worried that Ron followed you to that restaurant up there the other day? Am I right? You were afraid he saw you go to your little rented cottage? That's where you went after you had lunch that day?"

"That's right."

"What can I do?"

I handed him a sheet of paper with the address of the cottage and a penciled map of the confusing little lanes of Chautauqua. Our cottage was on Kinnikinic near Lupine. It backed onto the sprawling open space that led up to the Flatirons. "Drop us at the front door of the Chautauqua Dining Hall now like you're leaving us off for dinner and then drive right back out and kill a little time. Sometime in the next fifteen minutes or so come back and leave our things on the porch of the cottage. The porch is screened in but the door is always open. Be as inconspicuous as you can be. Don't linger there. Don't knock. There's a back door Landon and I are going to use to get in. We'll enter from the hiking trail."

"Food?"

"Already stocked."

"Money?"

"I have plenty."

"Really? I can get you some."

"Really, I have a lot. Thousands."

"That's serious. And after tonight?"

"We'll see."

He nodded. "How do I get in touch?"

I reached into my purse and grabbed a pen and another scrap of paper. "Here's the number at the cottage—don't worry, it's in the owner's name, not mine. If you need to reach me, call me twice a minute apart and let the phone ring once each time, then hang up. That will be the signal. We'll meet at Dushanbe—you know, the tea-house—exactly one hour later."

"You'll do the same with me?"

"Yes."

He reached across the front seat and touched my hand. "The other thing I said I'd do? I'm still waiting to hear about the guy who whacked your husband. You know, his current intentions."

I forced a smile. "Thanks," I said. I thought I knew Ernesto Castro's current intentions.

Carl checked his mirrors and began to pull away from the curb. He asked Landon if her seat belt was clicked. I wouldn't have guessed that hit men were the kind of people who checked their mirrors and insisted that children fasten their seat belts before they pulled away from the curb. Two minutes later we were gliding to a stop in front of the Chautauqua Dining Hall. I got out of the car and encouraged Landon to let go of the dog. She gave Anvil a last hug and kiss, and then one or two more.

Carl said, "Bye, Peyton. You take care."

"You too, Carl. Thanks for the help. And Carl?"

"Yeah?"

"Great dog."

"Thanks." He smiled at me.

Landon said, "Yeah, Uncle Carl. Anvil's a great dog."

Carl said, "You know, maybe it was just an asshole who broke into your house. Maybe it was nothing."

I leaned into the car. "I wish that were true. But I think somebody was trying to send me a message, Carl. It's my job to hear it."

And with that, we were off on our adventure. I reached into my purse for two lollipops.

I only had one.

I gave it to Landon.

She would have preferred a Twix, but I didn't have any of those.

2

Barb was munching on what she'd promised herself was her absolute last slice of pizza when the phone rang. She paused Will Smith on her DVD and said, "Hello." She expected some news from the front desk. She didn't expect a voice call from Atlanta.

"It's Prowler."

Barb sat up straighter. She moved the laptop from her thighs to an empty spot on the mattress on her right.

"Yes."

"Tomorrow."

"Time?"

"Before she's home from work. Midday would be ideal."

"Same as we originally discussed?"

"Make it look just like what we know about New Orleans. Your equipment is ready?"

"Yes."

"Don't bother to confirm. I'll get my confirmation on the news. Your departure plan?"

"I'll return my rental car to DIA. Take a bus to Colorado Springs. I'll fly from there to Columbus. From Columbus I drive home."

A loud pounding on the door interrupted their conversation.

"Somebody's here. Probably housekeeping. Anything else?"

"Have a good trip."

Carl Luppo paused after pounding on the door of the motel cabin. He'd heard her talking. He knew she was in there.

CARL LUPPO DIDN'T like road work. He never had. Thought he probably never would. And this felt like road work. He was in a town he didn't know too well. He was visiting a strange motel. And he was calling on a woman he didn't know at all.

This definitely qualified as road work.

He allowed himself a moment of self-doubt before he pounded for the second time on the heavy wooden door of the cabin at the Foot of the Mountain Motel. The effort reverberated up his arm to the shoulder that he had bruised an hour or so earlier in his ill-fated attempt to bust down Peyton's front door. No way he was putting that shoulder into this monster door.

No way.

Through the closed door a voice, almost feminine, almost without accent, said, "What do you want?"

"I'm Phil—I'm from Blackjack. We delivered you a pizza before. Turns out there's like a problem."

Carl saw the woman's eye shadow the peephole in the middle of the door. He stood his ground but made certain that she couldn't see his hands. The gloves he was wearing might make her suspicious.

She said, "You're not the kid who delivered my pizza."

"Exactly. That's the problem. I'm his manager. He's disappeared. We can't find him. We need to talk to you."

"I don't know anything about it. I can't help you."

Carl shrugged, just in case she was watching. "I don't find him on my own, I'm going to have to call the police."

After a delay of about ten seconds, the door opened maybe a foot. Carl smiled. Until then he hadn't seen the woman out of her car. She was a small person, maybe a little thick in the hips. He liked his advantage sizewise.

Weaponswise? The jury was still out. But Carl suspected that the advantage wasn't his.

She smiled right back at him. Her eyes said she didn't really mean it. Carl noted that.

With barely disguised attitude, she said, "What can I do for you? He was here—what?—over an hour ago. He delivered my pizza. Mushroom and Canadian bacon." She hooked her thumb over her shoulder, pointing at the box behind her on the bed. "Then he left."

Carl was analyzing the situation while he listened to her speak. He'd already seen both her hands. They were empty. The part of the room he could see was neat except for the pizza box and a couple cans of soda on the floor by the bed.

He'd already decided that he thought maybe they should talk.

He took a half-step into the doorway, making certain his heavy shoe would block the arc of the door before it could find his face.

Her eyes flicked up to Carl's eyes, the long muscles in her legs and arms tensed, and she spun on the ball of her right foot, turned rapidly to her right, and lunged behind the open door.

Carl was impressed by the woman's quickness, but he had anticipated the move she made behind the door, and he had her face down on the floor and was on top of her in five seconds. He kicked the door closed behind him while he put some serious pressure on the back of her neck with his forearm. He knew it probably felt to her like her spine was about to snap like a pretzel stick.

He felt like a gorilla again.

It had been a while but, he thought, it was just like riding a bike.

From his vantage on top of her he could see a camera. Even though it was on top of a chest of drawers across the room, he could tell it wasn't the familiar shape of his old 35mm Canon.

He said, "You been taking pictures?"

He released just enough pressure so she could talk. "I'm a tourist for Christ's sake—tourists take pictures," she said.

Carl ignored her protests. It was apparent that she wasn't frightened enough yet. That happened sometimes. Especially with pros. Not as often as you might think, though. Carl said, "That's one of those new digital cameras? You use it with that computer? It develops them electronically? Is that how it works?"

"Something . . . ahhhhgh . . . like that." She rasped, "Yes, yes, it's a digital camera. You can have it, the computer, too. Oh my god! You can have anything you want."

Carl slowly increased the pressure on her neck. "I'm glad to hear you say that. Cause it turns out I do want something. Not your camera though. I think what I want is some information."

Desperation and relief in her voice, she said, "Anything."

"Who you workin' for?"

He felt her muscles slacken, and then she farted loudly. Carl smiled to himself. Aside from having to tolerate the smell, he thought, it was better than a fuckin' lie-detector test.

He gave her five seconds or so to decide to respond to his question before he renewed the pressure on her spine. He was out of practice and hoped he didn't cross the line unintentionally. His experience had taught him that the bones tended to snap loudly when he crossed the line.

Just like a saltine—no warning.

After a moment the woman kicked the floor two or three times with the toes of both feet, alternating her legs, like a baby throwing a tantrum. Considering that it might be a message from her indicating a tendency toward future cooperation, Carl lightened up a little with his forearm.

She coughed and made choking noises.

Carl said, "I really can't understand a thing you're saying."

"I'm a fifth-grade teacher," she said, her voice as raspy as a man dying in the Mojave.

"Yeah, and I'm a priest who works with lepers." He paused. "'Cept I'm not as patient or as generous as Father Damien, you know what I mean? That's a .22 pistol on the table behind the door. What's a teacher need with one of those?"

She panted. Grunted. But she didn't answer. Carl didn't care. He knew the .22 was a rotten gun for a teacher to carry for protection. But it was a great gun for an assassin planning some close-up work.

"So let's start with an easier question. What's your name?"

"Barbara, Barbara Turner."

"You been taking pictures of a friend of mine, Barbara Barbara Turner. Notice that wasn't a question. But this is: Why don't you tell me why you been taking pictures of my friend?" He put a few more foot-pounds of pressure on her neck. "I should probably tell you—one more lie and you're dead."

She spit out a single word. "Assignment."

Carl sighed. He was getting into the rhythm of this. So was she. He shrugged, though from Barbara's position she couldn't witness it. "Not a lie exactly. But not terribly forthcoming either. Did I mention I have a knife in my pocket? Let's say you cut the crap or I'll cut your hamstrings. Horizontally, not vertically. One at a time. How's that?"

She farted again.

Carl was growing confident that this woman wasn't accustomed to in-her-face violence. If their roles were reversed he knew he wouldn't be giving an inch. He'd be taunting her, busting her chops, daring her to kill him. He knew he'd go out with attitude.

He said, "Good. I'm thinkin' maybe we understand each other. Who gave you this assignment?"

"Prowler."

"Prowler? Huh? Who the fuck is Prowler? What is that? Is that a first name or a last name?"

"Don't know. It's all I have. He's a guy in Georgia."

"Georgia? Where?"

"It's in the South."

He had to restrain himself from pounding her in the face. "I know where fucking Georgia is. I'm asking where in Georgia."

"Near Atlanta. That's all I know. He runs this agency I . . . work for sometimes. I've never met him."

"Why?"

"Why haven't I met him? He likes it that way. So do I."

"Not why haven't you met him, why did he send you to take pictures of my friend? That's a normal thing for fifth-grade teachers to do on vacation? I'm supposed to believe that?"

"I don't know. He never tells me why. I don't ask. A client . . . made a request, I guess."

"You guess? So what kind of agency is this you work for?"

"We do investigations."

"Investigations?" Carl's voice aptly conveyed his skepticism.

"We find people. Information."

"Yeah right. So how do you reach Prowler with this information?"

"Phone. E-mail."

"Does he already have the pictures you took? You sent them to him over the computer? On the Internet, like?"

"Yes."

"You want to give me Prowler's number?"

She spit out the number and the e-mail address, and Carl had her repeat them twice more while he committed them to memory. Memory calisthenics was something he had practiced while he was in the penitentiary after he'd read some of John Lucas's memory books.

"You're doing much better. Let's not lose any momentum here. So I'm wondering something else. You have a partner? Somebody you're working with on this assignment from this guy in Georgia called Prowler?"

"No, no, no. I always work alone."

"No guy with black lace-up shoes?"

"What? No, no. I promise. It's just me. I work alone."

Carl weighed her response for honesty. "So there's nobody you sent to visit my friend tonight?"

Fear swelling in her voice, she said, "I swear."

He thought she was telling the truth. But her answer worried him. If the guy who threw mattresses and tied up Peyton wasn't with Barbara Barbara Turner, who was he with? Was it really a marshal?

Something else was worrying Carl. He was straddling a line that he'd never expected to straddle again in his life. He was going to have to decide whether this woman lived or whether she died. Either way, he knew that Barbara Barbara Turner wasn't going to complete the hit on Peyton. If Carl allowed this woman to live she'd get out of town as fast as she could. But Prowler would interpret the leniency as a sign of weakness on Carl's part. Carl knew that his appearing weak wouldn't be helpful to Peyton's longtime survival.

And appearing weak wasn't exactly part of Carl's persona.

"What else can you tell me? I'm looking for something that might increase my compassion, maybe."

Barbara Turner was silent. Carl guessed at the pathway that her thinking was taking. Should she be a hero and suffer like hell? Or should she give it up and suffer only a little bit?

Carl allowed her almost half a minute, then said, "Well?"

"Prowler once said she had to be done at the same time as two others. I don't know anything more about it, but obviously there're others involved."

"But you don't have anything to do with the others?"

"That's right."

"And he said 'the same time'? Prowler said that?"

"Yes."

Carl considered his next question carefully. "So you were going to kill her? My friend?"

They both felt the hesitation. They were both aware that the other one felt the hesitation.

"Yes," she blurted. "Yes. Yes. Yes. I was."

"When?"

"Tomorrow."

Barb knew she was dead before her neck snapped.

3

It was late, after eleven o'clock, when Alan Gregory flicked off the lights and climbed into bed beside Lauren. He kissed her on the lips and then he kissed her about five times on her taut belly. He said, "Good night, both of you. I love you."

Lauren rolled from her back to her side so she was facing him. She said, "Did you decide to call Sam about that . . . patient?"

The room was too dark and his eyes hadn't adjusted. He couldn't see any definition in her eyes. "What?"

"You were thinking of calling Sam Purdy to send a patrol car by that patient's house? Did you end up calling him?"

"No. She never called back."

"So you think that means she's okay?"

"That's what I usually try to tell myself."

Lauren rearranged the pillows she used to support her abdomen and her legs. "It could mean the opposite."

With a little mirth injected into his tone, he said, "It would be awkward for me to get through life thinking that way. I try to interpret not hearing from patients as a sign that they're doing well. The alternative is unnerving."

She said, "Oh." The single syllable expanded like a gas, filling the entire room. He had no choice but to inhale her doubt.

He asked, "What does that mean?"

"I don't know. Maybe this isn't a usual patient."

"Maybe," he said.

She asked, "Do you ever get feelings?"

"Like intuition? Those kinds of feelings?"

"I guess."

"Sometimes."

"Me, too," Lauren said.

The phone rang.

Alan answered, listened for a moment, covered the receiver with his open palm and said, "It's for you, sweets; it's police dispatch. You're on call tonight? I didn't know."

First she nodded, then she shook her head. As she reached across him to grab the phone, she explained, "I'm backup."

Into the phone she said, "This is Lauren Crowder." For about a minute she listened without asking a single question. Finally she said, "Of course, I'll hold while you patch me through."

A MINUTE OR so later she threw back the duvet that covered her visibly pregnant body and swung her legs over the edge of the bed. She forced a smile onto her face as she handed Alan the phone so he could hang it back up.

"I'm either too old or too pregnant for this," she said.

"What is it?"

"Apparent homicide at a little motel at the west end of Arapahoe. The Foot of the Mountain. Do you know it? I'm wanted at the scene."

"Yeah, I do know it. It's charming, but I don't think that's the point. Why don't you get somebody else to do it? Who's your backup tonight? Call them. I'm sure they'll understand."

"I told you already, I *am* the backup. Fred's catching tonight, but his wife's out of town and his kid's real sick. I think she has the croup. It's a small crime scene; my part shouldn't take that long."

"It's a homicide, right? You'll be gone until the middle of the night, and you know it." He paused before he added, "You won't catch the case, will you? You're about to go on maternity leave."

"No, I'm just covering for Fred. There's no way that they would assign me a homicide this late in my pregnancy."

"Was that Sam on the phone? Is this going to be his?"

Their friend, Sam Purdy, was one of the felony-team detectives eligible to catch homicides. She nodded. "That was Sammy. I'll say hi for you."

Five minutes later she was dressed and out the door.

4

Alan was still awake when Lauren crawled back into bed at a quarter to three. All she had to say about the murder at the motel was that no witnesses had come forward, and that it didn't look like it was going to be an easy case unless the victim's husband or boyfriend did it.

He asked if she was going to catch the case.

Lauren said, "I already told you no." Her tone clearly indicated she didn't want to discuss the motel murder anymore.

Alan rubbed her lower back for a few minutes as she struggeld to find a comfortable way to rest her big belly on a pillow. After a minute or two, she stuffed another one between her thighs.

From the rhythm of her breathing he could tell that she found sleep long before he did.

The alarm stunned them awake after only a few hours.

5

Ron Kriciak pulled his pickup truck down Peyton's street at seven-twenty on Wednesday morning and slowed to a stop a couple of doors away from her town house.

He was uncomfortable with the level of monitoring he was doing with Peyton. In most circumstances Ron was a proponent of allowing the witnesses he was watching to make it or break it on their own. He didn't like sitting on his witnesses like a damn chicken on an egg, but the message he was getting from Fenster Kastle was clear: If Peyton sneezed, Kastle wanted Ron close enough to hand her a tissue.

Since Peyton hadn't answered her phone when Ron had called at eight forty-five the night before, he figured he'd better stop by, check on her, make sure that everything was okay.

Five seconds after he eased the truck to a stop, it was clear to him that everything wasn't okay.

The front window of the town house was broken out.

Ron stopped the truck and felt for the weapon in his shoulder holster before he killed the engine. He pulled latex gloves from under the seat. Despite an acute sense of alarm, he managed to approach the house with practiced nonchalance. On the porch, he dialed Peyton's number on his cell phone with one hand while he tried the doorbell with the other. The doorbell rang loudly through the missing window. But no one came to the door. After the phone pealed three times, Ron held the cell phone away from his ear and listened to the ringing that was coming from inside the house. When the answering machine kicked in, he reached into his jacket pocket and yanked out the latex gloves, pausing to snap them onto his hands. He tried the front door knob. It was locked. Ron couldn't decide if the locked door was a good sign or a bad one. In the end he figured it didn't really matter. He pulled his gun from its holster, checked the slide, reached through the broken window, and let himself into the house.

. . .

OTHER THAN THE broken glass on the floor below the window, Ron saw no immediate signs of damage. In his peripheral vision he noticed that some flowers and water had been dumped on the living room carpet. He wondered about it but couldn't generate any hypotheses to match that evidence.

He sniffed the air but his nose found no clues.

With a fingertip he caressed the safety on his handgun to convince himself it was off before he moved past the dining room toward the kitchen and family room.

Trouble.

The pantry door was open and groceries were spilled all over the floor. Spatters, smears, and streaks of blood led from the pantry toward a door on the far side of the kitchen. Ron guessed the door led to the garage.

A crystal vase lay on its side in the kitchen sink. Ron remembered the flowers and water that he'd seen on the floor in the living room. He had *A* and he had *B*. But he still wasn't sure what they added up to. He didn't have *C*.

On the coffee table in the family room lay an open copy of John Irving's *The Cider House Rules*. The center of the book had been hollowed out with a razor. The cache was now empty.

Ron debated following the blood. He didn't; instead, he backtracked and climbed the stairs, hoping he would find Peyton and the kid. Fearing he would find Peyton and the kid.

Walking into the master bedroom he said, "Shit."

Used duct tape was strewn about the room. Two distinct bundles of sticky gray bands lay in the middle of the carpet and one smaller piece of less than six inches in length rested closer to the window. The mattress, box spring, pillows, and bedding were tossed haphazardly all over the floor. A metal bed frame and oak headboard sat naked across the room.

Ron surmised a struggle had taken place in the room and guessed that the duct tape had been used to restrain someone.

Peyton?

As good a guess as any.

The master bath was, to Ron's eye, unremarkable.

In his cursory examination he didn't notice that it contained neither a hairbrush nor a toothbrush.

Down the hall he found that the girl's room was messy but intact. The bed had been slept in.

Ron retraced his steps, descended the stairs, and once again pondered all the pieces of the puzzle. He couldn't get them to configure into a recognizable form.

He decided that it was time to follow the blood and check the garage.

He crossed the kitchen, opened the door to the garage, and flicked on the overhead light. Peyton's car was in the center of the space, which was designed to hold two cars. Ron being Ron, he noted that the sedan needed to be washed. But he was surprised that the vehicle was there at all. By then he'd expected to find it gone along with Peyton.

He blinked twice as though clearing his vision would make the vehicle disappear. Even after he blinked though, the sedan was still there. And it was still dirty.

Ron stepped down a single concrete step into the garage. Without opening the doors he peeked into the car. The interior was empty.

He moved around to the driver's side, opened the door, leaned inside, and popped the trunk latch before he stepped to the back of the car.

As he raised the lid he said, "I don't believe this."

He used his gloved fingers to check the man in the trunk for a pulse before he flipped open his cell phone and hit the speed dial for Fenster Kastle's number in Washington, D.C.

FENSTER WASN'T AT his desk. It took someone over a minute to locate him.

"It's Ron Kriciak and this isn't a secure phone, Fenster."

"Yes."

"I'm at her house. It's not even eight o'clock in the morning here and it appears that she's gone absent. Circumstances unknown. One of ours—repeat—one of ours—is unconscious in the trunk of her car.

Apparent head injury. Hell, *definite* head injury. House shows signs of break-in and struggle."

"Which one of ours?"

"You want a name?"

"No, I want hobbies and make of car. Then I'll try and guess the guy's identity. Lordy."

"He's a local guy named Ficklin. You know him?"

"First name?"

"Ernest. Ernie."

"Should he know where she is? Is he on this client and somehow I don't know about it?"

"No way," admitted Ron.

Kastle exhaled loudly. "Get him some medical help and do it quietly. Once he's in the hospital, get a guard on him and isolate him like he's POTUS and the rest of the world has malaria. You understand what I'm saying? The second he's alert and talking, I want to know. Don't even think about talking to him before I do."

"Yes, sir."

"Back to our friend. Is she on the run or has she been abducted?"

"I couldn't say."

"Then guess."

"There's duct tape in her bedroom. It looks like it was used as a restraint. I'd guess abducted."

The line went quiet long enough for Ron to become nervous all over again.

"I want to know what happened in that house, and I want to know where she went, with whom, and when. Any resources you need locally, we'll arrange. Are the local authorities involved?"

"It does not appear so."

"Good. Keep it that way."

"Sir."

"I want updates on a secure line on the half-hour starting at eight-thirty your time."

"Yes, sir."

6

Dr. Alan Gregory was about a dozen or so blocks away from Peyton's cottage in Chautauqua. He was in his Walnut Street office, only a few minutes into his second psychotherapy appointment of the day. Over his patient's left shoulder he noticed a little light flash red on his office wall, indicating that his *next* patient had arrived. The red light distracted him briefly because it appeared to indicate that his next patient—a woman who had never been on time for anything in her life—had actually arrived forty minutes early for her appointment.

His current patient was relatively new to his practice—this was only her third visit to his office. She was a thirty-four-year-old single woman named Kelli Wynton who was suffering during a relatively chronic phase of what he liked to call *Self/Savvy*-itis. He suspected that as a younger woman Ms. Wynton may also have endured the common, milder form of the disease—*Cosmo*-itis—and may indeed have been one of those troubled adolescents who suffered from the earliest known form of the illness—*Seventeen*-itis.

Ms. Wynton's conception of her mental well-being was largely shaped by her reading of her own inadequacies based on articles and surveys in the latest issues of the popular women's magazines. That limited perspective left her totally immune to recognition of the impact of issues that may actually have been germane to her mental health.

While Dr. Gregory was distracted by the little red light beaming on the wall, Ms. Wynton was talking about the methods she was employing to get men to call her back after the first date. The methods apparently weren't working with anything approaching a satisfying degree of certainty.

The therapist's eyes left Kelli's as the red light flashed off, then on again. He hoped she hadn't noticed.

The patient had just begun explaining with apparent pride that she got a lot of first dates. Two, most weeks. Sometimes three.

A minute into her protracted conclusion that the frequency of first dates must mean she was an attractive person, the light flashed off again, then immediately on once more. Dr. Gregory heard a distant thumping bass begin powering its way through the well-soundproofed walls of the office suite. His patient didn't seem to take any notice of the percussion.

Dr. Gregory listened to the muffled sound of his partner, Diane, calling out from the hallway outside his office, "Excuse me, you can't go back there. No! Don't go in there; he's in session."

Seconds later the door flew open and Ron Kriciak walked in. He was wearing a paisley tie on a chambray work-shirt and some green cotton pants that had never seen an iron. He held his arms away from his sides and puffed out his chest like a chimpanzee. "I need to talk to you," he said, nodding to Alan Gregory. His voice was accusatory—the tone a parent might employ when bursting into a teenager's room just after receiving a phone call from the principal.

Trying to remain calm, Alan stood and replied, "This is not okay, Ron. I'm with someone right now. If you need to talk with me, you can call and make an appointment like everyone else." To his patient, Alan said, "I'm sorry for the interruption. I'll handle this as quickly as I can."

"I called. I got your damn recording. This cannot wait for you to return my call 'as soon as possible.' It's an actual emergency. A real live life-and-death emergency," Ron said.

"Then go have a seat in the waiting room. Give me a few minutes to wrap this—"

Ron said, "No." He turned to the patient and a badge materialized in his hand. "Ma'am? I'm a U.S. marshal and this is official government business. Would you please step out of the office for a moment and wait down the hall in the waiting room for your doctor? I appreciate your cooperation. He'll be with you as soon as he is done cooperating with me."

Alan faced Ron and said, "No. *You* go wait in the waiting room. She and I will find a quick place to stop and I'll be right with you."

Kelli Wynton stood and moved toward the doorway. "No, no, no. I think I'll just go," she said. "Really, it's not a problem for me." She almost sprinted out the door in the direction of the waiting room. She hadn't bothered to collect her purse or the top to her pale blue sweater set.

Alan saw Diane loitering in the hall outside the office, her cordless phone in one hand, the other poised above the alarm-system panic button that was mounted on the wall. He raised a palm, encouraging her to hold off.

"Ron," he said, "what the hell do you think you're doing busting in here like this?"

"She's gone. Peyton has disappeared. We can't find her."

Alan immediately thought about her phone call the night before and her sense that someone from the Marshals Service was following her. He tried to comprehend the gravity of what Ron was telling him. He turned to the open doorway first and said, "I think it's okay, Diane. Thanks for your help." She frowned at what she perceived to be her partner's total lack of judgment and moved out of his sight down the hall. Alan didn't hear her office door close and assumed that Diane was loitering in the hall within listening range.

Alan faced Ron and asked, "I don't get it. What do you mean that Peyton's disappeared?"

"I went by her house this morning. She wasn't there. Her house is a shambles. Broken glass, tossed furniture. That's the kind of disappeared that I mean."

"Jesus," Alan said.

"So do you know where she is?" Ron demanded.

Alan shook his head, then explained what the gesture actually meant. He said, "Ron, you've been dealing with Teri Grady for a while on other cases. I'm sure you know that I couldn't tell you even if I did." He hoped Ron was able to translate those words into, "No, I don't know where she is."

Ron folded his arms and tilted his head to one side. "You *are* going to tell me what you know."

Alan thought Ron looked like a bouncer. "First, how about you tell me what you know. And don't threaten me, Ron. I don't react well to it."

"Don't be cute, Doctor. She may be in serious danger."

"I'm hearing that from you loud and clear. Please understand that. But if she is, I know nothing about it." He wondered if that was exactly true. Peyton had told him the night before that she was concerned that someone was following her around with a camera. It had been his impression at the time that Peyton thought it was someone from WITSEC.

Ron asked, "Do you know any reason that she might have run?"

"Run? What makes you think she ran? I thought you were worried that she might have been abducted or killed. You said her house was busted up."

"If she's been abducted, then she's already dead. If she ran, I still might be able to save her sorry ass."

Alan moved across the office and shut the door. He pointed to the couch and said, "Have a seat."

Ron sat on the middle of the sofa and spread his legs so that there were about thirty inches between his knees. He leaned forward and rested his weight on his elbows, and the paisley tie he was wearing hung down between his legs like an extra-long floating punctuation mark.

Alan spoke slowly, carefully. "I don't think I know anything that can help you find her, Ron." He let his words settle.

Ron raised his chin. Alan thought he was still trying to look intimidating. "I'll get a court order to make you talk if I need one. I'm not going to mess around with you in these circumstances. There's a different set of priorities here."

Alan struggled to decide whether or not Peyton would want him to trust Ron Kriciak with more information. "There are? I'm sorry, but it doesn't work that way, Ron. I don't know if you've been down this road before, but I have. The courts might subpoena me but they can't make me talk. I won't divulge confidential information from her therapy sessions. The only reasons I could breech her confidence would be if she were in imminent danger, if she threatened someone, or if she hurt a child. That's it. But even that's irrelevant in this circumstance because I don't know anything that will help you find her or help you explain why she is missing. I wish I did."

"She hasn't said anything about feeling like she's in danger? Nothing along those lines? She hasn't mentioned anyplace she might go if she was frightened?"

Alan exhaled and then took a deep breath before he said, "I've gotten the impression from earlier conversations with you that you perceived Peyton as still feeling vulnerable and . . . distrusting of almost everybody, you guys in WITSEC included. I have no reason to argue with that impression. Is that clear enough for you?"

Ron nodded as though he finally heard. "But where she might go if she panicked? She hasn't said anything about that?"

"I don't know anything that can help you there. Nothing."

"Has she had specific concerns about us? About the Marshals Service?"

Alan's eyes said "yes."

Ron said, "Shit." His left foot began tapping. "Has she reported seeing anyone from her previous life?"

Alan stared at him. "I can't tell you what she reported to me. I will state again that I don't know anything to explain the current circumstances other than to support your earlier impressions that she remained frightened of the people who are after her and she remained suspicious of the Marshals Service."

Alan expected that Ron was about to become exasperated by his repeated protestations of privilege. But, instead, Kriciak seemed to be getting the hang of how to translate the conversation.

"Nothing?"

"Sorry, nothing."

"You screwing with me? This is an official interview. I'm a federal officer. I'll get your ass."

"I'm not screwing with you, Ron. Has she done this before? Disappeared overnight?"

Alan noted a hesitation before Ron responded. "We don't watch her all the time. She might have been gone some night. She certainly hasn't reported her window being busted before."

Alan said, "Maybe she went someplace she would feel safe. There's a possibility this could be nothing, then, right? There could be a reasonable explanation."

"Her front window was busted out. Her bedroom furniture was all over the place. There was blood."

"Her car?"

"It's there."

"When's the last time you heard from her, Ron?"

"She was seen yesterday."

Alan noted the awkward construction. "And . . . ?"

"And what?"

"And did whoever saw her yesterday notice anything out of the ordinary in her behavior?"

Ron hesitated again but said, "No."

"Have there been new threats against her?"

"This is my interview."

Alan allowed his mind to find an innocent explanation. He said, "Let's both of us pray that she met a guy, and that her daughter's at a friend's house at a sleepover. Let's pray that's what this is."

Ron stood. "She never talked about being somewhere else to feel safe? Even just in passing?"

"Sorry, Ron."

A MINUTE LATER, Dr. Gregory escorted Kelli Wynton back down the hall into his office. Again, he apologized for the interruption.

She said, "It's fine. It was all kind of exciting." She hesitated. "He's really what he says he is?"

Dr. Gregory nodded.

"Are you in, um, some kind of trouble with . . . him?"

"I do some consulting work for the Marshals Service. The interruption was the result of an unfortunate misunderstanding."

"Oh," she said. "Oh . . ." She reached up and touched the soft spot below her left ear with the index finger of her right hand. "I didn't notice he was wearing a ring. Do you know if he's seeing anybody?"

7

Ron Kriciak used a pay phone, not his cell phone, to call Fenster Kastle in Washington, D.C. Ron was put right through to Kastle in his office in the U.S. Marshals Service.

"You talked to her shrink?" Kastle asked.

Ron said, "Yeah. Just now came out of his office. I don't know if he knows anything or not."

"What do you mean?"

"He's smart enough to know he doesn't have to talk to me, but he seemed to be trying to let me know that he doesn't know anything that might help us. He seemed genuinely surprised by the news."

"We have any leverage with him?"

"Not sure. His wife's a DA. That might help. I'm going to call the woman he's filling in for and see if she has any ideas on how to move him."

"News from our client's town house?"

"Nothing. Still don't have any idea what came down there. Two different intruders is the way it looks. Our guy is only one of them and he's still unconscious. We have word of a cab picking her up last evening at her town house at nine-twenty, taking her and her daughter either to the airport or to the bus station. We're trying to ascertain which."

"I bet bus. She'd need ID at the airport. You're following up on routes and drivers?"

"I agree with your assessment. And yes, we're looking at what directions she could have gone at that time of night."

"The local police are staying away?"

"So far."

"What was our guy doing in that house, Ron?"

"He's not talking yet. I could only speculate."

"Then speculate."

"He didn't like the fact that she was under our protection in the program. He was in her house either to scare her or to plant something that would make her look like a security risk."

Kastle waited. "Yes? You know something else. Don't be playing with me, Ron. It's not a level field we're on."

Ron exhaled. "One of Ficklin's friends lost his job with the program after the stink that our client made to Congress. Ficklin moaned about it constantly."

Kastle growled. "How did he find out she was there?"

"Don't know."

"Find out."

"Yes, sir."

"Keep me informed, Kriciak."

"Yes, sir."

eight

THE TRAIN IN THE PARK

I

My plan for disappearing with Landon covered the basics. Shelter, food, money. It didn't cover the dead time in between.

Landon and I had grown oddly accustomed to being prisoners. Slaughter, Louisiana, had been a prison for us. Boulder was a prison. Bigger, nicer—sure. But a prison's a prison.

This musty old cabin in Chautauqua was going to be a whole different kind of prison. It appeared that for a while we were going to be confined to this cell for twenty something hours a day. That left a lot of dead time.

The time that came between eating-time and sleeping-time.

I had packed our travel Scrabble game, which Landon loved to play. I enjoyed playing Scrabble slightly less than my daughter did, partially because I hadn't beaten her since the day after her eighth birthday. As an alternative to Scrabble we'd gotten into the habit of playing gin rummy games to a thousand. I could still beat her at that occasionally.

The cottage's game cupboard also came with an incomplete set of dominos, a peg-deficient game of Parcheesi, and a Monopoly game that belonged on "Antiques Roadshow."

And we had books. Landon and I, we always had books.

That first night in the cottage I slept on a daybed in the main room and awoke early, my T-shirt stuck to my back. Landon was curled on her side on the double bed in the solitary bedroom. I'd been too paranoid to open any windows the night before, so the cottage in Chautauqua was stuffy and smelled of a half-century of summer sweat. The furnishings in both rooms were Mission pieces, old and scratched and proud. I had a sense that Myrna, my landlord, didn't have any idea how valuable they'd become over the years.

I peed and threw water on my face before I set a kettle on the stove for instant coffee. I ate applesauce from a little plastic tub with a flimsy plastic spoon. The sweet fruit tasted so good I opened a second plastic tub and finished it before the water rolled to a boil.

The telephone rang, and I was so startled by the noise that I almost screamed. The ring wasn't the familiar electronic chirp of my phone at home, but was instead an old-fashioned *rrrrrrrring*. If I disassembled the big black phone that sat on the end table by the sofa, I knew I would actually find a bell inside.

I waited for a second ring, but the phone rang only once. I found my wristwatch on the little table by the front door and watched the second hand sweep smoothly around the clock face. As the second hand moved, I parted the curtains on both sides of the living room and examined the quiet little lane in front of the cottage. The same few cars were visible that had been visible the night before. I didn't expect to see anything suspicious, and I didn't.

After a little less than one full rotation of the second hand the bell blasted again. *Rrrrrrrrring.*

I waited. No additional sounds.

Carl.

It was seven twenty-three. I'd been on the run less than twelve hours and he already wanted to talk.

. . .

OKAY, IN HINDSIGHT maybe I should have prepared Landon for the wheelchair.

When I went into the bedroom to rouse her after Carl's call she awakened cranky and disoriented. No, she wasn't eager to have her hair darkened to black. She didn't like the sunglasses I'd picked out for her. She thought the clothes I'd chosen were "the epitome of disgusting."

Studying spelling had swollen Landon's vocabulary beyond reason. Frequently I was proud. Often I was amused. Occasionally I was annoyed. This was one of my annoyed times. I said, "It's *e-pit-o-me*, not *ep-a-tome*."

"What-ever. Then these clothes you want me to wear are the *e-pit-o-me* of disgusting."

I told her that was the point. She looked at me as though I was insane, and for the fifth or sixth time in twelve hours I wondered if I was.

I actually thought of calling Ron Kriciak and asking for his help. One phone call, and Landon and I would soon be in the back of a U.S. Marshals Service van with two or three armed babysitters. The van would have opaque windows, and my daughter and I would awaken the next day in Omaha or Fresno or Walla Walla.

There was only one problem. I knew in my heart that there was a fifty-fifty chance that the man I'd last seen in the trunk of my car *was* a U.S. marshal. Were I to call Ron, I would have even less confidence that WITSEC and the marshals could protect us than I'd had when we'd arrived in Boulder. And I still wouldn't have any idea why Ron had been following me around town or why the man with the black lace-up shoes had been hiding under my bed.

LANDON'S HAIR FRESHLY dyed, mine under a beret, I coaxed her onto the wheelchair and began the long journey into Boulder from our Chautauqua cottage. Landon pouted for the first six blocks, wouldn't even play spelling games with me. She somehow managed to find at least three opportunities to use the word *epitome* in a sentence. Each time her pronunciation was perfect.

She seemed especially annoyed that the wheelchair didn't come equipped with a steering wheel.

I cursed Robert and missed him like a drowning man misses air.

THE OLD CHAUTAUQUA site enjoys prime Boulder real estate near the top of Baseline Road just before Baseline begins its steep ascent into the foothills of the Rocky Mountains. The turn-of-the-last-century Chautauqua complex of meeting rooms, auditoriums, and small summer cottages fills a few precious acres that stretch below the vast open space that leads up a steep slope to the base of the vaulting Flatirons. The Chautauqua site is high, with spectacular views to the west, north, and east. It's isolated on the very edge of town. There's precious little traffic.

From the moment I found the ad for the cabin in the want ads, I thought it would be a great place to hide for a while.

But it's a long way on foot from Baseline Road to the Dushanbe Teahouse. By the time I'd pushed Landon's wheelchair as far as the commercial district on The Hill, which was still a few blocks from the teahouse, I'd already decided that I was going to need to come up with a different meeting place for any future meetings with Carl Luppo. I'd also decided that on our return trip, Landon and I were going to take the city bus system as far back toward Chautauqua as we could. The route from Chautauqua to downtown Boulder was almost all downhill. The route from downtown Boulder back to Chautauqua definitely wasn't.

WE DIDN'T MAKE it to Dushanbe on time. The plan called for our arrival sixty minutes after Carl's twin phone calls. We actually arrived eighty-five minutes later. I paused on the sidewalk outside the teahouse to remind Landon to act cool when she spotted Carl. I wheeled her inside, and I immediately saw Carl despite the large crowd in the room. He had two empty espresso cups on the table in front of him. As we walked in he looked up toward the door, gave us a cursory glance, then checked his wristwatch and returned his attention to the morning paper.

He hadn't recognized us. Amazing.

It was the wheelchair. It was Boulder. It was the wheelchair in Boulder. People didn't want to stare. People didn't even want to see when there was a kid in a chair. I patted myself on the back for that one.

I pushed Landon toward the table. Carl didn't look up until we were five feet away. I said, "Hi."

Landon smiled for the first time all morning.

Carl almost laughed out loud when he finally recognized us. With a quick motion he folded up the newspaper he'd been reading and stood to greet us. "You have a seat, both of you. Or one of you. I guess one of you's already sitting. Whatever, I was starting to worry."

"It's a long walk," I said.

"Oh, oh. Of course, of course. What do you want? Coffee, tea? The espresso's okay. Hot chocolate for my little friend? What's it gonna be? The pastries are pretty good, considering."

I assumed he meant considering they were made in Colorado and not wherever he was really from.

A gorgeous young waitress approached us. Her waist-length hair was the color of the flesh of a bing cherry. I ordered tea. Landon ordered a decaf mocha—thank you, Robert—and a chocolate croissant. I thought she was acting a little precious for Carl's benefit, but I wasn't about to call her on it. At least she'd found a reason to stop pouting and she hadn't forced "epitome" into a sentence since we'd arrived.

Landon leaned forward on her chair and whispered, "Where's Anvil? Did you bring him?"

"No, sugar, he's at home," Carl said. "I knew I was going to be busy today. I have some appointments later on this morning. He doesn't like it when I'm running around too much."

A minute later the woman with the beautiful hair brought us our drinks. I thought Carl was showing a little nervousness as he held up the newspaper and asked, "You seen the morning paper?"

I shook my head. He handed me his folded copy of the *Boulder Daily Camera*. "Page one," he said.

My instantaneous fear was that I was going to discover that my photograph was placed prominently on the front page. But it wasn't. The only picture I saw was a fine color shot of a golden retriever romping in Boulder Creek. There were three articles that began above the fold. I scanned the headlines quickly, reaching a rapid conclusion that Carl wasn't really trying to draw my attention to the follow-up story on the latest terrorist bombing in the Middle East or to the exposé the *Daily Camera* was doing on problems in the county clerk's office.

The third story above the fold was about an apparent murder at a motel in west Boulder. A woman from Indiana named Barbara Turner who was in town for meetings at the university had been found in her motel room with her neck broken. The room showed signs of a struggle. The police were thinking the crime might have been committed during a burglary.

I read on and found that I had started tapping my right foot to control my mounting rage. Landon was peering up at me from over the top of her big coffee cup. Despite my efforts to mask what I was feeling, she noticed something in my face or eyes and said, "What is it, Mommy?"

I said, "Nothing." I said it with the kind of disingenuous voice I used when I was stopped by a cop for speeding. The voice I used when I said, "Is there a problem, Officer?"

The newspaper article explained that the murder had taken place the previous evening at the Foot of the Mountain Motel. Had Carl mentioned the name of the motel where he had followed the woman who had been tailing me with the camera?

I didn't think he had. Just that it was on the west end of Arapahoe. Which is right at the foot of the mountains.

Without gazing up, I touched the newspaper and with forced civility I asked, "Carl? Is that the . . . um . . . same motel?"

"Same as what?" Landon asked enthusiastically.

Carl said, "It is."

"Same as what?" Landon demanded more assertively.

I looked at Carl with as much intensity as I dared muster. The determination in his expression matched my own. I shook my head as I mouthed, "Did you?"

Landon's eyes darted from my face to Carl's and then back again. Loudly, she said, "Did he what?"

For a moment, Carl didn't say a word. Then he said, "Not in front of the kid. Never, ever, talk in front of the kid."

Landon said, "That's not fair. That's the *e-pit-o-me* of not fair." I thought that her words were perilously close to a whine.

Carl momentarily ignored me and spoke to Landon as though she were his favorite niece or granddaughter. He said, "You know what I missed doing last night? I missed having someone like you to throw a baseball around with. You like to play catch?"

Landon said, "I'd rather play soccer. You're pretty good for . . ."

She was going to say "an old guy" or something like that and caught herself. But her words just hung there; she didn't know how to end her sentence.

Carl smiled at her before he looked at me and slowly closed his eyes.

I felt a chill and a deep ache in my chest and gut. My mouth opened in a silent scream and every bit of color in the flamboyantly decorated teahouse disappeared and turned to khaki.

THERE'S A LITTLE park that runs between Thirteenth Street and Broadway across from the teahouse. I pushed Landon's wheelchair down the walkway so that she could look at the ancient locomotive, passenger car, and caboose that are on display in the park, and then I walked away from her so that I could talk privately with Carl. I found it amazing that Landon was so intent on staying in character that she would stay put in the chair.

When we were about a hundred feet away, she yelled, "Hey, you're not going to just leave me here, are you?"

Everyone within shouting distance stared first at her, then at Carl and me. I felt about as inconspicuous as if I were wearing a WITSEC sweatshirt.

Or a bull's-eye.

CARL SAT ME down on a bench above the banks of Boulder Creek and waited a good twenty seconds for me to say something. Below us the snowmelt-swollen creek flowed hard and fast through thick brush. The setting was so serene it almost distracted me. I was pretty sure that Carl was expecting me to launch into an attack and vilify him for the murder at the motel. But getting out of the crowded teahouse and sitting by the creek had pacified me somewhat. I was willing to listen.

I glanced up to check on Landon. She was precisely where I'd left her. All I said to Carl was, "Go on."

He shrugged. Opened his hands. Closed them. "The woman with the camera yesterday? The one I said was following you? She was a pro. You know what I'm talking about?"

He looked at me, fixed his eyes on mine. I shook my head.

"She was working for a man she called Prowler, in Georgia, near Atlanta. Like I said, she was a pro. There's a hit out on you. She was here in town to clip you. She didn't know the client." He picked up a twig from the bench and twirled it between his fingers. "I didn't go there to whack her—I'd feel better if you believed me on that—but if I let her live, you were going to die today, Peyton."

I was barely surprised. My lips were stuck together. I had to separate them with my tongue. I said, "Of course there's a hit out on me. And Ernesto Castro's the client. He hired her." My voice couldn't carry all the despair I was feeling. Castro had found me already. So quickly, so easily. There was no hiding from him.

"Don't think so," Carl said.

"Why?"

"Two reasons. First, like I said, she was a pro. People like this Prowler and this woman, Barbara Turner, wouldn't come cheap. We're talking major bucks. Your guy doesn't have that kind of cash. Am I right?" I nodded. "If it was him ordering a hit, he'd use a hoodlum, somebody he knows from inside the can or somebody from the drug world. Like he did when he tried that botched thing with your daughter in . . . where was that you were living again?"

"Slaughter. Louisiana."

"Yeah, like that f—, excuse me, screw-up."

"But Robert was killed by a pro."

"He was, yeah. Maybe your guy still had grease then, right? Or somebody owed him a favor? He'd been making a lot of cash moving dope. Probably had a stash he was dipping into. But later on? After he was in the state prison? And you were, you know, in Slaughter. That work in Slaughter was amateurs. What Castro tried there shows that whatever well he was dipping his bucket in was dry a long time ago. It isn't him who hired this guy Prowler in Georgia."

I considered the argument. "Did you learn anything from the woman about this guy Prowler?"

"Got his phone number and e-mail address. Won't help for long, though. The trail from Barbara Turner to Prowler will be cold already. Nonexistent soon. You can bet on it. Anyway, given my peculiar circumstances, I can't exactly expect much help from the cops about Prowler."

I remembered that I had, until very recently, been an officer of the court myself. A friend of the cops I was now avoiding. "You said there were two reasons you were sure Ernesto Castro wasn't Prowler's client. What was the other?"

"Because Prowler's client wanted some other people hit same time as you. People somewhere else. He told this Barbara Turner you had to be done at the same time. Who else would Castro want hit? Nobody. He's out to punish *you*. Just you."

What Carl was saying didn't make sense. I asked, "Then what others were supposed to be killed?"

"The business doesn't work that way. Barbara Turner wouldn't know that side of it. She'd only know her assignment."

I tried to make sense of what Carl was saying. Who else could Ernesto Castro want to kill besides me? And if not Castro, who else could a renegade WITSEC marshal want to kill besides me?

I said, "The man last night at my town house? The one who attacked me? He was with her? He was working with Barbara Turner?"

"No."

I jerked my head to the side and glared at Carl. I lowered my voice as I said, *"What?"*

"She said no."

"And you believe her?"

He made sure I was still looking at his face before he said, "I was being pretty persuasive."

I shuddered and felt gooseflesh cover my body. "Who was the man at my house then?"

Carl shook his head.

I was lost. I tried to be deliberate in my thinking, to question my assumptions. But I stayed lost. The pieces didn't seem to fit. Almost offhandedly I asked, "How was she going to kill me?"

"There was a gun in her room. A .22 pistol. It's a killer's gun. I imagine you were going to get it like your husband got it."

"And a silencer?"

"Yeah, I found a suppressor, too. A good one. Sleek. Made by someone who knew what he was doing."

"Was she going to kill Landon?"

"You know, I didn't ask." He grimaced. "That's important. I'm sorry. I should have asked. It's not like me."

"If there's a next time don't forget to ask," I said and stood to rejoin Landon by the old locomotive.

I was halfway back to my wheelchair-bound daughter when I saw the other pieces as clearly as if they were clouds against the blue sky that framed the foothills of the Rockies. I yelled back over my shoulder at Carl, "I think this might be about Khalid. I need to find a pay phone. Fast."

I didn't know what it meant when Carl responded, "You know, I think I need one too."

As I ran back toward the teahouse I heard my daughter yell out, "Don't you two even think about leaving me here!"

2

Prowler's phone rang about eleven-thirty Atlanta time. He guessed that Krist was calling with an update or a confirmation about the two jobs he was doing in Florida. Prowler pressed a button to answer the call. Into the microphone of his headset he said, "Prowler."

A voice Prowler didn't recognize responded. "Prowler, good. Listen. You don't know me, but I thought you'd want to know that your friend Barbara Turner's dead. I'm telling you since apparently you're like her closest thing to next of kin or whatever. Be apprised that I have her stuff. *All* her stuff. Well, all her important stuff, anyway."

Prowler flicked a switch that would distort his voice for the duration of the call. *Apprised?* He said, "Who are you?"

The man said, "Not important. Let's just say I'm someone who doesn't like what you're up to."

Pause. Prowler said, "And you think I'm up to what?"

"Don't bullshit me, Mr. Prowler. I know who Barbara was. I know what she did for a living. I know who she was after out here. I know your name and I know where you do your business."

"What's your name?"

"What's yours?"

"What do you want?"

"It's what I don't want that should concern you. I don't want my friend bothered again. I definitely don't want the pleasure of meeting Barbara Barbara Turner's replacement. I don't want any more of your people around here. If I do, the result will be the same. Then I'll come looking for you because you've been uncooperative. Is that understood?"

Prowler said nothing.

The voice said, "Good."

Click. Dial tone.

Prowler rocked back on his chair and curled the microphone of his headset away from his lips. He flicked the switch to mute the voice distortion. To no one in particular he said, "Damn."

He reached a quick decision: he had to raise Krist and postpone the Florida action until he'd spoken with his client and received fresh instructions.

Briefly, he pondered his own vulnerability as a result of the apparent debacle in Boulder. What could this guy have taken from Barbara? Her camera? After the download she would have cleansed the disk. Barbara was savvy and reliable. She would not have forgotten the protocol. Her computer? Without the correct password, the hard drive would self-format after the second try at unauthorized entry. Any attempt to open the case? Same result. Anyway, she was too smart to leave incriminating data on her hard drive. Her weapons? No concern there. Neither the gun nor the silencer was traceable. Her cell phone? A clone.

Fortunately for Prowler, other than knowing that he was somewhere in the greater Atlanta metropolitan area, Barbara Turner had no idea where Prowler's business was physically located. But the guy on the phone had obviously managed to get Barbara to divulge Prowler's phone number. Barbara, Prowler knew, was someone who would be quite reluctant to part with the number. Prowler assumed that meant that the man on the phone was someone willing to use torture as a motivational tool.

Which meant that the man was someone like himself, thought Prowler.

Once more he said, "Damn."

OVER THE NEXT five minutes Prowler scoured the web for news on Barbara Turner's death. The *Boulder Daily Camera* website provided almost all the information he needed to know about her murder.

He pondered the situation for an additional minute before he took action. Prowler assumed that if the U.S. marshals had any idea what Barbara Turner was up to, then they had probably already moved Peyton Francis someplace new and that she and her kid would have new identities before they saw the next sunrise.

He'd have to start his search for them all over again.

There was no conceivable way he could coordinate the three contracts under these circumstances.

He had to call off the two hits scheduled for that morning. He paged Krist.

Krist didn't respond.

He paged him again.

Prowler waited.

3

Andrea's phone rang only once before her secretary answered. She told me that Andrea hadn't come into work that morning.

I felt a tidal change immediately. A whale was surfacing so close by that I could feel its spray on my face.

I identified myself as an old friend of Andrea's and asked, "Did she call in sick today?"

"No, but last night when she left she said she wasn't feeling well. I'm guessing that she's home in bed."

"What kind of not well?"

"Sore throat. Achy. You know."

"Have you tried her at home?"

"No. I assumed she was resting."

I USED MY 7-Eleven phone card to try Andrea's home number. Three rings. Four, five . . .

Seven . . . eight.

Andrea was one of those people who set their answering machine to pick up after an almost interminable number of rings. "Cuts down on messages from the impatient," she'd explained.

Nine.

I steeled myself for her eventual message, wondering if she'd changed it since the one she'd recorded using the Julio Iglesias background music. I hoped so; I hated cute answering-machine messages.

"Hello," she said, finally.

The sound of her hoarse voice brought a huge smile to my face. I wanted to hug her over the phone. "Andrea? It's Kirsten." I stumbled over my own name.

"Kirsten? Hi. I mean, Peyton."

"You don't sound good."

"I'm sick. I think I have the flu. Or some viral knockoff that's undistinguishable from the real thing."

"I'm sorry."

"Could be worse."

It's about to be, I thought. The whale hadn't left my bay. I saw it breach nearby. "Listen, honey, this is going to sound weird, okay? What I'm about to tell you? Try and keep an open mind as you hear it."

She coughed.

"There's somebody after me here, you know, where I'm living. Somebody new, if you can believe it. Not the same people."

"*What?* Somebody new is trying to kill you?"

Hearing her say it out loud made it seem even more real. I hugged myself with my free arm. "The woman didn't actually get a chance to try—she's dead now. That part's a long story. The important part is that she wasn't after me because Ernesto Castro sent her. You with me so far?"

"I'm trying. Are you and your baby okay?"

"So far, we're fine. Fine. The point I'm trying to make is that I think she might have been after me because of Khalid. Because of the letter Dave got and the phone calls that you and Dave have been making about the problems with the investigation. You still follow?"

I thought I could feel her voice quiver, but I detected almost no hoarseness as she said, "Yes."

"Before she . . . died, this woman who came to Boulder to kill me said that I was supposed to be killed at the same time as some . . . others."

"She told you this?"

"No, not me. Someone's been . . . helping me. She told him about it after some . . . coercion."

"And what? You think it was Dave and me? We were supposed to be the other ones?"

I judged her voice to be only mildly disbelieving.

"I do believe that. Yes. At least I think it's possible. I'm really, really afraid that it's possible."

"I should call Dave."

"Yes, you should. I'll call you back in five minutes to hear what he has to say. Is that all right?"

She coughed.

· · ·

ON THE ADJACENT phone, Carl had already completed his call. He waited for me to hang up and said, "I called this guy Prowler. Warned him off. Probably won't do any good, but I wanted him to know that I got his woman to talk. That's important for him to know. Might create some doubt. Some hesitation. At least he has to wonder what it is I know."

I tilted my head toward the pay phone I'd just used and said, "That was my friend Andrea in Florida. I think she might be one of the ones who was supposed to be killed first. She's calling a friend of ours, a man we both think might be the other one. I'll call her back in a minute to see what he has to say."

Carl's expression was dubious. He said, "You'll explain all this to me later, of course?"

"Of course."

He fought a yawn. "I think I'll go see Landon over there while you make your other call."

Aware at some level that I was sending a hit man to baby-sit my daughter, who was currently pretending to be crippled, I said, "Thanks, I'm sure she's getting antsy over there all by herself."

I COULDN'T WAIT five minutes, I called Andrea back after three. Her line was busy. I tried again at five minutes. Still busy.

Eight minutes, same result.

Finally at eleven minutes and twenty seconds, my call went through.

Andrea answered in tears. She said, "Kirsten?"

"Yes?"

"Dave's dead. What do I do now?"

FROM WHAT I could glean from Andrea, who'd just heard the whole story from Dave's almost hysterical wife Vicki, Dave Curtiss had started his day with the before-work routine that had marked a few thousand mornings before it and should have marked at least a few thousand after. Up at six forty-five. First cup of coffee standing in the kitchen in his boxers. Shower, shave. Shirt fresh from the laundry. Suit that probably should have already gone to the dry cleaners. Discarded three ties before he found one that wasn't stained. Kissed his wife. Teased his oldest daughter about the latest boy who was calling her morning, noon, and night. Second cup of coffee with some toast and butter and a glance at the *Wall Street Journal.* Didn't touch the fresh fruit cup that Vicki had prepared for him.

The *Today* show played in the background. Dave probably didn't hear a single word that Katie said.

By eight o'clock Dave Curtiss had gathered his briefcase, searched half the house for his car keys, and said good-bye to his family in the kitchen. He walked through the small mudroom and down two concrete steps to enter the garage for a ten-minute drive to his office.

That's where Vicki found him about nine-fifteen when she went to run her first errand of the day. Dave was slumped sideways on the front seat of his Lexus, most of his big body bent over the center console.

At first she thought he was just trying to find something that he'd dropped on the floor of the car.

I TURNED TO go find Carl and Landon after I hung up the phone.

I had to cross Thirteenth Street to get back to the park. I didn't remember seeing any cars coming, but I'm not sure I really would have noticed. By the time I was halfway to the old locomotive Carl hurried across the lawn to meet me.

I was fighting hyperventilation. I managed to say, "He's dead. My friend Dave Curtiss is dead. It's a long story, but I think everything has to do with an old murder case we prosecuted together back in Florida."

Carl took both my hands and led me across the park to the bench by Boulder Creek. He sat me down. To clear my head, I asked how Landon was doing.

"Happy as a clam. She's studying spelling, if you can believe it. Never seen such a thing."

I smiled weakly.

He said, "Now tell me, how was your friend killed?"

"How?"

"What method?"

Not, "What happened?" Not, "Why?" But, "How?"

"His wife told my other friend that the paramedics thought it was a heart attack. She found him this morning slumped over the wheel of his car in their garage. Dave has a history of heart problems."

Carl nodded. "They probably used drugs. It'll be hard to prove unless the cops are looking for it. Your other friend? The one you called first? She was involved with this old case, too?"

"Yes."

"So why does somebody want you all dead?"

"We're pretty sure a man was framed for murder years ago. We think by the police. We were involved with the prosecution. The three of us were going to start trying to get the conviction overturned."

"Why?"

Carl seemed sincerely puzzled. I tried to explain. "The man who was convicted for the crimes is about to be executed. None of us could let that happen. We were planning a campaign to reopen the case."

Carl's expression betrayed nothing as he said, "But you could all live with this guy being in prison for all these years? That didn't bother you none?"

I felt defensive as I said, "The man who was convicted is not a good man. He's a . . . criminal. He deserved to be in prison." My explanation sounded righteous and hollow simultaneously. Especially given the fact that the man who comprised my audience of one was also once a criminal who some other prosecutor had decided deserved to be in prison.

Carl let it slide. "You have evidence to support your new point of view? I'm guessing you don't."

I shook my head. "We have an idea where to look for evidence. Whom we might talk to."

"I assume that what the three of you have been planning wouldn't make the police who investigated this very happy."

"No."

"So I'm left to what-do-you-say—surmise—that it's a cop that hired this Prowler?"

I nodded. "That's what I'm guessing."

"You think you know who?"

I nodded again.

"How sure are you?"

"Why?"

"Curious."

"Pretty sure."

"Put a number on it. Like 99 percent sure?"

"Ninety percent sure."

Carl took a long slow breath. On the exhale he said, "This cop have a name?"

"Mickey Redondo. He's a detective."

"Tell me about Mickey Redondo."

I did. I told him what I knew about Mickey. It wasn't much. Carl asked a few more questions. I remembered a few details about Mickey, his family, and his kids. I filled in where I could.

When I was done he said, "But your friend's okay as of this morning? The one you talked to."

"She has the flu."

"The flu?"

"She stayed home from work today with the flu."

"She live in a house or apartment?"

"Condo."

"Big building?"

"Big enough."

"Havin' the flu may have saved her life."

"That's what I told her, too."

Carl said, "I'm going to give you some ideas for her. You need to call her back and tell her what to do."

"Okay," I said. "What?"

"She should call the police and make up some story about being afraid after her friend died. Ask for protection. I bet one of Prowler's people is waiting for her to come out of her house. If there's somebody there, they need to see the cops arrive."

"What are you going to do?"

"I'm going to call Prowler again. Mention the name of that cop you think is dirty. Create some, what-do-you-say, turmoil."

Below us the water was still rushing over the smooth rocks in Boulder Creek. Until that moment I hadn't heard a single sound as the torrent flowed nor had I noticed the passing of a solitary drop.

CARL AND I arrived at the pay phones again. I tried Andrea's number. It was busy.

I said to Carl, "Her line's busy. Maybe she's already calling for help. Before I call her back, I need to know something." I touched his arm near his biceps. "Are you doing okay? About last night, I mean?"

His eyes narrowed. He said, "I don't know what you mean. The thing at your house?"

I flicked a glance his way so I could gauge his sincerity. "I'm talking about what happened at the motel on Arapahoe. Are you feeling all right about what happened there last night?"

I saw his Adam's apple pop as he swallowed and watched him wet his lips with his tongue.

"*Feeling* . . . all right?"

"When we talked last week, you said sometimes it's hard . . . you know, afterward. Emotionally, I mean. You talked about playing catch with your kid and cooking ziti. I was just wondering how you were feeling today, that's all. I'm . . . concerned." I stared at the creek, then at my fingers. I was beginning to feel awkward and uncomfortable.

"Penne," he said. "It's different from ziti. They're both little tubes but one has ridges; the penne does. And it's cut at an angle like. The other one's plain, you know, smooth, and it curves a little. I use penne more; I kinda like the way the ridges catch the sauce."

"I never knew the difference. I'm sorry."

"It's nothing." He touched me on the arm. "Peyton, listen to me. I've hurt a lot of people in my life. That's the truth. I have. But I've helped more people than I've hurt. You may not want to believe that, but it's true. I've saved more people than I've killed. And last night wasn't about hurting somebody. It was about helping somebody, saving somebody."

Was I supposed to say "thank you"?

He said, "But thanks for asking. I'm seeing Dr. Gregory later. You know."

I didn't know, but I dropped it. Mustering the energy to extend compassion to a killer the first time had taken all my emotional reserves. I couldn't do it again.

I just couldn't. Even though the hit man had probably just saved my life.

4

Andrea's line was still busy when I called a second time. I was growing more and more agitated. I stood by Carl's side and listened as he made his second call to Prowler. Carl dialed the number from memory.

I don't know how Prowler answered, but Carl began his end of the conversation by saying, "It's Barbara's friend from Colorado. You remember—from before? Good. Thought you might remember me. Listen, there's somethin' I forgot to tell ya, earlier. . . . You don't mind? This isn't a bad time for you? . . . You're sure? I don't want to interrupt somethin' important."

Carl's tone had taken on a different cadence. He was clipping his words, dropping consonants. It was a fresh melody swollen with attitude. He sounded like a mobster from the movies.

As he listened to whatever Prowler was saying in reply, Carl rocked his head back and forth slowly, and rolled his eyes as though he found what he was hearing to be tedious.

"Good, good. I'm glad to hear that. . . . What did I forget? Here's what I forgot. I forgot to ask you to give my regards to Mickey. You'll do that for me, right? . . . His son's still at Duke I hear. Electrical engineering or something like that? Do I have that right? Daughter's about to graduate high school? A father should be proud, real proud of kids like that."

As Prowler responded, Carl's eyes flashed a little surprise.

"You're askin' me Mickey *who*? What do you think, Mickey fuckin' Mantle? Mickey fuckin' Mouse? How many Mickeys you and I both know, Prowler? Don't pull my chain. I get short of patience. You can ask you friend Barbara Barbara Turner about my patience."

Carl hung up.

When he turned to me and spoke again, his voice had evened out, the odd cadence again submerged. Like one of my whales. He said, "Message delivered. Just like Western Union." He paused. "Or e-mail. Whatever."

MY TURN. I glanced over my shoulder to check on Landon. It appeared that she was still studying her spelling lists. I owed her big time for her cooperation. Maybe I'd find a way to get her some sushi.

Out of the corner of my eye I noticed that Carl was doing that neck-stretch thing again. I turned back and punched in the long string of numbers that would connect me to Florida.

"Andrea," I said, "it's me again." She'd answered after half a ring.

Her voice was thick and heavy, as though she'd been drinking. I hoped it was the flu, not alcohol. She needed to stay sober for what was going to happen next. Her words came out in a burst. She said, "Hi. First thing is, I'm really, really scared, like terrified. Got it? Second thing is, you think Dave was murdered, don't you? You don't think it was a heart attack?"

I forced much more calm into my tone than I was feeling. My instinct was to counterbalance Andrea's anxiety in the same manner that Robert had often tried to counterbalance mine. He used to joke that once freed, my anxiety tended to act like a balloon while the air was escaping.

Andrea's too.

I replied, "I think it's possible that Dave was killed. In case that's true—and we don't know that for sure—you and I need to be especially careful. First thing is that you need to get some protection.

Here's what you're going to do: As soon as we hang up you need to call the police, tell them how frightened you are, tell them that you and Dave had received threats about an old case—even use Khalid if you want. Have the police come over and get you and help you find someplace safe to stay for now. Okay? Can you do that?"

"Yes, yes, yes. I'll—"

I heard a quick intake of breath, a loud thud, and a sound like someone spitting.

"Andrea? Andrea?"

No answer. Not another sound from Andrea.

I shouted, "Andrea!"

Seconds passed while I strained to hear another sound come from the speaker that I was pressing hard against my ear. I shouted, "Andrea!" again. An elderly woman walking on the sidewalk toward the teahouse tried to ignore my outburst, but failed.

In my ear a hard click was followed instantly by the sound of the dial tone. For some reason I thought it was odd that the phone hadn't even been jostled on its way back to the cradle.

I dropped the receiver and covered my mouth with both hands. I said, "Oh dear God, no."

Carl said, "What? What?"

"I think they just killed her. While I was talking to her, I think someone killed her."

"What?"

"She just stopped talking, right in the middle of a sentence. I heard some funny noises—like a slap, some spitting—and then the line just went dead."

He grabbed me by both shoulders and stared intently into my eyes. "You got her address?"

"Yes, yes, of course." I said, already digging into my purse. He didn't have to ask another question. Immediately, I called the familiar number of the Sarasota Police Department and said I'd heard a woman screaming bloody murder inside a condo on Longboat Key. I gave Andrea's address. They tried to get my name and number, but I just told them to hurry. Then I hung up.

Carl said, "Given the present circumstances, you've been in one place way too long. We should both get out of here. You want a ride somewheres for you and your kid?"

Numbly I said, "Yes, that would be nice." I turned to walk back to retrieve Landon and her wheelchair.

She was gone.

5

Krist finally returned Prowler's page.

"Where the hell have you been?"

"I was already visiting my second cousin when you paged me. Couldn't exactly pull out my cell phone and chat."

"Visiting? Her home? I thought this was going to take place out in the open. You said something about water?"

"Her routine changed. She stayed home today. I had to alter the plans to keep on schedule."

"Are you on your cell right now?"

"Yeah. But don't worry, it's a fresh clone."

"Doesn't matter. I want you to pull back."

"What do you mean, pull back?"

"Retreat. We've lost the coordination on the other end. We're going to have to regroup."

"I can't pull back. Like I said, I had to go to plan B, but it went okay. The visit's done on my end. I'm on my way to do the drop."

"You've run both errands?"

"As ordered."

"Damn. Where are you now?"

"I'm on my way south to the Everglades. I'm planning to do a little sight-seeing. Maybe feed some wildlife."

Prowler growled, "I don't want any evidence of this . . . surfacing. Not now. Not next week. Not ever."

"In that case I'll forgo putting a cross up where I leave the remains. It's usually a dead giveaway."

"I'm not in the mood for your humor. And I think I'm going to need you to run another errand right away. The one that was supposed to be done along with yours. That target's on the run, so this new errand's going to be out of town. Call me on a land line when you're free."

"It'll be a couple hours till I can get down there and get everything into small enough sizes to feed the alligators."

Prowler shuddered at the image, hung up, and said, "Damn."

TWO MINUTES LATER Prowler was about to call his client and give him the bad news about Colorado when the phone rang again. This time it was Marvin calling from Washington, D.C.

Prowler hadn't correctly guessed the identity of the caller.

Marvin said, "My man just phoned. Half the building is acting crazed. They're burning up the e-mails between headquarters and the field, especially Colorado. It looks like they can't find her."

"What do you mean they can't find her?"

"The marshals have lost her. She split from the place where she was living sometime last night, and she's gone into hiding somewhere else. My guy's take is that he thinks that internal security was breached, that somebody in WITSEC found out where she was and it freaked her. She ran. They're checking buses and shit. He says they're using all their resources to track her down."

"They're sure she's gone and not . . . *gone?*"

"No, they're not sure. They are considering that option as well. But so far, no evidence."

"Call me when they find her. Especially if they find her body."

"Immediately. Prowler?"

"Yes."

"I told you my man was good."

Prowler grunted and disconnected the call without responding.

. . .

PROWLER ADJUSTED THE microphone on his headset, punched in the number for his client's pager, left an emergency code, and then he waited. The return call came in eighty-eight seconds.

"Prowler."

"What's up?"

"You on a land line or a cell?"

"Hard wire. Pay phone."

"My man on the ground in Colorado is history. The target's status is unknown. There's a small chance that the errand was run for us by someone else. What's more likely is that she's on the loose from her handlers."

"What about Florida?"

"The local errands have been run successfully."

"Shit. This was supposed to be timed with precision. I can't believe you blew this."

"Excuse me?"

"You have intelligence on her whereabouts?"

Prowler wondered if the man was attempting to be sarcastic. "We're right on top of it. We know what the marshals know. They're scouring the country looking for her. When they find her, if she's alive, we'll deploy immediately. If she's dead, everyone's concerns are moot."

"You'll deploy? If they find her first, they're not going to let her surface for weeks. Maybe months, Prowler. They'll put her and her kid in a safe house with full-time U.S. Marshal babysitters. You need to find her first, not second. Once she learns what happened to her friends and puts two and two together, then she's really, really going to start singing."

Prowler knew the man's conclusion was absolutely right, but he was loath to acknowledge it. He kept his silence.

The man prattled on. "You've already broken our contract, you know. Timing, as the lawyers like to say, was of the essence."

"You're threatening not to pay me?"

"Quite the opposite. I'll be making the second payment as soon as we get off the phone. What I want you to do is go and earn it. Page me immediately when you have an update."

Prowler had a physical repulsion to being ordered about. He felt the tendons in the front of his neck tighten. He said, "Before you hang up, there is one additional piece of news you might want."

"Yeah, what's that?"

"The man who apparently killed my operative in Colorado? He seems to know your identity."

"*What?*"

"He phoned me to inform me of the failure of the mission in Boulder. By the way, be assured that this was a reliable man I had in Colorado—getting my phone number from him would have required significant persuasion, I can assure you. Anyway, the man on the phone told me to be sure to give his regards to 'Mickey.' Didn't use a last name. But he did go on and mention something about your children. Seemed to know details about their lives. You have a son at Duke apparently? An electrical-engineering student or something like that? The man on the phone suggested you should be very proud of him."

The man laughed nervously. "Are you making this up, Prowler?"

"*Au contraire.* I have the entire conversation on disk. You want to hear it yourself?"

"Who was it? A marshal?"

"I doubt it. But you may end up wishing the U.S. marshals were your main problem."

"Why? What are you talking about?"

"I don't pretend to know the man's identity. But to me, it sounded like somebody connected."

"Connected? What do you mean? Like a gangster?"

"Yeah, a wiseguy, like Robert De Niro."

"How would she be involved with somebody in the mob? That doesn't make any sense at all."

"My thoughts exactly. She's a prosecutor, right?"

"Yes, she's a goddamn prosecutor."

"Makes no sense."

"A wiseguy warning *me?* What kind of mess have your people gotten me into? What kind of half-ass operation you running, Prowler? How badly does that ship of yours leak?"

"We don't leak. That's precisely why you should be worried. Your name is written down exactly nowhere in my files. Nowhere. Not on a single sheet of paper. Not in a single computer file. In fact, I don't even know your whole name. The operatives in the field never learn the identity of the client, so they can't divulge it, even when they are captured and . . . tortured. Which I think my man was, by the way."

"What are you saying?"

"That it appears that your worst fears are coming true. This man who called me identified himself as a friend of our friend in Colorado. Which I assume means that she knows what he knows. She gave him your name. Which means what, exactly? Given that he knows your identity, it means that she probably knows your identity. And that means that these lawyers you want dead seem to know exactly who they're after. And maybe why."

"Jesus. He really mentioned Duke and engineering, right?"

"That's right."

"Jesus, Jesus."

Prowler clicked off the line before his client did. He sat back in his chair and rotated the mic of his headset so it hung in the air below his chin. He pushed his wheeled chair away from his console and closed his eyes.

He didn't tolerate failure. And this whole account was beginning to smell like failure. He had to find Kirsten Lord or Peyton Francis or whatever her newest name was before the U.S. Marshals found her.

She had a fifteen-hour head start but was probably limited to road or rail travel. Did she have fresh ID? He didn't know, but he had to assume that she did.

Prowler got up from his chair and walked to the far side of the office, where he stood in front of a huge map of the United States that almost covered a large wall. He began to calculate radii from Colorado's Front Range, pausing from the task only long enough to remove a tiny bottle of Coca-Cola from the undercounter refrigerator on the adjoining wall. The Coke was a little seven-ouncer, the kind they used in vending machines when he was a kid. The perfect size for a soda bottle. Every sip of a seven-ouncer was sharp and cold and sweet all at once. There was no deterioration in flavor or carbonation as he drank. The iced glass was exquisitely designed to maintain the perfect temperature of the beverage.

He flipped off the cap with a bottle opener—the old-fashioned way—and drained the bottle in two long draws as he stared at the map.

The bottle still in hand, he began to smile.

He knew exactly where to find the woman and her daughter. He touched the tip of the bottle to the correct spot on the map before he began the short walk back to his perfect desk chair.

6

"Carl, she's gone. Landon's gone!"

"*Every precious thing I lose, you will lose two.*"

Carl had been standing with his hands in his pockets and was looking down at his feet, pondering something through a vision of concrete and asphalt. At my words he jerked his head up and said, "What the . . . ?"

We both began running. Ernesto Castro's words hovered over my head like Satan's halo.

"*Every precious thing I lose, . . .*"

A chain-link fence about four feet high surrounds the train that is on display in the center of the park. The area between the train and the creek—where Carl and I had been sitting earlier—is mostly grass.

"*. . . you will lose two.*"

Landon wasn't in the open area. We had to get all the way around the train to search the other side of the park.

I yelled, "You go that way," while I pointed to the near edge of the fence. I assumed I would be a faster runner than Carl and I'd already begun to sprint toward the far edge of the fence surrounding the train.

Whales, whales, whales. They were everywhere, I swear. It almost felt as though they'd beached themselves in my path and I had to dodge them as I ran.

Less than a minute later, Carl and I met on the other side of the three-car train. Neither of us spoke; we both just shook our heads, our eyes frantically searching for any sign of Landon. I immediately took off toward the big white bandshell and tiny amphitheater that separates the northern edge of the park from the heavy traffic on Canyon Boulevard.

Landon, still in her wheelchair, was ten feet from the stage, listening to two boys a few years older than her. They were performing rap.

They rapped badly. They danced badly.

But they were game.

I reminded myself to breathe. I reminded myself to leave my terror at the door. I reminded myself that this—all of this—was already much, much too hard for a little girl.

Carl joined me at the rear of the amphitheater. He was breathing hard, like an athlete after a long run.

I said, "Let's give her a minute."

He said, "Yeah. She can probably use one."

CARL DROVE US west on Arapahoe before turning left on Ninth. He turned right at the southern edge of the old pioneer cemetery. I asked him to stop and pointed out a little grocery store on the corner behind us. "Next time we need to meet, let's meet there, okay? It's easier for me."

He said, "Sure," and headed farther west into the confusing streets on the other side of the graveyard. He stopped his car in the shade of an elm that was badly in need of pruning and suggested I get out of the car.

Landon said, "Not me, right?"

Carl answered. "That's right. We won't be long."

She mumbled something that I was certain I would have considered snide. In other circumstances I would have called her on it. Not that day.

I climbed out of the car. Carl did, too. We stood leaning against the trunk, staring back toward downtown.

"What're you going to do?" he asked me.

"I need to find out what happened to my friends. That's first I guess."

"Doesn't sound good. What you heard on the phone doesn't leave me thinking you'll learn good things."

My voice shook with reverberations of suppressed rage and with the hydraulic pressure of thwarted tears. "What would they do to her, Carl? If they were to kill her in those circumstances. In her condo like that. How would they do it?" I shivered at my own words.

He shrugged. "Depends what their intentions were. Sometimes you want people dead and you want everyone to know it. Sometimes you want 'em just to disappear like you vaporized them."

"Dave Curtiss's death was . . . clean, right? The heart-attack thing? They wanted that to look like natural causes? Not to draw attention?"

"Yeah, that was clean."

"So they went to some trouble to make that look like something natural. Let's assume they wanted Andrea to be clean, too. How would they do it?"

"If it was me? Given that what you heard on the phones was probably their backup plan—seeing there was no way for them to know she'd stay home sick from work—I probably would have done something straightforward and quiet." He raised his chin and glanced quickly at me. "I would have strangled her. Probably with a wire. Had something all ready for her body."

"What do you mean?"

"Even though it was the backup plan, I still would've been ready to go in if I needed to. Disposing of the body is the complicated part. I probably would've gone into her building dressed like a repairman, you know, maybe had a washing machine or a refrigerator with me on a dolly. Once she was clipped I would've stuffed her inside, then rolled her back out inside the appliance. No one would have given it a second thought. You walk into a building with a refrigerator, nobody's surprised when you walk back out with a refrigerator. Then I would've stashed the body where nobody would ever find it."

"It's that easy to get away with it?"

He shrugged. "I never got caught." He allowed that thought to permeate my membranes before he said, "Stranger hits are hard for the cops. Motive is elusive. Unless you get sloppy, it's easy to get away with it. Well maybe not easy. But if you're careful, not too hard."

As a prosecutor I knew that, of course. But I didn't want it to be true about Robert's killer. I was still hoping and praying to see the man in the chinos join Ernesto Castro behind bars.

Carl continued. "After you find out exactly what happened to your friend, then what are you going to do?"

"For now? Try to stay hidden."

"What about the guy who's about to fry in Florida? You going to forget about him?"

"No, I'm going to need to get some help with that."

"What kind of help? Something I can do?"

"No, I wish. Andrea and Dave were going to do all the legwork on the case. They were down there; they knew the players. Dave had already talked to Mickey Redondo's old partner. He was helping us.

"Let's face it, given what's going on with me, I can hardly go to Florida and start asking around about this old case. If I'm going to be effective down there, I'm going to need a lawyer, somebody who has a privilege to protect. Somebody willing to go to Florida for me. Somebody willing to go to bat for me."

He grunted. "And for that guy who's about to fry."

"Yes," I acknowledged. "And for Khalid."

"There might be someone."

"What? What are you thinking, Carl? Do you know a lawyer who can help me out?"

"No, not exactly. What kind of lawyer are you looking for? What about a lawyer like you? A prosecutor. Would that work for what you need?"

"Sure. If they'd be willing to do what I want. A prosecutor would understand my position."

"Then I might know of someone you could talk to."

"You know prosecutors? Of course you do. What? Federal prosecutors? U.S. attorneys? The people you testify for? Who?"

"No. I'm thinking about Dr. Gregory's wife."

I almost laughed. "Excuse me."

"Dr. Gregory's wife is a DA. Here in Boulder."

I couldn't believe what I was hearing. "How do you know that?"

"I'm not a . . . trustful person. I checked him out before I started seeing him. She's a DA. Doesn't have the same last name as him. I have it written down at home. Trust me, I know what I'm talking about."

I didn't doubt it for a minute. "Do you know her, Carl?"

He shook his head. "Not personally. Wouldn't be hard to make her acquaintance, though."

A FEW MINUTES later Carl dropped Landon and me at the entrance to the Dining Hall at Chautauqua. It was risky; I felt very exposed being dropped off in broad daylight in front of a dozen people, but I didn't feel that I had the physical energy required to push Landon up the steep hill that led from Baseline Road to our cottage. The walk from the Dining Hall would be much easier.

I had already begun to rethink the wisdom of sticking Landon with the wheelchair.

After Carl drove away, I pushed her and her wheelchair over to Kinnikinic and then up toward Lupine and our little cottage, smiling at a couple of my new neighbors along the way.

Once we were inside the screened-in porch, Landon vaulted out of the chair, spun on me and said, "This is so, *so* not fair."

I replied, "Yes, you're right, it is. It's the epitome of unfair."

She surprised me by smiling. She said, "It's not only the epitome. It's the entire paradigm."

She pronounced it *para-diggim*.

I didn't correct her.

TO MOLLIFY HER I played, and lost, three quick games of Scrabble before she decided to withdraw to the bedroom with her portable CD player and the latest Harry Potter.

I made tea from a Lipton tea bag that I guessed had been in the back of an upper cupboard in the cottage's kitchen since the early part of Lyndon Johnson's presidency. I carried my mug out onto the screened-in porch and lay back on an old wooden chaise that was covered with cracked vinyl cushions that were the color of dried parsley. The chaise was much more comfortable than it looked.

The screened-in porches that were so common around my new home kind of threw me. Before I'd discovered Chautauqua, I hadn't seen a single screened-in porch in Boulder. Nor had I seen many bugs. Certainly not like the South.

The neighborhood of my little safe house was pure Norman Rockwell. Across the way, I watched as a big sister pushed her little sister in a stroller, an old one, almost a buggy, not one of those strollers that look like they're made for day hikers. The sisters were coming right at me down Lupine. The big girl was singing a song that was making the little girl laugh. Across the street from them a woman about my landlady's age was hanging bed linen on a clothesline that was strung between two trees.

The sheets were white. Just white.

None of the cars I could see that were parked on the narrow lanes of Chautauqua was a new model. Not even close. Although real estate in Boulder was absurdly expensive, this wasn't a rich neighborhood. The tiny lawns were ragged. No air conditioners hummed.

If I ever got to stay in Boulder, I thought it might be a perfect place for Landon and me to have a life.

Having a life, now that was a fantasy.

I closed my eyes and wondered if Carl Luppo was right, if Dr. Gregory's wife could really help me.

I ALMOST FELL asleep while I was thinking about getting older.

I had been looking at my hands and noticing that my once almost flawless skin had begun to stretch and wrinkle. Each morning when I woke, the mirror revealed that my eyes and the corners of my mouth sagged slightly in places they were once taut. My butt was busy proving the law of gravity.

That's what I was thinking when a whale breached and came into view. It was a gorgeous beluga.

.   .   .

THE NIGHT BEFORE he was killed, as we were getting ready for bed, I was standing at the bathroom sink vainly lamenting the loss of my youth to Robert, who was leaning back against the headboard of our bed, reading a report for work. I was bitching and moaning and prattling on, but I didn't think he was really listening.

Silently he joined me in the bathroom. I watched him approach me in the mirror. Without warning he lifted my nightgown over my head so that I stood before him completely naked. He leaned around me and he lightly kissed my scrubbed face, touching his lips to the wrinkles at each corner of my mouth, and then to the tiny ridges that had recently developed on the outside of my eyes.

Next he lowered himself to his knees and placed his lips on my belly where, once flat, it was now gently rounded. With his large hands he turned me around and kissed my gravity-challenged ass.

When he stood again to face me, he moved his lips to within an inch of my ear and he whispered, "Your beauty has changed, K. It has not diminished."

The memory brought on tears, and the tears chased the whales away.

I FELL ASLEEP on the porch.

My last waking thought was that Carl Luppo had killed someone for me.

I couldn't find a compartment in my life where such a thought could fit.

chapter
nine
HOUSE CALL

I

Midday, Alan Gregory's pager alerted him to a message from Ron Kriciak. He returned the call only a few minutes after he felt the pager vibrate on his hip, and just before the arrival of his one-o'clock patient, Carl Luppo.

Given the contentiousness of their confrontation earlier in the day, Alan decided to try mending fences by trying to be overtly cordial with the marshal. He replied to Kriciak's curt greeting—"Kriciak"—by saying, "Ron, nice to hear from you again. It's Alan. How you doing?"

Ron wanted none of it. "Heard anything from her?"

Alan fought a sigh. "As I explained earlier, I couldn't say if I did, Ron. Unless she gave me her permission to talk with you, of course. If she does call me, I'll be certain to ask her if it's okay with her for me to call you." All the information Ron needed to answer his original question was readily available in the faint etchings between those lines. Alan hoped Ron recognized it. He asked, "You guys hear anything?"

Ron didn't answer his question. "Then you'll page me the second you hear from her?"

"The second she gives me permission."

Ron hung up. Alan concluded that cordial hadn't been the best possible strategy for dealing with him.

CARL LUPPO WAS right on time for his appointment. As he sat in his usual place on the sofa across from his therapist, Dr. Gregory thought his new patient seemed upbeat, less somber than usual.

As though he could read his doctor's mind, Carl started off by saying, "I been busy. I like being busy."

Dr. Gregory waited. Carl waited. The doctor's anxiety exceeded his patient's. Finally, Alan Gregory said, "You've been busy. What have you been up to?"

"Helping a friend. Somebody who needs some assistance."

He found it odd that Carl was suddenly being coy with details. "You've talked before about a young woman you've been spending time with? The one with the 'issues.' The one who you think isn't scared of you. Is that the friend who you've been helping out?"

Carl smiled. He said, "Yeah. I feel useful with her. I don't feel that too often anymore."

Dr. Gregory misread Carl's intention, thought he was talking about feeling useful, not about the girl. He said, "The marshals find you useful, don't they? The testimony you give?"

Carl shook his head. He had been talking about the woman. "It's not the same. I do that for the U.S. attorney because I said I would. I'm doing this for her because I want to. It's different."

Dr. Gregory finally recognized that he had encouraged Carl on a detour and that Carl had immediately drawn him back to the girl. Alan Gregory waited for his patient to demonstrate his intended direction.

"Listen, I want to clear something up. I tell you something, you don't tell anybody else, right? Not Kriciak? Not Kriciak's boss. Not anybody?"

Dr. Gregory tried not to look taken aback. "Unless it involves child abuse or imminent danger to you or someone you're threatening, no, I don't tell anyone without your permission."

Carl held up a hand. "Just so we're clear—I mean in case there's any question—you don't have my permission. Okay? No offense, of course. Now tell me about 'imminent danger.' Sounds like a hurricane warning. What exactly does that mean? Imminent danger?"

"Let's say you told me you were planning to go out and kill somebody. I'd have an obligation to warn that person beforehand or tell the police so that they could protect him . . . or her."

Carl raised an eyebrow and tucked in his wide chin. "Now why would I tell you something like that?"

"I'm not saying you would, Carl. What you disclose to me is totally up to you. I just used it as an example of imminent danger."

"And this is the same kind of example you might have used with somebody else? Somebody whose background is a little different from my own?"

Dr. Gregory thought about it, understood Carl's defensiveness. But he said, "Yes, I often use the same example when this question comes up."

Carl pondered his response. "But if I told you something else—something not about somebody getting whacked, but something that the marshals would really, really like to know from me, you still wouldn't tell them? I'm talking about something that's already happened, not any of this imminent danger bullshit."

Carl didn't curse much in therapy. His therapist noted the profanity before he responded. "Not without your permission, no. I wouldn't divulge it."

"Now how about a whatchamacallit, a hypothetical? Let's say one of your patients knows something about another one of your patients—let's say they're acquaintances, like."

Dr. Gregory sensed that his patient was looking for an acknowledgment. Warily he said, "I'm not fond of hypotheticals."

"I'm not fond of hemorrhoids, but so far I haven't found that to be much of a protection."

He smiled. "Yes?"

"Hypothetically? You couldn't divulge what this one patient of yours said about this other patient of yours? I mean since they're both patients, right?"

Dr. Gregory felt a trap being sprung. He had no idea how to avoid tripping the wire. He said, "If I understand your question correctly, you're right—I couldn't divulge anything about either patient. But I might have some questions about the nature of the relationship. Between one patient and another, I mean. And I might question whether the relationship between the patients was in the best interest of the psychotherapy."

Carl said, "Yeah?"

He nodded. "Is there something you want to tell me, Carl?"

Carl shook his head. Stared. Finally, he said, "I ever tell you I got a dog?"

2

Landon didn't want to go out again if she had to use the wheelchair. I couldn't really fault her because I didn't want to go out again if I had to push the darn thing back up the hill with her in it. So I decided that she'd recovered from what ailed her and asked her if she wanted me to start calling her Lourdes.

She didn't get it and didn't seem to think I was particularly amusing, even after my explanation.

But she did agree to come with me to meet Carl, this time at four-thirty at our newly arranged meeting place, Delilah's Pretty Good Grocery, which was much closer to Chautauqua than was the Dushanbe Teahouse. In order to arrange the rendezvous, I'd called Carl's home number twice around three-thirty, hanging up each time after one ring.

I tried to lure Landon on the errand with hopes of seeing Anvil, but she was in one of those preadolescent spaces where hope wasn't a sufficient motivation for her. Wasn't even a planet in her universe. So I told her that if she cooperated during our visit, I'd buy her something too sweet for words.

She told me that I was using hyperbole. She pronounced it "hyper-bowl."

I said, "Yes, I am exaggerating. But the word you're using is hyper-bole. It's pronounced hy-per-bow-lee."

She shook her head at me and said, "Whatever."

IN MY BRIEF time in town I'd discovered that, much to my sur-prise, Boulder still had a few little places like Delilah's dotting its hip landscape. Delilah's was an aging grocery/sundry/convenience store in a cramped but wonderful old stone building that was on the corner of Ninth and Euclid smack in the middle of the thriving residential portion of the neighborhood that Boulderites call The Hill. Delilah's was part gathering place, part community bulletin board, and part 7-Eleven, but without the plastic and the corporate panache. You could get a half-gallon of milk, a loaf of bread, leave a card up to sell a bicycle, find out where to get your navel pierced, and discover at what time at least eleven different yoga classes were meeting.

Best of all in my mind, Delilah's Pretty Good Grocery was, geo-graphically at least, all downhill from our cottage in Chautauqua.

I WAS MORE nervous during this excursion than I had been during the morning outing with the wheelchair. Earlier at the teahouse with Carl, I think I had myself convinced that the marshals would have been convinced that Landon and I had left town the night before. Now, I wasn't so sure I was as clever as I thought I'd been. And Andrea's ap-parent death in Florida had left me shaken and feeling even more vul-nerable, if that was possible.

I kept trying to picture Prowler and his minions and could only con-jure images of an army of Carl Luppos.

Landon and I walked down the hill and hung out inside the store waiting for Carl to arrive. My daughter was agonizing between an oat-meal cookie the size of a Frisbee or a good old-fashioned Butterfinger bar. I could tell she was hoping I would tell her she could have both. Her eyes told me that her father would have.

She was probably right.

Thanks, Robert.

Hello, Mr. Whale.

My heart leapt when Carl Luppo walked into the store. My heart didn't skip in fear, but in an oddly-defined gratitude. Even affection, I think. The man had become a kind of icon to me. He was protector, guide, mentor.

I wasn't beyond seeing the irony: I was running from a hit man into the arms of a hit man.

He was wearing a baggy plaid shirt and a green-and-blue ball cap that read "AF." I'm sure Carl didn't know that by doing his clothes-shopping at Abercrombie on the Pearl Street Mall, he had ended up dressed way too hip for his age.

Landon said, "Cool hat, Uncle Carl. Did you bring Anvil?"

He touched the brim of his hat. "Thanks. He's in the car. You can say hi to him a little later, okay?"

Carl approached me and kissed me on my cheek. I was left almost breathless by his greeting. I wasn't sure why.

"What's up?" he asked.

I handed Landon two dollars and told her to choose what she wanted from the endless snacks before us. As she spun away from me I added that Carl and I would be out on the porch of the store talking. Once outside we sat facing Euclid. Each of us focused our attention on every pedestrian who loitered on the sidewalk, every driver who slowed or parked in front of the store.

I said, "I like your idea about approaching Dr. Gregory's wife. I want to meet with her, see if she's in a position to help me. Did you get her name when you went home?"

He nodded as though he'd expected the question. "Lauren Crowder. She's . . . Boulder County Assistant District Attorney Lauren Crowder."

"So she works at the Justice Center on Canyon?"

"Wouldn't know about that," he said. "Kind of thing you'd know better than me. You're not thinking of going to see her at her office, are you?"

I had been. I said, "That wouldn't be smart, would it?"

"No." He paused. "Where she works? My guess is that there are lots of cops. Lots of lawyers. Not too good if someone like you wants to stay anonymous. You want to know where they live?"

"You know where they live?"

He shrugged.

I asked, "Would you take us there?"

"Now?"

"No, tonight, when they're both home from work."

"Sure. I'm not doing anything. Be worth the effort just to see the look of surprise on Dr. Gregory's face." Carl smiled in a way that made his eyes seem heavy. He and I had never talked about the doctor we shared.

Just then Landon walked out the door with nine cents in change, the cookie, *and* the candy bar.

Carl asked me, "Is it okay for the kid to take Anvil for a little walk now? I'm sure he'd like that."

Of course I said yes. I followed them across the street to Carl's car, which was parked by the wrought-iron fence of the cemetery. Anvil was elated to see us coming. As soon as Carl opened the door, Landon scooped the dog up in her arms. Carl clipped a leash onto Anvil's collar and lowered him to the sidewalk.

Immediately my introverted daughter asked Carl, "He's a boy, right? Why doesn't he have any balls?"

Carl looked at Landon with a critical eye. Then he said, "Oh, Anvil has balls, my little friend. He just doesn't have any nuts."

LANDON AND I parted from Carl and Anvil after a leisurely walk through the old Columbia Cemetery. My daughter and I took back streets as we strolled up the hill to Chautauqua hand in hand, friends again. We talked about school and boys and bad men and lying.

Later, back at the cottage, we made a dinner out of the contents of cans and boxes and ate on the porch while we played Yahtzee. I scanned the road constantly for cars and hoped that Landon didn't notice.

She beat me two out of three. And she probably noticed.

After dinner, at seven o'clock, we found Carl's car parked a block north of Baseline on Grant, exactly where he said it would be. He waved to us from the driver's seat and we climbed in. Anvil went immediately for Landon's lap.

I said, "I hope Dr. Gregory and his wife are home."

Carl smiled as if he already knew.

HE DIDN'T NEED a map to find the house, which was in a part of town I'd never visited. Carl drove away from the mountains and then back up into the hills that formed the eastern side of the Boulder Valley. The last turn took us onto a dirt-and-gravel lane, which curved back toward the Boulder Turnpike. Flanking the end of the lane were two houses, one up the hill, one down. The road dead-ended at a barnlike structure just beyond the houses.

Carl said, "Believe it or not, they live in the little house."

The little house wasn't that little unless it was being compared to its grander neighbor. Dr. Gregory and his wife lived in a stone-and-siding-covered single-story house that meandered unevenly from gable to gable, as though it had been constructed over time by many different owners. The steep gable over the entry was trimmed in a way that matched the gable over the separate garage, which appeared newly built.

To Landon I said, "Honey? Why don't you leash Anvil up and walk him around this clearing here between the houses, okay? Don't go far."

"And watch out for foxes, babe," Carl added. "I've seen some foxes wandering around here, and I'm afraid Anvil would make some pretty appetizing fox food."

"Foxes," she said. "Sweet."

As Carl and I approached the door of Dr. Gregory's house, the sun was just beginning to fracture as it sank between the sharp peaks of the distant Continental Divide. The sky above the mountains was devil blue and Confederate gray. The view was breathtaking.

"Let me do this," Carl said as he hit the button by the door.

I didn't hear the doorbell ring. All I heard was a terrific commotion and the resonance of a dog's bark that seemed to vibrate all the way into the marrow of my bones.

A woman's voice, sharp but calm. "Quiet . . . Good . . . Sit . . . Stay."

The barking stopped.

Eyes peeked out from a small fan-shaped window at the top of the door seconds before the door opened. The woman smiled pleasantly and said, "May I help you?" as her striking violet eyes danced from Carl to me and then back to Carl. Finally her attention came back to me and her eyes stopped, narrowing.

Warily, I looked at the dog, which resembled a small bear. The dog was using every bit of its power to fight its instinctive desire to bark and to charge and to have either Carl or me for dinner.

"Yeah," Carl said. "Yes, yes. I think you can help us."

The woman standing in the doorway had short black hair and a lovely face. Her feet were bare and she wore red capri pants and a billowing cotton top. She was also very, very pregnant. Her eyes took on a quizzical twinkle and she said, "Do I know you?"

She was talking about me. I spoke for the first time, trying to squeeze the anxiety from my voice. I said, "No, I don't think so. I don't think we've met. I'm new in town."

She nodded but her eyes said she disagreed with my assessment.

Carl said, "We are sorry to bother you, but my friend needs your help, Miss Crowder. Your legal help."

The woman stepped back in a way that was almost reflexive, and the dog tensed. She spread her hand in front of the dog's snout and it whimpered. The woman shifted her gaze once again to Carl before she returned it to me and smiled. She held out her hand and said, "Won't you come in, Ms. Lord. I'm Lauren Crowder."

I felt my heart race in panic at the sound of my real name. Somehow I managed to reach out and shake her hand before she offered it to Carl.

He took it awkwardly and said, "I'm Carl Luppo. It's a pleasure."

She pulled the door the rest of the way open and said, "Give the dog a minute. She'll get used to you. Her name is Emily."

Carl held out his hand for the dog to sniff and said, "Don't worry about me. I love dogs."

Lauren said, "Unfortunately, the problem is that Emily doesn't always love humans."

I stayed back a step.

Lauren gazed past me and smiled once more. She said, "Is that your daughter out there, Ms. Lord?"

"Kirsten. But please call me Peyton, if you don't mind. And yes, that's my daughter. That's Landon."

"Bring her in with you. The little dog, too."

"The big dog won't mind?" Carl asked.

"No, Emily's cool with little dogs."

"What is Emily?"

"Emily's a Bouvier. A Bouvier des Flandres. A Belgian sheep dog."

"Her bark is worse than her bite, right?" Carl joked.

Lauren said, "I doubt that, actually. Although she's never bitten me, I'm relatively certain that her bite is much more unpleasant than her bark."

THE HOUSE WAS simple but elegant. Even as day rushed toward dusk, long streams of light flooded into the space. The floors were polished hardwood. A newly refurbished kitchen opened to a dining room and living room that were each framed by huge windows facing the Front Range of the Rockies. The area that would typically comprise a dining room was filled by a huge pool table.

Carl held Anvil while the big bear dog danced at his feet. Landon held my hand. Lauren invited us to sit.

I was anxious waiting for Dr. Gregory to walk in and find Carl and me in his house.

"You recognized me?" I said to Lauren as I took a seat beside my daughter on the sofa.

"Twice now, actually, though you look a lot different now than you did the first time I saw you on the news. The other time I saw you, you were leaving my husband's office. I recognized you then from your pictures. I was quite . . . I don't know . . . captivated by all that you went through earlier in the year. You know, with your work, and your family. I'm so sorry about what happened to your husband."

"Thank you. I don't really know how to ask this, but has Dr. Gregory . . . I don't know . . . ?"

"No, he hasn't said anything. My husband doesn't talk about his patients with me," Lauren said as she smiled at Landon. "Are you hungry or thirsty? Can I get you something? I bet I have a pop if it's okay with your mom."

Landon said, "No, thank you."

Lauren raised her eyes to me and asked, "You would like my legal advice on something?" Her tone was generous and cordial, the kind of tone that a lady in the South would use to offer me more tea.

I pulled Landon close to my side and said, "Is there someplace she can go while you and I talk? She has some books she brought with her. They'll keep her busy. She won't be a problem, I promise."

"There's a room downstairs with a television, maybe she would like to go down there and—"

Just then Dr. Gregory interrupted. The intrusion of his soft voice startled me. He said, "Why don't I take her with me? I was going to go over to Adrienne's house for a little while. Maybe Landon would like to meet Jonas. I'm sure Jonas would love to meet her and get to know the dog." He lowered his gaze to Landon. "Jonas is younger than you, Landon, but that boy sure loves dogs."

Dr. Gregory was standing in an open doorway on the far side of the room, wearing a T-shirt over a pair of green sweatpants. He was barefoot and his hair was wet as though he'd come straight from the shower. He stepped forward into the room and said, "Lauren, you'll be okay here with your guests?"

She said, "Absolutely."

He looked at Carl and said, "Hello, I'm Alan Gregory."

Carl waved and said, "Hey. Carl Luppo. This here is Anvil." I could tell Carl was fighting a smile.

I steeled myself and said simply, "Hello." I was trying to read Dr. Gregory's eyes for surprise or disdain or fury or something. But I couldn't read his eyes any more than I could bring myself to call my therapist Alan.

3

Prowler abhorred witnessing violence that he wasn't personally perpetrating, and he couldn't tolerate the site of blood that he wasn't personally spilling.

For the two hours and fifteen minutes that he waited impatiently for Krist to call him again, Prowler fought off images of what the man was actually doing to dispose of the woman's body down in Florida. In his mind, Prowler kept seeing big curved blades, like machetes, and neat little saws that were intended for pruning hardwood trees. He fought off mental images of the dead woman and intrusive thoughts of his neighborhood butcher quartering a chicken. He kept recalling cinematic versions of the behavior of hungry alligators.

Prowler tried to divert his attention from the carnage by surfing the web while he sipped from a little bottle of Coca-Cola in an effort to try to settle his stomach.

KRIST FINALLY CALLED again midafternoon.

Prowler started speaking before the man had a chance to begin expounding on the details of his final errand in the Everglades. "You're going to Boulder, Colorado. If you leave right away you can still get a flight out to Chicago or Atlanta and make a connection from there. I have the schedule in front of me. Do you want me to pick a flight?"

"I thought you said she split from Colorado last night."

"Turns out that's exactly what she wants everybody to think."

"You're sure?"

"You're traveling on my dime. Of course I'm sure. I've e-mailed you all the information about your new cousin. You need to know that she has a kid with her, a nine-year-old girl."

"And?"

"And nothing. The kid's not important to me. She's collateral. Whatever happens, happens."

"Gotcha."

"By the way, I forgot to tell you, I think the woman has someone helping her. The guy could be connected."

"What do you mean 'connected'?"

"Mafia connected. Barbara's dead. I got a call from the guy who's responsible. He sounded to me like he could be a wiseguy. All accent and attitude. A tough guy. Lots of threats."

"You shitting me? How did he find you?"

"She must have given me up."

"Doesn't sound like her. Was she tortured?"

"That's what I'm thinking. Still doesn't fit. I'm working on the angles. But be careful when you get there. This guy could be a wild card. As you know, I don't like to gamble."

"I don't like it either, Prowler. The fee on this is going to be double. If it turns out that I have to do this wiseguy, too, then it's triple."

Prowler sighed and said, "I don't care." But he was beginning to think that it might be easier just to forgo his agency fee, whack his client instead, and forget the rest of the job. "I've already sent the file your way. You'll get fresh leads as I develop them. Check in when you arrive in Boulder."

Prowler settled his fingers on his mouse and clicked three times to set up the task he wanted the computer to perform, then he clicked once more to begin it.

The high-fidelity speakers on each side of the room came to life with Carl Luppo's voice.

"Don't bullshit me, Mr. Prowler. I know who Barbara was. I know what she did for a living. I know who she was after out here. I know your name and I know where you do your business."

"What's your name?"

"What's yours?"

"What do you want?"

"It's what I don't want that should concern you. I don't want my friend bothered again. I don't want the pleasure of meeting Barbara Barbara Turner's replacement. I don't want any more of your people around here. If I do, the result will be the same. Then I'll come looking for you because you've been uncooperative. Is that understood?"

Prowler fingered the buttons on the mouse and clicked twice more, playing the digital recording again. Each time he listened, he was more and more certain about his conclusion.

Although usually not one to talk to himself, Prowler said, "This man with her may be cruel, but he's not so clever. He calls me the morning after the murder and tells me that the two of them are still in Boulder. Which means that once again I have my haystack. All I have to do is find a couple of needles."

He paged Marvin in Washington, D.C., and asked for an update from the U.S. Marshals Office. "You talk to your guy again?"

"Just hung up with him."

"And?"

"He's tapped in to the max. They're throwing internal security to the wind. He's seeing all the e-mail that's flying around. They've lost her. Can't get a lead from anybody. They've got their people out every-where. They've talked to the cabbie who picked her up at her place last night, her boss at work, her neighbors, her daughter's teacher, her shrink, her babysitter, her—"

"Her shrink? She's seeing a shrink?"

"Yeah. That's what my guy says."

"Name?"

"Just a sec. Guy's name is . . . Alan Gregory. Dr. Alan Gregory. Alan with one *l*, you know A-l-a-n?"

"He's in Boulder?"

"I guess. I didn't ask. I can confirm that if you want."

"Don't bother. Is Dr. Gregory a fed?"

"No. Apparently he's private."

"I need more data. Anything you get. Don't wait for me to call. I want updates as soon as you have them."

Prowler ended the call without saying good-bye and, using the web, began compiling information about Dr. Alan Gregory of Boulder, Col-orado. Ten minutes later he e-mailed the data—a rather complete dossier of professional and personal information—to Krist as an attach-ment to a simple message that read, "I think this should help you out."

Then Prowler paged his client and waited less than a minute for his return telephone call.

"Here's the status. The marshals don't know where she is. But we do. We found her. She's still in Boulder. I have my most senior man on the way."

"Do you know where in Boulder she's hiding?"

"Not yet. But . . . we think her shrink might tell us."

"She's seeing a shrink?"

"We have reliable information she's been seeing a Dr. Gregory. Dr. Alan Gregory."

"Let me know what he says as soon as you talk to him."

"Don't worry."

"My friend has transferred the rest of the money, Prowler. I'm not worried. If I were you, I'd be worried. He doesn't like to be disappointed."

4

After my therapist left the house with my daughter and both dogs in tow, Carl asked Lauren if he could shoot some pool while she and I talked. I thought I felt her hesitate before she told him to go ahead. She looked at the pool table the same way Robert used to eye his sixty-four Porsche when someone asked if they could take it for a spin.

Me? I was grateful that Carl wasn't going to try to intrude into my meeting with Lauren.

As Carl went about the business of retrieving the balls from the pockets and setting up a fresh rack of balls on the table, Lauren took my hand and led me from the sofa outside to a narrow deck that fronted the living room. The deck hung over a sea of grasses that bordered the highest reaches of the Boulder Valley and offered a view of a thousand mountains and a lifetime of sky. "It's why we live up here," she said. "Every night at sundown I get a reminder of why we live up here."

"It's . . . gorgeous," I said, before quickly adding, "I'm feeling so sorry that we came. I didn't know you were so . . . pregnant."

She laughed and placed her hands on her womb. "You think so? Maybe just a little bit," she said.

"When are you due?"

"Not until late September, if you can believe it. Which means I'm going to get even bigger. And don't apologize for coming to see me. I'd like to try to help you. I really would."

"You don't know what I'm going to ask of you."

She appeared unconcerned. "I assume you want some advice."

I shook my head. "I wish it were that simple. It's not. I need some help—some real help—to try to save someone's life."

She smiled a little. "And you think you need a lawyer for this? Maybe I could put you in touch with a cop."

I shook my head. "It's about a man I helped put on death row. He doesn't belong there." I let those provocative words hang in the air, hoping for a reaction, but she was almost as good at screening her feelings as was her husband.

All Lauren said was, "Yes?"

"Do you know about my situation? Why I'm in Colorado?"

"That you're in hiding? There have been rumors around our office—I'm guessing you know that I'm an assistant DA with Boulder County—that you were placed in the Witness Protection Program after your husband was murdered."

"Actually I didn't go into the program until after there was an attempt to kidnap my daughter. But, yes, I'm in the Witness Security Program. Or I was." I sighed. "Listen Lauren, before I go any further, I would like your assurance that this is a consultation between attorney and client. Quite simply, I need the protection of your privilege. If you don't agree to help me after you hear what I have to say, I will understand completely and our relationship will end here tonight. But either way, I need to know that what I'm about to tell you is protected communication."

She touched her lips with the fingers of one hand. "Okay," she said. "For this moment at least, I'm your lawyer."

"I don't even know if your husband knows this, but as of yesterday I'm on the run from the Marshals Office, from WITSEC. That's the Witness Protection Program. My participation in the program has been controversial from the start, and some things have happened that have convinced me that the marshals can't guarantee that Landon and I will be safe from, I don't know what else to call it—retribution from within that organization."

"I know about your history as a critic of the Witness Protection Program. I always considered your position to be a valorous one."

"Thanks, I guess. I've come to believe that the line that's strung between valor and stupidity is incredibly easy to trip over. Because of the national attention my criticism of WITSEC received, some of the marshals hold me responsible for budget cuts, job losses, demotions—you name it. There're a lot of people in the organization who don't feel that Landon and I deserve their protection. Because of our notoriety, when we entered the program we were placed in a special category of protected people whose identities and whereabouts are supposed to be shielded from all but a few people within the United States Marshals Office."

"Okay. I'm with you."

"Last night, just about this time actually, someone—there's a reasonable possibility it was a marshal—broke into our home. I think he was just trying to give us a message that we weren't really safe in WITSEC. Well, I'm not stupid, I heard the message. We ran. We left the place where we were living and went into hiding from everyone who's after us, including the Witness Protection Program." I pointed over my shoulder at Carl who was lining up a long shot. "My friend's been helping us."

"Carl?"

"Yes."

She nodded. I could tell she had a few questions about Carl Luppo that she was wise enough not to ask. She said, "And now you're in my home. What is it you want from me?"

I began, "There's a man named Khalid Granger who is about to be executed by the State of Florida. I've come to believe that there's a reasonable likelihood that he's not guilty of the crimes for which he's been sentenced. I want you to help me try to stop that execution."

I'd already made a decision not to presuppose what Lauren Crowder's bias about capital punishment might be. I'd considered, and ruled out, the option of questioning her about her political views before I asked her for help. I hoped it didn't matter what she believed about the death penalty; I wanted someone who would help me do the right thing. Period.

"How would I do that?"

"I think the lead detective on the case, a man named Mickey Redondo, is dirty. I believe, as do the other two prosecutors who worked on the case, that Mickey set Khalid up. Why? I don't know. How? We have some ideas."

She held up her hand to slow me down. "Wait a second. Where are these other two prosecutors now? Why can't they help you out?"

I started to cry. "I think they were both killed this morning." I wept as I added, "They were my friends."

WE TALKED FOR most of an hour. After around forty-five minutes I heard Dr. Gregory return home with a little boy, Landon, and the two dogs. Over my shoulder I watched as Carl gave Landon a cue stick and began teaching her something about shooting pool. Lauren noticed, too. I don't think she was accustomed to nine-year-old girls getting lessons on her pristine table.

The most difficult part of the conversation with Lauren was avoiding the parts about Prowler and Barbara the hit woman and Carl Luppo's visit to the motel on Arapahoe. I didn't want to reveal either my identity or my location to the local police, and I didn't want to say anything that might lead anyone to suspect Carl's involvement in the murder at the motel. All I told Lauren about the most recent events was that since Dave Curtiss had died and Andrea had disappeared so suspiciously that morning, I feared for my own safety as well. I could tell that she sensed I was being evasive about something. It made us both uncomfortable.

At one point she interrupted and asked me if her husband knew anything about Dave's death and Andrea's disappearance. I told her no, to the best of my knowledge, he did not.

When I was done with the story, she said, "Can I summarize this,

Peyton? The man who originally threatened you, the one you think had your husband killed? You assume that he's still after you?"

"Ernesto Castro. Yes. I have to assume he's still after both of us. Landon and me."

"Okay. In addition, you have reason to believe that the Witness Protection Program is no longer able to guarantee your security? That there might even be people inside the program who are eager to compromise your security and leave you at risk from Ernesto Castro?"

"Yes. My best guess is that I was assaulted by a marshal last night."

"And now, you also have come to believe that this detective in Florida, Mickey Redondo, has either killed, or perhaps arranged the murder of two prosecutors in order to protect himself from accusations of impropriety in regard to this old murder case? Correct?"

"That's right."

"And that leads directly to the conclusion that Mickey Redondo— or someone doing his bidding—is probably out looking for you, too."

"That's my fear, yes."

Lauren shifted her weight before she pulled herself to her feet by tugging on the railing of the deck. She looked down at me and smiled. "Will you excuse me for a moment? I have to pee. I actually can't believe I made it this long. I haven't gone this long in two weeks." She reached for the door, paused, and said, "Peyton? Why do I get the feeling that you were the kind of girl who got herself into trouble by having two dates to the prom?"

HALF A MINUTE later the door opened again and Dr. Gregory took his wife's place out on the deck. He was still wearing the same sweatpants and T-shirt that he had been earlier. But his hair was dry. He said, "Your daughter's great, Peyton. We had a wonderful time next door."

"Thank you. She is wonderful. At least most of the time."

He said, "Jonas's mom is a doctor. She got called into the ER, so Landon and Jonas are both here with me. They're downstairs; they're having fun together."

"Great."

"We need to talk, don't we? You and I?"

I nodded and fought fresh tears. I did want to talk with him, but I wanted to talk about being terrified for Landon and about losing my friends in Florida and about the incredibly jumbled feelings I was having about Carl Luppo and what he had done for me. But that's not what Dr. Gregory meant by his offer. He wanted to talk about my showing up unannounced at his door with Carl Luppo, and he wanted to talk about why I was meeting with his wife.

I grabbed a DumDum from my pocket, unwrapped it, and asked him if he wanted one. He shook his head. I placed the candy on the middle of my tongue and twirled the stick twice. This one was lemon.

"There's an ethical code that governs my work, as there is with yours," he began. "One of the ethical principles—one of the benchmark ethical principles—of my profession is the prohibition against psychologists having dual relationships with any of their patients. What that means in practice is that I'm not permitted to provide clinical care to anyone with whom I have any other kind of relationship. *Any* other kind. Does that make sense?"

The words made sense, but I wasn't ready to respond to him quite yet, so I shook my head.

"It means I can't do psychotherapy with the guy who cuts my hair. I can't do an evaluation on the son of my best friend. I can't provide consultation to my banker's staff."

His argument was persuasive. I was standing in the middle of the railroad track and I could see the train coming, so I admitted the obvious. "And you can't provide help to a woman who's a client of your wife."

He nodded.

I shifted the location of the lollipop in my mouth, then removed it and tilted the little yellow orb toward him. "Who says I am?"

"You're not?"

"I didn't say that. I guess I'm trying to find out how you were reaching your conclusion."

"Excuse me? You're denying that you've come here tonight to ask my wife for legal help?"

His voice betrayed some frustration. I considered the break in his demeanor a victory. "I'm not denying anything. I'm not admitting anything. I'm only wondering how you reached your conclusion. All that seems apparent to me is that I came by your home to see your wife. Whether she and I are anything other than casual acquaintances is a matter of conjecture. In a town the size of Boulder, I'm sure you occasionally have professional relationships with people who are casual acquaintances of your wife." I felt like a lawyer for the first time in months.

He quickly regained his composure, which had only slipped about three degrees. While he moved his hand back and forth in the air between our chairs he asked, "Is this going to be a control issue between us?"

Was that an accusation or was he intentionally providing me with a way out of my dilemma? I honestly couldn't tell. I asked, "Does psychotherapy usually come to an end on control issues?"

"Usually not, no. But sometimes."

I decided he was offering me an escape route. I said, "Then I'm afraid that it looks like this is going to boil down to be a control issue." I put the lollipop back in my mouth.

He stared past me, into the darkest part of the sky. After half a minute or so he said, "There's something else, though. We're going to have to talk about your relationship with . . . Carl."

I nodded and opened my eyes widely. "Because?"

I knew that he couldn't admit to me that Carl was his patient. That would breach Carl's confidentiality. And if Carl had already told Dr. Gregory that he and I were friends, Dr. Gregory couldn't tell me that, either. The fact was that Dr. Gregory and I couldn't talk about Carl Luppo until I brought him up and even then Dr. Gregory couldn't admit that he was treating Carl.

Dr. Gregory was stuck. I could tell from the look on his face that he knew he was stuck, too.

He said, "Ron Kriciak is looking for you."

"I guessed that he would be. It's possible that a marshal—one of his colleagues—broke into my house last night. Landon and I left the place where we were living. I don't have much faith that WITSEC can protect me any longer."

"Ron seemed sincerely concerned."

"I'm not convinced. He may be or he may not be. Some of his colleagues certainly are not."

Dr. Gregory digested my words. "Kriciak would like me to let him know if I hear from you."

As evenly as I could, I asked, "Will you do that?"

"Not without your permission."

"Good. You don't have it."

He almost smiled. "For some reason I suspected that," he said.

I sucked hard on the lollipop. So hard that my cheeks went concave. I said, "Are we okay? Doctor and patient okay?"

He shrugged. His shrug was not as grand a gesture as Carl's. He asked, "We have trust issues. We have control issues. I'm not convinced we can work them out, but I'm unwilling to decide tonight that we can't. Are you planning to keep your next appointment?"

"That may not be . . . judicious on my part. I'm trying to keep a low profile. Do you ever do any work over the phone."

"In an emergency, I have."

I had hoped our discussion would end up somewhere in this vicinity, and I knew what I was going to propose. "I think this is an emergency. Can you give me a phone number that you actually answer? One that doesn't go to an answering machine. I'll call you on your pager first and leave you a four-digit message. That will be the time I'll call back."

Before he had a chance to agree or disagree, Lauren walked back out onto the deck. Dr. Gregory offered her his seat. She lowered herself gingerly and said, "While I was inside? I got a phone call from a man named Ron Kriciak. He said he was an inspector with the U.S. Marshals Service."

My lungs seemed to purge themselves of oxygen. Had Ron found me and followed me here already?

Dr. Gregory was still standing beside his wife. He said to her, "Really? Ron Kriciak called for you?"

"Yes, he asked for me. Wanted to talk one law enforcement officer to another. *Mano a mano.* He hinted that he'd like me to use my influence to ensure that my husband cooperate fully with reasonable requests for information from the U.S. Marshals Service regarding his clients."

I sighed, relieved that Ron was still looking for me.

Dr. Gregory said, "And you told him . . . ?"

"That my husband is a stubborn man who tends to be resistant to most forms of cajoling."

"Most forms?" His voice momentarily took on an unfamiliar—for me at least—teasing quality.

She teased him right back, saying, "That's right, most forms."

Dr. Gregory said, "It's not the first call like that Kriciak has made today. Teri Grady got one, too. She phoned me late this afternoon to give me a heads-up that Ron was pressuring her to pressure me about the exact same thing."

Lauren asked, "How is she?"

To his wife, Dr. Gregory said, "Sick of bed rest but she's doing okay. She asked about you and said to say hello."

I asked, "Who is she?"

Dr. Gregory opened his mouth as though he was going to answer, but he didn't speak. Lauren said, "Teri Grady's a psychiatrist in Denver. She's on pregnancy leave from her position as the regional psychiatric consultant to the Witness Protection Program. My husband has been filling in for her during her absence."

I said, "Oh."

The people from WITSEC were definitely trying to find me. They were pressuring my doctor and now they were pressuring my new lawyer. But at least it didn't seem like they knew that Landon and I were still in Boulder.

5

Though the night had turned cool, Lauren opened all the windows in the bedroom before she stripped off her nightgown and climbed into bed.

"You're hot?" Alan asked.

She nodded and gestured at her gut. "I don't just have a bun in the oven. Sometimes I think I have an oven in the oven." She busied herself with the complicated task of arranging pillows to support her body's unfamiliar form.

When Lauren was done with the pillow gymnastics, Alan started to rub her lower back and said, "You can't help her, babe, you know that, don't you?" His inflection made it clear that he was saying that she shouldn't help, not that she wasn't able.

Lauren intentionally ignored the clues in his tone. She asked, "What do you mean I can't help her? I don't know any such thing."

"I mean it's too dangerous. For you and for the baby."

Lauren sighed, then stilled her breathing. "This is . . . awkward territory for us, Alan. Let's be careful here, ourselves. There are certain things about the work we do that we can't discuss with each other. We've always respected that." She was glad that the lights were off and that she was facing away from him on the bed. She didn't want him examining her eyes for truth.

He said, "I am being careful and I'm trying to be discreet. All I'm saying is that her life is much too dangerous. You shouldn't be involved."

"And you should?" As soon as the words were out of her mouth, she wanted them back. They sounded childish.

"I didn't know what I was getting into. I think you do."

"Maybe I do. But I don't see how you might know what I am or I am not getting into. I haven't told you anything. And if she's told you anything, you can't talk about it with me."

"The very fact that you aren't willing to talk about it tells me that you're involved professionally with her. That's all I need to know to make me concerned for you and our baby."

"Is it?"

"What does that mean?"

Lauren felt trapped. She'd just succeeded in getting the pillows just right—for a few blessed moments her womb actually seemed to be floating in zero gravity. But she felt a strong need to be facing Alan to continue this conversation. "Come over to my side of the bed for a second," she said.

"What?"

She laughed. "Get out of bed and come over here. I want to look at you, and I have these damn pillows in a position that's almost Zen in its perfection and I don't want to move."

He climbed out of bed, avoided tripping over Emily on the way, and knelt beside his wife. "You know you look lovely. Cindy Crawford has absolutely nothing on you," he said.

She laughed again. "Although I think I like having you kneeling naked at the side of my bed pretending that I'm beautiful, your flattery won't work."

He smiled. "You look lovely whether my flattery works or not."

Lauren got serious. "Ever since I saw her in your office, I've told you that I wanted to help her, didn't I?"

"Yes, you did."

"Given an opportunity, I'm not going to turn my back on her."

He touched her naked abdomen.

"Don't play the baby card on me, Alan. I'm as capable of taking prudent risks as you are."

"You sure you want to use me as a comparison?"

"You know what I'm saying."

He touched her nose and then her lips before he said, "She doesn't know what's out there. I don't know what's out there. The marshals don't know what's out there. How can you possibly decide what's prudent?"

ten

A BAD CASE OF STREP

I

Jeremiah Krist's road style was completely antithetical to that of Barbara Turner. While he was on assignments, Krist preferred to travel like a business executive. Whenever possible he chose big, anonymous hotels, and, using one of his many fake identities, he booked every detail of his travel in advance over the Internet. On this trip he was a purchasing manager for Texas Instruments.

His flight from St. Petersburg into Chicago was delayed by thunderstorms, and he barely made the last connection of the day from O'Hare to Denver, sprinting down the jetway with about thirty seconds to spare before the cabin doors were sealed. Once safely on the ground in Colorado, he drove his rental car—a big Mercury—away from Denver International Airport and took it directly to the Omni Interlocken Hotel in Broomfield, about ten minutes east of Boulder on Highway 36.

Krist had chosen the Omni because it was big, it was new, it catered primarily to travelers doing business in the adjacent Interlocken Business Park, and because every guestroom was equipped with a T1 Internet line for rapid connections to his laptop.

Krist was asleep in his fourth floor room by midnight. He set his travel alarm for five-thirty. He'd asked for a western facing room, knowing that he'd wake up to a stunning view of the Front Range.

The first thing Krist noted at breakfast was that doing business in Colorado didn't seem to require a business suit. Despite the fact that the hotel catered to out-of-town visitors to the big corporations that had sprawling campuses in the nearby business park, only two of the thirty or so business people he spotted in the hotel restaurant were wearing business suits.

And they were both women.

Ties, too, seemed to be optional. He guessed that only about half the men were wearing neckties.

Back up in his room after breakfast, Krist traded in his brown suit for khakis and a black blazer—the paraphernalia of Krist's line of work required a jacket, after all—but he ditched his tie. A quick glance in the mirror convinced him that he now looked the part of a businessman from Texas with an appointment at Sun Microsystems or Level Three Communications.

Krist booted his laptop and checked his e-mail for fresh updates from Prowler. Nothing new had arrived since he'd gone downstairs for breakfast, so he reviewed the information that he'd already been sent about Dr. Alan Gregory and decided that since he had only one lead, there was no reason not to follow it.

FORTY-FIVE MINUTES LATER, Krist found a parking spot at a meter on Walnut Street in Boulder and made his way up the sidewalk to the building that his records showed housed Dr. Gregory's office. Once there, Krist climbed the wooden stairs of an old Victorian house. The sign outside indicated that Dr. Gregory shared the office with another psychologist, a woman name Diane Estevez.

From the porch, Krist peered through the front window into a parlor/waiting room that was separated from the rest of the house by a closed door. In the waiting room, a woman in her fifties was sitting on a burgundy sofa reading the *New Yorker*. She glanced up at him for a second before returning her attention to the magazine.

No secretary or receptionist that Krist could see.

He walked back down Walnut and found a pay phone near Ninth Street. He called Dr. Gregory's office number and got a recording. Jeremiah Krist hung up before the beep.

Probably no receptionist.

Using the sidewalk on the opposite side of the street, Krist walked back toward Dr. Gregory's building. A man with a ponytail and a dangling gold earring shaped like a whale's tale was stepping out the front door of the Victorian. A young woman—no more than nineteen years old—was heading up the steps. She had a tiny leather backpack strapped to her back.

The man held the front door for her as she entered. He smiled at her. She didn't seem to notice.

Krist kept walking.

Although he wasn't averse to being the beneficiary of miracles, he didn't have any illusions that his target was going to conveniently arrive at Dr. Gregory's office for her regularly scheduled appointment. Nonetheless, Krist had been hoping to find a clinical operation that was a little less opaque than Dr. Gregory's appeared to be. A conveniently bored secretary or receptionist could have filled him in on a lot of details of what was where and who was who behind the closed door that led away from the waiting room.

Frustrated, Krist decided to check out Dr. Gregory's house, hoping, in the end, that it might turn out to be the more efficient place for a chat.

ON THE WAY to Dr. Gregory's home, Krist got lost twice after he turned off South Boulder Road. The secondary streets in this part of the country were poorly marked, and Krist was almost certain that the map he'd downloaded off the Internet lacked at least three of the little lanes he passed. In his head he was already drafting a scathing critique that he would e-mail back to the company that provided the map.

He drove on. It appeared that the lane he was on dead-ended near the last two residences, precluding a casual drive-by. The lane widened between the two houses. After that, a small turnaround in front of a barn marked the end of the road.

In front of the larger of the two houses, a young boy was playing a version of Frisbee that required him to try to get the flying disk to land in one of various laundry tubs that had been scattered around on his front lawn. The game seemed to require a lot of running and jumping and squealing. A woman—from her grim countenance Krist guessed she was chronically depressed and in her thirties—sat in the shade offering occasional encouragement that sounded to Krist like, "There you go, Jonas."

Krist held the car's speed under ten miles per hour and tried to look lost. He gripped his rental car map in one hand and kept twisting his head around as though he were hoping he might stumble upon a landmark.

Once he was opposite the house, the boy named Jonas stopped running and tossing Frisbees into laundry tubs, and he froze his eyes on Krist and the Mercury.

The woman took her eyes off the child, rested her hands on her lap, and stared at the car as though she hadn't seen one in weeks.

Krist spotted the brass number on the house behind them and knew that it wasn't the number for which he was searching. Dr. Gregory lived in the other house. Krist threw the map down as though he were disgusted and proceeded to the end of the lane where he pulled the big car into a creeping U-turn that carried him right past Dr. Gregory's front door. On his slow pass-by he endeavored to memorize every detail he could about the house and the locale.

One of the first things he noted was a small sign by the front door announcing that the home was protected by an alarm monitored by a company called Alarms Incorporated. He also noticed a chain-link dog run.

Inside the run was a big bucket for water. But no dog. Krist guessed that Gregory would be the kind of guy who would own a golden retriever or a black lab.

Without another glance at the woman or the boy, he made his way back down the lane.

Other than the presence of an alarm, and the possible presence of a dog, Krist couldn't have been more pleased with what he had learned. Gregory's house wasn't exactly in the middle of nowhere. But it was close enough to the middle of nowhere for what he had in mind for later that day.

HE DROVE BACK toward Boulder and stopped in a parking lot on Twenty-eighth Street about a block away from the local Hertz office. He tugged on the latch that would pop the hood of his Mercury, climbed out of the car, and opened his pocketknife. After a moment's deliberations, he sliced a hole in one of the hoses that circulated coolant to the radiator.

As soon as he confirmed that antifreeze was dripping freely from below the car, he squeezed back behind the wheel and drove straight to the rental car company lot where he traded his defective Mercury for a huge GMC four-by-four.

Now, in Boulder, he'd fit right in.

2

The morning after our visit to Dr. Gregory's house, Landon woke up with all the signs of strep. Fever, sore throat, stomachache. I knew the contours of my daughter's strep symptoms as well as I knew the signs of my menstrual distress.

And sometimes it seemed as though she got strep as often as I got my period.

I also knew the treatment she would need. The doctor would look at her throat, feel her nodes, give her a rapid strep test, and begin an overnight culture from a swab from her throat. As soon as the rapid strep showed positive—and it would—the doctor would prescribe erythromycin twice a day for ten days. After one day of medication

Landon would no longer be contagious to others. After three doses of medication she would no longer be punky to me.

Both were important milestones.

The consequence of not promptly treating strep infections is rheumatic fever. Not treating Landon's strep was absolutely not an option.

The trouble was that I didn't know how to get her the medicine she needed. I didn't think I could risk walking into a doctor's office or emergency room. Surely, as soon as I went to register Landon as a new patient, my WITSEC-provided identification would be entered into some computer system that was on-line with some other computer system, and our presence would be red-flagged by some vigilant U.S. marshal who was assigned to stare at his computer monitor until the name Peyton or Landon Francis showed up someplace.

I knew that it was possible that I could get away giving both Landon and myself new fake names and then paying for her treatment with cash, but what if they asked for ID? I didn't know what I'd do, so I didn't want to risk it if I had other options.

I thought I had one. I called Dr. Gregory.

HE HADN'T YET left for his office when he responded to my page.

"I need a favor," I said.

"What would you like me to do?" he asked with absolutely no inflection in his voice.

"Landon has strep. She woke up at five with all the symptoms. I'm bothering you because I'd like your help with two things. One, would you please tell Jonas's mom that her son has probably been exposed?"

"I can give you her number if you'd like."

"I'm happy to tell her myself, but the second favor is something I need from you. Would you please ask her if she'll prescribe some erythromycin for Landon?"

"Adrienne—that's Jonas's mom—is a urologist, not a pediatrician."

"It doesn't matter. She can still prescribe. And I know the dose. Landon gets strep two or three times a year."

"Adrienne doesn't even treat Jonas herself, Peyton. She takes him to a pediatrician for stuff like this."

"My . . . position is delicate, Dr. Gregory. I can't exactly take Landon to a pediatric clinic, can I?"

He was silent for a moment. "Let me make a call, try to find her. How can I reach you?"

"I'll call you back in ten minutes. How's that?"

"Make it five, but Peyton?"

"Yes?"

"What I've just agreed to do? This is outside the boundaries of the therapeutic relationship. I'm not comfortable with it. You and I are going to have to talk about what's reasonable for you to expect from me."

"The circumstances are unique," I argued. "I don't have anyone else to turn to . . . who knows my position."

He started to say something else and then said, "I'm going to have to tell Adrienne something to get her to agree to do this. That has to be okay with you."

"Is she discreet?"

"Better. She's a closet anarchist."

"Go ahead."

I CALLED HIM back in five minutes.

"Adrienne's already at the hospital. She won't be coming home until a few minutes after six tonight. That's early for her. She agreed to bring home two rapid strep tests with her—one is for Jonas—and she'll bring some erythromycin samples. She asked if Landon could take pills or if she needed liquid."

"Pills are fine."

"She wants to know Landon's actual birth date and her weight."

I told him.

"She wants to see Landon herself. You can be at her house at six then?" he said.

"Yes."

"Do you need a ride?"

Was he offering? "No, thank you. I'll call my friend."

I thought I heard him sigh.

IT WASN'T EASY but I waited until the middle of the day before I called the district attorney's office and asked to speak to Lauren Crowder. When I called I was put right through.

Immediately she said, "Peyton, I don't have anything."

"I'm sorry if I'm being impatient. It's just—"

She cut me off. "It's not that. I know that time is tight. I made some initial calls, but I didn't get anywhere. That retired cop who was helping your friends? I tried him first."

"Jack Tarpin."

"Yes. His wife says he's gone for a couple of days."

"He runs fishing charters."

"That's what you said before. I put a call into that guy at Northwestern, too. You know him? That journalism professor whose students have gotten so many men off death row in Illinois? He hasn't called me back yet. I'm hoping for some advice from him on how to proceed. I also have some calls into the Southern Capital Punishment Project to see if they are in a position to help us with Khalid. But based on what you've told me so far, mostly things depend on the cooperation of the ex-cop, on Jack Tarpin."

I asked, "What about Pat Lieber? The man who made the phone call to Mickey Redondo?"

"I'm checking on that, too. I have a law student doing some research about him from public records. This all takes time. I can't just pick up the phone and call him out of the blue and ask him if he recalled bribing a detective on a murder case, can I?"

"No," I said, "you can't do that."

I ARRANGED TO have Carl pick Landon and me up at Delilah's Pretty Good Grocery at a quarter to six. While we were waiting for Carl to arrive, Landon managed to make her throat sound as rough and raspy as a cat's tongue in order to con me into a ginger ale. I hated myself when her histrionics worked. As she contentedly sipped her drink through a straw, I bought every newspaper I could find, looking for news about

Khalid, or about us. I scoured *USA Today* for anything about Andrea's disappearance or Dave Curtiss's death.

I found nothing.

But the *Boulder Daily Camera* had two prominent follow-up stories and a sidebar about the recent murder at the Foot of the Mountain Motel. The gist of the articles was that the police were stymied by the crime. Motive was particularly elusive. The sidebar was a soft piece about the dead teacher's former elementary-school colleagues in Texas. Although they hadn't worked with the victim in over three years, they were—each and every one of them—totally shocked and dismayed at her violent death.

Aren't they always?

Carl pulled his car to the curb in front of Delilah's right on time. I wondered whether punctuality was a universal trait among members of La Cosa Nostra. Somehow I doubted it, although I could see how it could be of logistical benefit to hit men.

I smiled when I saw that Anvil was accompanying Carl. The dog was so happy to see Landon that I was afraid his little heart was going to burst with joy.

I was almost that happy to see Carl. When I climbed onto the front seat next to him, I leaned over and kissed him on the cheek. It confused me, I think, almost as much as it confused him.

His eyes softened as he asked, "So how you feeling, baby?"

My breath caught in my chest. I didn't know if he was addressing my daughter or me. Landon spared me humiliation when she rasped, "Okay. The ginger ale really, really helps. Thanks for bringing Anvil, Uncle Carl."

He touched me on my knee. His fingertips felt hot. "And what about you? You holding up?"

I nodded and put my hand on top of his.

AS WE DROVE the last hundred yards to Dr. Gregory's house I could see that he and Lauren were just getting home from work. The garage was open and each of them was carrying a briefcase as they walked to their front door. Her briefcase was at least twice as thick as his. They stopped when they noticed Carl's car approaching.

Lauren waved. My God, she looked pregnant. She was fighting that third-trimester waddle I remembered too well.

Dr. Gregory didn't wave. I knew that he was no longer comfortable with his role in the drama that had become my life. The truth was that I lacked sympathy for his position. My thought was, welcome to the club.

I think Carl was sensing the same reluctance from Dr. Gregory that I was. He said to me, "You know what? I think I'll stay in the car with the kid till we know the game plan."

"That's fine. I'll go find out what's happening, where I should take Landon for her test." I opened the door and got out of the car.

Dr. Gregory said, "Hello, Peyton. Adrienne's not home, yet. She's going to be late. Just got a call."

Lauren raised her cell phone. "Don't worry, it's not a big deal. She's always late. This time she got called to the hospital to remove a pickup stick from an eleven-year-old boy's penis." She held up a hand as though she were about to be sworn in as a witness. "I kid you not. How's your daughter feeling?"

I could hear Landon all the way from the backseat of the car as she said, "Oh, that's gross."

I couldn't help wincing at the pickup-stick story myself. I answered Lauren. "Landon's uncomfortable, but she'll feel better as soon as she gets some antibiotics. I'm sure that she's feeling better than the little boy with the pickup stick in his . . . penis. Thanks for asking."

Lauren said, "Why don't you all come inside, get something cool to drink? It's a warm evening."

"You know," I said, "I think I'd be more comfortable out here."

Lauren flicked a look at her husband. It was a "that's your fault, *honey*" look. "How about Landon coming in, then? It's way too hot for her in the car. Let her come inside to the air-conditioning and lie down while we wait for Adrienne. She said thirty minutes. But with Adrienne the first number you get usually doesn't mean too much. It's kind of like the sticker price when you're buying a car."

Before I had a chance to answer, Landon popped out of the backseat with Anvil tight in her arms. "Sounds good to me," she said. "Hello, Ms. Crowder. Good evening, Dr. Gregory."

God help me, she'd remembered their names *and* remembered her manners. I actually thought she was about to go southern on me and tip into a curtsy.

I said, "You really shouldn't be around her, Lauren. With the strep, you know?"

She hesitated for a moment. "You're right. Tell you what," Lauren finally said to me. "Give me a few minutes to change my clothes, and then you and I can go for a walk with the dogs, Peyton. We have some things to talk about. Landon can come inside with Alan. If she feels up to it, she can play some pool. That way I won't be exposed. Hi, Mr. Luppo." She waved at Carl.

I watched as he waved back unenthusiastically.

Lauren flicked another glance at her husband—this one was a warning glance—before she faced Carl again and said, "You're welcome inside, too, of course, Mr. Luppo."

"Call me Carl, please. I'll think about it," he said with the thickest accent I'd yet heard come out of his mouth.

Landon took Dr. Gregory's hand and together they walked in the front door a few seconds after Lauren. Carl climbed out of the car and stood next to me.

He said, "Weird, this whole psychotherapy thing, huh?"

"Absolutely. I don't know how to act around him."

"You supposed to act?" he asked.

I allowed his words to reverberate, listening for an echo of sarcasm. I couldn't detect any. "Don't think so, not literally," I said. "But I've never been in this situation before."

"Me neither. It's like he can't get over the fact we're friends. You and me, I mean."

"Something tells me it's not that simple."

Carl acted surprised by my statement. "What? Us being friends? You think it's more complicated?"

"I meant more complicated for him. To have two patients who are friends. I suppose it raises issues."

"*Issues?* You don't think?" he said, his voice tailing away.

"What?"

He hooked his thick thumb at me and then curled it back toward himself. "That he's thinking that, you know, there's anything else between . . . you know . . . us. I'm talking . . . you know. That he means *that* kind of complicated?"

I blushed.

"Us? I, um. Of course . . . Well."

"Yeah. Me, too," Carl said. "Me, too."

3

Krist had arrived back in Spanish Hills shortly after four o'clock in the afternoon. He'd followed the dirt lane toward Dr. Gregory's house but instead of continuing all the way to the end of the road, he turned west at the final intersection, pulling his big vehicle down another scraggly country road until the four by four was invisible to anyone heading toward Gregory's house. Then he drove a little farther.

The lane he was on ran in a mostly southerly direction on the Rocky Mountain side of Dr. Gregory's house, but the road curled to the west before it reached the point where it was opposite the house. The field between the road and the house, which was perched on a gentle slope, was carpeted with waist-high grasses and was devoid of structures. Dr. Gregory's closest neighbor to the west was well over two hundred yards away.

Krist pulled his vehicle behind a berm of soil that had been cut into place by a piece of heavy equipment. He thought that an unskilled road grader operator had probably created the berm. Krist climbed out of the car, grateful for the man's incompetence.

The late afternoon sun radiated fiercely as Krist tugged a bright orange highway vest over his head. In case anyone grew curious about his presence on the road, he set up a surveyor's tripod on the western shoulder for cover. He alternated his attention between the surveying scope and some compact binoculars as he methodically plotted the architectural details of Gregory's house and the topographical details of the surrounding land. Twice over a period of about twenty minutes he moved the tripod and pretended to take new readings.

Once his surveillance was accomplished, Krist packed up his tripod, climbed back into the truck, and followed the lane as it wound farther to the west. It looped around for almost half a mile before it spun back to the north and connected to a paved road that led to an intersection with South Boulder Road.

He now had identified two avenues of exit, his personal minimum for any contact that had the potential to get violent. The planned interview with Dr. Gregory certainly had the potential to get violent. Krist hadn't been able to imagine a single scenario that would leave Dr. Gregory alive once the doctor had been enticed to give up Kirsten Lord's current location.

Krist's logic was simple. Alive, Gregory could warn her about what was coming. Dead, he couldn't.

Although Krist hadn't had the luxury to invest sufficient time to determine Dr. Gregory's work schedule, he was proceeding under the assumption that the doctor worked something approximating a regular day and didn't expect Gregory to arrive home for an hour or two. With that cushion of time to kill, Krist circled back around behind Gregory's house, again pulled his big car back to the shelter of the earthen berm, dumped his orange vest, yanked a gray-and-green daypack onto one shoulder, and began hiking across the field below Gregory's house. He took long strides, acted purposeful, marching directly to the lower level of the house. Most of the way he followed a narrow trail cut through the grasses by small animals. Once at the house, he peered through the windows on the garden level and then hoisted himself to one of the two decks that protruded from the upper level.

Had it not been for the likely presence of a burglar-alarm system, Krist would have just broken into the house and waited inside in comfort. But the shadows below the deck would be a pleasant enough place to kill some time while he waited for Dr. Gregory to get home from work and disarm the alarm.

.   .   .

DR. GREGORY'S DOG, Emily, had been sleeping in the master bedroom when she heard, or felt—or both—the arrival of an intruder on the deck off the living room.

Emily was a Bouvier des Flandres—a Belgian sheepdog. Although her size and shaggy profile might evoke comparisons to an Old English sheepdog, in demeanor Bouviers have much more in common with another herding dog of European ancestry, the German shepherd. Like the German shepherd, Bouviers possessed an edginess, a wariness, a willingness to mix it up. Some police jurisdictions used Bouviers for police work.

If she didn't know you, Emily could be mean.

As Krist was climbing onto the deck, he hadn't heard the dog approach the sliding glass doors behind him, but when Emily started barking ferociously twelve inches from his ear, Krist left his feet as though his shoes had been equipped with ejection devices.

When he spun to see the source of the commotion, Krist's hand was already molded firmly around the grip of his handgun. Looking down at the animal on the other side of the glass, he thought for a moment that Dr. Gregory had a pet bear. The dog that had lowered itself onto its rear legs and was yelping and baring its teeth was a compact, powerful animal with perfectly upright ears, no tail, and a long beard. Krist guessed the dog's weight at close to one hundred pounds.

Each bark shook Krist like a sonic boom. The explosions came at him like machine-gun fire.

"Damn," he said out loud. "What the hell are you?"

Krist assumed the dog wouldn't quiet until he climbed off the deck. He lifted his leg back over the rail and lowered himself to a position in front of the basement level of the house, which was exposed on the western slope below the twin decks.

As the dog's barking began to slow, Krist began to consider plan B. Plan B would definitely include something for the dog.

Krist leaned against the side of the house and listened for the sound of approaching cars.

4

Krist heard the popping of gravel on the lane before he detected the noise of a car engine. Initially, he thought that two cars were arriving at the Gregorys' house. But a third soon followed.

He wasn't pleased. He hadn't been counting on a crowd to be around while he and Gregory chatted.

By the time he'd managed to edge around the side of the house far enough to try to see who had arrived along with Dr. Gregory, Krist heard the buzzer on the home's alarm system blare. Within seconds, it was quieted. To Krist that meant that Gregory or his wife, or both, had entered the house and hit the code to still the alarm.

Just about then, two sharp barks like thunderclaps echoed from the dog. But only two. Krist quickly decided that someone was with the Gregorys, and that whoever was with them wasn't a total stranger to the dog.

Krist backtracked toward the deck. Plan B had accounted for Gregory's wife, and for his dog, but not for any unexpected visitors.

The plan was malleable, though. Krist knew that the primary variable was going to be the amount of carnage he left behind after his conversation with Dr. Gregory.

WHILE HE'D BEEN waiting for Gregory to arrive home, Krist had spent his time accomplishing two tasks. He'd cut the cable that carried the phone company signal to Dr. Gregory's house and to the nearby neighbor's house. And he'd destroyed the latch that held one of the basement windows locked. With Gregory home and the alarm deactivated, Krist made his next move, sliding the window open and poking his head through the opening into the house's garden-level basement.

He didn't see or hear any signs that anyone had come down the stairs, so he pulled his body through the window and waited just inside, listening specifically for sounds of the dog descending the stairs to eat him. While he listened he held his handgun at the ready, the barrel pointed at the foot of the stairs.

Nothing.

From the furnishings in the room, Krist surmised he was in a guest suite of some kind.

Above his head he heard footsteps crossing the floor and he heard muted voices. He edged silently across the room to the base of the stairs and waited while he tried to ascertain whom he was about to meet when he climbed upstairs.

Somewhere close by at the top of the stairs, a woman called, "Emily? You want to go for a walk?"

Krist listened as the dog's feet scratched maniacally at the wood floor in a desperate effort to get to the door before the woman changed her mind about the excursion. The woman said, "Good girl. Good girl," before she adjusted her tone and yelled, "Alan, we won't be gone too long, maybe a half-hour. I bet we'll be back before Adrienne gets home. See you guys soon."

Guys, Krist thought. *She'd said "We." She'd said "Guys."* Then he wondered, *Who the hell is Adrienne?*

The front door opened, then closed.

Krist assessed the situation. The good news was that the damn dog was gone. The bad news was that someone—an unknown someone—had stayed behind with Dr. Gregory.

Krist didn't hesitate. According to what Dr. Gregory's wife had said as she walked out the door, Krist had only about thirty minutes to convince Dr. Gregory to divulge Kirsten Lord's current location. By the end of those thirty minutes, the wife would be back from her walk with the devil dog and someone named Adrienne would arrive to complicate Krist's life even further.

Jeremiah Krist knew that by the end of those thirty minutes Dr. Gregory would have revealed Kirsten Lord's secrets. And Jeremiah Krist knew that Dr. Gregory would be dead.

Krist edged slowly up the stairs.

The upper landing was near the front entryway of the house. Gun at the ready, Krist paused and looked toward the big glass windows to the west. He spotted the pool table he'd spied earlier from outside, and he saw the deck where he'd been standing when he was scared half to death by the bear dog.

He didn't see any people.

The first doorway on his left led to a modern kitchen—granite countertops and brand-new appliances. Krist poked his head far enough into the room to assure himself that no one was there. The big room by the windows was empty of occupants, too. A hallway on the far side of the big room led, Krist assumed, to the bedrooms. The house had to have bedrooms.

That's where he expected he'd find Gregory.

Which left one person unaccounted for. His wife had said, "See you guys soon."

Guys. That meant someone besides Gregory.

Krist padded silently across the floor to position himself while he waited for Gregory, and that someone else, to emerge from the bedrooms. Krist had chosen to wait in a corner behind the pool table. He'd be behind Gregory as the doctor emerged from the bedroom.

Two steps before Krist had reached his goal in the corner, he heard Dr. Gregory call out, "You want something cold to drink? Would that feel good on your throat? But I don't know if we have any ginger ale in the house. You want orange juice?"

Krist spun and faced the opening to the hallway that led to the bedrooms.

In two seconds Gregory emerged from the doorway. He didn't see Krist standing in the corner. Gregory didn't show any hesitation at all; he walked purposefully toward the sofa on the other side of the room.

Krist's eyes followed. That's when he saw that there was a person lying under a blanket on the sofa.

Does Gregory have kids I don't know about? Krist wondered. *Is Prowler's intelligence that faulty?*

A little girl sat up from under the blanket and faced Gregory. She looked past him, saw Krist.

Krist felt it physically as the little girl pointed at him and said, "Is that the bad man, Dr. Gregory? I thought he was supposed to be big."

5

After a few minutes Lauren came back outside carrying Anvil in her arms. They were preceded by the big dog, Emily, who had extended the cord on her retractable leash as far as it would go. The dog looked strong enough to tow a car.

Carl took Anvil from Lauren's arms and clipped a leash to his collar. The poodle pranced at Carl's feet, his tail erect and wagging and his long nose in the air. "I know you two need to talk about the legal stuff," Carl said to me. "I'll hang back behind a little bit, if you don't mind. Out of listening range. Anvil and me could use the exercise. The walk will do us good, and he has to do his business."

Carl was asking me whether or not it was acceptable with me that he come along as my bodyguard. I said, "Thank you, Carl."

Lauren narrowed her eyes slightly at our interaction. I thought she nodded just the slightest bit, too, but I wasn't sure. Suddenly she moved one hand to her protruding belly. "Oooh," she said with a high voice, "I just got whacked."

Carl looked away, trying to pretend that he hadn't heard what she'd said.

I, too, paused in reaction to Lauren's choice of words and swallowed before I exhaled. To mask my discomfort I unwrapped a Dum-Dum and placed it on the center of my tongue. This one was apple. Not my favorite flavor. I offered a lollipop to Lauren and Carl, but apparently neither shared my addiction.

Impatient to begin her walk, Emily led us all down the lane.

Although we were moving along in the final sharp rays of a late-day sun, the skies to the north of us were as gray as wet ash, and lightning bolts were etching shock cords of fire in the clouds. Vertical pinstripes of virga marked the boundaries of the storm like an aerial picket fence. "Is that storm coming this way?" I asked.

"No," Lauren said. "It will head either north or east. They rarely come south from there. We're not in any real danger."

I almost laughed at the naivete.

With high clouds to the west and the massive storm shadowing the plains to the north, the imminent sunset was choreographed to be magnificent.

CARL AND ANVIL kept their distance, allowing Lauren and me to gain thirty or forty yards on them.

I asked Lauren how she was feeling.

She smiled at me and said, "The pregnancy? Fine. Good. You know—you've been there. I get tired and my back hurts a lot of the time. I can't get half my shoes onto my feet. I'm good and ready to deliver the baby, but the baby's not quite ready to be delivered." The dog suddenly lunged forward so forcefully that I was afraid it was going to separate Lauren's shoulder from its socket. She didn't seem to mind. "Listen," she continued, "I'm still waiting to hear from Jack Tarpin but in the meantime, my law student? His name is Arturo Mota. I told you I had him checking public records on Pat Lieber."

"Yes," I said. "The football coach." I realized that I was reading hope into her tone.

"Arturo is as sharp as coral. Best law student I've ever had. Anyway, in one hour on the computer he managed to get everything I'm about to tell you. What appears to be most important about what Arturo learned is that Lieber's wife has a younger brother. Current age is thirty-six, thirty-seven, something like that."

"Same as me. Same as Khalid."

"Yes. The same as Khalid."

We walked a half dozen more steps before she continued. "The wife's brother's name is Princely Carter. He's currently residing in the state prison system in the Commonwealth of Virginia. He's been there since 1995. And, conservatively, he's expected to be there until at least 2007."

"I bet he doesn't call himself Princely inside." I don't know why I felt compelled to make a joke about it, but I did.

She said, "I think that's a safe bet. He's in for armed robbery. Hit a combination convenience store/gas station in Richmond in the spring of 1995. Turned out he made the mistake of hitting the place right at shift-change. The clerk's husband was a Richmond cop who was just showing up at the store to give his wife a ride home from work. Didn't much like Mr. Carter pointing a gun at her."

"I hate it when that happens."

"No doubt Princely felt the same way."

"No doubt."

As her story progressed, my pulse was outpacing my feet and I was lagging behind Lauren because the big dog was pulling her along like a propeller at full throttle. We'd just reached an intersection with another dirt and gravel lane. I followed Lauren as she tried to keep up with a determined Emily bulling around the bend onto the new road. At the turn, I looked back and saw Carl and Anvil keeping pace a few dozen yards behind us. Anvil kept a showy, perfect stride on Carl's left side.

At that moment it was difficult for me to see why science was convinced that the poodle and the Bouvier shared membership in the same species.

A hundred yards or so down the road, Emily stopped in her tracks and started sniffing the left side of the dusty roadbed. It gave Lauren a welcome chance to relax her arms.

I caught up with her after a few steps. "You probably see where I'm heading with my story about Princely," she said.

"I can guess. The day of the murders, the day Khalid was arrested? If the phone call to Mickey Redondo happened the way we think it happened, this brother-in-law, Princely, may have been the offender in the homicides in Sarasota. Pat Lieber somehow knew about the murders—if that's the case, I assume he heard about it from Princely. He called Mickey, and suggested to Mickey that he would be rewarded handsomely if Mickey were able to keep his wife's brother's name out of it. As a theory it covers most of the bases."

"I see it almost the same way. But I doubt that Lieber gave up his brother-in-law's name on the phone that day. My guess is that Lieber asked enough questions of Mickey to find out that there was a suspect that Mickey liked for the murders. From there he just encouraged Mickey to make sure the case stuck against Khalid."

"You're probably right. A couple of big questions remain. Can we put this Princely Carter guy in Sarasota that day? And can we find some evidence of the payoff Mickey received from Lieber?"

"Arturo's looking, trying to see if Carter has any priors anywhere in South Florida, especially in Sarasota County. Also checking previous addresses. Knowing Arturo, I bet he has something for me tomorrow."

"Have Mr. Mota check Manatee County and Charlotte County as well. There should also be some record of the quid pro quo. Mickey had to get something out of this. Money can be traced."

"Maybe. But my experience here is that it's much harder to do that kind of checking without subpoenas. I don't think we'll see any evidence of a money trail unless we can prove some of these other things first. You know, first we have to get a judge to see it our way."

"Wait, Lauren. You said this Carter was picked up in Virginia for an armed robbery, right?"

"Yes."

"At a convenience store?"

"Mm hmmm."

My breathing grew shallow. I felt the same way I had when I'd first moved to Boulder and the altitude had stunned me when I tried to jog—there wasn't enough oxygen available to feed my lungs. "He used a gun?" I asked.

"Yes."

I waited for her to look over at me. A few seconds later my silence drew her gaze like a magnet draws steel. Her eyes were arresting, a deep violet that glimmered almost as black as the light off her sable hair. I said, "At the beginning of the robbery did he shoot out the lens of the surveillance camera?"

Emily started off again, yanking Lauren down the road. She lunged to keep her balance. Over her shoulder, she said, "Took him two shots, but yes. Now how did you know that?"

I was startled as Carl suddenly appeared right next to me. Anvil brushed against my leg like a cat.

Carl asked Lauren, "You know this car?" A big green sports utility vehicle was parked off the side of the road. The car was partially concealed by a shoulder-high mound of dry dirt.

"No, I've never seen it before. Emily and I do this walk almost every day. We never see cars parked around here." Her voice lacked alarm. She hadn't spent enough time swimming with whales, I thought. Lauren pointed up the hill. "There's no reason for anyone to park here. The closest house to where we're standing is ours."

Carl handed me Anvil's leash and shaded his eyes while he peered through the smoked glass on the passenger side of the car. "It's a rental, there's a map on the seat," he said. "And the back is full of surveyor's shit. That doesn't wash." He looked around. "Where's the damn surveyor and why's he using a rental?" He wasn't really talking to Lauren or to me. He was talking out loud to himself.

While we all stood watching Carl further examine the interior of the car, the big dog, Emily, moved off the road into the tall grasses that led up a gentle slope toward the house that Lauren shared with her husband, my doctor. The dog almost disappeared. She was visible in the hay the way an alligator is visible in the water.

Lauren saw me watching the dog and explained, "She follows the fox trails up there sometimes. The red foxes make her crazy."

Carl stepped away from the car. "I don't like what I'm seeing here. I'm going back. I want you both to stay away from the house, you understand? Till I tell you it's okay, you stay away from that house."

He was talking mostly to me.

I asked, "What are you thinking, Carl?"

"The car is bothering me. I don't like that the girl's up there." He pointed at the house. He was talking about Landon.

I said, "Do you think—"

Lauren interrupted. "You think someone's here? At my house?" She was incredulous, not yet terrified.

Carl centered himself between us and looked at me. "You don't go up there. No matter what, right? Till I say it's okay?"

I couldn't respond. My soul had suddenly begun to ache as though it were convulsing. I was swimming in the roughest of seas and I was being buffeted by the swells of at least a dozen whales.

A chorus in my ears shunted out every other sound. All I heard was Ernesto Castro's promise. *Every precious thing I lose, you will lose two.*

"Landon," I said. I'd intended to scream her name but I wasn't able. It was as if I suddenly didn't know how.

"Alan," Lauren said. "Oh my God! Should I go to a neighbor's house and call the police?"

Carl looked at me, then back at Lauren. "Probably wouldn't be the best thing, given the circumstances. Me being here. Her being here. You got a gun up there in the house?"

I was "her."

Carl was surprised, almost shocked, when Lauren answered his question about the gun by saying, "Yes."

"What is it and where?"

"It's a little Beretta. A .9mm. I have a carry permit for it, but I don't bring it into the house when there are kids there. I left it in the car because of Landon. It's locked in the glove box of my car."

"It's loaded?"

"Of course."

"You got a car key with you?"

"No."

He said, "Take care my dog," and took off onto the fox trail into the sea of grasses.

As defiantly as I could, I called after him, "I can't leave Landon there, Carl. I'm coming with you."

He stopped on the trail and froze me with a stare I'd hoped never to see from him. "Pay attention to me. You paying attention to me?" His eyes narrowed. "Good. If I'm right about what I'm thinking and someone's here, then they're here for you. Once they get you, all bets are off. Anybody else who happens to be in the vicinity is as good as dead. Your kid, your doctor, your lawyer, anybody else. You want to save some lives, you stay away from the damn house."

He lowered his head and ducked down, his arms swinging out to the side as he lumbered up the hill.

Lauren said, "He looks like a soldier."

"Or a gorilla," I murmured, almost involuntarily.

"What?" Lauren said.

Every precious thing.

Every precious thing.

6

For a bad man, Krist *wasn't* big.

In the sensible Mephisto walking shoes he had chosen to wear for what he now hoped would be the conclusion to this adventure, Krist topped out at around five foot four. In his entire life he'd never weighed more than one hundred and twenty pounds. Nature's inclination toward irony had dictated that he be compensated for his diminutive stature by being granted an oversized head and ears that could catch enough air to sail a dinghy on a still day.

Only thirty-four years old, his once blond hair had already turned the gray of tarnished silver.

DR. GREGORY DIDN'T immediately comprehend Landon's question about the "bad man."

"What do you mean?" he asked her.

Landon pointed. "That man behind you. I thought the bad man would be bigger. Didn't you?"

Krist said, "Turn slowly, Doctor. See for yourself."

Alan Gregory held his hands out from his sides and rotated ninety degrees. He did it slowly, as directed. He turned his neck the rest of the way so he could spot the man standing in the corner behind the pool table. The man held a handgun, an automatic. Gregory noted the elongated barrel and thought, *silencer*.

Gregory said, "What do you want?"

"Her mother. I want her mother." Krist was still celebrating the presence of the little girl in Gregory's living room. He couldn't believe his good fortune. He'd come here as a long-shot way of finding his target. Now he figured he would be on his way out of Colorado within hours.

Landon started to whimper. "Don't hurt my mommy," she said. "Don't hurt my mommy."

Krist stepped two steps closer, paused, and then stepped one more time. He smiled at Dr. Gregory and said, "Dr. Gregory? I'm waiting for you to tell me where I can find her mother."

Gregory tried to think. The gun that the man was pointing at him didn't help him focus. Gregory was terrified by his options. Landon was in serious jeopardy already. Peyton was certainly dead the moment she walked in the door. Lauren and his unborn child were likely casualties, too. Alan Gregory made a choice. He said, "She's on the run. My wife and I are watching her daughter for her."

The grin still on his face, Krist raised the gun up so he could site it, adjusted the aim just once, and pulled the trigger. A *pfffft/clap* sound was almost lost in the ensuing *thud*. A shell casing ejected from the gun and landed on the floor beside one of the legs on the pool table.

Landon screamed. "He shot Daphne."

Daphne was Landon's teddy bear. The bear had been snuggled tightly in the crook of her left arm.

Krist said, "I'm a very good shot. Next time you're uncooperative with me, I won't hit the bear."

The grin had degenerated into a smirk. Gregory thought that the man was enjoying himself. He also assumed that the next shot would be directed at Landon, not the bear.

Dr. Gregory said, "She's on a walk with my wife. They shouldn't be gone very long."

"Your wife said around thirty minutes. We're probably down to twenty-five by now."

"Probably."

"That big dog of yours, too, right?"

"Yes, the dog is with them."

"Who's Adrienne?"

"My neighbor across the way. She has nothing to do with this."

"Everyone who shows up at this house from this point on will be considered to have something to do with this."

Gregory felt sweat dripping down the crease of his back.

Landon held up her bear and said, "She's not dead. Daphne isn't dead. She's only wounded. You have to hit them in the head to kill them."

The bad man smiled at the girl's conclusion about guns and bullets,

6

but he addressed Dr. Gregory. He said, "I don't think you're lying to me at the moment. But in case you are, here is the reason you are still alive: If I discover that you've lied to me, the first thing that will happen is that you will tell me the truth, then you will die slowly and painfully. If it turns out you've already been truthful, you'll die the same death as Daphne."

Landon said, "Daphne is not dead. See?" She spun the bear and pointed it at Krist. The hole from the slug was almost invisible in the toy's abundant fur. "As a matter-of-fact, Daphne is the epitome of not dead."

The man ignored her. "So is there anything you would like to add to what you've told me, Dr. Gregory?"

Gregory thought, *This man doesn't know about Carl.* "No," Gregory said, "I have nothing to add."

"Good. Put your hands on your head and go sit in that chair." Gregory moved closer to Landon. The man said, "No, not next to her. That one, there. Yes . . . good." He inhaled deeply. "I like that smell. Cordite. Don't you?"

Landon whispered, "Is he the man who shot my daddy?"

"I don't think so, honey." What Alan left unsaid was that he thought this was the man who was going to shoot her mommy.

The man asked, "You have a cell phone in the house?"

"It's in my car. In the garage. I leave it there most of the time."

"Your wife? She have one?"

"Yes."

"Where is it?"

"I'd have to check to be sure, but it's probably charging on a little desk in the kitchen." He tilted his head toward the front of the house in the general direction of the kitchen. "She charges it every day when she gets home from work. The charger's on the desk."

The man backed away toward the kitchen. Without warning, he ducked inside for a moment and returned a few seconds later with Lauren's flip phone. "This is it? Your wife's phone?"

"Yes."

The man dropped it on the hardwood floor and pounded on it with the heel of one of his Mephistos. It skittered away in one piece. He retrieved it, and after looking around for a hard vertical surface to fling it against, he threw it as hard as he could into the floor. The phone busted into three pieces.

"That should take care of the phone problem. You expecting any visitors besides this Adrienne person your wife was talking about?"

Alan saw Landon begin to open her mouth. He cut her off before she could say something that might reveal Carl's presence. "Adrienne's a doctor. She's coming over with a strep test for the girl. She's the only visitor we're expecting tonight."

Krist smirked. He said, "No one else is coming?"

"No. We're not expecting anyone."

Krist said, "But then again, you didn't exactly expect me, did you?"

7

As Carl trudged up the hill he figured he was either being totally paranoid about the car with the surveying equipment, or he was about to meet a pro, most likely somebody Prowler had sent to clean up after what happened to Barbara Barbara Turner.

Carl was still a good fifty yards from the house when he spotted the telephone cable dangling like squid-ink spaghetti from a weathered post on the far side of Gregory's house. That's when Carl knew for certain that he wasn't being paranoid about the car. He stared at the cable for almost ten seconds, then muttered, "I'd only go to that kind of trouble if I was planning on camping out in there." His conclusion: Prowler's new pro wasn't sure what he was going to find inside the doctor's house. So the guy had prepared himself for a lengthy stay.

Carl slowed his pace as he approached the garden level of the house. Even though the basement window lock had been jimmied by a careful person, Carl recognized the damage immediately. Nonetheless, Carl was impressed by the quality of the work. Not surprised, but impressed. This wasn't some bozo with a hammer and a rag.

Carl circled the house on the north and entered the Gregorys' garage through the side door. He paused and perused the good doctor's inventory of garden tools, ultimately choosing a hatchet that looked old enough to have belonged to Gregory when he was a Boy Scout.

Carl recognized his doctor's car. It was on the far side of the garage. The car closest to the side door of the garage had to be Lauren's. The passenger-side door of the car was locked. The driver's side door wasn't. Carl let himself in, slid onto the driver's seat and tried the glove box door. As Lauren had promised, it was locked.

Without hesitation Carl swung the hatchet against the lock. He didn't get much of an arc in the confined space inside the car and the blade on the ax was so dull that the first stroke barely dented the hard plastic on the dashboard. He flipped the hatchet over and pounded at the little door three more times—*whap, whap, whap*—with the blunt back side of the tool.

The door popped.

He reached in and grabbed Lauren's Beretta, checked the magazine, and flicked off the safety. Then he chambered a round, placed the gun on his lap and checked his pulse. Calm and steady at seventy-eight.

"It's just like riding a bike," he said to himself, and he retraced his steps toward the basement window with the jimmied lock.

CARL COULD BARELY wriggle through the opening. His shoulders got stuck first. After he finally got them through, his hips got caught. Eventually, he had to twist sideways to get inside the damn house. As he lowered himself headfirst to the carpeted floor of the basement, he concluded that the new guy that Prowler had sent was either a snake or a midget.

Carl lifted himself from his prone position and a single loud thud shook the floor above his head. He froze and began to count. The counting was a prison reflex—he used to time the approach of the guards as they neared his cell. When his count reached the number thirteen, Carl heard another sound upstairs, this one sharper, as something hit the same location on the floor.

Carl sprinted toward the staircase.

He was close to them now.

Now he could hear voices.

He began to climb the stairs. Two steps from the top he heard Prowler's man say, "But then again, you didn't exactly expect me, did you?"

8

"They may not have expected you," Carl said. "But I did."

Carl Luppo hadn't stayed alive in La Cosa Nostra for so many years by playing fair. Once he saw the gun that the man was pointing at Dr. Gregory, Carl didn't wait for the guy holding the weapon to turn around to even the odds. Carl shot the man right in the back, grouping three slugs between the man's shoulder blades into an area about the size of a navel orange.

Maybe a grapefruit.

Lauren's Beretta had roared in the confined space, and the smell of burnt powder hung in the air like a metallic mist.

Though his ears were ringing, Carl thought he could hear Landon screaming from across the room.

He said, "Dr. Gregory? Is the girl okay?" But he couldn't even hear his own voice, let alone the doctor's reply.

9

Time stood at attention. Perfectly still, like the guards outside Buckingham Palace.

What are those guys called anyway? Oh, it doesn't matter.

Every precious thing . . .

Every precious thing . . .

From the moment Carl Luppo had begun crabbing up that hillside of golden grasses until the moment I heard the gunfire explode from Dr. Gregory's house could have been a minute, an hour, a day, a year.

All I know is that it was a lifetime.

After Carl warned us to stay away from the house, Lauren had tugged me and the two dogs back up to the intersection of the dirt lanes. She wanted to be in position to flag down Adrienne before her neighbor drove unwittingly into whatever was happening in the house.

We stood there waiting to learn what was happening to my daughter and her husband. We talked little, and I can no longer remember a word that passed between us while we paced at the intersection of the lanes. I do recall the fading light—the night was more than halfway done stealing the relics of the day. And I recall my fear that the sunset was a metaphor for something I didn't want to imagine.

Lauren held Emily's leash. I squeezed Anvil in my arms. The rapid pace of his heart—faster even than my own—helped me pretend that I was calm.

The sudden sound of the gunfire that came from the house caused both Lauren and me to jump back as though we were dodging bullets. The big dog's ears went down and she whimpered.

An instant later Lauren yelled, "Alan!" and began to run down the lane.

I said, "My baby!" and I dropped Anvil to the ground. I was past Lauren in a second, the dog beside me on my left.

Everybody knows that in the face of panic, mothers can outrun mere wives.

And I like to think I can outrun an eight-months-pregnant woman any day of the week.

chapter eleven

SUBURBAN BLUES

I

As I burst in the front door the smell hit me first.

Burnt powder.

Maybe twenty feet from the door I saw a man sprawled on the floor. He was bent in ways that proclaimed death, an arm twisted below him, his neck wrenched sideways. The back of the taupe sofa behind him was polka-dotted with dark spots of different sizes. I knew the spots were his blood. The man's face was turned away from me but he was small, too small to be my doctor, too thin to be Carl Luppo.

I wanted to scream for my daughter but I didn't know what I'd walked into, and I didn't want to put her in any more danger than she was already in.

Every precious thing . . .

Lauren joined me in the open doorway. I watched her eyes as she saw the man who was dead on the floor and then as she spotted two handguns lying on the table near the top of the stairs. One of the two pistols was elongated by a silencer. She covered her mouth with her spread fingers and quietly said, "Oh my God."

Emily began barking at the corpse on the floor. The dog was baring her fangs, ignoring commands from Lauren to quiet. Lauren used all her strength to control the leash. Anvil joined in the chorus of barking, but his yip was high-pitched and lacked fervor. His heart wasn't really in it.

I think he was just trying to belong.

Carl heard the commotion the dogs were making and stepped into the doorway that led to the living room from the deck. "Hi," he said. "I was outside trying to signal you guys everything was over up here."

The dogs quieted. I wasn't at all sure why.

I spit out the solitary word, "Landon?"

He tilted his head. "She's good. She's back in the bedroom with the doctor. We didn't think she should be here with . . . you know . . . the guy."

"Did she . . . ?" I couldn't finish my own thought.

Carl knew. He said, "She heard what happened but she didn't actually see anything. The jerk shot her bear."

"He shot *her bear? Daphne?*"

Lauren said, "My husband? Alan's okay?"

"Absolutely, absolutely. Things got a little testy . . . but . . . hey, you know. It turned out for the best."

I looked at the man on the floor. "Carl, who, um, is he?"

Carl shrugged. "Didn't give his name. Some guy with a gun. He was here to do a piece of work and he was looking for you, Peyton. He told Dr. Gregory he was looking for you."

I started to shake. I started to cry.

Lauren's voice was hollow. She said, "We need to call the police."

Carl said, "Yeah. But the phones are dead. He cut the lines. Busted up somebody's cell phone, too."

Behind me, I heard a car approaching on the lane. Emily turned her head and growled.

Lauren put her arms around me to try to provide some comfort. She said, "That'll be Adrienne with the strep tests. She'll have a phone. You don't know her but my guess is she'll be pissed off that she missed all the excitement."

To no one, to myself, I said, "I need to calm down, stop crying, so I can go see my baby."

"Sure, sure," Lauren said. As she embraced me I could feel her baby kicking at the walls of her womb.

A car door slammed.

Ten seconds later Jack Tarpin walked in the door of the house.

Immediately I pushed Lauren away from me and I stopped crying.

My first thought was that Jack hadn't changed much in all these years.

2

My second thought?

Jack was wearing chinos.

I swear. Also, beat-up old boat shoes without socks and a striped polo shirt that had once been brown and yellow but was now beige and off-white. But most definitely chinos.

Jack Tarpin was a fresh whale dressed in chinos.

That's how I knew that he was here to kill me.

I said, "Jack."

I USED EVERY bit of self-control I had in order to refrain from running wildly toward the bedrooms to find Landon. I didn't even flick a glance that way.

Jack said, "Hello, Kirsten. I'd say 'good-to-see-you after all this time' but it's really not." He puffed a little air through his nostrils in some expression of derision. "All these years and you can't let something go. Don't know if it makes any difference to you, but the cops never trusted you." He filled his cheeks with air and then exhaled through pursed lips. "You two ladies step away from those guns there on that table, please."

Before he even finished his sentence, I heard a clatter behind me and turned my head to see Carl's wide back and shoulders as he crossed the narrow deck and launched himself headfirst over the railing.

I hadn't seen Jack holding a gun—I don't know where on his body he'd had it stashed—but before I turned back to him, he unleashed a round that whizzed right past my head. The roar caused my gut to grip.

He'd shot at Carl.

Before I had a chance to scream, Jack was past me, running toward the glass doors. He hurdled the sofa like a steeplechaser, and his front shoulder sent the screen door off its tracks as he blasted toward the spot where Carl had propelled himself from the deck.

I yelled, "Carl! Watch out!"

Jack spent about five seconds scouring the area below the deck, but the night was upon us and he apparently didn't see anything he thought was worth shooting. I watched him touch a spot on the railing with the pinky of his free hand. He lifted the finger until it was just below his nose and he sniffed. When he looked up again, he narrowed his eyes and raised the gun so it pointed right at my belly.

"I take it that was your wiseguy?" he said to me.

"What?"

He raised his pinky in an odd salute. "I think I got him. There's some blood out here."

He started to laugh, but he stopped as soon as he was far enough back into the room to focus his eyes on the dead man who was on the floor by the sofa. It was as if he was seeing the guy for the first time.

"Hell's bells," he said, shaking his head. "I sure wish I knew what the hey was going on here." He pointed at the man with the barrel of his handgun. "Who the heck is this?"

Neither Lauren nor I answered.

He raised his voice. "The dead guy. Who is it?"

I said, "Somebody broke into the house. My friend shot him."

Jack seemed to consider my story while he rubbed his face with the heel of his free hand. More to himself than to Lauren and me, he said, "Another one of Prowler's, I bet. I'm glad I came."

Lauren said, "What?"

He shook his head. "I want you two to go lie down on top of that pool table over there." He waved the gun. "Go on, the both of you.

Where I can see you. I sure didn't expect such a crowd at this place. Thought it was just going to be me talking to some doctor." He ran the fingers of his free hand through his thick white hair and sighed. "I have to take a minute to figure out exactly how I'm going to do this and have any prayer of getting away with it."

I comforted myself with the knowledge that of all the things that Jack had been accused of being during his less-than-illustrious career—drunk, coward, incompetent—he'd never been accused of being a genius.

Lauren's skin was so pale I was afraid she was going to pass out. I led her by her clammy hand and helped her climb onto the felt-lined slate of the pool table. She never relinquished hold of Emily's leash. The dog was uncharacteristically restrained.

To me Lauren whimpered, "He can't kill my baby, can he? He won't kill my baby?"

Jack spoke again. "While I'm thinking here, you go ahead and put your arms over your heads, you know, like you were doing jumping jacks or diving backward into a pool or something." We did. He said, "Good. Stay that way."

It seemed to me Jack was making a mistake by ignoring the big dog. But then I didn't know the dog very well. Still quiet, Emily was sitting at the far end of the pool table. Anvil was right next to her.

My thoughts leapt back to Landon.

Every precious thing . . .

A few seconds later Lauren surprised me by saying, "It was you who got the call that day, wasn't it? It wasn't your partner."

From my position on the pool table I couldn't see Jack's face. I actually didn't even know where he was in the room. Seconds passed and I was almost convinced that he wasn't going to answer her.

Finally, he said, "So you know all about it, do you? You must be the lawyer who was talking to my Pamela." His voice was as melodious as a brogue.

"Yes."

"Well, I'm sorry you're here today, little lady. What a mess to be a part of. A bun in the oven, too. I'm very sorry you're here. I'm sorry for both of us." He paused. "A little more sorry for myself than I am for you, but I'm sorry nonetheless."

As though she hadn't even registered the threat Jack was making, Lauren pressed him. "You got the call from Pat Lieber, though, right? That day at the station. You're the one who re-did the GSR? Then you set up your partner in case things went wrong?"

Jack didn't answer.

"Just tell me if I'm right."

The lilt disappeared from Jack's tone as he replied, "Shut up, why don't you. I'm thinking, here."

I raised my head and saw that Jack was sitting across the room on a straight-back chair. He'd chosen a position where he could not only see outside toward the deck in case Carl returned, but he could also keep an eye on the front door and on the stairs that came up from the basement.

I craned my neck a little farther—the two guns that had been on the entry table were no longer there.

Jack was well armed.

I lowered my head and prayed for Landon.

I wondered about Dr. Gregory.

I wondered about Carl.

I prayed some more.

Jack stood and stepped close to the pool table. I raised my head again so that I could see him. He had a big automatic handgun in his right hand. He asked, "Is there anybody else in this house. Like back there?" He was pointing at the hallway that led to the master bedroom.

Toward Landon.

I said, "No. No one else is here."

"Where's your kid, Kirsten? You have a little girl."

I hesitated a split second as I constructed a lie. Jack saw me hesitate.

"She's here, isn't she?" he asked, even before I could tell him my lie.

"No," is all I said. The solitary word was more protest than denial. I raised my voice. "No! No! Don't go in there." Dr. Gregory and Landon had to have heard me.

They had to.

Jack was already moving past the pool table toward the bedroom. He stopped. "Get up," he commanded Lauren.

When she'd struggled to her feet, he placed her in front of him as a shield and began pushing her down the hallway toward the bedroom. Over his shoulder he told me not to move an inch or he'd kill my daughter.

I stayed on my back on the pool table and prayed while I steeled myself for the roar of a gun.

Emily barked. Anvil yipped, too.

3

Alan had, of course, heard the roar of the shot that Jack Tarpin had unleashed at Carl Luppo as Carl dove off the deck. Immediately, Alan had spirited Landon outside onto the master bedroom deck and lowered her over the side, eventually dropping her to the ground, and he hoped, to relative safety.

Alan followed Landon over the railing. He found her underneath the deck sitting next to Carl Luppo.

"They shot Uncle Carl," Landon said in a rapid whisper. "But he's not going to die because they got him in the leg, not in the head. My daddy was shot in the head, and that's where they have to get you if they want you to die."

Carl said, "That's not exactly true, pumpkin."

Alan said, "How bad is it, Carl?"

Carl flicked a glance at Landon. "Not good," he said. "Not good. He didn't hit me with no .22. I'm losing some serious blood here."

Alan lowered his head and tried to examine the wound, which was high on Carl's thigh a few inches below his buttocks. Carl already had his belt wrapped around his leg near his groin as a tourniquet.

"Who's in there with them?" Alan asked. "Who shot you?"

"Peyton called him Jack. I don't know. You gotta go do something for the women, Doc. Take my gun."

"You have a gun?"

"I borrowed it from this woman I met recently. Don't ask. You don't want to know."

Alan said, "I have a phone in my car. I'm going to call the police."

"You don't have time. That man's here to kill Peyton. He's not going to let your wife witness that and live. He'll kill her too."

Alan looked at Carl while he weighed the gun in his hand. "Is this ready to fire? I don't know much about guns."

Carl checked to make certain a round was chambered. "Yeah, it's ready. But it's a .22. A small caliber. You're going to have to get close enough to the guy to hit him in the head."

"What are you talking about?"

"He's a big guy. This thing doesn't have stopping power like a .38 or a .44 or even a .9mm. You'll have to get him in the head to make it stick so he doesn't turn around and get the women after you shoot him."

"I told you," said Landon.

Carl gestured behind him. "The basement window is open. You can go back in that way if you want."

Alan swallowed and considered his options. "If I have to get as close as you say, I'm thinking of another plan. Take care of Carl, Landon, okay?"

She said she would.

Alan took off around the house. He arrived out front just in time to see the headlights of Adrienne's Chevrolet Suburban bouncing down the lane. Instantly, he revised his plan and jogged out to meet her car.

ADRIENNE AGREED TO hit the doorbell that was next to Alan and Lauren's front door before she ran back over to her house. She promised to call 911 on her cell phone as soon as she was safely inside with Jonas and his nanny.

While Adrienne hit the bell, Alan waited crouched down low in the driver's seat of her Suburban, which he'd parked ten feet from his front door. The .22 pistol that Carl had given him was tucked between his right thigh and the seat of the car. The engine was running. The headlights were on. The brights were on. The huge vehicle was in four-wheel drive. And it was in gear.

Alan could barely see over the rim of the dashboard. But he could clearly see the fan-shaped window that was cut high into the front door of his house.

He fixed his eyes on that window, and he waited.

4

While Jack and Lauren were gone searching the master bedroom, time stopped for me again. I don't know how long it actually took them to come back into the room. It felt like a year or two.

But it was probably a minute or so.

Jack immediately ordered Lauren back onto the pool table and then walked out of my line of vision.

He said, "Where's your kid?"

"With friends," I said. I'd anticipated the question and had a pack of lies all ready to go.

He didn't ask for any more of my lies though.

For two or three minutes the room was as quiet as the night. The only sounds I heard were the dogs breathing and the pounding of my heart.

Finally Jack said, "We're going to have to go someplace else. I don't want to do what I have to do here."

"You mean kill us?" I said. I don't know why I wanted him to admit his plans, but I did.

Before he could respond, the doorbell rang and the dogs started barking as though the world was ending. Emily tore off toward the front door. Lauren barely had time to grab the handle on her leash. The dog almost succeeded in yanking her master off the table. I kept a firm grip on Anvil's lead so he couldn't take off toward the door.

"You know who that is?" asked Jack over Emily's barking, which was almost cacophonous.

Lauren raised herself to her elbows and said, "My neighbor's coming over. She's a doctor. She's dropping something by on her way home from work. She doesn't know about any of this. Just go to the door and tell her I'll call her later. If you want me to, I'll do it."

"Stay where you are. What if I don't answer?"

"She heard the dogs. She may come in to get them. Her son likes to play with our dogs."

"She has a key to your house?"

"Yes, she has a key to the house."

Jack Tarpin faced us. "Either of you two moves, you're dead."

I said, "We're dead anyway."

With the gun in his hand he walked toward the front door.

I whispered to Lauren, "How far is the drop off the deck?"

"About ten feet."

"We have to do it."

She grabbed her belly. "My baby. She won't make it if I jump."

"Maybe not," I said. "She definitely won't make it if you don't. He's going to kill us."

"Alan will come."

"No, Lauren," I said. "We have to jump. I'll help you over the rail. On three. One, two—"

Before I could say "three," the front of the house seemed to explode and bright lights flashed into the room. The roar was deafening and a cloud of dust billowed back into our faces.

I grabbed Lauren's arm and yanked her toward the deck.

5

Alan saw a shadow fall across the window that was cut into the door a split second before he saw the pink face that followed.

He didn't hesitate.

He pounded on the gas pedal of Adrienne's huge Suburban. The front end seemed to falter momentarily before it lurched across the few feet of gravel and hopped up the solitary step to the porch. The two decorative columns that supported the entryway blew away from the path of the car and a moment later the blunt face of the Suburban decimated the doorway of the house. Alan sat back against the seat and braced himself for the explosion of the air bag. When it came, it still stunned him.

The front door and its entire frame collapsed inward. The car hesitated once more. Alan sat up higher in the seat and kept full pressure on the gas. He thought he heard a scream but the echo of the airbag detonation and the noise of the destruction were too intense for him to be certain.

Ten feet or so into the house the Suburban came to a grinding stop.

Alan grabbed the gun that was wedged beneath his leg and climbed out the driver's door into the destruction of the entryway of his house.

Frantically he searched the rubble in front of the Suburban for signs of the man with the pink face. The air was thick with dust and the brash glare from the headlights reflected back into his eyes. He spotted a weathered boat shoe near his own feet. Then he found the collapsed front door. It was resting almost flat on the floor. The man was not underneath it.

Alan leaned over to search beneath the car. He felt a hand close hard around his ankle. Before he could react the hand yanked him from his feet.

As he fell he saw the orange disks of Emily's eyes as she peered through the dust and debris. Her mouth was opening and closing as she barked, but Alan couldn't hear her roar.

The gunfire was too loud.

The man with the pink face was trapped beneath the Suburban. One of his hands gripped Alan's ankle like a vise. The other hand, pinned by part of the front-door frame, held a semiautomatic pistol. The man was firing back toward Alan, but the arm with the gun was totally restrained by the door frame, and the man couldn't rotate his wrist quite far enough to aim correctly to hit his target. With each shot, though, he was getting closer.

Alan lifted the .22. Through the haze and dust he spotted the man's head and chest beneath the oil pan of the Suburban's engine. Alan raised his gun, the barrel only three feet away from the man's head, maybe four. He leaned back and aimed, remembering Carl's warning that he had to be close enough to be certain he could hit the man's head.

The man fired again. The bullet whipped into the wall inches from Alan's chest.

Alan closed his eyes and fired.

He didn't open his eyes again until the grip relaxed on his leg.

Finally, he heard barking and in the distance, sirens.

chapter
twelve
ON KINNIKINIC

I

The State of Florida executed Khalid Granger early on the morning of my thirty-sixth birthday, three days shy of his own.

I stayed up late the night that he was electrocuted. I sat in front of my new computer, glued to the Internet, waiting with futility for word that the governor of my home state would show enough courage to spare the life of a very bad man who absolutely didn't deserve to die at the hands of the people.

The final word from his spokesman was that the governor went to bed at his usual time. It was much earlier than I went to bed that night. I'm afraid that the governor slept better than I did, too.

Did he sleep better than Carl Luppo?

Or better than Ernesto Castro?

I somehow doubted it. I was already of the belief that all hit men sleep like babies.

. . .

LAUREN AND I had tried. God, had we tried. I thought we had a good story. A great story even. But, in Florida, during every autumn football season, our culprit, Pat Lieber, was more popular than God. And the truth was, we didn't have a bit of actual proof to back up our claims that Lieber had bribed Jack Tarpin to set up Khalid Granger for the murder of the two Mennonites in the Sarasota convenience store.

Lauren told me that what we really had was the best recipe for slander that she'd ever seen in her life.

I heeded her frequent pleas for caution, so we proceeded carefully. But we made scant progress.

We were able to prove that Jack took a phone call from Pat Lieber at the police station on the day of the crime. The timing though? We could never pin that down with any certainty. What was said? Lieber certainly wasn't talking, wasn't even returning our messages. My last attempt to reach him by phone earned me a referral to an attorney in a Miami law firm. The lawyer specialized in libel and slander cases.

Jack Tarpin, of course, wasn't talking either. Jack had died in the ruins of Alan and Lauren's entryway from a single gunshot to his head.

Pamela, Jack's widow, freely admitted to us that she had written the letter to Dave Curtiss about Khalid's innocence. At the time she thought, of course, that by writing the letter she was not only being a good citizen but was also blowing the whistle on Mickey Redondo, not on her own husband. Her admission didn't matter, though; everything she knew about the case was part of the assortment of lies that had been packaged and wrapped by her now dead husband. She wasn't able to tell Lauren and me anything that assisted us.

Police firing-range records confirmed that Jack and Mickey had gone to the range the night of the murders to practice shooting. It was an act that one of their colleagues told me was, "Absolutely inexplicable the night of a double homicide. Meshuga. I don't know what they were thinking."

Mickey Redondo maintained all along that he didn't know a thing about what Jack might have been up to. He didn't remember anything about spilling coffee and switching out the GSR envelopes. Mickey never wavered from his position that Khalid Granger was as guilty as an adolescent at confession and that Jack Tarpin wasn't smart enough to frame a picture, let alone an innocent man. I think one of two things was true: Mickey was either an integral part of the whole mess or he was just too humiliated to admit that he'd been duped by someone he disrespected as much as he disrespected Jack.

Sometimes I figured the first was true; other times I was sure it was really the second.

We were able to discover that during the winter after the murders in the convenience store Jack's oldest son received a full-ride academic scholarship to the University of Tennessee, which happened to be Lieber's alma mater. Pat Lieber, it turned out, had written a glowing letter in support of the scholarship application. An admissions officer admitted to us off the record that Jack Tarpin's kid was "barely deserving" of the award he'd received. Had the grant process been corrupted? No one was saying. We couldn't prove that it had been. But Lieber's recommendation letter in support of Jack's son's application was so laudatory it glowed like the Hope diamond in the noonday sun.

Was that surprising? Only if you considered the fact that we were never able to ascertain that Pat Lieber had ever actually met the young Mr. Tarpin.

Lauren and I suspected that the scholarship was the payoff that Lieber arranged for Jack Tarpin's help in framing Khalid. As a payoff, the strategy was elegant. No money ever actually changed hands. No financial transactions could be traced by zealous prosecutors.

Like us.

And Princely Carter? He was a veteran, an MP for God's sake. Why was that information important? Because of the medals Princely earned as a marksman.

On the pistol range.

The whole thing smelled. Lord, it smelled.

But it didn't stink enough to save Khalid. The surprising truth about reversing a sentence of capital punishment is that it requires more evidence than getting the conviction in the first place.

. . .

I HADN'T SEEN Carl since the night the ambulance took him away from Dr. Gregory's house. For weeks his last words rang in my ears. The words weren't even intended for me. As he was wheeled into the back of the ambulance, he'd yelled to Lauren. He'd said, "Take care my dog."

Not to me. To Lauren.

Take care my dog.

THE WHALES HAD stopped ambushing me.

It took a few days for me to notice that I was no longer being constantly buffeted by the impact of beasts surfacing suddenly in my proximity. The memories, the gentle ones and the sad ones, the ones that made me smile and the ones that made me cry, now swam with me most of the time. Right out in the open. When I bothered to scan the horizon of my life, I could see them clearly in front of me or watch them out of the corner of my eye as they flanked me. They were always there. I could *feel* them.

That's what was different. I could feel them.

The feelings were there to remind me of the people I had loved. There to remind me of the people who had loved me. There to remind me of the losses I had suffered and to remind me of the losses I had dodged.

I treasured them all. Welcomed them all.

I somehow discovered the capacity to cherish the time I'd had with Robert rather than using all my energy ruing the circumstances that had caused me to lose him. I allowed myself the freedom to admit how he'd confined me with his love, and also to acknowledge the ways he had saved me with it.

I accepted the role my timidity had played in the death of Khalid Granger. And I vowed not to raise a timid child.

Given who my child already was, it was the easiest vow I'd ever taken.

2

Ron Kriciak visited me on what would have been Khalid's birthday. Ron didn't call first; he just showed up at the door of the screened-in porch of the little cottage on Kinnikinic. Amy was playing with a girl she had met down the street.

"May I come in?" he asked.

I stepped back and left room for him to enter.

"May I sit?"

"Of course," I said.

He moved a few steps to the sofa. "You and . . ." He snapped his fingers, searching for a name.

"Amy. My daughter's real name is Amy."

"You're well?"

"We're well," I said. "Considering."

"Yeah, considering."

"What about you, Ron?"

"I'm uh . . . I don't know. I'm different since that night. Different. Have to admit." Ron had shown up about thirty minutes after Dr. Gregory crashed his neighbor's car into the house. About twenty-nine minutes after Dr. Gregory shot Jack Tarpin to death. Ron and I hadn't talked much that night. His hands had been full as he was counting dead bodies and bullet holes, trying to piece together precisely what had transpired. I also suspected he was busy fighting ambivalence about whether to fulfill his sworn duty to protect Carl and me or just go ahead and kill us himself.

"I think we all are," I said. I could tell I was making him more uncomfortable than he already was. That was okay.

He cleared his throat. "This is an unofficial visit."

"Yes, Ron, I know. We don't have any official business any longer." I tilted my head across the room. "I got the paper." The paper was pressed behind glass in a cheap frame I'd bought at Walgreen's. It was hanging above the sofa like a diploma from a mail-order university.

He crossed his right leg over his left knee and tugged at the sock above his hiking boot. "I want to apologize for letting you down. That's why I'm here. I didn't take the risk from inside the program seriously enough. I'm sorry. I should have suspected someone might . . ." His voice trailed off. "What happened that night at your house, that never should have happened."

I felt the reverberation of his apology all the way to my toes, as though Ron had struck my skeleton with a tuning fork. He was talking about the man who had been under my bed. The man who'd bound me with duct tape.

I nodded and asked something I'd been eager to know. "Tell me something. Was he there to hurt us? Amy and me?"

He shook his head. "No. He says no. He just wanted to spook you. Scare you out of the program. Convince you that we couldn't protect you."

"Why?"

"You know the WITSEC heads that rolled after the stink you made in New Orleans? All the guys who were canned after your report to Congress? One of them was one of his friends. Our guy—the marshal—who busted into your house says he was just getting even."

I nodded. I'd suspected as much. Finally I said, "Thank you for the apology, Ron."

"I meant it," he said.

I looked back up, and before I'd even considered the question, I asked, "Carl Luppo?" I was aware that I was trying to sound less eager than I was. "Do you hear from him at all? He's feeling better, I hope."

Ron answered as though he'd been waiting for me to ask. "Yeah, he's feeling better. He's recovered from his wound. That's what I hear, anyway. You can probably guess he's not one of my witnesses anymore." Ron paused. "You risked a lot for him."

"Did I?"

I suspected that Ron was referring to the deal I struck with WITSEC after the near-catastrophe at Dr. Gregory's house. The deal was that I would ask for the paper from WITSEC and leave the program voluntarily if, and only if, WITSEC didn't punish Carl Luppo for having been in contact with me. My leverage? If WITSEC didn't take my offer, I planned to go public with the fact that one of their own marshals had assaulted me in my home while I was under government protection.

WITSEC took the deal.

"Leaving the program? I'm still not convinced it was the best choice you could make. You could both still be in danger. Both you and, um—"

"Amy."

"Yeah, Amy. Anyway, I'm curious why you would do that for him. For someone like Carl."

Do what? Risk my life for him? I can't imagine why.

"I hardly knew Carl Luppo," I said.

"Yeah," Ron replied. "That's the story I keep hearing."

THE PHONE RANG an hour or so after Ron left the cottage. It only rang once. I'd been outside on the porch and the line was dead by the time I got inside to answer. A minute later it rang a second time. I was ready.

"Hello," I said.

"So it's me," he said. "How you doin'?"

"Hi Carl," I said, trying not to squeal in delight. "It's so good to hear from you. How's your leg? Is it healing okay?"

"Almost as good as new except it looks like it got shot up. My first bullet hole comes after I'm retired. Who would have guessed? Your little girl, she's good?"

"She'll be fine, Carl, thanks to you."

"Me? I don't know about that. We all did some things that night. You, me, her, the doctor, everybody."

"I said, 'Thank you,' Carl. Be gracious, okay?"

"Okay, then, you're welcome. Hey, I got some news you might want to hear. Apologize for it taking so long, but with everything that's been going on . . . ah, you know. Anyway, I finally found out about that old grudge you were worried about. Well, it melted after all. Just as I'd suspected—it turns out it was carved of ice, not stone. I talked to some people who talked to some people, you know what I mean? These people, they applied a little heat to the man in question, and the grudge he had against you, it . . . it melted. Let's just say it melted."

I exhaled as though I'd been punched in the gut. "Ernesto—"

"Yeah, yeah. We don't have to use names. You know who I'm talking about. It's over with him. The old grudge? It's over. He has other things to worry about. New things. More immediate things that might affect his day-to-day comfort and his sense of long-term security, you know? You and your girl, though? You're safe."

"You're sure?"

"Absolutely. You can take it to the bank."

"Thank you, Carl. God, thank you. It's hard to believe. I feared he'd never go away." I could hear Carl breathing. I imagined the smoothness of his skin and the scent of him in his car. The lemon and the vanilla. "What about you? Are you safe, Carl?"

"Me? Sure. Where I'm living now ain't Boulder, but it's all right. I'm finding my way. Opening up to people a little more; that's something I learned in Colorado. May I ask you a question?"

"Sure."

"You ever talk to Dr. Gregory? How's my dog?"

LAUREN HAD HER baby four weeks early. Despite the premature arrival both mother and child were doing fine. The baby was a beautiful girl that she and her husband named Grace.

In my heart, I felt that Lauren and I were destined for a rare friendship. Given the circumstances that had thrown us together, we had mutually agreed to start the relationship slowly, but the pull between us had the force of gravity. We talked almost daily. I relished the tug, and I began to feel that the friendship cavity that had been created by Andrea's death was sure to fill. The recess was disappearing smoothly, the contours diminishing gradually, the way footsteps disappear in the sand.

After Dr. Gregory crashed the car into the house that night I'd helped Lauren over the deck railing and I'd used strength I didn't really have to lower her from the deck so that she only had to fall a few feet to the ground. When we finally got down, we discovered that her daughter seemed to be fine. And so did mine.

. . .

LAUREN'S HUSBAND, ALAN, was no longer my therapist. After that night at his house, we both knew he could never be. I worried sometimes what it was like for him after he'd killed Jack Tarpin. He never told me, of course. That wouldn't be his way.

But I guessed it was hard for him. I'd come to believe that at some level it was hard for Carl, too.

The killing, I mean.

Dr. Gregory suggested a couple of other people in town for me to see for continuing treatment. I was seeing one of them. A woman.

With the whales no longer waiting in ambush, though, I wasn't sure I would choose to be in psychotherapy much longer.

acknowledgments

This book could not have been written without the assistance of some people I am not free to name. Given their circumstances, it isn't prudent for me even to list their initials. But they know who they are. I thank them for their generosity and their candor. Although this book is in no way their story, they taught me things that I had absolutely no other way to learn.

Support takes many forms. The kind that is most intrinsic to me is the encouragement and direction that I receive from family and friends. Thanks to Harry MacLean, Elyse Morgan, and Tom Schantz for their early critiques. Enduring thanks to Patricia and Jeffrey Limerick, for the first step up, and to Stan Galansky, for his medical wisdom and wonderful tales of urological mayhem. And, as always, special gratitude is due to Rose Kauffman, Alexander White, and Sara Kellas.

Dave Curtiss and Vicki Switzer made a generous contribution to charity in order to attain the dubious distinction of having their names used as characters in this book. I thank them for their public spirit and their blind courage.

The act of publishing a manuscript has a single goal—making the finished book as strong as it can be. With this book I had wonderful help in achieving that goal from Lynn Nesbit, Steve Rubin, Shawn Coyne, Kate Miciak, Nita Taublib, and Irwyn Applebaum. I'm indebted to them for their contributions.